Everything I Can See.

Acknowledgements

To my husband, as always, without your encouragement, I wouldn't be where I am today. Thank you.

To my children, Lexus, Alicia and Dwayne. I wouldn't be able to name any characters without your input.

To my bestest friend ever, Michelle. You have been and always will be my sister. You are amazing!

To the #WritingCommunity on Twitter. Without your continued support, I wouldn't have been able to push through the self-doubt.

To two of the most fantastic beta readers, Eva Laudriec and Elizabeth Holland. You have both been an amazing support to me on my journey and I am truly blessed to have support like you both.

<u>Chapter One</u>

Chylla threw the spear again, this time hitting her target.

"How many times did it take you?" Aquilia laughed.

"I'm old," Chylla remarked in her defence.

Both women laughed. They had spent so much time together over the years; they knew when the other was joking around. They were more like sisters that a Queen and her protector.

"Come on, let's get some lunch. I need to check in with Zeke at the comms room. The Belasic Armada has been leisurely passing by every other week. I think they are planning something," Aquilia informed her.

"Let's hope not. With Nymeria and Celest still on their honeymoon, we are short up front, unless…" Chylla stopped mid sentence.

"No. Absolutely not," Aquilia quickly stated.

"Oh come on. You know how good they are," Chylla smiled.

"No. Scarlex and Eliontara are not ready. Not yet anyway." Aquilia replied as she turned towards Zeke's door.

Just as she reached for the touchpad, an explosion rocked the Palace.

"The children!" Aquilia exclaimed. She spun round, her long scarlet hair wrapping itself around her. She ran as fast as she could to where her children were studying with Halana.

"Halana, get the children to the bunker, quick," Aquilia ordered.

"What was that noise Mummy?" Scarlex asked.

"Nothing for you to worry about at the moment sweetheart," Aquilia smiled at her. "You go with Miss Halana and I'll come and find you shortly."

Scarlex and Eliontara both followed Halana without further question. They had seen attacks come and go over the past few years, this wasn't new to them.

"Your Highness. I will keep them safe," Halana said, gently touching Aquilia's arm. "Come now children. You heard your mother, let's go."

Scarlex and her brother had never questioned Aquilia's commands. They knew that she knew best.

"Oh, it never works!" Bella cried.

"It takes time child," Benzyline soothed her. "Have faith in yourself."

"How can I? It never goes right. First it dyes my hands green, then my hair orange and now it explodes!" Bella said, tears streaking down her face.

"What on Dionne happened here?" Layson asked, wafting the smoke away from his face.

"Oh Layson. Nothing is going right," Bella replied.

"She needs more practice, that's all," Benzyline told him. "She's too much of a perfectionist. I'll go find Aquilia. Explain the commotion. I hope it hasn't caused too much of a fuss."

Layson crossed the room in a few strides and took his wife in his arms. "She's right. You need to relax when you're practicing; maybe it will all go to plan then."

"And if it never works?" Bella sobbed.

"We will make it work," Layson whispered.

Aquilia keyed in the code for the comms room and waited for the door to open. Inside she found Zeke carefully watching the monitors. She peered over his shoulder but nothing seemed to be happening.

"Zeke, were we just attacked?" Aquilia asked.

"No Your Highness, nothing has passed my screens. Did you feel the jolt too? I thought it could be a tremor of some kind. I read somewhere that Earth has the, a lot," he replied. He scanned the surrounding area for any sign of a threat but there appeared to be nothing.

"It's very strange," Aquilia whispered. "Let me know is anything shows up."

Zeke nodded and turned back to the monitors as Aquilia left the room. As the door closed behind her, she could hear her named being called.

"Benzyline what is it?" Aquilia asked as the old woman approached her.

"It's Bella. She tried the same potion again and caused an almighty bang," she replied.

Aquilia looked at her dead in the eyes and tried not to lash out. "Benzyline, what have I told you about practicing magic in the house?" Aquilia questioned.

"Oh Your Majesty. Bella is quite keen to learn," Benzyline replied.

"I know, but it's too risky in the Palace, especially with the children around. I had to send them into the bunker because I thought we were under attack again," Aquilia told her. "I don't mind Bella practicing, that's why we built the outhouse. It's reinforced just in case things, you know, blow up."

"You're quite right Your Highness. I'm very sorry," Benzyline said.

"Go to Bella and take her outside," Aquilia laughed.

"Right away," Benzyline smiled.

Aquilia could never stay angry and anyone for long, unless they had done something terrible. Like her Uncle Altair. He was dead, but she wished she could bring him back just to kill him all over again. Sometime she wished none of her past had happened. Sometimes she was glad it had, because without her past, she wouldn't be who she was today.

Zeke settled back in his chair, his eyes never leaving the monitors. He studied them, checking for anything out of the ordinary. He had seen a few abnormal things go past. Like the double decked spaceship that flew past over five months ago. That image would never leave his memory. It was the most unusual colour. The top deck was green whilst the lower deck was purple. Zeke shook his head to rid the memory from the front of his mind. He checked one of the other monitors. Nothing seemed amiss there either. As he turned to check the monitor that surveyed beyond Jupiter, an army of ships caught his eye. Grabbing his radio, he called for his dad.

"Dad, you need to come quick. Something isn't right up here," Zeke said.

"On my way son," Layson replied. He quickly kissed Bella on the head and ran off. "Stay safe."

Layson ran through the Palace, almost colliding with Chylla on the way.

"Whoa, where's the fire?" Chylla laughed.

"Sorry," Layson shouted back to her. "Zeke needs me."

Chylla stopped for a second. 'Why would Zeke need Layson so urgently?' She thought to herself.

She followed Layson towards the comms room. He went inside but left the door open a little. Chylla knew not to eavesdrop but she was worried. Zeke never called for his dad to look at anything unless it was serious.

"You see what I mean?" Zeke asked Layson.

"Yes, I see. Where are they heading?" Layson questioned him.

"I don't know. They won't respond. I've tried everything Dad," Zeke replied.

Layson took a deep breath, "OK. Radio The Queen and tell her, try not to panic her. I will try and get everyone to the bunkers without too much alarm. Its better we move early than risk any casualties."

"And you need me where?" Chylla asked as she entered the half open door.

"Anywhere and everywhere," Layson replied.

"You got it," Chylla said. She saluted Layson and left.

"How long do you think she was there for Dad?" Zeke asked.

"The whole conversation kid, but don't worry. She's been doing this a very long time!" Layson smiled.

Zeke smiled back and turned towards the monitors. The fleet of ships were getting closer by the second.

"OK ladies and gentlemen if I could have your attention for the briefest of moments," Chylla announced over the loudspeaker. They had one fitted to save time. It would usually take a few hours to inform everyone. Now they announced things this way.

"Thank you. I would like you all to make your way, slowly and rationally to the nearest bunker. I don't want to cause alarm but this is for your safety." Chylla continued.

The people of Enceladus made their way towards the underground bunkers that had been built over the past few years. Aquilia had designed them so that she could protect as many of her people as she could. Chylla watched as everyone filed sensibly towards the bunkers. Those more able were helping those more vulnerable along the way.

"How is it going?" Aquilia called over the radio.

"It's going well Your Highness. Try not to worry," Chylla replied.

"Very well. Thank you," Aquilia said. She turned her attention back to Zeke. "How is it looking?"

"It's hard to say. One minute they look like they could attack at any second, the next they look like they are miles away. Is this some sort of trickery?" Zeke asked.

"Of that I am unsure. Do we know anything about them?" Aquilia asked.

"Dad is trying to find out now, but I haven't seen anything like this before, and I've seen some wild things from this seat," Zeke told her.

Aquilia sat on the chair next to him. Memories flooding back of the times she sat in Zeke's chair next to Zeebrakaan, whose chair she sat in now. Zeke had never once sat there. He left it vacant as a tribute to his predecessor.

"And the longer you sit there, the wilder it will become," Aquilia smiled. "You have a gift Zeke. You stepped into this role with ease and have made it your own. You would have made Zee very proud, just as you have your parents."

Zeke blushed, "gee, thanks Your Highness. I really don't know how to reply to that. I am grateful that you gave me a chance to help out here."

"I'm glad I took a chance on you. You haven't let me down yet," Aquilia said.

The radio beside Zeke crackled to life.

"Zeke, I found them," Layson called. "I'm on my way."

Chapter Two

"Are you sure Your Majesty?" Chylla asked. "It seems a long way for them to come."

"Layson identified their ships. He used the telescope that Sinclair designed to read the tail codes," Aquilia replied. "We need to get someone up there to negotiate, they aren't responding to our calls."

"I could go myself, I mean, Nymeria and Celest are due back tomorrow, but I don't think we have until then," Chylla offered.

"No, I'd rather you stay here with me. I'll send Onyx Abyss Alpha up," Aquilia replied. "Plus, I have an idea."

Aquilia set off towards the comms room. She had decided it was time to see what Zeke was really made of. Upon opening the door, she noticed how much attention Zeke paid to the screens, he had a notepad beside him, jotting down times and movements.

"Zeke, how do you feel about your own mission?" Aquilia asked.

Zeke almost fell off his chair. "Do you think I could do it? I wouldn't want to let you down Your Highness."

"Follow me," Aquilia told him.

"Who will mind this place? I can't leave it unattended," Zeke told her.

"I will take things from here," Chylla replied as she breezed into the room.

"Not that chair, please. It was Zeebrakaan's. I'd rather you took my chair," Zeke said. He was unaware of the reaction he would receive.

Chylla nodded her head slightly and sat in Zeke's chair.

"Thank you," he said.

Aquilia led him towards the ship of Onyx Abyss Alpha. "I want you to travel with them."

"To where exactly?" Zeke asked nervously.

"Up there. You are to find out, first hand, why they are here," Aquilia told him.

"And if they don't tell me?" Zeke asked.

"Then we will never know," Aquilia smiled. "There is no passing or failing here Zeke. Know that, whatever happens up there, you tried. That's all I ask of my crew."

Zeke nodded. He must have nodded too many times because he began to get dizzy.

"Now, this is Balzar, he is the Captain. Run everything by him first," Aquilia told Zeke.

Zeke shook Balzar's hand.

"Welcome aboard Zeke," Balzar said. He had a deep commanding voice. "Anything you need, just ask."

"Thank you," Zeke said softly.

Aquilia moved around the ship with ease. "This is Matro, he is basically you," she laughed. "He is the ships technician."

Matro nodded towards Zeke and then turned back towards the screens.

Zeke looked around the ship in awe. He had seen it fly before but this was the first time he had actually set foot inside or even stood anywhere near it.

"You like what you see?

Zeke spun around but saw no one.

"Down here."

Zeke looked down. He was surprised. "I'm sorry. I didn't..."

"See me? It's OK. I get that a lot. I'm Mitzi," she said, holding out her hand.

Zeke bent slightly to shake it. As he did, he saw something within her. He wanted to recoil from it but didn't.

"So, first time huh?" Mitzi asked.

"On here? Yeah. It's amazing," Zeke replied.

"Follow me. I'll show you some more whilst Queen Aquilia briefs Balzar on our mission," Mitzi led him deeper into the ship. "We won't be up there long, hopefully, but if we get waylaid, you can sleep here," she explained, pointing out a row of beds that folded out when they were needed.

"That's pretty cool," Zeke exclaimed.

Mitzi laughed, "That's not even the cool part!"

"Huh? You gotta admit, it is pretty cool," Zeke laughed.

"He's fitting in well," Balzar said.

"I hoped he would. How are you Matro?" Aquilia asked.

"Doing OK so far Your Highness, thank you for asking. Will he be my replacement?" He replied.

"He will. You just inform me when you're ready to hand over the chair," Aquilia smiled. "It will be a like for like replacement. You will be stationed on Enceladus, within the Palace walls."

Matro nodded. "I think I will be ready after this last mission Your Majesty."

"Very well. I shall leave you all now. Watch him Balzar. He's family," Aquilia warned.

"Yes Ma'am," Balzar bowed.

As Aquilia left the ship, Balzar retracted the steps and prepared the ship for take-off. She watched as it lifted higher into the sky, the afterburners lighting up as they switched to Hyper Jump. Aquilia made her way back to the comms room just in time to see them approach the ever nearing ships.

"Does he know yet?" Chylla asked.

"Not yet. Let's see how he does up there," Aquilia replied. She sat herself in Zee's chair and watched the event unfold.

"How long do we have to stay here Miss Halana," Scarlex asked. She had become quite twitchy in the past few minutes.

"I'm not sure sweetheart. I guess until you mother says it's safe to emerge," Halana replied. She hadn't heard any other explosions since they had left the Palace.

"Why don't we practice our moves whilst we wait," Eliontara suggested. "It will be good to pass the time away too."

Scarlex nodded. She wasn't a huge fan of closed in spaces but she knew her mother had sent them here for their own safety.

Eliontara took his starting stance and began his moves. He spun in a circle twice; bent low to the ground with his right foot far out behind him, then pounced on his left, somersaulting twice in the air before landing on his right foot and taking up a defensive stance.

"You're turn," he told is sister.

Scarlex stood on her left foot, holding her right above her head; she held her fist out and sprang from her toes, landing just before the wall. She ran up the wall. One step. Two. Sprang into a back flip and landed in the splits with her fists still out.

Halana clapped with enthusiasm. "You are both very good and quite agile!"

"What's agile?" Scarlex asked, wrinkling up her nose.

"It means flexible," Halana informed him. "You can both move with such fluidity."

"We used to watch mother all the time. She is quite agile too, isn't she?" Scarlex asked.

"She certainly is. She was once like you both. Eager to learn and keen to please. She has come such a long way since those days, but, she is so proud of you both," Halana told them.

Scarlex huddled up to Halana. "I don't like it down here. I don't feel like I can breathe properly."

"Come now Scarlex. Let's try to calm ourselves down a little. Eliontara, come and sit with us please," Halana asked.

Eliontara did as he was asked and held his sisters hand gently. "Try not to worry Scar. We will be OK. I promise you."

"I hope you are right," Scarlex replied. "I really hope you're right."

☐ ☐ ☐

As Onyx Abyss Alpha made its way towards the fleet of ships heading for Enceladus, Zeke started to get nervous.

"When we arrive, Zeke, you're to head up the questioning," Balzar informed him.

"I'm not sure I'm the right person for that," Zeke told him. "I wouldn't even know where to start."

"It's easy. Trust me," Mitzi said. "You just have to find out what their plans are."

'Easy right?' Zeke mimicked.

"I know how you feel," Mitzi said. "I've been there."

"What do you mean?" Zeke asked.

"I'm the interrogator on this ship," Mitzi shrugged.

Zeke tried not to laugh but a giggle escaped. "I'm sorry. I just don't see it."

"There's a lot you don't know about Mitzi, but, right now, isn't the time to learn. There'll be time for that later," Balzar said as he pointed out how close they were.

Zeke took some deep breaths and tried to practice what he would say. He didn't even know who he had to talk to.

"Don't try and practice. It never works," Mitzi whispered.

"How did you..?" Zeke began but Mitzi just winked at him. He had a lot to learn about this mysterious being.

The closer they got, the more nervous he became. He watched as they pulled alongside the head ship. He climbed aboard a separate pod and entered the ship via a side hatch.

"I am a representative from Queen Aquilia of Saturn and Enceladus. I request a response on you planned actions," Zeke told the captain.

The captain looked down at Zeke and was silent for a second, as if deciding whether to answer him or ignore him.

"Hmm, I'm Captain Valex. I come from planet Vortula in the Amexia Galaxy. We have come seeking special water from Dionne. Our King is gravely ill and only that will save him," Captain Valex explained.

"If you had explained this when I called via the radio, we could have arranged for this to be brought to your ship and then you could have been most of the way home by now. Do you have any proof that this is your assignment?" Zeke asked.

Captain Valex produced a video transmit from a doctor who stated that only the water from Dionne would save their leader. Zeke nodded his acceptance and radioed back to Chylla.

"They need water from Dionne for their leader. He is gravely ill and only that will save him. How do we do this?" Zeke asked.

"I will send what we have left of the Stealth Raiders to Dionne; it will be faster that way. I will then have them deliver it to you," Chylla replied.

"Very well. I will wait until it has been delivered before I leave the ship," Zeke told her. He turned back to Captain Valex and explained the plan.

"Thank you. We will hold course here until the water is delivered. Have you any ideas how we can make it back quicker?" Captain Valex asked the worry was clear to see across his face.

"I'll see what I can arrange," Zeke told him.

He walked away from the Captain and radioed Chylla again. "Is there any way we can get them back any faster?

"I can think of one way, but it's going to be a huge ask. Hold on," Chylla replied. The radio fell silent for a while.

"Where are you going?" Aquilia asked as Chylla stood to leave the comms room.

"I need to speak with the Higher Elders. The captain has requested a faster travel time. Normally on Saturnites and Enceladant are allowed to use Hyper Jump, but I am going to request that Captain Valex be able to use it to get home," Chylla explained.

"Do you think that is wise?" Aquilia asked. "I mean, we don't even know these beings."

"I know. The Higher Elders can dig deeper into them before they make a decision. It will take the Stealth Raiders at least another half an hour before they have enough of Dionne's water to serve its purpose," Chylla said. She left the comms room and proceeded to the meeting room. She hoped they could help, especially as they once needed help from a far off land. The help didn't arrive in time, but she knew if that had contacted the far off galaxy in time, it probably would have saved their beloved Queen Quintara.

Chapter Three

"Zeke, are you there?" Zyra called over the radio.

"I'm here," Zeke replied.

"I have authorised a Hyper Jump for our friends. This will only work once and YOU are to initialise it," Zyra explained.

"I'm not sure I know how to," Zeke replied. "I've never done that before."

"Don't worry. Chylla will talk you through the controls. You will need to be on Onyx Abyss Alpha for it to work. Now, The Stealth Raiders should be with you any second. Hand over the water and bid them farewell," Zyra told him.

"Understood," Zeke replied. He placed his radio back into his pocket. "I believe Dionne's water will be here momentarily. I will then set you to Hyper Jump so you can return hastily."

"I appreciate all the help you have given us. We give you this as a token of our gratitude," Captain Valex handed him a golden chalice encrusted with emeralds.

"There is absolutely no need for this," Zeke replied looking at the chalice in awe.

"Please. Accept it and hand it to Queen Aquilia," Captain Valex bowed his head.

"Very well, I will pass over your gratitude. Now, let's get you home," Zeke told him.

Zeke bid his farewells to the crew of Captain Valex's ship and left via the side hatch to return to Onyx Abyss Alpha. Once aboard, he radioed back to Chylla to ask for instructions.

"Are you in front of the controls?" Chylla asked.

"Yes," he replied.

"OK. I want you to press the blue button, three times. Then the yellow one twice. You got that?" She told him.

"Blue three times and yellow twice. Got it," he replied. "Wait! Which yellow button? There are two."

"It's the one on the left," Chylla told him.

Zeke steeled his nerves and pressed the correct sequence. "Now what?" He asked.

"Now, move the ship so that it faces Captain Valex's and press the red button," she told him.

He took holder of the ship's steering column and turned the ship so it faced head on to the other. He then pressed the red button. A burst of light emitted from the front of the ship and radiated over Captain Valex's. Within a few seconds, the other ships were gone and all that was left was wide open space.

"Well done Zeke. Time to come back now. We have something to discuss," Aquilia radioed to him.

"Yes Ma'am. I'm on my way," he replied.

"You did good," Mitzi said as he sat down for the return trip.

"Thanks. I was so nervous. I didn't know what to expect," he replied. "So about you?"

"There will be plenty of time for that another time. I know what you saw. I know what gift you possess," she told him with a smile.

For the rest of the journey, Zeke watched as Saturn spun below. He missed his old house, but he had come to love his new one. He wondered if his cousin, Evadene missed her home and, most importantly, her mother, Halana.

"We're nearly back. You all good?" Balzar asked him.

"I'm as good as I can be, thanks," Zeke replied.

"I know what you left behind. I know it was hard, but look at what you have now. Maybe one day you'll visit again. Maybe one day you'll see that things aren't so different up here," Balzar said. "But know, there are a lot of people around who come from far and wide, if you ever need us, we're here."

"Thank you, I may take you up on that one day. Right now though, I best hand this over. I can get quite clumsy when I'm nervous," Zeke thanked him.

Onyx Abyss Alpha landed perfectly and the stairs to the ship descended onto the landing bay. As Zeke made his way down, he said goodbye to the crew and thanked them for their hospitality.

Aquilia met him at the bottom of the steps and nodded towards Balzar. "Follow me Zeke. We have some matters to discuss."

"Should I be worried?" Zeke asked.

"It just depends how you will take this. It is a big decision to make," Aquilia replied.

Zeke followed his Queen towards the meeting room. He had begun to worry about what Aquilia wanted to discuss. He frantically wrung his hands together in nervousness.

"Try not to worry Zeke. It will be totally your decision," Aquilia smiled. She held the door to the meeting room open for him to enter first.

The room hadn't changed much. The same white table sat at the centre of the room. The white walls making the room seem bigger than it was. He half expected an ambush from the Higher Elders as he took a seat at the table.

Aquilia sat beside him. She still had a smile on her face. "Now Zeke, I need you to listen to me very carefully before jumping to a decision."

Zeke nodded.

Aquilia was worried about how he would react at being stationed *on* Onyx Abyss Alpha full time. "OK, I'm just going to come out with it. Matro has been grounded. We need a full time technician on Onyx Abyss Alpha and I think you will be perfect for the job. It's higher pay than here in the Palace but due to some health conditions, the doctors have grounded Matro. Would you like to take the job?"

Zeke sat in stunned silence. "Who would take over here? I mean, there's no one qualified. I would have to train someone and fast. How long before you need an answer?"

"Slow down Zeke. It would be a straight swap. Matro would be able to take over from you on Enceladus and you would take over from him up there. It's simple. Do you want to talk to your parents about it? We have some time," Aquilia replied.

"Erm, yes, can I?" He answered.

"Of course. You know where to find them," Aquilia said as he ran off in search of Bella and Layson.

"I hope he takes the offer," Quintara's voice came over the intercom.

"Who knows Mum; maybe he'll want to stay here, then I will have to look for and train someone else," Aquilia sighed. "I hope he accepts. It's a great opportunity for him."

Zeke wandered through the Palace in search of his parents. The whole time, Aquilia's words were ringing through his head. *"You would be perfect for the job. On Onyx Abyss Alpha."*

It wasn't long before he found his Dad. Exactly where he always was. Sat behind Sinclair's old desk.

"Dad, are you busy?" Zeke asked, lightly tapping on the door.

"Come in son, never too busy for you. What's up? You look like you've been told that the world is ending," Layson said, gesturing for Zeke to sit in the chair opposite him.

Zeke took the seat but then lost his nerve to ask his father what he thought of Aquilia's offer.

"Spit it out Zeke. I can tell when something is bothering you. Out with it," Layson told him.

Zeke looked his father in the eyes. "Queen Aquilia has offered me a job."

"Well, you already have one. What is different about this one?" Layson asked.

"It's on Onyx Abyss Alpha. I would be the ships technician," he replied.

"What's happened to Matro?" Layson questioned. "Is he OK?"

"Matro is OK. The doctors have grounded him though, something to do with his health," Zeke told his father. "I don't know whether to take the job or not."

"I would say the choice is yours, but I know how good you are at your job. Queen Aquilia knows too, that's probably why she offered it to you first and didn't advertise it," he told Zeke.

"I told her I would chat with you and mum first; do you know where she is?" Zeke asked.

"Probably in the outhouse that Queen Aquilia built for her to practice in. She was trying the same spell in the kitchen and created a blast," Layson informed him.

"So it was Mum that made the noise!" Zeke laughed. "I'm going to find her and ask her opinion. So you think I should go for it?"

"I certainly do son. You will be great at it," Layson told him. "I'm sure you will love travelling around."

"Thanks Dad. Talk to you later!" Zeke shouted as he ran down the corridor.

Layson laughed as he shook his head. He was happy Zeke had settled in well here. A shrill tone broke through his thoughts. He picked up the clear phone which rested beside him.

"Hello," he answered.

"We need Zeke and fast. Is he still with you? Aquilia replied.

"No, he's just gone off to find Bella. I'm sure I can catch up with him pretty quickly. Is it urgent?" Layson asked.

"Indeed. Be as fast as you can, meet us at Onyx Abyss Alpha." With that the line went dead.

Layson didn't miss a beat. He rose from his chair and sprinted after Zeke, shouting his name as he ran.

Zeke had just made it to the outhouse when he heard his father's shouts.

"Dad, what is it?" Zeke asked, helping his father sit on a nearby wall.

"Aquilia called. You're needed urgently. You are to meet her at Onyx Abyss Alpha," Layson panted.

"But I haven't spoken to Mum yet," Zeke replied looking anxious.

"The Queen said it is urgent. You're mother will understand," Layson told him. "Go. I will talk to her."

Zeke nodded once and ran in the direction of the launch pad.

Layson quickly gathered himself and knocked on the door of the outhouse. Bella answered, her face covered in white powder.

"What is it Layson, you look worried," Bella asked, shaking her head to release some of the loose powder.

"It's Zeke. He has been offered the position of technician on Onyx Abyss Alpha. He is worried how we will react to him being away a lot of the time. I've told him I believe he is a perfect fit for the job. He was on his way here to talk to you about it, but he has been summoned by Her Majesty," Layson explained.

"Oh my boy! Working on Onyx Abyss Alpha! It makes my heart flutter. Of course he must accept, but what of Matro?" Bella asked. "Is he OK?"

"He is my love, but he has a few health conditions. Zeke told me that the doctors are going to ground him, which means the ship needs a new tech," Layson explained. "When he returns, I will send him to you. How are you getting on?"

"Slowly, but I'm taking my time now. I will come and find you later," Bella replied and she closed the door.

Layson wished he hadn't believed everything Altair had told him before about Queen Quintara and King Elio. He imagined how his life would be back on Saturn. He still had his monthly injections to keep the Dark Wolf at bay. It had only been seen once since the battle against Altair. Layson was glad it was under control. He liked his life here.

"Your Majesty, I came as fast as I could," Zeke announced as he reached the launch pad.

"Ah Zeke. Thank you for getting here so quickly. We need you to get on board right away. Matro has taken a turn for the worse and we are needed on the boarders of Pluto," Aquilia told him.

Zeke nodded once and began to climb the steps.

"Your Majesty, there has been major casualties on Pluto, we must move immediately," Balzar told her.

"Then off we go," Aquilia replied. "I will stay in contact."

She closed the hatch and Zeke settled into the seat vacated by Matro.

"It works the same way as Enceladus," Mitzi said from beside him. "Looks like we're gonna be working together!"

"Seems like it," Zeke smiled. Something about her settled his nerves.

"What's happening out there Zeke?" Balzar asked, guiding the ship through the space junk that had accumulated over the centuries.

"It's not looking good," Zeke replied. "There's over a hundred ships descending on Pluto. What could be there that they could possibly want?"

"I don't know, but we are about to find out," Balzar replied.

As Zeke looked up from his monitors, a huge ship came into view. An ominous looking being stared straight at them.

Chapter Four

Halana had become worried about how long they had been underground. She pulled her phone from her pocket and hoped to get a signal from so far down. She dialled Queen Aquilia and waited for a reply.

"Halana, what is it?" Aquilia answered.

"Is it safe to bring the children out yet Your Highness?" Halana asked.

"Out? Oh my, you are still in the bunker?" Aquilia exclaimed. "Yes, yes, absolutely. It had completely slipped my mind. We had an issue with Pluto. In fact, meet me in the dining hall."

Aquilia hung up the phone and rushed from the comms room where Chylla held the fort.

"Come now children. Your mother says it is safe to emerge," Halana smiled. "Scarlex, are you OK?"

"Yes Ma'am, just feeling a little breathless," she replied.

The children followed her to the surface, gulping large amounts of air as they did.

"Go slowly children. Your brain will go fuzzy if you feed it too much as once," Halana warned them. "Why don't you head off and finish your sculptures, I'm sure Aunt Evadene will be delighted to see what you have achieved."

The two children ran to the art enclosure, scarlet and blue hair bouncing around as they ran. Halana shook her head and made her way to the dining room to meet with Aquilia.

"What have you made Scar?" Eliontara asked, lopping his head side to side.

"It's supposed to be Mother, but I don't think I have quite got the dress right. Do you think you could help me out?" She asked.

"I can try," he replied grabbing a handful of clay. "If we add a bit more flare here, and, using this palette knife, insert a fold here, I think you've got it just about right."

"Thanks brother! It looks amazing, now I just need it to dry so I can paint it," Scarlex said in amazement. "You really are talented."

"You have your talents too sis, maybe you are yet to discover them fully, but they are there," Eliontara smiled.

"Do you think we will be able to visit Aunt Evadene soon? I miss her and Uncle Janus," Scarlex asked.

"I'm sure mother will let us visit again soon. Let's get this finished so we can call Aunt Evadene later and show her," Eliontara said.

As they worked, a mysterious figure watched them from afar. Careful not to be spotted, the being camouflaged themselves against the backdrop of the plants.

"I can see them Master. What be your orders?" She hissed.

"Keep an eye on the girl. She is hiding something," came the reply. "She harbours something deep within that will inevitably become handy should we need to fight."

"Indeed sir," she replied.

She continued to watch the children. Taking in the ways in which they moved and communicated with each other. When she was finally satisfied with her recon work, she slithered away and returned to her Master in order to share her findings.

"Your Majesty, what has happened?" Halana asked as she sat with Aquilia in the dining room.

"Halana, thank you for coming. Matro has been taken gravely ill. We had news from Pluto that someone has instigated an attack and we have had to send Onyx Abyss Alpha there," Aquilia began to explain.

"So who has taken over poor Matro? Will he be OK?" Halana asked.

"Zeke has taken Matro's place. I had asked him before we found out about Pluto, but whilst he was checking in with Layson and Bella; we received word on the impending attack. I had no choice but to send them off to find out exactly what is happening," Aquilia explained.

"Have we heard back from them? Do we know anything further about the army?" Halana asked. She threw questions left and right.

Aquilia held up her hand. "I know you have a soft spot for Zeke, but I trust Balzar and Mitzi to keep him safe."

Just as she finished her sentence, Chylla radioed through. "We have word from Balzar."

Aquilia gestured for Halana to accompany her to the comms room. Halana worried about a lot of the younger ones on Enceladus. She followed Aquilia as she made her way through the Palace, silently hoping that Zeke and the others were safe.

"What do we have Chylla?" Aquilia asked as she sat in Zee's chair.

"I'm not sure. We received this video not more than a few minutes before I radioed you," Chylla pointed to the monitors in front of her, and played the clip.

"This is Onyx Abyss Alpha. We are requesting backup assistance immediately. Contact with enemy is imminent. Search UAO773."

"That was Zeke," Halana cried. "Has there been any more contact?"

"I'm afraid not. It's been radio silence since that video was received," Chylla replied.

"We should get Layson to run a check on the code that Zeke said. I don't want to worry him so we will have to keep this to a minimum," Aquilia told them. "It is strictly a need to know basis."

"But I think they need to know!" Halana cried. "He is their son for crying out loud. Wouldn't you want to know if it was one of yours?"

"Of course I would, but right now, we cannot allow anyone to know the details. Not yet. As soon as we figure out who the army belongs to, we can then take the next steps," Aquilia replied. "Have Nymeria and Celest arrived back yet?"

"I called them back urgently, they should arrive momentarily," Chylla replied.

"Thank you. Halana, run this message to Layson and ask him to check out this tail code as quickly as physically possible. Where are the children?" Aquilia asked.

"In the Art enclosure. They are finishing their sculptures to show Eva later. I'll run the message up and wait until he has something to show," Halana replied. "I promise I will not utter a word."

"Thank you," Aquilia whispered. "I'm going to check on the children."

Halana left the comms room and made her way to Layson's office. She made it just as he was returning from his brief visit with Bella.

"Ah Layson, just the right man for the job," Halana smiled.

"Halana, lovely to see you. How can I help?" He reciprocated the smile and allowed her to enter his office first. "Please, have a seat."

"Thank you. I have a tail code, sent from Onyx Abyss Alpha. How fast can you do a search?" Halana asked, handing over the paper.

"It will take me mere seconds to have the information needed. Is this the reason for Zeke being called up so urgently?" Layson asked.

"I believe he is attending some recon for the Queen," Halana lied. She hated lying, but Aquilia had asked her to keep things secret for the time being so she would obey.

"I'm glad he has been offered this position. I really think it will be good for him to get off the rock for a while. He needs to be around others," Layson spoke whilst he searched. "Ahh, here we are." He printed off the necessary information and handed it over. "Please inform me of his return."

Halana nodded and took the paper from his outstretched hands. "Thank you Layson. I will certainly let you know when he returns." Her eyes wandered to the window as she watched another ship land.

Layson turned to see Nymeria's ship descend and land. "I thought they weren't due back until tomorrow? What's happening?"

"I'm not sure. I will find out and inform you," Halana lied again. "Thank you for the information." She smiled as she strode from the room.

Halana made her way back to the comms room and handed the paper over to Chylla. As she read over the information, Chylla's hand covered her mouth. "It can't be."

"Can't be what?" Nymeria asked from behind Halana.

"The army which is attacking Pluto. It's Foltuna from Gaxotroid Andromeda," Chylla informed her. "They have taken Onyx Abyss Alpha hostage."

<u>Chapter Five</u>

"Right, listen up. Onyx Abyss Alpha is now in a hostage situation. We are its only backup. This is what you trained for," Nymeria shouted.

Before her stood an over one thousand strong army, consisting of The Stealth Raiders and the additional trained personnel. All eyes were on her as she explained their plan of action.

"We are not to alarm Foltuna, but we are to make our presence known," Nymeria continued. "Stealth Raiders, we are to circle the main ship. Use cloaking to hide our presence until they make a move. No-one moves until *I* give the order, understood?"

"Yes Ma'am" they shouted in unison.

"Right, fall out!" She shouted.

The deafening noise of over a thousand boots marching out of the military hall made Aquilia cover her ears. She had heard it many a time with drills and training, but her ears would never get used to the noise.

"Are you OK Your Highness?" Halana said as she gently touched Aquilia's arm.

"Yes, sorry Halana. The noise, it just becomes too much," Aquilia replied.

"Let's go somewhere a little quieter. Maybe we should check on the children," Halana smiled as she guided the Queen away from the thunderous steps.

"Zeke, it seems your plan worked. The video was received by Enceladus. Let's hope they work out what to do," Balzar said.

"I hope so too. I'm just glad they haven't tried to come aboard yet," Mitzi whispered.

"Everything will be fine Mitzi. Try not to panic," Balzar said softly. "It's not like last time."

Zeke knew what he meant. When he had briefly held Mitzi's hand earlier that day, he had seen everything. From the way she was bound, to the look on her face. He could tell something like this is terrifying for her.

Mitzi turned to see him watching her. "I know what you saw," she whispered.

"Saw? Me? I didn't see anything," Zeke protested.

"I'm Alphir. I know you are part Alphir," Mitzi replied.

"Why are you here and not back on Alphitrax?" Zeke questioned.

"Alaysia thought it best I train with the Enceladants. She saw that I had a talent and sent me here," Mitzi explained.

"I signed her up for Onyx Abyss Alpha when I saw her interrogate a prisoner we were holding for questioning after the first attack on Enceladus after Aquilia was crowned," Balzar said.

"The Neptunites? I thought no prisoners were captured?" Zeke asked.

"There was only one. She was caught trying to break into the Queen's personal quarters. Celest and Nymeria caught her, took her to the dungeon and placed me on guard," Mitzi explained. "I could hear her muttering some inaudible things, so I shackled her to the wall and questioned her."

"It was amazing; you should have seen how the woman just gave up all the information. It's something I've never seen before. That's what I knew, I just *had* to have Mitzi on my team," Balzar smiled.

"And Matro?" Zeke asked. "He is great at his job right?"

"Oh beyond any doubt, he's one of the best. It's a shame that, for his race, he suffers some rapidly declining health issues, much like the one he is having now. Man, I hope he's doing OK," Balzar replied.

Zeke stole a glance from the side window, grateful to see an armada of ships making their way towards them. "I think we have company."

Mitzi climbed on Zeke's lap to get a better view out of the window. "Sorry," she smiled.

"It's OK," Zeke laughed.

They watched as the ships got closer, not too close, but close enough that Zeke could make out Mythia's in the centre seat of the head ship.

"If they are there, where are The Stealth Raiders?" Balzar asked.

"I don't know, but if I know Nymeria and Celest as well as I think I do, they won't be far away," Zeke replied.

"We have them in our sights," Celest announced.

"OK, slowly move around, I need to see exactly what we are up against. There was no word on how many ships there were," Nymeria replied.

Celest manoeuvred the ship so that it moved amongst the armada as it sat just above Pluto. A plume of smoke billowing from below signalling that they had already launched one attack, Nymeria would make sure they didn't launch another. With the ship covered by the cloaking technology, they worked their way around the mass, finally settling right at the centre.

"OK, seems the lead ship is currently stationed next to Onyx Abyss Alpha. We could easily take these out and then work on the lead ship?" Celest suggested.

"Seems too risky, any other suggestions?" Nymeria asked.

"I do have one," came a small voice from the back.

"Come forward" Nymeria ordered.

A young boy, maybe only around twelve or thirteen made his way forward. "Sorry for speaking out of turn."

"No, please, what did you have in mind?" Nymeria asked.

"Well, as you can see, this ship here," he pointed at the one closest to their left side. "Is leaking some sort of fluid. Maybe if we ignite a flame, it may just take out the rest for us?"

"What's your name?" Nymeria asked.

"Shlysta Ma'am," he replied.

"You may have a point Shlysta. Let's give it a go. Celest, move us back as soon as I ignite the flame. Everyone, brace yourselves," Nymeria announced.

"Will I be punished if it doesn't work?" Shlysta asked as he made his way back to his seat.

"Absolutely not. Everyone is entitled to have suggestion," Celest smiled.

"OK. Everyone ready?" Nymeria asked.

She held the flare gun tight, aimed it at the leaking ship, said a quick prayer and pulled the trigger. The red flame ignited the other ships leaking fuel and caused a chain reaction.

Celest quickly moved their ship as far as possible before almost twenty ships became a huge fireball. As ships exploded left and right, Celest managed to avoid being hit by flying debris. She watched as doors flew past The Stealth Ship at a rate of knots, just skimming the top of her ship. She pushed the controls forward causing the ship to nose dive before another hunk of metal skimmed past her on the right.

"This is getting dangerous," she said.

"Isn't that just part of the fun?" Nymeria smiled.

Celest knew what she meant. They had been in worse danger before now, but never part of a huge fireball.

A large piece of the ignited ship flew under them, crashing into their lead ship, rendering it useless. Celest brought her ship up alongside it and Nymeria climbed aboard.

"You are to state your grievances with Pluto," Nymeria ordered.

"Our fight is with them, not you Stealth Raider. Mind your business," the Captain of the lead ship replied.

"Then we take you in for questioning. Celest, hook us up," Nymeria radioed. "I'll take it from here." Nymeria gestured for her crew to restrain the captain and his crew.

Celest tethered her ship to the lead ship of Foltuna and towed it back to Enceladus.

"Chylla wanted me to allow Scarlex and Eliontara to get involved with The Stealth Raiders, but I feel they are still so young," Aquilia told Halana as they sat at the crystal fountain.

"Young? Scarlex and Eliontara young? Don't let them hear you say that," Halana laughed. "Isn't one of the youngest only around twelve?"

"Shlysta? Yes, but he is different," Aquilia replied.

"Is he? Or is it because he isn't your child?" Halana smiled. "It's completely understandable, you want to protect your babies, but you promised not to treat them that way."

Aquilia sighed. "I did, didn't I?"

Halana smiled. "You are a brilliant mother. I don't doubt that your own parents are beyond proud of how well you are doing."

"Mother never says anything personal anymore. It's like she has completely forgotten that I ever existed, especially since I told her about me being Alphir," Aquilia said as she hung her head down.

"Try not to be too disheartened Your Majesty. It is probably a lot to take in," Halana said as she gently touched Aquilia's shoulder.

Aquilia looked up at the sky just as The Stealth Raiders broke through the atmosphere. They were towing another ship behind them, with Onyx Abyss Alpha bringing up the rear.

"What on...What is this?" Aquilia cried.

She radioed through to Chylla demanding answers.

"I tried to reach you Your Highness. They captured the lead ship of Foltuna and are bringing its captain in for questioning," Chylla replied.

"Thank you Chylla. I assume Mitzi will be in charge of questioning?" Aquilia replied. She knew Mitzi could do a great job and would have the information out of them in seconds.

"Indeed Your Highness," Chylla replied.

Before anyone could say anything else, an ear shattering horn blasted through their thoughts. As Aquilia and Halana picked themselves up from the floor, a ship, almost three times the size of Onyx Abyss Alpha entered their atmosphere. The Stealth Raiders quickly towed the lead ship away with Onyx Abyss Alpha following along behind.

"You are to let my leader go," came a booming voice.

"Not until they answer my questions. You do NOT, and I repeat, DO NOT have permission to land. I suggest you wait them out where you are or return later," Aquilia fired back.

"And who might you be woman?" A male voice asked, clearly annoyed by her orders.

"I am Queen Aquilia of Saturn and Enceladus. I will only warn you once more, make your choice," Aquilia replied, her eyes now flickering red.

"I don't take orders from women, especially not small women like you. I will take my ship and I will leave," the man shouted.

Aquilia rolled her eyes which were now flaming red. "I swore she wouldn't rear her head again but *you* just made me change my mind."

Within a heartbeat, The Phoenix had broken through and was now ship to beak with the bigger ship.

"You had a choice and you chose wrong," she thundered. "Now you leave without a choice."

She grabbed the ship with her talons and flung it out of the atmosphere.

No-one moved an inch. Not even Halana. Something was dreadfully different about The Phoenix. Something Halana couldn't quite put her finger on.

<u>Chapter Six</u>

"Did that just happen?" Mitzi asked Zeke.

"Yes, it did. Did you miss the entire fight against Altair?" Zeke asked.

"I missed the major parts," Mitzi said lowering her eyes.

Then it hit Zeke. What he had seen earlier that day. He wanted to reach out to her but he was afraid of what would happen.

The ship landed and Mitzi made her way to the interrogation room, closely followed by Zeke.

"I have to do this part alone, I'm sorry," she said as she turned to face him.

"Absolutely. I'll wait in the canteen, will you come by after?" Zeke asked.

"I guess. I'll see you then?" Mitzi replied, blushing slightly.

Zeke turned towards the comms room. He would check in with Chylla first before grabbing something to eat in the canteen.

As he entered the room, he overheard Chylla on the radio to Zyra.

"I know she said she would keep it under wraps but I think he just pushed her too far," Chylla said.

"It wasn't a good move. Now he has something over her should they ever come to blows again. She must be more careful," Zyra replied.

"I'll speak to her," Chylla said.

"See that you do. You are the only one left from the original Elders who taught her, you should be keeping a better eye on her!" Zyra scolded her.

Zeke had become angry but he didn't speak out of turn. He waited for Chylla to finish her conversation before announcing his arrival.

Chylla placed the radio down and put her head in her hands. 'How am I supposed to keep an eye on her when she's the Queen? I can't exactly punish her for anything she does, it's her world!' She said to herself.

"It's hard isn't it?" Zeke whispered.

"Zeke. How long have you been there?" Chylla asked.

"Long enough to hear you being scolded by Zyra," he replied. "Does she have any idea how hard it is to protect a world and its entire population?"

"It's not as simple as that Zeke and you know it," Chylla told him. "She is the Higher Elder. We bow to her."

"Not Queen Aquilia. We bow to Queen Aquilia. I understand that you loyalties lie with the Higher Elders, but mine lie with the Queen," Zeke said. He smiled at Chylla before leaving and getting some lunch before meeting back up with Mitzi.

"So, you refuse to give your name and you refuse to answer any questions regarding your mission freely?" Mitzi asked.

The man refused to reply.

"Well, I guess we have to do this a different way," Mitzi said. She turned away from him and rolled her neck twice to the left and once back to the right. Her eyes turned black and she lashed a forked tongue. "I'll ask again. What is your name and what is your mission?"

The man turned physically orange with fright. "My name is Yasha. I'm from the Foltuna Armada and we had Intel that one of our fugitives was being harboured by Plutons. We were told to go and extradite him back to Maxidus."

"Now, that wasn't so hard was it," she hissed.

Yasha was visibly shaking in fear of her. His skin had lost it purple tone and had turned a burnt orange colour. He was sweating more than any other alien being had before and his eyes kept rolling back into his head. Mitzi became worried. She radioed through to Zeke.

"I think you need to come and see this," she said.

"I'm on my way," he replied. He put the sandwich down he was eating and ran to the interrogation rooms.

Mitzi didn't have time to change to her original form before Zeke arrived but he didn't seem fazed by her appearance.

"How long has he been like this?" Zeke asked, laying him down on the floor.

"I don't know. Only a few minutes. I got the information out of him and he just started sweating like that and his eyes. What's happening to him Zeke?" Mitzi said, panic filtering through her voice.

Zeke looked at her in her current form. "What are you?" He asked.

Mitzi had been warned to be very careful who she informed of her form. "I'm....I'm a Slizard."

Zeke had read about them in Evadene's books. They were formed as part serpent, part lizard. They possessed a rare genetic dysfunction meaning they could survive in any climate or atmosphere.

"I'll take him to medical, but I think I know what's happened," Zeke told her. "Don't blame yourself." He smiled at her as he carried Yasha to the medical suite.

Mitzi watched as Zeke left and turned the corner. She slowly morphed back into herself and left the room. As she walked she looked out of the windows of the Palace at the surrounding gardens. She spotted Scarlex and Eliontara in some form of enclosure. She walked towards them but was stopped by Zeke.

"They worked out what was wrong with him," Zeke said.

"What was it?" Mitzi replied, looking over his shoulder at the two Royals.

"His kind doesn't react well to Slizards. Now, the doctor asked if he had come into contact with any recently. I know it's customary not to reveal anyone's form unless given prior permission so I kept it quiet," Zeke answered her. His eyes followed hers. "Ah, Scarlex and Eliontara. Queen Aquilia's children. They are finishing their sculptures for my cousin."

"Your cousin? Who is that?" Mitzi asked.

"Evadene. She is the Duchess of Astrodia," Zeke said proudly.

"I believe I have heard of her. I had no idea she was a relation to you. Maybe I am in the presence of Royalty also?" Mitzi gestured to him.

"Oh no. My dad was friends with Altair, until he came to his senses. I'm not even remotely royal. Stands me no chance with the girls," Zeke laughed. "They seem to only be interested if I am part of the Royal Family."

Mitzi looked at him in the eyes. "I'm sure the right girl will come along when you least expect it. Anyway, now you are the technician on the ship, you won't have to worry about girls for a while. You won't be on land enough to keep up," she laughed.

Shrugging her shoulders she walked back to Onyx Abyss Alpha.

"I haven't spoken to my mum about it yet," Zeke whispered.

Zeke walked back towards the ship with his head hanging low. He really didn't know what to say about the job that Aquilia had offered him. He would love the chance to travel with Onyx Abyss Alpha, but what if something happened here and he was needed. How fast could that ship actually go without the need to clearance for Hyper Jump?

As he turned the corner he came face to face with Balzar.

"What's up with Mitzi?" He asked.

"The being she interrogated has a bad reaction to Slizards," Zeke replied.

"Ah. So you know?" Balzar asked.

"Yeah, Mitzi told me. I haven't told anyone else though, not even the doctor. Even if the Maxidum does say anything, the doctor will probably put it down to cloudy brain. He's not exactly in the right frame of mind to describe *exactly* what he saw," Zeke smiled.

"So, they're from Maxidus? Interesting. Look, we're grounded for a few hours. Why don't you go off and see your family?" Balzar offered.

"I think I will. I haven't even spoken to my mum about taking the job yet," Zeke replied. "Thanks."

Balzar nodded towards him and turned in search of Mitzi. He knew something like this was bound to happen soon. He just hoped he could smooth it over with her before they left again later. He could do without her going into hibernation on him whilst they were away.

Aquilia landed softly next to Halana and transformed back to her Enceladant form.

"What was that?" Halana asked as Aquilia's wings finally tucked themselves away.

"He was being a brat! I asked him nicely," Aquilia shrugged.

"And what if Freefla had just so happened to go past? You know how sneaky he is," Halana said angrily.

"He didn't though so..." Aquilia shrugged.

Halana lifted her arms in the air. She didn't even have the words. "There's just...Oh forget it." She said and turned to walk away.

Aquilia studied her for a moment. "Why is she so angry?" She asked herself out loud.

"Maybe you should see Chylla, she will bring you up to date," Zeke said as he walked past.

"Why?" Aquilia asked.

"I think its best you hear it from her," Zeke replied. "Have you seen my mum?"

"The outhouse. Thanks Zeke," Aquilia answered.

"Anytime," he replied as he walked away.

Aquilia made her way to the comms room. She needed to know what Zeke meant. As she got nearer, she could hear raised voices.

"And how exactly am I going to stop her?" Chylla asked.

"Any way possible. Even if you have to lock her up," Quintara replied.

"I won't do it," Chylla said. "She is the Queen. I cannot go against her."

"And you are *FORBIDDEN* to disobey orders from the Higher Elders, are you not?" Quintara replied through gritted teeth. "If she lets that thing loose again, who knows what could happen or *who* it could get back to."

Chylla shook her head. "I will talk with her, but I cannot promise anything."

"Then you best be *very* persuasive," Quintara replied and closed off the connection.

Aquilia stepped inside the room quietly and sat down next to Chylla. "I think we need a little chat, don't you?"

Chylla looked up and into Aquilia's electric blue eyes.

"How much did you hear?" Chylla whispered.

"Enough. Now. Talk," Aquilia replied, narrowing her eyes at Chylla.

Chapter Seven

"Mum, are you here?" Zeke called out as he neared the outhouse.

Bella flew out of the door with a smile. "Zeke! How is it?"

"How is what Mum?" He asked.

"Oh you know the big open space!" Bella smiled.

"You know?" Zeke asked.

"Your father mentioned it earlier. I'm so proud of you!" She beamed.

"You don't mind if I accept? What if something happens here and you need me?" Zeke asked, worry slipping through.

"Oh Zeke! I think your father and I are old enough now to look after ourselves. You deserve to go and see what's out there," Bella told him as she hugged him tight.

"Thanks Mum." Zeke whispered as a solitary tear fell from his eye. "I'll check in when I can."

"I know you will darling," Bella said as she stroked his hair.

"Well, I best let Queen Aquilia know that I will accept the position," Zeke smiled.

Bella watched Zeke walk back to the Palace before heading back into the outhouse.

"Are you OK dear?" Benzyline asked, rushing to her side.

"Oh, don't worry. Just watching my only child take a leap off a small rock," Bella smiled.

"Zeke? Has he fallen? Does he need assistance?" Benzyline asked.

Bella laughed. She clasped Benzyline by the shoulders and looked her in the eyes. "Do you remember when Lyra first moved out of the house?"

"She never moved out. I kicked her out before she married that vile man," Benzyline replied. "But I do remember when she became her own sorceress."

"That's exactly how I feel now," Bella replied.

"But Zeke isn't magic, is he?" Benzyline asked as she looked out of the window. "He looks relatively normal if you ask me!"

Bella laughed even harder. "Oh Benzyline! Zeke has been offered a job aboard Onyx Abyss Alpha as the technician."

"Well, you could have lead with that," Benzyline smiled. "He deserves it. He is such a good spirit. He will do just fine up there, you'll see."

Bella turned back towards the table and continued practising the same spell. This time, it worked.

"Ha! Maybe you just needed to take a load off your mind dear," Benzyline laughed.

Both women sunk to the floor with their backs against the wall and breathed a sigh of relief.

"Right," Bella said as closed her eyes. "What's next?"

Benzyline stared wide eyed at her. "Next? Oh no dear. Now you must rest. An Alphir cannot perform so much magic at once. You must rest."

As she looked over at Bella, she had fallen asleep right where she sat. Benzyline didn't want to wake her so she silently crept out of the outhouse and back to the Palace. As she approached, she could hear raised voices.

"So you think you can just lock me up?" Aquilia shouted at Chylla. "Do you really think that would hold me back?"

"That wasn't my idea Your Highness, that came from Quintara," Chylla argued back.

"Of course it did. Even though I am now the Queen, she is *still* trying to control things," Aquilia argued. "Why can't she just let me do things my way?"

"Because, as The Higher Elders, we are here to make sure you do the right thing," Zyra interrupted.

"The right thing? Am I not allowed to make mistakes? Does everything have to be perfect?" Aquilia demanded.

Chylla hung her head. She didn't know what to say. She knew Aquilia was right, but she couldn't go against what The Higher Elders asked of her.

"Now, all of a sudden, you are silent Chylla. You have nothing to add to this?" Aquilia asked her.

"Your Highness, I am ordered to protect you. With you flaunting you inner power, you are putting the whole Kingdom at risk," Chylla replied. "I cannot help but wonder if The Phoenix now controls you and not you controlling it."

Aquilia was shocked. "You seriously think I would jeopardise the kingdom? I'm surprised at you. All of you. I fought for

this Kingdom. Just as I fought for Astrodia, and now, this."
Aquilia said. "I'm disappointed."

Aquilia turned to leave the comms room, knocking down
Benzyline in the process.

"Your Majesty," Benzyline bowed. "Whatever is the matter?"

Aquilia calmed herself before relaying everything to her.
Benzyline tipped her head sideways and gave a half smile.
"You control The Phoenix. Not the other way around. Why
don't you go and see Zeke before he leaves with Onyx Abyss
Alpha."

"Leaves? Did he accept the job?" Aquilia asked.

"From what I have heard, yes, but I suggest you pay him a
visit before he departs," Benzyline bowed again before
walking away.

Aquilia made her way towards the launch pad, in search of
Zeke.

"Balzar, has Zeke boarded yet?" Aquilia asked.

"Not yet Your Highness. We aren't due to leave for another
twenty minutes. I was just giving her a quick spring clean,"
he replied, holding up a purple feather duster.

Aquilia laughed, "Balzar, you realise we are in the middle of
winter."

"Better to start early than not at all!" Balzar laughed. "At least she is ready for whatever is thrown at us."

"Indeed. Where do you think he would have gone?" She asked.

"Try the medical suite Your Highness. I believe he may be visiting Matro," Mitzi said as she sat on the top step on the boarding stairs.

"Thank you Mitzi," Aquilia smiled and she turned for the medical suite.

"You OK Mitz?" Balzar asked genuinely concerned for her.

"Me? Yeah, I'm just dandelion," Mitzi replied, the frown never leaving her face.

"You like him don't you? Afraid he will reject you?" Balzar asked.

"Why do you have to be so good at reading minds?" Mitzi looked up at him. "I'd kick u around but...well...you're up there and I'm down here."

"Oh Mitzi. I can't see why he wouldn't like you. You're kind and considerate...at times," Balzar laughed when Mitzi threw him the side eye. "All I'm saying is see where things lead."

Mitzi sighed audibly. "Maybe. I mean, if Hula can love you, there's hope for all of us, right?" She laughed.

Balzar playfully nudged her elbow and winked at her. "You'll be fine kid. Just wait and see."

Aquilia rushed into the medical suite just in time to see Zeke emerge from the emergency room. He had streaks down his face.

"Zeke, what is it?" Aquilia asked as she rushed to his side. "Is it Matro?"

"He's gone Your Highness. They said his health had deteriorated so much; there was nothing they could do for him. They put him in a deep sleep but his heart stopped just after. I held his hand right to the end, just so he wouldn't be alone. Did I do the right thing? He doesn't have any family," Zeke sobbed.

Aquilia gathered him up and hugged him tight. "I'm sure Matro felt your presence. You did the right thing," she whispered.

"I want to take the job. I want to continue Matro's legacy. When do I start?" Zeke asked.

"Right now, in fact, Balzar and Mitzi are already on board. They just need their technician and they are ready for lift off," Aquilia replied.

Zeke nodded, turned back to look at Matro, just as the doctors covered him over with a bow of their heads, and then made his way to Onyx Abyss Alpha.

It was time for his new adventure to begin. It was time for him to make his own way in life. Time for him to shine.

Chapter Eight

"How did he seem to you?" Mitzi asked as they scanned the surroundings of Maxar.

Zeke kept his eyes on his monitors as he answered. "He was peaceful. I stayed with him the whole time. He was never alone. I promise you."

Zeke had broken the news to Balzar and Mitzi just after they had exited Encelandus's atmosphere. Mitzi had broken down and Zeke had held her whilst she cried, avoiding skin contact at all costs. Balzar had been a little quieter. He had set the ship to autopilot and withdrawn to his own quarters.

"Do you think Balzar will be OK?" Zeke asked her.

"He'll just need some time to come to terms with things. He and Matro go so far back," she replied.

As Zeke concentrated on his monitors, a red light flashed up front. "Mitzi, what's that light?"

"Oh no, that's the collision alert. I'll have to get Balzar," she said, panic dripping through her voice.

Zeke watched as she scurried away, only to return seconds later with Balzar on her heels.

"OK, looks like there is an asteroid heading our way. Zeke, do we have a speed or heading?" He asked.

Zeke scrolled through the monitors, frantically searching for anything that would answer his question but there was nothing that jumped out at him. "There's nothing on screen sir."

"What do you mean? There has to be something there," Balzar demanded.

Zeke checked again, this time zooming in on the surrounding area, again, finding nothing that put their ship in danger. He shook his head. "I've zoomed in at up to 250x zoom and there is nothing there. Not even a speck of space dust."

Balzar stepped towards the monitors and looked at them. He saw nothing that resembled an asteroid or a ship. This confused him. He stared out of the window, hoping to catch a glimpse of whatever had set of the sensors. He narrowed his eyes in order to have a better field of vision. Nothing jumped out at him. Nothing made itself known to him. He was stumped. "Can you run a fault diagnosis?"

Zeke nodded and loaded up the programme. He typed in the instructions and started the scan.

"What else could it be Bal?" Mitzi asked softly.

"I don't know. I had the maintenance done on this ship before we left. There were no faults listed and everything cleared the tests," Balzar replied.

"Nothing is showing on the faults sir," Zeke said. "Could it be something outside?"

"Good question. I'll load up the cameras and see what shows up," Balzar replied. He walked to the front of the ship and pulled up the heads up display. After selecting a few of the options, the screen displayed the outside of the ship. What he saw astounded him.

"How do you think he is doing up there?" Bella asked Layson as they lay under the stars.

"I'm sure he is doing great. It's his niche; he can operate any scanner in this universe and the next. Try not to worry," Layson replied kissing the top of her head.

After watching the dusk fall, they headed back home. After packing the picnic basket away and rinsing the dinner plates. Bella headed off to bed. She drifted off into a fitful sleep. Tossing and turning back and forth.

"Something isn't right. Too many alarms"

"How do we stop them?"

"I don't know. We've never had this many going off at once."

"What do we do? We're too far out for anyone to reach us."

"We just have to wait them out and hope they stop on their own. What do the monitors say?"

"Nothing is showing up. There's no sign of anything heading our way. We seem to be alone up here."

"What's that?"

"Oh no! Get down!"

"Zeke!" Bella screamed.

"Bella! What is it?" Layson mumbled through his sleep.

"I just had the worst dream ever," Bella cried.

Layson took her in his arms and rocked her gently. "Tell me about it," he whispered in her ear.

"Oh Layson. I feel so stupid. I dreamt something bad was happening to them up on Onyx Abyss Alpha. I know Balzar wouldn't let anything happen to them," Bella cried. "But it felt so real!"

"Why don't we go and see Chylla, would that put your mind at rest?" Layson smiled.

Bella nodded so hard she gave herself a headache. They both got dressed and made their way to the Palace. Bella kept looking up as they walked, wringing her hands together with every step. Layson pulled her closer, rubbing his hands up and down her arms and they walked. The closer to the Palace they got, the more worried Bella became. She could see staff members rushing around inside. This seemed so unnatural for this hour of the night.

"What's happening Layson?" Bella whispered. "Please tell me everything is OK?"

"I'm sure it's fine darling. Let's see who we can find," Layson replied.

They opened the door and walked into chaos. There were a mass of beings everywhere. In every direction someone else was shouting instructions.

Layson grabbed the first person he could see, "Lopin, what's going on?"

"I can't really say sir. You will have to find someone higher up than me. I'm just to get everyone into bunkers," Lopin replied.

"Thank you. Carry on," Layson said.

Lopin nodded and ran off.

"Layson?" Bella asked.

"I'm working on it sweetie," he replied.

Layson led Bella deeper into the Palace. He could see the mass of people rushing around. He had dragged Bella halfway towards his security office before being stopped by Yinix.

"Sir, we are in the midst of a major incident. Did you not check your messages?" She asked.

"No, why would I have needed to?" Layson replied pulling his phone from his pocket. Looking at the screen he noticed there were almost seven missed calls and equally as many messages left. "What's going on?"

"I think you should go in search of Chylla. She will give you more information than I can," she replied.

"Thank you Yinix, carry on," Layson told her as he pulled Bella towards the Comms Room.

"Chylla!" Layson shouted.

"Bella. Layson. We've been trying to contact you for hours," Chylla replied. She dragged them both inside the room and closed the door.

"What is going on?" Layson demanded.

"There's been a malfunction. We are trying to establish what happened but we can't get back in contact with them." Chylla replied.

"In contact with who?" Bella whispered. "It's Zeke isn't it? What's going on?"

Chylla's head dropped. She found it hard to nod.

"Oh my," Bella said as she sunk to the floor clutching her chest. "My baby."

"We received a video from Onyx Abyss Alpha just over 2 hours ago. They say the collision alert system is showing up but there is nothing showing on the monitors. Zeke says there is nothing around them but stars, not even a speck of space dust," Chylla informed Layson. "We are trying to run diagnostics from here but everything is showing at green and working perfectly."

Layson ran his hand through what little hair he had and clung to the back of his neck. "May I?" He gestured the system in front of her.

"Sure," Chylla replied and vacated the seat. She watched as Layson typed in a few commands and a whole other diagnostics system appeared on the screen. "What's that?"

"It's a program I wrote with Sinclair before his untimely passing. It gives us a way to access the mainframe of Onyx Abyss Alpha without any outside interference. No-one aboard the ship will know what we are doing," Layson explained without taking his eyes off the screen.

Bella watched her husband work, yellow tears streaking down her face. She felt so guilty about encouraging Zeke to take the job. She wanted him to be back here, safe and sound at home, where she could keep an eye on him. She continued to wring her hands together. She paced back and forth outside the Comms Room before being led away by Halana.

"Come dear; let's get you something to calm those nerves. I'm sure young Zeke is holding up well," Halana whispered.

"I feel so terribly guilty. I feel I pushed him into it and now it's *my* fault he has problems," Bella cried. "What can I do?"

Halana looked at Bella with kind eyes. "My dear; there is not much we can do from here but wait for answers."

Bella sat on the chair provided by Halana. Her leg bobbing away with nervousness. She chanced a glance out of the skylight, hoping to catch a glimpse of anything that was happening above.

"You'll not see anything through that dear," Halana told her as she handed Bella a cup of freshly brewed Lavender tea. "They aren't even in this Galaxy."

Bella almost choked on her drink. "Where...Where are they?"

"Maxar Galaxy. About one light year from here," Halana explained.

Bella closed her eyes as more tears fell. She sobbed until she couldn't sob anymore.

"What has got you in such a bother?" Halana asked, gently touching Bella's arm.

Bella turned to her and sighed. "I had a dream, and this was it."

Halana looked at her in shock. "Tell me about it, please."

Bella looked Halana in the eyes as she spoke. She wanted to see her reaction to the dream she had had.

<u>Chapter Nine</u>

"I don't understand why it's still going off. I can't figure it out," Balzar said. "Do you think the video reached Enceladus?"

"The delivery report says it arrived. I can't see if it's been read though," Zeke replied. He looked over at Mitzi. She was huddled into the corner of one of the seats at the front of the ship. She looked scared. "Hey Mitz, you OK?"

She looked at him, her blue eyes wide with fright, and shook her head aggressively. She was visibly shaking. He held his hand out to her. She debated taking it, looking between Zeke and Balzar.

"You need comfort Mitz. Go," Balzar told her.

She took Zeke's hand and bounced onto his lap, her arms wrapped around his neck. "Can you still work with me clinging to you like this?" She asked.

"You're fine Mitz, anything to stop you shaking," he smiled at her. He worked with ease as she slowly trembled less and less. As he typed commands into the computer system, he could gently hear her breathing become deeper. She had drifted off to sleep. "Is this normal?" He asked Balzar.

"For Mitzi, a lot of her trust issues come from her parents. They believed she had a deformity. That's why she was so small. Unbeknownst to them, three generations back on her father's side, there were a generation of smaller beings, what we now call Squinks. She has tried to research everything but she hasn't found much," Balzar explained.

"I hope she wouldn't be offended by you telling me about her, would she?" Zeke whispered.

"I would have told you myself if you'd asked," Mitzi answered him with a smile.

"If all this hadn't had happened; I might just have done!" He replied. "I thought you were a Slizard?"

"I can transform into one or the other, depending on what I'm doing at the time. The Slizard comes from my mother's side, the Squink from my father's. I use them both to my advantage," Mitzi explained.

"Wow! You learn something new every day," Zeke smiled.

A beeping from his console tore him away from her eyes. He could see a green cursor moving around his screen. Suddenly, video link appeared. Zeke watched as the pixels arranged themselves to show his father.

"Zeke? Are you there?" Layson asked.

"Dad, yes, we're here," Zeke replied.

"Ahh yes so I see, and who is that climbing over your shoulders?" Layson asked with a smile on his face.

"This is Mitzi, the ship's interrogator and Balzar, the ship's captain is here too," Zeke replied, smiling back.

"Perfect, because I will need you all," Layson told them.

Halana's expression never faltered the whole time Bella explained her dream.

"And now look what's happening. It's all my fault," Bella cried.

"You didn't cause the alarms. You haven't done anything wrong Bella," Halana told her, softly holding her hands. "Zeke is a good boy. A calm boy. He will work things out."

"Do you really think so? He's only young. Should I really have sent him away?" Bella asked.

"You are a great mum Bella; never question what you do for your child. We do these things to ensure our children's happiness. Look at Evadene and me. All my grandchildren live on another planet. We stay in contact. If I had my way, they would all live up here, but I had to let her decide, and I gave her my blessing. If I hadn't, she probably would hate me forever," Halana said, shrugging her shoulders.

Bella thought for a moment. Maybe Halana had a point. Children fly the nest at some point, but not all of them end up in situations like Zeke.

"Stop thinking negatively, I can see the red mist descending!" Halana smiled.

Just as Halana spoke the words, Chylla burst through the canteen door.

"Layson got him," she said.

"What do you mean? He's back?" Bella asked excitedly.

"No, but Layson has managed to contact him, he's alive. They all are. I have to find the Queen and inform her immediately," Chylla replied.

Bella took a deep breath in and tried to contain her tears, unable to define if they were tears of joy or relief.

"Can I speak with him?" Bella asked.

"If you go to the Comms Room, I'm sure Layson will allow you a few seconds," she replied with a smile.

Bella looked at Halana, smiled and ran to the Comms Room.

"So what are we up against Dad?" Zeke asked, Mitzi still on his lap.

"I'm not sure yet son. Sinclair and I designed a whole new diagnostics system for all the ships just in case the on board ones malfunctioned," Layson replied.

"Is that what you think is the problem?" Balzar asked.

"I believe so. From my screen here, I can see that five sensors have gone down, whether they have broken off or are fully malfunctioned, I couldn't say, but I'm going to see what I can do from here. Any of you done a space walk before?" Layson asked.

"A what?" Mitzi questioned.

Layson laughed. "It's when you venture outside of the ship whilst in space."

"Are you clinically insane?" Mitzi asked, moving her little face closer to the camera.

Layson looked into her blue eyes. She was a really pretty being. "I'm not insane little one. It's something astronauts from Earth do all the time. They repair their space station whilst it's in space. They built it there."

"What is this magic you speak of?" Mitzi asked.

Layson laughed. "Oh young Mitzi, there is so much more to learn about life and our neighbours."

Mitzi looked at him with a straight face. "You realise I'm one hundred and seven, right?"

Layson instantly stopped laughing. "Excuse you?"

Zeke was surprised too. Balzar, however, seemed amused.

"Oh come off it Mitzi. Tell them how old you really are," he said.

Mitzi giggled, "OK. I'm only eighteen."

Layson smiled. "You will have to meet Evadene. She will show you so much History, it's unbelievable. So, anyone fancy it?"

"I'll go. I'm the Captain. Can you talk me through it?" Balzar asked.

"Absolutely! Go suit up whilst Zeke gets our comms ready." Layson replied.

"Dad, are you sure about this?" Zeke asked as Balzar attempted to pull on his spacesuit.

"Piled on a few pounds there Bal?" Mitzi laughed.

"Shut it you," Balzar laughed. "I've got it back to front!"

"Yeah, sure you have," Mitzi giggled, She pounced back up onto Zeke's lap and curled up.

"Cute little thing ain't she?" Layson asked.

Zeke looked down at Mitzi sleeping on his lap. He couldn't help but smile. His dad was right. She really was cute.

"Think yourself lucky Zeke. She doesn't trust easily," Balzar said as he clapped Zeke's shoulder.

"I heard that," Mitzi whispered.

"You were meant to, now sleep. You need to recharge," Balzar told her.

Mitzi snuggled herself back down and drifted off to sleep.

"Right, let's get this done," Balzar said.

Balzar made his way towards the hatch that opened into the dark abyss outside. He took a deep breath and turned the wheel. Zeke watched him through the round window, signalling thumbs up; to tell Balzar they were ready.

"OK boss. What do I do?" Balzar asked Layson over the radio.

"I need you to tether yourself to the outside of the ship; we don't want you taking your own trip, do we?" Layson laughed.

"I hope not sir," Balzar smiled.

"Right, now, move along to the front of the ship and tell me what you see," Layson instructed him.

Balzar floated along the outside of the ship, waving at Zeke as he passed the window. Zeke waved back before settling back into his chair with Mitzi still cradled in his hand. She stirred slightly but then drifted straight back off again.

"Zeke, you there?" Layson called.

"Right here Dad, what have we got?" He replied.

"It's not good," Balzar replied. "It seems we have lost the sensors completely, the entire cabling system has gone too. There's a strange substance on the front of the ship. It's gold and shimmering. I've never seen it before. I'm going to scoop a sample and have it checked when we return to Enceladus."

"Will we need to go back to get repairs?" Zeke asked.

"That's an idea, but not practical at the moment. With the sensors out we would be in incredible danger. Layson will talk me through a quick fix. Something that will enable us to get home in one piece, I hope," Balzar explained.

"What's happening?" Mitzi yawned.

"Balzar is outside the ship. My dad is going to talk him through a way to fix the ship so we can go home and get the sensors fixed. Recharged now?" Zeke said.

"More than I was. Before you ask, it's because I'm so tiny that I have to rest quite often. It doesn't affect my work. I normally rest whilst we travel but today was different, especially with it being your first proper mission with us and with the loss of Matro," Mitzi replied.

Zeke smiled at her then turned back to the monitors. He watched as Balzar followed every instruction Layson gave and then double checked everything again. He turned towards the ships main window and gave the thumbs up. They were ready to go home.

As Balzar made his way back inside the ship, something heavy knocked them off course. Balzar quickly climbed back aboard and joined Zeke and Mitzi on the bridge.

"What was that?" Balzar asked.

"I'm not sure. Nothing showed up on screen, but I'm scanning the area," Zeke replied. "Dad, are you still there?"

"I'm here son, what's up? Is Balzar OK?" Layson replied.

"I'm fine. Back aboard and safe. Something hit the ship and now, we've been thrown off course. I will attempt to rectify it now," Balzar replied.

"The monitors aren't showing anything Dad. Something is majorly wrong up here," Zeke told him. "We need to get home."

Mitzi slinked towards Zeke, climbing up to his shoulders and putting her tiny arms around his neck, "I'm scared Zeke." She whispered.

Zeke gently lopped his head to one side, just enough to softly touch her white hair. "I won't let anything or anyone hurt you." He smiled.

She tried to smile, but it didn't reach her eyes. As she turned to watch Balzar attempt to correct their heading, her eyes were drawn to the window up front. She daren't move to look closer but she was almost one hundred percent sure, something was looking at her. She began to shake more than before, pointing her small fingers towards the window.

"It's here," Mitzi whispered.

"What is?" Layson asked. "What has she seen?"

Zeke tried to block her line of vision but she looked straight through him. "What's here Mitzi?"

"The Wigfya," she whispered again.

Balzar turned at the sound of the word. "HIDE!" He shouted at her.

Mitzi scurried away looking like a frightened hamster.

"Balzar?" Zeke asked.

"I'll explain later, for now, we need to get her out of here," Balzar told him. He turned back to the control desk and guided them away.

"I'll inform Queen Aquilia that you are returning. Stay vigilant," Layson told them before signing out.

"He's a great guy," Balzar told Zeke.

"Yeah, he is. He wasn't though. It took a lot to get him how he is now," Zeke replied, remembering all the stuff he saw when he first arrived.

"Let's go home Zeke," Balzar said with a smile, but no sooner were the words out of him mouth, were they thrown further into the abyss, this time to a darker part of the galaxy.

Chapter Ten

"We lost them Your Highness," Chylla whispered as Aquilia watched her children finishing up their sculptures. Her face dropped.

"What do you mean by you lost them? As in signal?" Aquilia asked.

"No Your Majesty. We lost them from the radar too," Chylla replied.

Aquilia tore her eyes away from her children and looked Chylla dead in the eyes, "how far?"

"They were around a light year away Your Highness. I wouldn't even want to guess how far they are now," Chylla responded.

Aquilia looked back at her children who were inspecting their own handy work. "Ready the Stealth Raiders. Inform Nymeria she will have two extra soldiers on this mission."

Chylla looked at Scarlex and Eliontara then back at Aquilia. "Are you sure Your Highness?"

"More than I've ever been but allow me to break the news to them," Aquilia said.

Chylla bowed her head and went off in search of Nymeria and Celest.

Aquilia looked over at her children, dreading letting them out of her sight, but also knowing they had trained so hard for this next step. "Children, come here please."

Scarlex followed her brother to her mother's side. "What is it Mum?"

Aquilia quickly swiped at a tear that had escaped her eye. "Can either of you remind me why you talked me into allowing you to train?"

"We wanted to be able to protect the people of Enceladus Mum, just like you and the Stealth Raiders," Scarlex replied, her blue eyes sparkling as she looked her Aquilia. "Why are you crying?"

Aquilia thought she had hidden her tears well but it seemed her daughter had a sensitive side. "There has been some trouble on Onyx Abyss Alpha. The Stealth Raiders are being prepared as we speak, but I want you both to join them. They made need some of your expertise.”

“We aren’t better than Nymeria and Celest, what could we bring to the table?” Eliontara asked.

Aquilia held his chin in her thumb and forefinger and forced him to look at her, “you are both more talented than you give yourselves credit for, and I am so very proud of you. The choice is yours, if you feel like you aren’t ready, no one will think badly of you.”

“I’m ready Mother,” Eliontara said, straightening his back. “How about you Scar?”

Scarlex thought for a second. She glanced towards the sky, then back at her brother and finally into her mother’s eyes, shaking her head, “I’m not ready yet.”

Aquilia’s eyes softened. “That is perfectly OK. I will not force either of you into a battle you don’t feel ready for.”

As Scarlex attempted to smile, her brother gathered her into a bear hug. “I’ll be back soon sis. Don’t miss me too much.” He laughed.

Scarlex hugged him hard, “don’t get hurt and don’t get into trouble. Remember the first thing Chylla taught us, back away from trouble and keep your head down.”

Eliontara nodded in understanding. “Where do I go Mother?”

Aquilia swallowed the lump that was forming in her throat before finally saying, "head to the furthest landing strip from the base. We keep it there so no approaching enemies can spot it from above."

He nodded once and ran off to collect some of his things. Scarlex instantly broke down in tears.

"What is it darling?" Aquilia asked as she pulled her close.

"I have a bad feeling about this Mum," she replied.

"Scar, you know Elion has trained hard for this day, as have you. He won't let anything stop him from returning. You and he had a very close relationship, he wouldn't allow anything to jeopardise that," Aquilia told her.

Scarlex tried to calm herself, but she had visions of something going terribly wrong. "Mother, where is Zeke?"

Aquilia froze. She had forgotten o inform them of Zeke's new position. "He is...Erm...He is now part of Onyx Abyss Alpha team. He is their new technician."

Scarlex sobbed again. "You didn't tell us that Zeke was in trouble!" She turned and ran from her mother's arms, almost toppling Halana over in the process.

"Oh dear Scar, what's got you so upset?" Halana called but Scarlex continued to run.

Aquilia sat on the edge of the fountain with her head bowed, her shoulders visibly shaking. Halana approached with caution.

"Your Highness?" Halana whispered.

Aquilia spun round to face her, her blue eyes encircled with red. "I've broken her trust."

"Nothing that cannot be fixed," Halana shrugged. "Believe me. As parents, we sometimes break their trust without meaning to. It's part of the job description I'm afraid."

"I wish I had told them both about Zeke before offering them up to The Stealth Raiders," Aquilia sighed.

"They are both going?" Halana asked, looking back towards the Palace.

"Only Eliontara. Scarlex says she isn't ready yet, and I respect her for that," Aquilia informed her. "What I didn't tell them was that Zeke was aboard Onyx Abyss Alpha and that The Stealth Raiders are on an outbound mission to save them."

Halana looked at Aquilia; she had come such a long way from the child who had taken the Kingdom on at just five years old. She was now a loving mother who doted on her children. She had taught them not to take anything they had for granted and to respect others the way they expected to be respected. They were, effectively, mini versions of Aquilia. "She will forgive you, just give her time."

"I hope you're right Halana," Aquilia smiled. "Thank you."

Halana reciprocated the smile and guided Aquilia off to the launch pad. "You got and see Eliontara off. I will speak with Scarlex."

Aquilia couldn't find the words to express her gratitude, so she hugged Halana tight. It brought a tear to Halana's eye. Aquilia had almost become a second daughter to her now that he own was a Duchess and living on Saturn with her own family.

"Where are we now?" Zeke asked, looking out of the ships side windows and then back at the monitors.

Balzar check the maps on the heads up display and shook his head. "I have no idea. I don't think I've ever been this far out before."

Zeke checked his charts and compared them to older ones that were saved onto the system. He was stumped. He couldn't see anything that looked vaguely familiar. "I'm worried. We seem to have been thrown completely out towards the deeper reaches of space. I wonder if we can transmit a signal towards any nearby planets or ships."

He sent out a distress signal, hoping someone, somewhere, would reply, but after what seemed like an eternity, no one responded.

"Looks like we are on our own kid," Balzar told him. "We will have to figure this one out ourselves."

Zeke tried not to look defeated. His first mission and he was already out of his depth.

"Try not to think so negatively young Zeke. We'll work it out," Balzar said as he clapped his hand on Zeke's shoulder.

"I hope so. By the way, what's The Wigfya?" Zeke asked.

Balzar closed his eyes and sat next to Zeke. "It's a long story son."

"We got some time to kill. Humour me," Zeke replied as he turned to face him.

"Let me get Mitzi. It should be her explaining all this," Balzar replied. He stood to extract Mitzi from her hiding spot. "You wanna explain The Wigfya?"

At first Mitzi shook her head, but after Balzar whispered something in her ear, she looked back at Zeke and climbed on to his lap.

"The Wigfya are Squink hunters. They can sense one at an almost five mile distance," Mitzi began. "They smelt me, but when I hide, especially *where* I hide, they can't smell me at all."

"What do they want from you?" Zeke asked. He had only ever met one other person in search of something that didn't belong to them and that was Freefla.

"They want to drain us of our magic. We don't possess a lot, but it's enough in one of us to keep them going for over ten millennia," she replied.

"How do you know this?" Zeke asked. "I'm sorry if I ask a lot of questions. I just need to know so I'm able to protect you if I need to."

"I tried to research my kind a while ago, but all I could find were posts from Wigfya in search of any Squinks," she said. "They even offered rewards for the whereabouts of any. It scared me, but I carried on looking. I found a little about them attempting to harvest magic from a different species but the magic didn't work so well for them so they referred back to Squink hunting."

Zeke was appalled. How could someone use something gifted to another person for their own gain without caring how the other species feel?

"I will do everything I can to protect you from them," he told her.

"We both will," Balzar added. "Whatever it takes."

Mitzi smiled. She had always felt part of the crew here on Onyx Abyss Alpha, but now, Zeke made her feel just that little bit more special and she was glad.

"Let's get to work Balzar. We need to work out how to get back into civilisation before they move on without us," Zeke announced. "You staying Mitzi, or going for some rest?"

"Do you mind if I hang around you for a bit? I feel a lot safer here," she asked.

"You can stay as long as you need," Zeke smiled. He turned to the monitors and began tapping away, multiple tabs opened as he searched for a way to get them home. He told himself that he would need to do some of his own research into Wigfya if he was to be able to protect Mitzi from them.

"I think I've found something," Balzar said, breaking through Zeke's thoughts.

"What is it?" Zeke called from his station.

"Come take a look," Balzar beckoned to him.

Zeke rose from his seat and felt a sudden pressure around his neck; he had almost forgotten that Mitzi clung to him. He smiled to himself as he made his way to Balzar's display.

"As you can see, there's a cluster of stars just left of where we are now, I can't make out anything at the centre of them so my guess is, if we aim, full throttle towards the middle, the directional pull will spin us around by ninety five degrees and catapult us back on track for home," he explained.

"You think it will work?" Mitzi asked.

"I don't think we have anything to lose. I say we go for it. If anything changes then we re-evaluate and try again. I'm going to try and send a message to my cousin, Evadene. I don't want to attempt to send a message to Enceladus and it be intercepted. Eva will understand what I say, it will be in code," Zeke explained.

He loaded up his mail account and typed in her email address;

Eva,

The black hole has light emitting from it. Return the message to the professors. I have seen it for myself.

Also, ever Wonder If Grandma Found Your Asteroid? Let me know!

Zeke x

"What was that? Does she really have an asteroid?" Mitzi asked.

Balzar laughed. "That's clever, do you think she will get the message and understand it?"

"We message like this all the time, its normal for us," Zeke replied.

"His cousin is the Duchess of Astrodia!" Mitzi exclaimed.

Balzar laughed, "who told you that?"

"She's right. My cousin is Evadene Valera. She is married to the Duke of Astrodia," Zeke confirmed.

Balzar looked shocked. "I had no idea I was in the presence of Royalty," he bowed.

"I'm not royal," Zeke laughed. "Just taken in by it. It doesn't change who I am. I love working for Queen Aquilia."

Balzar smiled. He was warming to Zeke. "Let's go home."

Chapter Eleven – Saturn

"Eva, there's an email for you," Janus shouted.

"Will you keep your voice down? Ammyn is trying to sleep!" Eva hissed. "Who is it from?"

"Sorry, I didn't know you were right behind me. It's from Zeke," he replied.

"Can you quickly read it for me, I'm just finishing up here and then I need to make some lunch," she asked.

Janus opened the email and quickly read the contents. "When do you get an asteroid?" He asked.

"A what?" Eva replied, turning her head to stare at him.

"Zeke asked if you've ever Wondered If Grandma Found Your Asteroid." He asked again.

"Let me see," Eva laughed clearly tickled by the wording. She laughed after reading the message. "I get it now. Sometimes Zeke and I talk in code, just in case someone tries to intercept our messages and pick up information on the

Queen. He's asking about The Wigfya. I wonder why he would want to know about them."

Janus smiled. "I'm glad you have a close relationship with Zeke. I didn't know if you would take to him after what his father did."

"It wasn't his fault, not really. Layson had a tendency to follow orders and that's what he was doing, thinking it was for the greater good. Only to find out that it wasn't. He has paid his dues and now Aquilia trusts him," Eva replied. "I'll just relay the message to Chylla."

"You think she will understand the code?" Janus asked.

"I'm going to call her, not message. No one can intercept the calls," she laughed.

Janus left to room to allow her some privacy to make her call. He went to check on their children, all doing their own little thing, except Ammyn. She was sleeping soundly in her bed, something she had done a lot of recently. He had checked up on her sleeping patterns with the Galactic Doctors, only to be told that it was perfectly normal for someone of her size to sleep a lot, it aided her growth.

"Chylla, its Eva. I've just have the strangest message from Zeke. Is he OK?" Eva asked.

Chylla delayed her answer a little too long and Eva picked up on it.

"What aren't you telling me?" Eva asked.

"I guess you will find out at some point. Zeke has taken over from Matro on Onyx Abyss Alpha. There's been some trouble and we are unable to contact them," Chylla told her. "Did you say you received a message from him?"

"Yes, he said they are fine and have a plan to return home. I was to tell you that," Eva told her. She kept the part about the Wigfya to herself for now.

"Thank you Eva. How are things in Astrodia?" Chylla asked.

"Everything seems more peaceful now. Lyra's clan has settled and made vast friends. They put on a show every other evening, especially for the children of the Kingdom. I can't imagine what this place would be like without them," Eva told her. "I can't stay long. The children are wearing me out!"

"I distinctly remember you saying you wanted them all," Chylla laughed. "Say hello to them all for me and also to Janus and Lyra. I'm sure Aquilia will be in contact soon."

"I have some sculptures to inspect later today, so I will call back in a few hours," Eva reminded herself.

"Very well. Thank you again for the confirmation," Chylla replied and closed the call.

Eva could tell there was more to tell but Chylla refused to say another word. She would confront Aquilia later when she inspected the children's sculptures.

<u>Enceladus</u>

"Your Highness. I have received word that Onyx Abyss Alpha is well and attempting a mission back home. Your orders for The Stealth Raiders?" Chylla asked as she came to a halt in front of Aquilia.

"Received word from whom?" Aquilia asked.

"Eva Your Majesty. She says Zeke messaged her and asked her to relay that they were safe and attempting to return home," Chylla replied.

"Very well. Order The Stealth Raiders to launch and guard the perimeter, they are to intercept any passing ships," Aquilia replied. She then turned back to the paperwork in front of her.

She thought back to the disagreement she had had with Scarlex earlier in the day. She still hadn't made time to fix that. She sighed and put her paperwork away. That could wait until she had fixed things with her daughter. She stood up from her desk and looked out over the courtyard below. Now split into sections, there was a section for art and sculptures, a section for archery and a section for reading, this sat right next to the crystal fountain. That was exactly where she found her daughter, curled up in the largest chair there; reading from one of the poetry books Quintara had left.

"Hey," Aquilia said softly.

Scarlex lifted her head slightly, her bright blue hair shimmering in the light. She smiled at her mother, but her smile didn't quite reach her eyes.

"Are you still angry with me?" Aquilia asked sitting down on the opposite chair. "Be honest."

"A little yes. You know how much Zeke means to us," Scarlex began. "I thought you would have at least told us you had offered him Matro's job."

Aquilia hung her head. "I'm so sorry sweetheart. I promised to never keep things from you both and I did just that. Zeke was very apprehensive about the job. He had to take some time to speak with Layson and Bella about it, but I was so happy he accepted. He is the right person for the job."

"I know Mum. It would have been nice to say goodbye though," Scarlex replied as she looked up into the sky. "Do you think he will be back? Especially as they are now in trouble."

"Chylla informs me that they have devised a plan to get themselves back, let's hope they can wing it," Aquilia smiled. "I promise never to keep things from you again."

Scarlex looked at her mother and saw how troubled she looked. "What is it Mum?"

"What's what darling?" Aquilia asked.

"Something is troubling you, what is it?" She asked again.

"I do have a lot of my mind sweetheart, but I don't want to worry you with my troubles," Aquilia smiled. "I'm sure I will work them out somehow."

"It's good to talk Mum. You told us that. You told us that you hated things being hidden away and that we were always to tell you things. Maybe you should heed your own advice," Scarlex smiled back.

Aquilia cocked her head to one side and stared at her daughter. "You remember too much young lady! Maybe we can have a chat later?"

Scarlex nodded and went back to reading her book. Aquilia remembered exactly when she told them that. She had been so angry with her parents for hiding so much from her, that she promised she wouldn't hide things from her own children.

Walking back to her office, Aquilia made a snap decision to visit her parents in the Higher Elders room. Standing outside the door, Aquilia didn't even have any idea why she was here, but she still entered the room and announced her arrival.

"I wish to speak with my parents," Aquilia stated.

"The Higher Elders are busy, you will have to arrange an appointment," Zyra replied over the intercom.

"I will stay here as long as it takes," Aquilia said as she sat in the chair designed for her.

"It may take a while," Zyra said, sounding slightly agitated.

Aquilia didn't reply. She just sat and waited. She knew Zyra hated people waiting in the meeting room. She knew Zyra would send her parents before long and she was right.

"What is it Aquilia? We have a lot to do here," Quintara asked.

"Is that it?" Aquilia asked. "You don't ask about your grandchildren, you never ask how things are going here. Now you're both gone, you just wash your hands of me?"

"Sweetheart, your mother and I miss you dearly, but we have no need to ask about things as we can see everything," Elio replied. "You are doing a fantastic job with the children."

"It's not the same Dad and you know it. You don't even ask to see them, to speak with them. They ask after you but I have to cover it and say you are really busy," Aquilia cried. "When really it's not that at all is it?"

"What do you mean?" Quintara asked harsher than she had wanted.

"As soon as you found out I was truly Alphir, you almost cut all contact with me. It was as if you were ashamed of me," Aquilia told her. "Is that what it is?"

Quintara looked at Elio and Elio looked back at her. Obviously there was something to be said and neither knew how to say it.

"Spit it out," Aquilia screamed.

"When we found out you were Alphir, it was as if you weren't truly ours," Elio said gently. "Even though your mother gave birth to you, finding out you were sent from another planet, well, it unsettled us."

"Unsettled you? Unsettled *you*? How do you think *I* felt?" Aquilia sobbed. "Knowing my parents weren't really my parents, that I was carrying children when I went on to fight my 'Uncle' for a throne I probably didn't deserve! How do *you* think *I* felt?"

Quintara and Elio were silent.

"Exactly. You didn't think about that, did you?" Aquilia cried. "I grew up, here. In this Palace surrounded by people I knew *nothing* about. I was five!" Aquilia said.

"Are we really going to go through this again?" Quintara asked, instantly sounding bored.

"I'm sorry if my feelings aren't important enough for you Mother, but they are important to me and to *my* children. If you don't want to hear what I have to say, then you don't deserve the title of Mum or Grandma," Aquilia cried. She stood and left the room.

"Don't you think that was a little harsh dear?" Elio asked Quintara.

"No. She is an adult now. She needs to learn that stamping her feet like a five year old will get her nowhere!" Quintara replied. "Now, let's get back to work."

Elio was surprised by his wife's reaction. He couldn't understand why she would shut Aquilia down like that. He rejoined The Higher Elders back at their work stations and continued his work. He would talk to Quintara later.

"Will we make it?" Mitzi whispered in Zeke's ear. She had taken up position on his shoulder whilst they flew, full throttle, into the centre of a cluster of stars, hoping the speed and directional pull would throw them back to Enceladus.

"I got everything crossed," Zeke smiled at her. He watched as Balzar pushed the controls forward, accelerating them to almost four hundred and forty thousand miles an hour.

"Brace yourselves," Balzar called. He directed Onyx Abyss Alpha into the centre of the cluster and let the forces do the rest. He let go of the controls and strapped himself into his seat.

Mitzi held onto to Zeke with all her strength. She was scared that their plan wouldn't work. She hoped to be back on some form of land before long. She watched as the darkness stretched out before them. The masses of stars getting closer and closer; they were almost upon the huge cluster that was their destination. The gravitational pull of the centre, began dragging them in. Balzar checked their heading and held his thumb up. They were on course. As the ship was dragged in, Zeke felt the pressure on his chest. He held Mitzi tight and shielded her away. He took one last look out of the front window before everything went dark.

<u>Chapter Twelve</u>

"Thank you Nymeria. I will let Her Majesty know right away," Chylla replied. She rose from her seat and made her way to Aquilia's office. The whole way there, she had a smile painted on her face. That soon dropped when she couldn't find the Queen at her usual place.

She searched the Palace from top to bottom, finding no sign of her. Chylla made a last minute decision to check with Halana. She wound her way to Halana's workshop, amazed by all the different gowns and sashes that Halana had made. As she turned in circles she briefly spotted Halana staring at her from the doorway.

"Something take your fancy Miss Chylla?" Halana smiled.

"Did you make all of these? From scratch?" Chylla asked.

“Absolutely! Not a store bought gown among them,” Halana replied. “Was there anything you needed?”

Chylla cleared her throat. “Actually there was. Have you seen the Queen?”

“Only briefly earlier today, but not within the last few hours. Is it something urgent? Have you tried her radio?” Halana asked.

“Multiple times but there is no response. Can you think of anywhere she would go?” Chylla replied.

“Hmm.” Halana sat on the footstool and looked out over the Kingdom. “It does seem to me that our Queen may have had an unsettling afternoon.” She pointed towards the reading corner, where Aquilia sat, huddled with Scarlex.

“Thank you Miss Halana. You have been a great asset,” Chylla bowed before heading off.

“I do hope it’s good news,” Halana whispered to herself. “She could do with some of that.”

Chylla made her way towards the reading corner. She was in such a hurry to inform the Queen of Nymeria’s report, that she forgot her manners.

“Your Majesty,” Chylla shouted across the courtyard. “Your Majesty we have news!”

As soon as Aquilia looked up, Chylla realised her mistake.

"I'm so sorry Your Highness, I completely lost myself there," Chylla bowed.

"What is it Chylla?" Aquilia asked as she stood.

"Nymeria has been in contact. There appears to be a fast moving object heading our way. Celest insists that it is Onyx Abyss Alpha," Chylla replied.

Aquilia pulled her radio from her dress pocket and called in Nymeria. "Ready The Stealth Raiders. If it isn't Onyx, shoot it!"

"But Mother, what if it shoots back? Eliontara is up there!" Scarlex announced from the chair behind them.

"He will be absolutely safe my darling. The Stealth Ship has the best force field defence this side of the Galaxy. He will be perfectly safe," Aquilia smiled. "Trust me."

Scarlex looked at Chylla for confirmation. "I watched Sinclair create the technology himself. No one has ever brought down our ships."

This seemed to settle Scarlex's nerves a little, but not enough to allow her to settle back into her book. Instead, she searched sky for any signs of life from the ships patrolling their world. Her eyes darted from left to right and back again. On her third sweep of the sky, she spotted what looked like a rock, hurtling towards them.

"Mum, what's that?" Scarlex asked as she pointed towards it.

Aquilia and Chylla both looked up. They pinpointed the fast moving object with ease. Aquilia nodded towards Chylla who radioed to Nymeria.

"What have we got?" Chylla asked.

There was no answer.

"Nymeria, this is Chylla. What have we got?" Chylla demanded.

She turned to Aquilia and shook her head. Aquilia took the radio from Chylla and called out, "This is Queen Aquilia. I demand you reply!"

"Queen Aquilia, I apologise for the delay. We were analysing the shape of the object. We can confirm that it is Onyx Abyss Alpha. We are worried it may not be able to slow enough to land without crashing. We are preparing to lasso and tug," Celest replied.

"Aim towards the far pads. The Stealth can only tug so much," Aquilia said.

"Yes Ma'am," Celest confirmed.

Aquilia handed back the radio, instructed Scarlex to bring Bella and Layson and meet her in her office. Scarlex nodded once and hurried away.

"What are you going to say to them?" Chylla asked.

"I will have to tell them the truth," Aquilia replied.

"Which is?" Chylla questioned.

"I don't know. We don't know fully what happened. We just have to wait until they land and then they can explain exactly what went on up there," Aquilia replied.

"Balzar, this is Celest. Can you hear me?" Celest radioed through.

"Celest, it's nice to hear a familiar voice. Do you think you can slow us down at all? We are on a speed reading of nearly seven hundred and fifty miles an hour and I don't think the flaps will slow us much more than around six hundred. We would crash," Balzar replied.

"We got you big fella!" Nymeria giggled. "Be ready for a lasso and tug!"

"Oh my favourite two words! Let's get this going!" Balzar laughed. "You two, brace yourselves."

Zeke buckled himself into his seat, quickly grabbed Mitzi and secured her in his inside pocket. He could feel her shaking against him.

"It's going to be fine. I've got you," he whispered.

"I'm scared. What if the lasso and tug doesn't slow us enough?" Mitzi asked.

"We have flaps too; they are slowing us down at the moment. We are down to six-nine-three. As soon as we hit five-ninety, the lasso and tug will slow us enough to land," Balzar explained.

"Have you done this before?" Zeke asked.

"Practised, but never this fast. It will be hit and miss, we have to get the timing perfect, one millisecond out and we're...well, you catch my drift right?" Balzar asked.

Zeke nodded. He didn't want Mitzi to hear what Balzar meant. He shielded her from the outside whilst trying to keep track of their speed. He watched it clock down. Six hundred and seventy three. Six hundred and forty eight. Six hundred. Five hundred and ninety five. Five hundred and ninety. Zeke felt the tug on the ship, his neck almost snapping as The Stealth ship pulled them back easing their speed down bit by bit. Four hundred and sixty five. Four hundred and thirty. Three hundred and fifty. Slow enough to land.

As they glided to a soft landing, Zeke finally looked down to make sure Mitzi was OK. She was sound asleep in his pocket.

"Does that happen often?" Zeke asked Balzar.

"When she is scared, yes. It's not often but a lot has happened over the past few hours, a lot more than has ever happened on a routine mission," Balzar explained. "Let's get her in to the Palace and see how she is from there."

Zeke nodded and unbuckled his harness, careful not to disturb Mitzi. He stood and made his way down the steps of the ship, greeted by Celest and Nymeria.

"Hey, what happened out there?" Celest asked, worry crossing her face.

"Once we have debriefed with Her Majesty, we will fill you in. Is there anywhere we can lay Mitzi?" Balzar replied.

"Follow me," Eliontara offered. He led Zeke to his own bedroom and offered up his own bed. "She will be safe here."

"Thank you Eliontara. Do you know where your mother is?" Zeke asked as he lay Mitzi down on the white satin pillow.

"I would imagine she would be in her office. Probably with your parents," Eliontara replied. "I admire you Zeke."

"Why is that?" Zeke asked. They walked together towards Aquilia's office.

"You are brave. You were in a place no one could contact you, and somehow you got a message out. How?" Eliontara asked.

"Having a good knowledge of technology is a good thing. I managed to get that message out using the signal bouncing around space. There are so many out there, but you have to be careful what you say, so many others can intercept it and cause trouble," Zeke explained whilst they walked.

Eliontara soaked up all the information Zeke gave out. He was eager to learn and be able to pull off something just as fantastic. As they arrived at the door to Aquilia's office, the door opened and Bella appeared. She looked towards Zeke and threw her arms around him.

"Oh you had me so worried!" She cried. "I had this awful dream and when we came to ask Chylla for a report on your mission, they explained what had happened. Then your father helped you and then you were gone!"

"It's OK mum. I'm back, and I'm safe. I'll explain more about it later but I need to attend debriefing first. Will you be at home?" Zeke asked.

Bella shook her head. "I'll be in the canteen waiting for you."

Zeke smiled, hugged her again and kissed her head. "I love you Mum."

"Oh you soppy thing," Bella swiped at her tears. "I love you too."

Zeke knocked before entering The Queen's office. Balzar already occupied one of the seats, Layson the other. Zeke stood between them, his hands behind his back.

"You're not on trial here Zeke. Please relax," Aquilia smiled. "Now, what exactly happened out there?"

"In all honesty Your Highness. I don't think any of us really know. One minute we were taking instructions from Layson and the next, well, we were in the middle of nowhere with nothing around us but wide open space," Balzar began.

"I managed to get a message to Eva using a signal that had been bouncing around space. I should have contacted here, but Eva's email was the first one I thought of," Zeke said.

"It doesn't matter who you contacted, the best thing is that you did and that we knew you were safe. So how did you manage to get back?" Layson asked.

"Balzar spotted a cluster of stars ahead of us. It seemed to be spinning quite rapidly. His idea was to power, full throttle, into the centre and let the force catapult us out. It was a really good idea and it worked," Zeke explained.

"That was dangerous Balzar!" Aquilia said. "What would you have done if it hadn't worked and it catapulted you off to another Galaxy?"

"We would have devised another plan to get home Your Majesty. My plans run A to Infinity. I will always find a way to return," Balzar replied.

"I must say. It was cleverly executed," Aquilia smiled. "You all did well today. Where is Mitzi?"

"Asleep in Eliontara's bed Your Highness," Zeke replied.

"Will she be OK?" Aquilia asked Balzar.

"I hope so Your Majesty. So much happened on our trip that I'm afraid she may never want to go up again," Balzar replied.

"Layson, would you give us a moment?" Aquilia asked.

"Absolutely. Glad to have you back son," Layson said as he clapped Zeke on the shoulder.

Zeke smiled at his father, but he knew what was coming. He knew what Aquilia was about to ask. And he had only mentioned this to one person. Evadene.

Chapter Thirteen - Saturn

"You don't think I did the wrong thing do you?" Eva asked.

"No. I think you did the right thing. You had to mention it. It would have eaten you up if you didn't say anything and something happened. Try not to worry dear," Lyra told her.

Eva sat at the table, finger knitting another pair of booties. She had taken up finger knitting whilst she was pregnant with Codex. It calmed her nerves back then but today it was making them worse. She had already dropped three stitches and she had only completed one row. When the phone rang, she dropped the whole thing on the floor. She had known the phone would ring eventually. She wasn't ready for the conversation though. Lyra left her alone to speak.

"Eva, are you there?" Aquilia's face appeared on the screen.

"I'm here. Did they get back safe?" Eva replied.

"We're here," Zeke answered.

"Oh Zeke. I'm sorry. I had to tell her. I hope you don't think badly of me," Eva blurted out.

Zeke laughed. "No. I'm glad you did. I wouldn't have known where to start. We're just waiting on Mitzi to arrive."

"No you're not!" Mitzi mocked as she swung up onto his shoulder. "Oh, hi!" She waved at the screen.

"Oh wow! I've read so much about your species. Are you OK?" Eva asked.

Mitzi shrugged, "Ahh, so so. I got a lot going on up here though," she replied, tapping the side of her head.

Eva smiled, "that's understandable I guess. Zeke and Balzar taking care of you?"

Mitzi smiled shyly. "You could say that."

Eva knew the smile well. Mitzi liked one of them. A lot.

"So Eva. What can you tell us about The Wigfya?" Aquilia asked.

"There are so many different things about them; I wouldn't know where to start. What do you need to know most?" Eva asked.

"How much danger is Mitzi in when we are out on missions?" Zeke asked.

"She is only in immediate danger if they can smell her. There are a number of things she can do to put them off her scent, but I'm guessing Mitzi already knows most of them," Eva replied.

"I do and I don't. I tend to hide behind all the food on board the ship. That way they only smell the food," Mitzi replied. "I don't really know how else to mask my scent."

Eva was worried. "Mitzi, did you parents ever explain about The Wigfya?"

"Only that they use Squinks power to make them stronger," Mitzi replied. "Am I missing anything?"

"In a way, yes. As you are a rare kind, being part Squink and part Slizard, The Wigfya feel you are one of the more important kinds to catch. They won't harvest your power, but they will run tests to figure how to clone your DNA. There is so much you need to learn about them. Would you like me to teach you about them and your own species?" Eva offered.

"Would we have time before our next mission?" Mitzi asked, looking between Balzar and Aquilia.

"You aren't due to take off for another three days. I think, if Eva has some spare time, you should learn as much as you can. All of you," Aquilia replied.

"If it's all the same, I'd like to conduct my own research," Zeke asked.

"That's perfectly alright. Balzar and Mitzi, I will arrange for you both to fly to Saturn and meet with Eva, she will bring you both up to speed with The Wigfya. Eva, send some information to me also. I think I should be prepared," Aquilia said.

Eva nodded and the call was disconnected. The room fell silent. Nobody seemed to know what to say.

"I think we have completed our debrief. Go about your other duties. Zeke, can you remain for a moment longer?" Aquilia asked.

Mitzi looked worried as she walked away with Balzar. "Do you think he will be OK?"

"I'm sure of it. Don't worry. Let's go back to the ship and quickly wipe things down, then we can head to the canteen for some food. How does that sound?" Balzar asked.

"Sounds OK," Mitzi said softly. She kept looking back the whole time they walked.

"Zeke, please, sit," Aquilia gestured to the empty chair.

Zeke sat down and looked at her. She seemed to never age. She still looked like the seventeen year old girl who battled for her birthright.

"Why do you feel the need to do your own research?" She asked.

"I just feel I could find out a little more than Eva is offering," Zeke replied, looking away from her prying eyes.

"Zeke, what aren't you telling me?" Aquilia asked.

"Nothing," Zeke replied.

"Zeke, there must be something. I've never come across you turning down advice from Eva," Aquilia pressed.

"I just want to be able to protect her! Is that too much?" Zeke cried.

Aquilia sat back in her chair. She looked at Zeke in a whole new light. "She means a lot to you?"

Zeke sighed. "I don't know why, but yes. I feel like I have to protect her at all costs."

"It is perfectly understandable. She is your crew mate and it's part of your duty to protect your crew mates. I'm sure you would do the same for Balzar," Aquilia said.

"Mitzi is different. Of course I would protect them both with my life, just like I would this Kingdom, but Mitzi, she's...she's special," Zeke said softly.

Aquilia's eyes softened. "I expected nothing less of you Zeke. Come, we must set you up in the library and technology room for you to research."

She gently touched his arm and he was momentarily transported to a different world. It showed a battle enraging and a downed Aquilia, just as they broke contact he saw a flash of white before being slammed back into reality.

"Are you OK?" Aquilia asked. "You left me for a second there."

"Yes Your Highness. Thank you. I was thinking about where to start with my research," Zeke replied.

Aquilia smiled. "I'll let you settle here and I'll have some food brought to you."

"Thank you Your Majesty," Zeke replied. He sat at the table furthest from the door, this way he wouldn't be disturbed by passing eyes.

"I've upset him, haven't I?" Mitzi asked Balzar as they buckled themselves in for their trip to Saturn.

"I highly doubt it. Zeke is a resilient boy," Balzar replied. "I'm sure he is still on edge from our mission. Try not to get yourself in a panic."

Mitzi looked out of the window as they shot off from the launch pad and up through the Enceladant atmosphere. She admired Saturn's rings as they Hyper Jumped through space.

"I've never really toured Saturn," Balzar stated. "How about we look around before heading to the Palace?"

Mitzi stood on the last step on the ship and stared at her surroundings. Everything seemed so different from Enceladus. The buildings were different. The people were different. Even though both worlds were ruled by the same person, it was such a stark difference.

"What do you think?" Balzar nudged her slightly.

"Huh? Yeah, a tour would be great," she said, still staring ahead of her.

"Let's go this way first," Balzar said pointing to his left.

Mitzi followed him, careful not to be left behind. They walked around the tiny village to the south of the city. It seemed run down and empty. That was until a small child popped out from behind a house.

"Who are you?" She asked, circling Mitzi and Balzar.

Balzar held his hands out to show he wasn't armed. "My name is Balzar. This is Mitzi. We are part of Onyx Abyss Alpha."

"Why are you here?" She questioned.

"We are on our way to the Palace to meet with The Duchess," Mitzi replied.

"Palace is the other way," the child stated. "Go back!"

"What's going on out here?" An older lady emerged from the building closest to them. She placed herself between the child and them. "Who are you?"

"I just explained to the child. We are part of Onyx Abyss Alpha. We are on a visit to Duchess Evadene," Balzar explained again.

"Then you should be heading back that way," the woman pointed behind them.

"We mean no harm," Mitzi said softly. "We haven't really looked around Astrodia before."

"That's no excuse. You are here to visit with The Duchess. So leave. We do not need the likes of Squink here," the woman spat. She grabbed the child and slammed the door in their faces.

Mitzi was visibly upset by her words. Balzar scooped her up and carried her towards the Palace.

"Try not to let people like that get to you. Some just don't understand." Balzar said.

Mitzi didn't answer; she just wished Zeke was here. He would have stuck up for her. They made their way towards the Palace with no further hassle. As they approached, a little purple haired child ran to them, her harms stretched out wide ready to be swung into the air. Balzar caught her, just before she tripped over a small rock, and swung her high in the air.

"Weeee!" The little girl squealed.

"Ammyn, you come back this instant!" Lyra called from the open doorway. "Oh! Hello. How can I help you?"

"I'm Balzar and this is Mitzi," he announced, placing Mitzi back on the floor. "We have appointments with Duchess Evadene."

"Ah of course. Onyx Abyss Alpha. Come in. I'm so sorry about Ammyn, she is an escape artist I believe," Lyra laughed. She bent down to Mitzi's level and smiled. "Squink I believe?"

Mitzi nodded. "Please don't be like the others."

"What others?" Lyra asked.

"We wandered to the south of the landing pad and were confronted by some people from the village there. They said they didn't need the likes of Squink there," Balzar informed her.

"Hmmm, did she have orange hair and green eyes by any chance?" Lyra asked looking at Mitzi.

She nodded again.

"Ah, that will be Shima. She is a nasty so and so. Ignore her. She was once an outcast herself," Lyra told them. "Follow me. I believe Eva has something all set up for you both."

Mitzi and Balzar followed Lyra through the Palace doors with Ammyn still in Balzar's arms; he looked different holding a child. They walked through the Palace, amazed by how bright it was. The layout was somewhat different to the Palace back on Enceladus. It seems Eva and Janus had been teaching there too. Mitzi wondered what happened to the school there.

"You made it! Oh it's lovely to meet you properly, come in," Eva beamed from inside the library room.

Mitzi walked in and looked up. The shelves towered above her, but then most things did. The books were all clean and in order. It seemed Eva was proud of her book collection.

"Mitzi, I've made you a bit of a booster seat over here, just so it's easier for you to reach the table top. I hope you don't mind?" Janus asked from behind her.

"Thank you. That's very kind. Could you give me a scoot up?" Mitzi asked.

"No need. I even installed a ladder for you to climb," Janus smiled.

Mitzi was surprised by how accommodating they were. "You aren't bothered by me being Squink?"

"Why would we?" Eva asked, clearly confused.

"It seems Shima has been at it again," Lyra told her. "I'll have a quiet word. You would have thought she would have learnt by now."

"Thanks Mum," Janus replied. "I'll leave you all to get on with it. I'll be in the kitchen if you need me." And with that, he scooped Ammyn into his arms and bounced off with her down the corridor.

Mitzi smiled. She loved the way he was with Ammyn.

"Now," Eva said. "Where shall we start?"

Chapter Fourteen

"I'm worried about him," Bella told Layson as they watched Zeke through the doors. "He is going to make himself ill at this rate!"

"Give him some space honey. He's probably still processing what happened up there," Layson replied.

Zeke could hear them whispering at the doorway. He wished they would leave him alone long enough for him to get some of the notes written up. He had found out so much about the Wigfya, probably more than Eva could tell him. He had dug so deep into the mainframe of Wigstar; he even had the names of the High Polar. He risked a glance towards the door just in time to see his parents walk away. He pulled his notepad from his rucksack and jotted down names. He decided to talk with Chylla in private and see if she knew any of the names or anything else about The Wigfya. He trusted her. Standing from his chair, he gathered his things, the remaining crusts of his sandwich, and his drink bottle and headed for the door. His next stop? The Comms Room.

Aquilia checked on Scarlex and Eliontara as they finished their studies. Halana had been teaching them in between her dressmaking, and she had been so good at it. The children took to her well.

"Your Highness," Chylla said from her side. "I have some news about Pluto."

Aquilia turned to face her. "Go on."

"The Foltuna were searching for a fugitive on Pluto. It turns out Plutons weren't harbouring him after all. He has been planet-jumping. I had a tracker placed on him when we discovered him jumping from Pluto to Fardex," Chylla explained. "Now he's just jumped from Jaskir to Wurdik, do we inform Foltuna?"

Aquilia thought for a second. She worried that Foltuna would attempt to attack any planet they approached in search of their fugitive. "No, send Nymeria and her crew to bring him back here. They can collect him from us and then they can be on their way."

Chylla nodded and went on her way. Aquilia looked back towards her children. She needed to speak with them about the future and everything that comes with being Prince and Princess.

"Chylla, do you have a moment?" Zeke asked as she made her back along the corridor towards the Comms Room.

"Accompany me Zeke," Chylla replied. "How is it that I can help you?"

Zeke chose his words carefully. He didn't want anyone to treat Mitzi any differently if they knew who and what she was. "What do you know about The Wigfya?"

Chylla stopped in her tracks. "Why do you ask about them?"

"If I tell you, you have to promise not to say anything to anyone," Zeke told her.

"Including the Queen?" Chylla asked.

"Aquilia already knows, I mean to anyone else," Zeke replied.

"I promise, please," she gestured to the Comms Room. "We can talk privately here."

Zeke sat in one of the chairs that was barely used. He swore he would never sit in Zee's seat. "Mitzi is part Squink and part Slizard. The ships we ran into before we were catapulted into who knows where, were The Wigfya. They were after

Mitzi. She and Balzar are now with Evadene, who is teaching them more about The Wigfya so we can ensure Mitzi's safety, but I want to know more. I need to know more. I have to protect her."

Chylla smiled. "I sense more than just crewmate protection. She means a lot to you?"

Zeke sighed, "as much as I want to ignore it, yes she does. I don't know why or how but it happened. I don't want any harm to come to her."

"It is understandable young Zeke. She is safe with Evadene, so you need not worry yourself now. I can see you want to know more so you can protect her when you are far from safety. Let me instruct The Stealth ship on its mission and I will inform you of everything I know," Chylla smiled.

Zeke sat back and watched her work. He wondered when Aquilia would train someone to take over here since Matro passed. Maybe Chylla would take over permanently. She instructed The Stealth ship to collect the fugitive from Wurdik and bring him to Enceladus.

"Now," Chylla turned to him. "Where shall we start?"

"Preferably at the beginning," Zeke laughed. He pulled out his notebook and showed her what he'd already found out.

"Wow, you sure have been doing your homework. Now, let's see who you've got here," Chylla laughed. She pulled his notebook closer and ran through the names. "Hmm...He's dead. So is he. She is still alive somewhere, not sure where though, but I can find out. He's still around, she's dead, I know I killed her," she smiled.

"Really? Why?" Zeke asked.

"A long time ago, she was sniffing around Ammyn. Long before Aquilia arrived. She said she smelt something, but Ammyn was Enceladant born and raised, not an ounce of Squink in her. Fixie here," Chylla pointed out her name, "thought she could snatch Ammyn and nothing would happen to her, Ammyn was all but a child at the time not a warrior bone in her, but we looked out for her. Fixie didn't stand a chance."

"Wow, you all really look out for each other don't you," Zeke replied.

"Just like you are doing for young Mitzi," Chylla smiled. "Now, we know who is dead and who still wanders, but, I wonder who else has joined up recently." She turned to the computer and typed in a code Zeke had never seen before.

"What does that show?" Zeke asked.

"Ahh, if I tell you, I'd probably have to kill you," she laughed. "I'm joking. It shows all the different armies and squadrons around, even from other galaxies. Everyone has access, it's nothing secret."

She searched for The Wigfya in amongst all the others listed and sat back in amazement.

"Well, I never expected that!" She exclaimed.

"What is it? Should we be worried?" Zeke asked.

"Oh no. Definitely not. They haven't grown much over the past three centuries or so, in fact, there are only around fifty or so of them left. I wouldn't be too worried," she smiled, but when she turned back to the screen the smile left her face just as fast as it had appeared. "Oh no. Oh this isn't good at all. Stay here. I'll be back." She ran from the room.

Zeke peeked over at the screen and froze when he saw the name. He knew this wasn't good in the slightest. He had to warn his father. He gathered his things and ran from the room, making sure to close the door as he left; it was one of the first things Aquilia had taught him when he took over from Zee. He ran as fast as he could to his father's office, bumping straight into Chylla and Aquilia as he rounded the corner.

"I knew you would look and that this would be the first place you ran to, but you can't tell him yet," Chylla warned him.

"Why not?" Zeke asked.

"It's best we find out exactly why he has been lying all these millennia and why he's joined The Wigfya first, after that, we will allow you to inform your father," Aquilia told him. She gestured to her private quarters, "we will talk in here where we won't be disturbed."

Zeke followed them inside and sat on the sofa by the window. He worried about what he was about to find out, but as he waited for Chylla and Aquilia to begin, he worried about Mitzi.

"So, let me get this straight. Squinks hold some form of magic which helps The Wigfya live longer?" Balzar asked.

"In a rock shell, yes, but there are so many other reasons that The Wigfya would hunt Squinks. I'm sorry Mitzi," Evadene looked at her. "I have to tell it how it is."

"It's fine. I understand, go ahead," Mitzi tried to smile.

Eva hated telling beings about others who hunted them, it made her feel bad. "So, The Wigfya like to keep trophies, and I don't mean like stuffed beings, they keep Squinks captive and experiment on them. I've heard they have been trying to clone Squinks for a while, they've never actually managed it but the technology is evolving rapidly."

"So I should be worried?" Mitzi asked.

"With Zeke and I around? I doubt it very much," Balzar replied. "We would do anything to keep you safe."

"How come Zeke didn't come with you two anyway?" Eva asked.

"He said he wanted to do his own research, probably doesn't want to be anywhere near me because of who I am," Mitzi said softly.

"You have a lot to learn about Zeke. He is the least judgemental being I know. He just has his own way of researching things. I'm sure he will be in contact soon," Eva smiled.

Just as she finished her sentence, Janus appeared at the doorway.

"Sorry, Mitzi, there's a call for you upstairs," Janus smiled.

"Oh, erm, thank you," Mitzi replied. She made her way down the small ladder and followed Janus to the upstairs living room.

"Shout me when you're finished," Janus smiled.

Mitzi nodded and went in the room. This one filled with paintings that made her feel like she was being watched everywhere she went. She looked around for the phone but it was nowhere to be seen.

"Mitzi, look here," Zeke called.

She spun around, stopping as she spotted Zeke's face on the wall behind her. "Wow, a screen built into the wall?"

Zeke laughed. "Eva loves her gadgets. She likes to be able to paint and talk at the same time. I wanted to ask if you were OK."

Mitzi smiled. "I'm doing OK. I've found out some stuff about The Wigfya that I didn't know before. Janus built me a special chair with a ladder."

"Janus? I didn't know he had a creative side," Zeke laughed.

Mitzi watched him laugh. Her heart warmed when he smiled. It skipped beats too. "Seems he is. Have you found out anything interesting?"

"Probably just the same as you. I just thought I might have been able to find out some hidden things, but it seems they want to stay hidden. I will keep searching. I just wanted to make sure you were doing OK," he replied.

"Eva knows her history, and she is so kind in how she explains things," Mitzi replied. "I should get back. I don't want to miss anything."

"Sure. I'll...Erm...I'll speak with you later?" Zeke asked.

Mitzi nodded before leaving the room. She followed the smell of cookies all the way to the kitchen where she found Janus with his head in a triple decked oven.

"You bake too? Wow, Eva married the rarest of all," Mitzi laughed.

"I have to make sure my family is fed," Janus smiled. "Mitzi, is something wrong?"

"With me? No, everything is...well...actually, do you have a minute?" She asked.

"Absolutely, here," he lifted her onto the countertop. "Speak away."

Mitzi felt she could tell Janus anything and everything. And she did.

Chapter Fifteen

"So are we sure it's definitely him?" Chylla asked.

Aquilia looked back over all the details she had in front of her, scanning all of them again just to be sure.

"Certain. There's no doubt about it," she nodded. "We have to tell him."

"I don't know how he is going to take it," Chylla replied. "Should we let Zeke tell him?"

"I think we should all be there to support him," Aquilia said. "I'll round up Zeke, if you can get Layson and Bella to the meeting room?"

Chylla nodded and went on her way. Aquilia would have to choose the right words to tell Layson this news. It would knock him out of this realm.

"Zeke, can you meet me in the meeting room with your parents," Aquilia called over the radio.

"Sure, I'm on my way," Zeke replied. He worried what it would be about. He hoped they had confirmed what they had read earlier. He began to dread how his father would react.

"Layson, Bella, could you join The Queen, myself and Zeke in the meeting room please," Chylla asked when she found them both.

They exchanged looks before nodding and following her.

"What is it about?" Bella asked continuously as they walked the short distance to the room.

"I'm afraid that will have to be explained by Queen Aquilia and Zeke," Chylla replied. "I'm sorry I cannot divulge any further details."

"I hope it's nothing bad," Bella whispered. "I don't think I can handle anymore bad stuff this week, or this year."

"Let's just wait and see darling. It could be good news," Layson smiled. He secretly hoped it was good news.

They entered the meeting room to find Aquilia sitting at the table along with Zeke. The looks on their faces didn't signal good news. Layson held the chair out for Bella and Chylla and then sat holding his wife's hand.

"Thank you both for coming. This is going to be a shock, but I feel its best coming from us then you finding out another way," Aquilia began.

"Please, don't sugar coat it, just be up front," Layson said.

Aquilia looked at Zeke and nodded.

"Dad, we have some news and it's not the best news," Zeke began.

"I knew it, I just knew it," Bella cried.

"Mum, please," Zeke said softly. He sighed before speaking again. "I remember you told me that your father died a long time ago."

"Yes, almost two millennia ago. Why do you bring that up now?" Layson asked. Hus hands beginning to shake.

Aquilia slid a red folder over to him and gestured for him to open it. His hands were shaking so much; he couldn't grip the folder properly and kept dropping it onto the table.

"I'm sorry," he kept saying, fumbling with the folder once again.

Bella took the folder and opened it to the front page. Her face drained of its entire colour. "Layson, isn't that...?"

Layson spun the folder round to see the page. His eyes almost fell out of their sockets. "It's can't be. He's dead."

"As you can see, he isn't," Chylla added.

Aquilia quickly looked at her.

"Sorry," she mouthed shrugging her shoulders.

"How long have you all known?" Layson whispered.

"Only about an hour. I found him whilst I was doing my research on The Wigfya," Zeke explained.

"The Wigfya? Why were you searching them up? They are nasty people Zeke," Bella said.

"I guess you will find out eventually. Mitzi is part Squink and part Slizard. The Wigfya..." Zeke began.

"Hunt Squink. I know Zeke. I know all about them. We had an invasion on Alphir over three centuries ago. I know Mitzi's family but I had no idea they were Squink. They aren't small enough," Bella finished for him.

"But that's just the thing Mum. Mitzi takes after the third generation of her father's side. The Slizard comes from her mother's side, but she can use both. I think she favours the Squink," Zeke explained.

"Is that the blue eyed girl?" Layson asked.

"Yes. I wanted to find out how to protect her should anything happen, especially if The Wigfya manage to capture her," Zeke replied.

"She seems very special," Bella said.

Zeke nodded. He didn't trust his voice not to break when he answered.

"Then we have to do everything we can to help you protect her," Layson told him. "Let's get to work,"

<u>Saturn</u>

"All of that huh?" Janus asked when she had finished talking.

"Pretty much yeah," Mitzi replied. "I'm sorry to have bored you with all that. I think I just needed to tell someone I wasn't so close with."

"Hey, you didn't bore me. It's absolutely OK to talk to others. How often do you let your guard down Mitzi?" Janus asked her.

"Never, well, sometimes around Zeke. I don' know what it is about him, but he really calms me down. It's like, I could be panicking about something and just his touch soothes me. What could that mean?" She replied.

"It means whatever you want it to mean," he smiled. "Why don't we head back to Eva and Balzar? I bet they're wondering where you have snuck off to."

"We weren't actually," Balzar replied as he walked through the door. "Mitz, why didn't you talk to me?"

"I didn't feel like I could Bal. You're like a big brother to me and I didn't want you to think badly of Zeke if nothing came about for us," she replied hanging her head.

"Oh Mitz," Balzar replied as he scooped her up in his huge hands. "Hula always said you'd have me crumbling one day, and here I am." He let tears escape his eyes.

Eva gently laid her hands on Janus's shoulder, "I think we should leave them alone for a while," she whispered.

Janus followed her out of the room before turning to her and asking "how did Mitzi seem to you?"

"I think she just doesn't know who she can trust. She has a lot of trust in Zeke and Balzar, but when I told her about The Wigfya, she seemed to, or more pretended, to know everything," Eva replied. "I'm worried about her Janus."

"I'm sure we can help her in some way," Janus smiled. "Let's see how we go from here."

Eva allowed herself to be guided back to the library where Janus sat her at the table and placed a kiss on top of her head. She settled her back against his chest and allowed herself a moment to recollect her thoughts. She wanted to help Mitzi in any way she could but she felt like she would be up against it. Mitzi was, in a way, her own worst enemy.

Mitzi and Balzar soon joined her back in the library. She smiled as they sat back down.

"Everything sorted now?" She asked.

"I think so. I have told Balzar everything I told Janus in the kitchen area. He thinks that I should talk to Zeke about it," Mitzi explained.

"Sorry, talk to Zeke about what exactly?" Eva asked.

"Oh, I thought Janus would have spoken to you about what I told him," Mitzi looked confused.

"I don't tell anyone's secrets. That is up to you to tell," Janus smiled.

"I thought all married couples shared everything," Mitzi shrugged.

Eva laughed. "I trust him enough for anyone to talk to him about anything. If they trust me enough, they will come to me too. Janus has enough knowledge to be able to help anyone out if they need it."

"I'm so jealous! I wish I had a relationship like yours," Mitzi sighed.

"Maybe one day Mitz, who knows," Balzar smiled.

Mitzi smiled back at him. Her mind flooding with images of her and Zeke on picnics, and jetting off the furthest reaches of space.

"You still with us Mitz?" Eva asked, waving her hands in the air.

"Huh? Oh sorry. I was somewhere else entirely," Mitzi blushed.

Eva smiled. "Let's get back to it shall we?"

Balzar winked at Mitzi as she climbed back up the little ladder to the seat made just for her. She settled back and made sure she listened to everything Eva told her. She would need to be aware of her surroundings if she was going to survive.

Enceladus

"So, he joined up around two millennia ago. He isn't quite the head but there's only two more higher than him. For him to rise in the ranks, those above him must be captured and killed," Layson read.

"Can't he just kill them himself?" Chylla asked.

They had transformed part of the Palace library into a research room and were huddled around the centre table.

"No, if it were that easy, he would have done it so long ago. Members of The Wigfya have to be captured by an enemy and killed before the person below can move up," Zeke explained.

"So, how are we going to stop them from hunting Mitzi?" Chylla asked.

"Who is hunting Mitzi?" Eliontara asked from the doorway.

Everyone turned to see him staring at them. No one knew how to answer him without giving away what Mitzi was.

"Erm...Well, there are some bad beings out there honey, and they aren't always kind to others," Aquilia tried to explain to him.

"Is Mitzi something different Mama?" Eliontara asked.

Aquilia looked at Zeke but refrained from answering straight away.

"There you are Elion. I've been looking everywhere for you," Scarlex called. "Why is everyone in here?"

"We're just having a meeting sweetie, nothing to worry about," Aquilia smiled.

"No they're not. They are discussing Mitzi. There's something different about her and they won't tell me what," Eliontara replied.

Zeke walked to the children and looked them in the eyes. "You know we can't discuss someone's form without prior permission right?"

Both of the children nodded. "It's not fair to tell everyone about someone as you might hurt their feelings," they both said.

"So you understand why we can't tell you anything about Mitzi without her say so. Maybe, when she is ready and not before, she might tell you herself," Zeke smiled.

Scarlex put her arms around his neck and hugged him tight. "She likes you," she whispered.

Zeke pulled away and smiled at her. He saw something, but what he saw worried him. He now had a choice to make, should he tell Aquilia what he saw, tell Scarlex what he saw, or keep this information to himself?

Chapter Sixteen – Saturn

As Balzar and Mitzi made themselves comfortable in the beds Eva and Janus had made up for them, Mitzi turned to Balzar and looked at him with a confused look.

"Do you think everyone is OK on Enceladus?" She asked.

"I'm sure they are fine Mitz, get some rest. Eva has some other stuff to show us tomorrow and I'm not sure about you, but I'm beyond tired," Balzar replied. "I'm sure if there was a problem, they would call."

"Maybe you're right. Sleep well Bal," she said as she closed her eyes and began to drift off to sleep. She tossed and turned to get comfortable, finally settling for the corner of the pillow.

The bed was gigantic compared to the one she would normally sleep in. She rolled up in the pillowcase and finally allowed sleep to claim her.

Balzar watched her settle before allowing himself to doze. He promised himself a few hours at most, just to make sure Mitzi stayed safe, but as he awoke the next morning, his worst nightmares had come true.

Mitzi was nowhere to be seen and her pillow had vanished. Balzar threw the quilt off and jumped out of bed, his whole seven foot three inch frame visibly shook with worry.

"Mitzi! Mitzi where are you?" He shouted.

"What's happened?" Janus asked as he ran into the room quickly followed by Eva holding Xandr who wriggled so much she had to put him down.

"I'm sorry if I woke you all, especially the children, but Mitzi isn't here," Balzar said, pointing to the bed in which she should still be sleeping.

"You didn't wake us. Xandr here decided it was time to get up around four hours ago," Eva smiled. "Janus, check the kitchen. I'll check the gardens. Balzar, check the room in case she found somewhere more comfortable. I know Squinks have a tendency to find places out of the way to rest."

Both men nodded and went about their given tasks. Eva swung Xandr up and nuzzled into his neck. "It's a good job you were awake!"

"I saw her," Xandr gurgled.

"Saw who sweetie?" Eva asked, suddenly serious.

"Mitzi!" Xandr exclaimed.

"Saw her where honey?" Eva didn't want to scare him but she was beginning to worry.

"She was in the hands of a red man. She was sleeping soundly. The red man told me to shush but he didn't look nice and that's why I woke up," Xandr explained with frown.

"Janus! Balzar!" Eva shouted.

"Have I done something wrong Mama?" Xandr asked, tears forming in his eyes.

"Oh no honey. No, don't think that," Eva cooed.

Balzar was first to arrive, shortly followed by Janus.

"What is it? Have you found her?" Balzar asked, full of hope.

"No. Xandr saw her just as he woke up. I think The Wigfya found her," Eva told them.

"Oh no. Oh please no," Balzar began to cry. "I'll never find her again. Oh, Zeke is not going to be happy about this.

Neither is The Queen. I'm going to lose my job, my house, probably even my wife."

"Balzar. This isn't your fault. No one will blame you. We all believed she would be safe here," Janus said, gently touching his arm.

Balzar threw his huge arms around Janus's neck and sobbed. "She's too special."

"I know big fella, I know. Let's get a call in to Enceladus and take it from there," Janus soothed.

"I'll make the call. Xandr, you go play with Codex and Jaxson," Eva told him.

Xandr nodded, ran to Balzar, hugged him and ran off to play with his brother.

"He's such a sweet kid," Balzar said, wiping his eyes. "I'm sorry for breaking down like that."

"Completely understandable," Eva said holding her hand up. "Never apologise for being a friend."

"What kind of friend am I if she was taken on my watch," Balzar asked, tears still welling up in his eyes.

Janus guided him to a chair that overlooked the gardens and sat him down. "You have to remember that none of this is your fault. You are just as entitled to sleep as anyone. The Wigfya got lucky, that's all."

Balzar looked across the Kingdom. He saw the people going about their daily life without a care in the world. As he looked towards the village he and Mitzi had toured before arriving at the Palace, he wondered if the woman there had informed The Wigfya about Mitzi's whereabouts.

"You don't think Shima could have told them, do you?" Balzar asked.

"I hope not. The people that live there are part of Lyra's clan. She would go explosive if someone betrayed our trust. Lyra pleaded her life for them to be allowed to return to Astrodia," Janus explained.

"Lyra is your mother, is that correct?" Balzar questioned.

"She is. She has done her fair share of bad things but I think she deserves a second chance, and, if I'm honest, I don't think I would have been able to get through the last few years without her, especially when you have a father like mine," Janus smiled.

"I'm glad you have her around. I lost my parent a long time ago and I always wish they had lived longer," Balzar replied.

He looked back over at Astrodia and sighed. He loved this Kingdom. He had always wished he had been born here and not on Enceladus.

He looked back towards the village on the south side. Something caught his eye. A hooded being running from a house towards, what looked like, a small pod, before shooting off into the sky almost undetected, but then Balzar spotted a fleet of pods on its tail within seconds. They stopped the pod and escorted it back to Astrodia. He hoped whoever or whatever it was, it had a good explanation for creeping around.

<u>Enceladus</u>

"What!" Zeke screamed. "How?"

"We're not sure. Eva told me that when Balzar woke up, Mitzi wasn't in her bed. He looked around with the help of Eva and Janus, but Xandr alerted them to a red man. He said the red man had taken Mitzi," Aquilia explained.

"Red man?" Zeke asked. "What red man?"

"We believe this may have been your grandfather," Chylla whispered.

"That man has is no relation to me," Zeke insisted. "What are we doing to find her?"

"We have sent The Stealth Raiders to Astrodia. They secured a pod that had no permission to be there and have someone in custody," Aquilia replied.

"I want to be there," Zeke said. He rose from his seat and prepared to leave Enceladus.

"I don't think that is such a great idea Zeke," Chylla said. "You may compromise the interview."

Zeke slammed his palm on the table and then broke down in tears. "We have to find her. She will be terrified."

"We will find her Zeke, but we need you with a level head to do it," Aquilia replied. She placed her hands over his and brought his head to hers. "I promise."

Zeke nodded. Aquilia had never broken a promise before and he doubted she would start now. He closed his eyes for a second but was brought back to reality with a bump. Had he really just seen that?

"Are you OK Zeke?" Aquilia asked.

"Y...Yes. I'm just worried and don't want to miss anything. I'm going to go and do some more research on The Wigfya. Maybe I can find out how to locate them," he replied. He picked up his backpack and left the room, making sure he was out of eyesight before shaking his head.

"Are you OK young Zeke?" Benzyline asked as he rushed past her.

He stopped just as she said his name, turning to face her with tears streaking down his face. He shook his head ferociously. She held his shoulders and took him into a side room. She sat him down and held his hands whilst he cried.

"She means something?" She asked.

He nodded.

"I can see it in your soul. You are a kind young man, but I see something more within you for Mitzi. They will find her, and you will help. I can see it," she told him.

He thanked her and sat with her for a few more minutes before excusing himself and heading off to his own room for some peace. He had to think of a way to find Mitzi.

Zeke paced his room for the millionth time but he couldn't work out how he was going to find her without the help of others. He opened his laptop and downloaded a tracking app. If Mitzi still had her phone, he could trace it. He rapped his fingers on the table as he waited for the file to setup. He was becoming impatient. When it finally finished, he quickly typed her number in but it failed to locate her. His head fell back against the headrest of his chair. A sudden knocking at his door had him jumping to his feet.

"Come in," he answered.

Layson opened the door slowly. "You OK son? I heard about Mitzi."

Zeke sighed audibly. "I don't know what to do Dad. This program can't even trace her phone."

"Can I take a look?" Layson asked, pointing to Zeke's laptop.

"Sure. Knock yourself out Dad," Zeke shrugged. He pulled up a chair next to his father and watched him work.

Layson, somehow, managed to re-code the programme making it stronger. He then re-entered the number and, bingo, a small blip appeared on the screen.

"Wow Dad, you'll have to show me how to do that someday," Zeke smiled. "I have to go."

Layson smiled as his son ran off to find Queen Aquilia and show her the location. He was proud of Zeke. He used to be so quiet and now, well now he was out there protecting others. *'How different things could have been,'* he thought to himself.

Zeke turned another few corners before running head on into Chylla.

"Whoa, what's the rush?" Chylla asked as she took Zeke's offered hand and stood up.

"I found her! Well, dad found her, but I know where they are. We have to go and get her. She'll be terrified, you have no idea what she's been through," Zeke spat.

"OK, slow down. Deep breaths. Go over that again, slowly," she smiled.

"Dad found Mitzi. I know where they are. She will be scared. She has been through too much already," he repeated.

"Zeke, even you don't know what she has been through, unless she has told you? Mitzi doesn't tell anyone anything," Chylla asked.

Zeke tried to look away but Chylla caught him under his chin and pulled him to look at her.

"What do you know Zeke?" Chylla asked.

"More than you could ever imagine. About everyone," he whispered.

Chapter Seventeen

"Ahh, the elusive Mitzi Chilo. I've been searching for you for too long," said a man with red skin.

Mitzi shook harder than she ever had before. She was inside of a small cage. It was no bigger than her, and every time she moved it swung from side to side. She pulled her little legs up towards her chin.

"Do you have any idea who I am?" The red skinned man asked.

Mitzi shook her head. "Should I?"

"Oh but I thought you had been searching up on us? Trying to figure out how to avoid us," he laughed. "You know, you wouldn't have been able to hide from us for long. We've been tracking you for the past two centuries. We've known every mission you have undertaken and followed you."

Mitzi shook even more. She needed some kind of comfort before things got worse. She worried that if things got worse,

what she would do to these beings and not have any
recollection of.

"Don't worry Mitzi, we won't hurt you. Well, not much
anyway, but you have some rest time. We won't make it back
for a while," he smiled. His teeth were green and filled with
yesterday's lunch.

He made Mitzi feel sick. She huddled up into a ball and fell
to sleep. She dreamt that Zeke had come to rescue her and
that she was snuggled into his neck.

Zeke slammed the door behind him and locked it. He had
nearly told Chylla everything. Nearly told her he could *see*
everything. He had seen a lot to do with her past life and her
future, but he hadn't wanted that burden. He wished he could
control this curse, but it was out of his hands, almost literally.

Chylla pounded on the door with all her strength, almost
taking it off the frame before Aquilia grabbed her hands.

"What are you doing?" Aquilia asked.

"He knows something about Mitzi and he won't tell me,"
Chylla replied through gritted teeth.

"What does he know?" Aquilia asked.

"He won't tell me. He said Mitzi has been through enough
already, but he hardly knows her!" Chylla answered, she

turned and began pounding on the door again. "If you don't answer me in the next second, I will take this door off!"

"YOU WILLNOT!" Aquilia shouted. "Chylla, go and calm yourself down before you say something you will regret."

Chylla stood with her mouth wide open.

"Go!" Aquilia demanded and she turned her back on Chylla.

Chylla walked away with her head low. *'What was I thinking? I've probably frightened him half to death,'* she thought. She went back to her own room and sat on the bed. She cried. It had been such a long time since she had fully cried. The last being when she had told Ammyn that she had hidden when Queen Quintara's mother had been kidnapped and killed. She let out every last tear before drifting off to sleep.

Aquilia gently knocked on Zeke's door and waited. She slid down the wall next to his door and waited. Waited until he was ready to see her. She didn't have to wait too long as he popped his head out of the door,

"Hey, you wanna talk about it?" She asked.

Zeke looked up and down the corridor, half expecting Chylla to ambush him.

"She's not here. Can I come in?" Aquilia asked.

Zeke opened the door wider to allow her to enter the room. She sat on the chair closest to the window and gestured for him to join her.

"What happened Zeke?" Aquilia asked.

"I told Chylla that dad located Mitzi and that we needed to find her and that she had been through enough and Chylla just went crazy. Asking how I knew about Mitzi's life and saying I would only know if she told me and that Mitzi doesn't tell anyone anything about her life. Then she asked what I knew. I told her I knew more than she could imagine. About everyone. That's when she chased me. I had to run," Zeke explained, worry crossing his face.

"Zeke, what did you mean? Is this something we should be worried about?" She asked.

"No, well, not really." He took a deep breath. "Do you promise to keep this a secret?"

"You know, that whatever you tell me is confidential and will never leave this room," Aquilia replied.

Zeke closed his eyes for a few seconds, if only to slow his breathing down. When he opened them, he looked deep into Aquilia's electric blue eyes. She had been so kind to him since he had arrived. He owed her this much.

"I have an ability. Maybe a gift, maybe a curse, but if I touch someone's skin, I can see either their past, or their future, which ever presents itself to me. I saw Mitzi's past," Zeke told her.

"This is why you never touch me, isn't it?" Aquilia asked.

Zeke nodded. "I don't want to see your future and I know most of your past."

"Who have you shared this with?" Aquilia asked.

"Halana. I showed her what her future would be like. Only a snippet. That's when I knew you were going to be a mother yourself," he replied.

"Anyone else?" She asked.

"I've told my parents. They believe that I have a gift, but, personally, I feel it is a curse. I don't want to see my loved ones futures, especially if they are horrid," he replied with tears forming in his eyes.

Aquilia hesitated for a second before grabbing his hand; He was teleported instantly to a battlefield.

'That's the wrong way. Run this way.

Shut down all the servers.

Turn the mainframe off, quickly, this virus is eating away at the software.

Where's Layson?

In the tech room. He's checking on the hard disks.

Your Majesty, we must get you into hiding.

No. I will stand and fight just like I did before. Nothing and no one will take my Kingdom. Here or on Saturn.'

Zeke pulled away quickly. He felt his heart rate notch up and he began to breathe rapidly.

"I don't want to know what you saw," Aquilia told him. "But I want you to know that no matter what, we never avoid contact."

"You don't understand. If I know what will happen I will try and change it and that can have disastrous effects on life itself. I will try to alter the outcome, especially if it is something bad," he explained.

"Then you must learn to let life run its course young Zeke. What will be, will be, no matter what you try, life outsmarts us. Just promise me, that if you ever feel trapped, you will come and find me," Aquilia asked.

Zeke nodded. "Can we look for Mitzi now?"

"Where is she?" Aquilia questioned.

Zeke opened his laptop and the tracking program. The blip flashing away in front of them.

"Judging by that, I'd say they were somewhere in the vicinity of Grazille Swirl and Hurtsa Galaxy. If we want to find her, we need to move quickly. I'll send for Balzar, Onyx Abyss

Alpha and The Stealth Raiders will Hyper Jump there and search the area. I assume you want in?" She asked.

"Yes. I won't do anything stupid. I will follow all orders and bring her home safely," Zeke replied.

"Then you better get ready. I'll summon the troops," Aquilia nodded.

After leaving Zeke's room, Aquilia met with Celest and Nymeria. She explained the mission and warned them to watch out for Zeke.

"Do you think it is wise him coming too?" Celest asked.

"I think he needs to. He feels responsible, plus, I think there is more than just 'crewmate' protection at stake here," Aquilia smiled.

Both women nodded then left to ready their ship.

"Mum," Scarlex said. "Can I go too?"

"Do you think you are ready?" Aquilia asked.

Scarlex nodded. "Can I go with Zeke and Balzar though?"

"I will request it to Balzar. As he is the captain, it will be his decision," Aquilia told her.

"I understand," Scarlex replied.

She and her brother each packed their backpacks and got themselves ready for the mission.

"Are you sure you're up for this sis?" Eliontara asked.

"I have to be. Mitzi is a good being. She needs good souls around her," Scarlex replied. She zipped up her bag and flipped it onto her back. She chanced a glance out of the window, just in time to see Balzar returning from Saturn. She hoped he would allow her to join him.

Scarlex and Eliontara arrived at the launch pads complete with their own backpack. Eliontara turned to Scarlex and hugged her close. "Stay safe sis," he whispered and then made his way onto The Stealth ship.

Aquilia approached her and placed her hand on her shoulder. "Remember when I told you I wouldn't treat you and your brother any differently to the other fighters?" She asked.

Scarlex nodded and looked up at her mother.

"That will never change. I will never lie to either of you and I will expect the same in return," Aquilia continued. "Balzar has, kindly, approved your request to join him and Zeke aboard Onyx Abyss Alpha. You are to follow his orders and, under no circumstances, are you to princess around. Is that clear?"

"Yes Ma'am," Scarlex threw her hand up in a salute.

"Climb aboard and introduce yourself," Aquilia told her. "And stay safe."

Scarlex watched as her mother walked back to the Palace and, to what she presumed would be the Comms Room. She climbed up the steps and through the doorway.

"Scarlex reporting for duty. Where do you want me?" She announced.

"Welcome Scarlex. You can put your bag here," Balzar pointed out. "And I think we'll have you up front with me. Zeke has eyes on the monitors so I could do with an extra pair up here with me."

Scarlex nodded, placed her bag down and buckled herself in for launch. As the ships lifted off in tandem, she could just make out Eliontara in The Stealth Ship sitting on the second row back from Celest. She settled back and waited for orders. She was now part of the army that protected Enceladus and Saturn. Lives depended on her and she didn't want to let anyone down.

Chapter Eighteen

"Wake up Mitzi. We've arrived!" The red skinned man called.

Mitzi stirred awake, suddenly disappointed that she wasn't wrapped up with Zeke and that she was still in this tiny cage. "Where are we?" She asked.

"You don't know?" He laughed. "Of course you don't, you've been trying to avoid this place at all costs."

Mitzi thought for a second, she knew she should have listened to Eva. Tears pricked at her eyes.

"Oh there's no need for that Mitzi. We're in Grazille Swirl. I'm sorry, I forgot to introduce myself. I'm Xeno," he informed her.

"What are you going to do to me?" Mitzi whimpered.

"Oh do stop pretending you're scared. We all know your kind isn't scared," Xeno laughed.

"My kind?" Mitzi asked. "What do you mean?"

"Squink. Squinks aren't scared, at least, not the ones I've met and, believe me, I've met a few over my time," Xeno told her. "I'll take you to our holding room. You might be a little more comfortable there." He picked up her cage and walked with her through the dimly lit corridors and into a small room. The window was covered with a cage like contraption. Small enough that she couldn't wriggle through.

He placed her cage down and opened the hatch. "I hope you will be more comfortable here. I'm sorry we had to transport you like that but we couldn't risk you biting anyone."

"I've never bitten anyone," Mitzi replied looking confused. "We don't bite."

"Ahh that's what the last one said and then, when we injected her, she turned on us and bit my lead lab operative," he replied.

"Didn't you think it could have been a reaction to be injected without permission?" Mitzi asked.

"Of course not. She had been docile up to that point. She was vicious," Xeno replied. "Now, get some rest. You have a long day tomorrow!"

With those parting words, he turned on his heel and left the room.

"Oh Zeke, where are you?" Mitzi whispered to herself.

"So I can see that there are a number of planets in this Swirl. I'm tracking the location. It's stopped!" Zeke cried. "She's close by. Let me just zoom in here."

"Excellent work Zeke," Scarlex said.

Zeke smiled at her. It was like looking at Aquilia.

"So where are we heading young man?" Balzar asked from the cockpit.

"To a planet called Orxon," Zeke told him. He looked over at the third monitor and typed in the planet. It brought up an overview of the planet. "That can't be right."

"What is it?" Scarlex asked as she scanned the view ahead of her. The stars were a multitude of different colours.

"It says that the planet has been uninhabited for over six millennia. If that's the case, why would Mitzi be there?" Zeke asked.

"Let's see if this telescope Sinclair built is any good. Scarlex, if you will," Balzar smiled.

Scarlex nodded once and activated the telescope. She stood next to Balzar as he looked through.

"Here, take a look and tell Zeke what you see," Balzar gestured.

Scarlex did as she was ordered and placed her eye on the eyepiece. Within seconds her vision cleared and she could see what appeared to be a whole community on Orxon.

"There is a huge building to the north of the city below. There are quite a few inhabitants below. It looks like the building is some sort of laboratory, I can see some rooms that are pure white," Scarlex explained.

"Wait, you can see that far?" Balzar asked as he looked through himself. "I can't see that."

Scarlex smiled at him. "Telescopic vision," she tapped her eyes.

Balzar laughed. "You're a valuable asset!"

"I'll help all I can. Can I look again?" She asked.

"Please do," Balzar handed back to her.

Scar, can you see if you can spot Mitzi through the windows?" Zeke asked.

"I'll try," she replied. She looked again through the scope slowly moving from window to window until she saw a flash of white. "Wait! I see her. She's on the third floor and, one, two, three, four, seventh room from the left, and Zeke, she looks terrified."

"Thank you Scar. You don't happen to have any other hidden talents, do you?" He asked.

"Let me see what I can do," Scarlex replied. She headed back to the scope and placed her eye on the eyepiece again. She lined up the scope with Mitzi's window and blinked seven times in quick succession. "I hope she was looking!"

Zeke smiled. "Your mum would be proud of you."

"Balzar, updates?" Celest called over the radio.

"We have her, she is on Orxon and Scarlex located her room. We are going to try and land somewhere inconspicuous," he replied.

"That's great news. Well done Scar," Celest called. "We'll follow you down and then we go get Mitzi back."

"No, we have to move carefully. She has been taken by some pretty serious beings. We can't just burst in there and break her out. We need a plan," Eliontara shouted.

"Elion, what do you know?" Zeke asked.

"I know enough. I know what these beings do to others and it's not good. If any of us get caught, we may never get home," Eliontara replied.

"OK everyone. Get planning," Nymeria called out. "All plans will be considered."

The crews of both lead ships began planning, along with Mythias's crew.

"I think I have something," Scarlex announced.

"OK, we're all listening," Celest replied.

"I do have one question first, is anyone among us a shapeshifter?" She asked.

There was silence from all ships. Scarlex looked defeated, that was, until a voice from the back of The Stealth Ship spoke up.

"I can," Shlysta announced.

Everyone on the ship turned their heads.

"You never mentioned that before," Nymeria said.

"I'm sorry. I didn't think it would change anything," he said as he hung his head.

"Oh, it doesn't change a thing," Celest smiled. "It's just sometimes nice to know who can do what, if anything, on the ship, especially at times like this."

"Shlysta, what do you need to be able to change?" Scarlex asked.

"Just a picture. I can practically morph into anything," he shrugged.

"Great, Nymeria, can you show Shlysta a picture of one of The Wigfya?" She asked.

"On it," Nymeria replied.

"So, I want you to morph into that. If we can get you into that building, we might have a shot at getting Mitzi out, but it's going to be a team effort. No one can take all the credit," Scarlex said.

"We got ya Scar," Balzar replied.

Nymeria pulled up a picture of The Wigfya for Shlysta to look at. He lopped his head from side to side, making sure to remember every inch of the picture. He stepped away and closed his eyes. Within a few seconds he had turned into one of them. He had red skin and gleaming green eyes.

"Oh wow!" Celest exclaimed. "If I saw you anywhere near Enceladus I'd shoot you."

Shlysta laughed. "Probably a good job I don't morph often."

"You're doing great kid," Nymeria told him. "Let's get you down there."

Shlysta smiled and prepared to leave the ship. As he walked down the steps, he quickly blended in with the scores of Wigfya all marching towards the big building.

"Oh no," Scarlex cried. "They scan their eyes as they enter!"

"Let's see what happens first. We can correct things if we need to," Balzar said.

They all watched as Shlysta made him way to the gate. He kept his face forward so as not to draw attention to the ships. The closer he got to the gate, the more worried Scarlex became.

"If he gets caught, I don't know what they will do to him," she whispered.

"Think positive Scar," Zeke smiled. "I have every reason to believe your plan will work."

Shlysta was next to enter the gate. He stood as they scanned his eye and waited for the result. He didn't give anything away he just waited patiently. After a few seconds, they waved him through. Scarlex let out a sigh of relief and sat back in the chair.

"OK Shlysta, we're looking for the third floor. Any chance you can get there?" Zeke asked.

"I'll try," he whispered.

"Scarlex, can you find him through the telescope and relay back to us what's happening? We didn't have enough time to fit him with a camera," Zeke asked.

Scarlex nodded and looked through the scope. "OK, he's heading to the stairwell. Wait, he's been stopped by someone. I can't hear what's being said. The other man is pointing to the stairs."

"I hope he hasn't been rumbled," Celest said.

"Wait, no, he's fine. He's heading up the stairs," Scarlex replied. She watched as he walked the corridor, looking in and out of each room just as the other Wigfya were doing. "He is certainly fitting in!" She laughed.

Zeke wished he could be the one to rescue Mitzi. He hadn't been able to think clearly since she had been taken and he could normally formulate a plan within seconds. This time, Scarlex beat him to it.

"He's found her!" Scarlex called out.

"Shlysta, you need to get her out of there and quickly. I don't know how you will do it but, well, hurry," Celest told him.

"Got it," he replied. He turned to Mitzi and opened his pocked. "Jump in," he told her.

"I don't trust you," she hissed.

"Pass her the radio," Celest told him. "Zeke, you need to convince her and quick."

"Mitzi, Mitzi it's Zeke. You have to go with him. He's with us," Zeke told her.

"Wait, you have Wigfya on your team?" She cried.

"No, no, definitely not! His name is Shlysta, he's a shapeshifter," Zeke replied. "You need to hurry Mitz. They're coming back."

Mitzi thought for a second before jumping into his pocket. "You better not drop or squash me!"

Shlysta smiled. "I got you. I wouldn't let anything happen to you. If I did, Zeke would surely kick me all over the place."

"You got that right kid," Zeke laughed. "Get her out of there!"

Shlysta moved silently along the corridor. He looked for a faster way out but it seemed there was only one way in and one way out, back through the front gate. He straightened up and walked towards the gate.

"Going so soon?" The officer asked.

"Family emergency. I'm sure it's nothing but the wife, you know, she panics too much," Shlysta laughed.

"I hope it's nothing serious," the officer said as he swung the gate open to allow him to go through.

"Hopefully not. I'm sure I will return soon," Shlysta said. "Thank you."

He walked away without looking back. He didn't want them to have any reason to follow him.

"Just a few more steps," Nymeria called over the radio.

As he walked up the steps and through the door of The Stealth Ship, Celest closed the hatch and powered up the ship, she didn't want to risk anyone catching up with him.

"Let's get her home!" Nymeria announced and within seconds, all ships were homeward bound.

<u>Chapter Nineteen</u>

"So how long do you think it will take them to get back?" Chylla asked.

"I really couldn't say. I hope that their ships have enough fuel for a Hyper Jump, otherwise we could be looking at months before they finally land back here," Aquilia replied. She looked up at the sky, willing there to be any sign of them, but there wasn't a speck there.

Feeling defeated, Aquilia turned back to her desk and continued with the poetry book she was reading.

'As if by magic,

The signs of life appeared,

Although some thought it was a trick,

All obstacles were cleared.

As on the horizon they were seen,

It all seemed so much like a dream.'

'Odd,' Aquilia thought to herself.

"Your Majesty, they are arriving! The first ships have broken through," Chylla called over the radio.

"I'm on my way," she replied, looking oddly at the book. "If you have some sort of power I will throw you!" She whispered.

She walked out to the landing pad and waited for the first ships to land. One by one they touched down. She eagerly waited for The Stealth Ship and Onyx Abyss Alpha to land. As soon as The Stealth Ship touched down, Shlysta ran from the ship to place Mitzi in the medical suite with Zeke not far behind. He had been the first off Onyx Abyss Alpha.

"Zeke, what happened?" Aquilia asked as he ran past her.

"I'll update you when I know she is OK," he called back. "Talk to Balzar and Scarlex."

Aquilia watched him run off and turned to Eliontara who was now at her side.

"It was tough on him Mum, give him a bit of time," he said with a smile.

She smiled back and gently touched his shoulder. "Where is your sister sweetie?"

"Right here Mum," Scarlex replied as she climbed down from Onyx.

"How did it go?" Aquilia asked.

"We worked as a team. Shlysta is a..."Scarlex began.

"We don't reveal other's secrets unless given prior permission Scarlex, you know that," Aquilia reminded her.

"Sorry Mother. I guess I'm just so glad we managed to rescue Mitzi, I lost myself a little," she replied hanging her head.

"I suggest you hold that head of yours up missy," Balzar said as he climbed down from the ship. "If it wasn't for your plan, we never would have gotten her out."

"Balzar, debrief when Zeke has finished checking up on Mitzi. I expect everyone who was involved to be there," Aquilia told him.

He nodded and went off to grab a drink before their meeting. Eliontara and Scarlex joined him shortly after.

"You two OK?" He asked as they both sat down.

"Are all missions like that?" Scarlex asked.

"Not all of them. Most of the time when we patrol, we don't come across another ship for days or even weeks on end," Balzar replied as he opened a box of Slinkies.

"Eww, how can you eat those?" Eliontara scrunched his face up.

Balzar laughed, "quite easily, look." He opened his mouth and tipped the entire packet in.

Scarlex laughed. She knew how much her brother hated the taste of Slinkies. He said they tasted of sand and flowers, not that he'd ever eaten sand and flowers before. Or so he claimed.

"Now now, what seems to be so funny?" Celest asked as she sat at the table and glanced from Scarlex to her brother and then on to Balzar.

"Oh Eliontara here doesn't like Slinkies," Balzar explained. "Says the taste horrible."

"Eww, they are nasty. They just have no taste at all," Nymeria agreed.

Celest laughed again, "*I* actually quite like them."

Zeke sat by Mitzi's bed as she slept. He watched her eyelids flutter as she dreamt. This was the first time he had seen her since she was rescued. He willed her to wake up so he could see for himself that she was still her. He had never questioned the doctors here before and he most likely never would, but he needed to see her awake to know for himself. He needed to see into her eyes.

"Come on Mitzi. Wake up. Please," he whispered. "For me."

He continued to watch her, unaware of Aquilia's presence in the room.

"You know, it was Scarlex's idea to send Shlysta. She had this whole plan, and it worked. We got you out. Now I just need you to wake up," Zeke said softly. He tried hiding the fact his voice was breaking up.

"You can cry you know," Mitzi smiled. She opened her big blue eyes and stared at him. "You're such a softie!" She climbed from the bed and wrapped herself around his neck. "I missed you," she whispered.

"Ahem, sorry to interrupt," Aquilia cleared her throat. "Is there any chance we could debrief sometime today?" She smiled

"Sorry Your Highness. I'll meet you in the meeting room. I just want to make sure Mitzi is OK first," Zeke replied.

"Mitzi is part of this too, if she has clearance from the doctors, she is more than welcome to join us," Aquilia smiled.

"Thank you Your Majesty," Mitzi said. She clung on tight to Zeke's neck as they walked through the Palace, rounding everyone up as they went. Those they couldn't find were contacted by radio.

By the time they reached the meeting room, all crew members were present. Aquilia closed the door and brought everyone's attention to her.

"Now, I know that mission wasn't exactly what anyone had in mind, but I believe everything went according to plan and luckily, you managed to save Mitzi," she said. "I know, certain members had bigger roles to play than others but I know you all worked as a team. Balzar, do you have anything to add?"

Balzar stood up and looked around the room. "Everyone in this room played their part today, and for that, I'm grateful. From Scarlex and her amazing plan, to Shlysta and his, added extras. We came together and rescued someone rather special, thank you."

Everyone applauded Scarlex and Shlysta, the latter of which blushed within an inch of his skin.

"Now, Mitzi, how are you feeling?" Aquilia asked.

"I'm a little drained, but I do have one question. How did you know who had taken me and how did you find me?" She asked.

"That would have been Xandr. Evadene and Janus's son. He saw the man take you and I think it spooked him a little, it's the first time he has seen someone with red skin. He stayed awake, whinging until Eva woke up to tend to him, that was when I noticed you missing," Balzar explained.

"So, I don't get how you managed to track me down," Mitzi said.

"That was me. I have a program that can trace phones by signal. Don't worry, I only use it if we have trouble. I couldn't get it to latch onto your phone so my dad recoded it and that how we found you on Orxon," Zeke told her.

"I'm glad you used it. I would have been...well, I don't know what I would have been had you not all turned up when you did. I do have just one more question," Mitzi said.

"Go ahead," Aquilia replied.

"Who was blinking at me through the window?" She cried.

Scarlex looked away. This was one thing she hadn't explained to her mother yet. She hadn't even had a chance to explain her telescopic vision.

"I think we'll let them come clean when they are ready," Zeke replied. "Let's find you a room and you can rest some more."

"Ma'am, how long are we grounded for?" Balzar asked.

"Probably a few days at the most, enough time for Mitzi to find her feet again," Aquilia whispered as Zeke carried Mitzi off to find a spare room for her. "He really has got something for her hasn't he?"

"I wouldn't know Your Highness," Balzar said, turning to look out over the Kingdom,

"What aren't you telling me?" She pushed.

"It's not my story to tell. Maybe, one day, one of them will talk," Balzar replied and he turned to leave the room. As he opened the door, he spotted Scarlex walking away.

"Hey," he called.

Scarlex turned and he could see she was upset.

"What's wrong?" He asked.

"Did you tell my mother?" She asked.

"About your ability? No. No, of course not. I know the rules as much as the next being. Haven't you told her yet?" Balzar asked.

"There's never really been a good time. She's a busy woman." Scarlex shrugged.

Balzar looked at her for a second. The only difference between her and The Queen was their hair colour. Scarlex had electric blue hair, which trailed down her back in a long braid and Aquilia had the brightest red hair ever seen. They both wore their hair in the same fashion and both were incredibly feisty for all the right reasons. Scarlex had The Queens eye colour and the same slim lips.

"I think, if you go and see her, she would stop everything she is doing, just to listen to you," Balzar told her.

"Do you think so?" Scarlex asked. "I'm not so sure."

"How about, I check if she is busy, and then get you in there?" He asked.

"You would do that?" She exclaimed.

"Absolutely. Just wait here, promise you won't run away," he smiled.

"I promise," she replied. As he walked back inside the room, she paced the tiny corridor, rubbing her arms from a cold that didn't exist.

"I'm sorry to interrupt again Your Highness," Balzar announced as he re-entered the room.

"How can I help you?" Aquilia asked sliding chairs back into their places.

"It's probably not my place to say Your Majesty, but Scarlex is outside in the corridor. She wants to speak with you, in private, but fears you may be too busy," Balzar explained.

"Send her right in; I'm never too busy for my children. Thank you Balzar," Aquilia replied. She pulled out two chairs and placed them at the table, not too far away from each other. She wanted Scarlex to feel special.

Balzar exited the room and gestured for Scarlex to go in. "She's ready for you. Be honest and don't be afraid. I'll be in the canteen if you need me afterwards."

Scarlex walked forward and stopped in front of him. "Thank you. It was a pleasure flying with you today. Perhaps I can do it again sometime?"

"Whenever The Queen allows it, you will be welcomed," he replied. He watched her walk in and closed the door behind her.

"Come and sit down darling. What did you want to speak to me about?" Aquilia asked, gently touching her daughters arm.

"It was me," Scarlex said.

"What was you sweetheart?" Aquilia said.

"I blinked at Mitzi. Mum I have telescopic vision and somehow I can emit light from my eyes. Is there something wrong with me?" Scarlex asked. She sounded a little frightened.

Chapter Twenty - Saturn

"Do you think they found her?" Evadene asked Janus as she paced the library for the thousandth time.

"If you're not careful we will have to buy another patch for that one you're wearing out. Have you thought to call The Queen and ask?" He replied.

"Oh now, why didn't I think of that?" Eva said sarcastically. "I didn't want to impose."

"Call her. It's the only way to set your mind at rest," Janus told her. He pressed the phone into her hands and left her to dial.

'I hate imposing on her, especially after a mission as big as this,' she thought. She dialled the number and waited for an answer. It rang for what felt like hours before it was finally answered.

"Hello," Halana answered.

"Mum?" Evadene questioned.

"Oh hello darling, how lovely of you to call. What seems to be the problem? You seem surprised to hear me," Halana laughed.

"I was hoping to speak to Queen Aquilia," she replied.

"Oh, she is speaking with young Princess Scarlex. Shall I get her to call you back when she is finished?" Halana asked.

"No, it's OK. Do you know if they managed to find Mitzi?" Eva asked.

"Oh yes dear. She is resting now, but they got her home in one piece," she replied.

"Thanks Mum. I'll call Aquilia later, I never did get round to looking at those sculptures," Eva laughed. "Talk soon." And she hung up.

Breathing a sigh of relief, Eva placed the phone back in its cradle and went in search of Janus. She was about to venture into the garden when a high pitched screaming caught her attention. It was coming from the children's room. She took the steps almost three at a time and slammed the door open. There she saw Ammyn. Sitting bolt upright. Her green eyes wide with fright.

"What is it sweetheart?" Eva asked and she tried to comfort her daughter.

"Red, orange, blue. Mama, bad people," Ammyn tried to explain. Ammyn hadn't grasped speech as well as her brothers and sisters, so each day Janus and Evadene would spend some time helping her elongate her sentences.

"OK sweetie, take a deep breath in and hold, and out. Now, let's try again," Eva smiled.

Ammyn did as her mother told her to, closed her eyes for a second and said, "there was a man, I think, he had red skin. He was with another who had blue skin and orange hair. They are bad people Mama."

"Were they here?" Eva asked.

"No. I saw them. In my dream. They were on a ship, somewhere out there," Ammyn explained, pointing up to the sky.

"OK sweetheart. Let's try not to panic for now, but if you ever have that dream again, you come find me or Daddy OK?" Eva said as she hugged her daughter close. "I will never let anyone hurt any of you."

Ammyn drifted back off to sleep so Eva softly closed the door as she left the room. She went to the garden to find Janus rolling around on the floor being clambered on by Codex and Xandr.

"Can I borrow Daddy for a second boys?" She asked.

Xandr rolled off Janus's back and landed face first on the floor. Codex seemed to think it was hilarious so he did the same. They both ran off together to play in the pool.

"Is everything OK?" Janus asked.

"Did you hear Ammyn scream?" Eva asked him. She kept looking round to Ammyn's room.

"I heard something but I couldn't hear much over the boys. Is she OK?" He asked.

"I don't know. I'm worried. She told me about a dream she had. It was about a red man and a blue man with orange hair. She said they were on a ship out in space somewhere," Eva looked worried.

"Maybe we should ask Aquilia to send the Wraith Doctors?" Janus suggested.

Eva nodded so Janus made the call.

<u>Enceladus</u>

"Hey! How did it go?" Balzar asked when Scarlex came into the canteen.

"Better than I expected. Mum is going to get The Wraith Doctors to talk with me after they return from Saturn," she replied.

"Why are they going to Saturn?" Balzar asked.

"Something to do with Ammyn. Auntie Eva is worried about her," she shrugged. "I'm sure she will be fine. Ammyn is a quiet girl."

Balzar thought for a moment. He remembered Ammyn running to him and him swinging her up, but she didn't really speak much. He thought about contacting Eva and asking if Ammyn was OK but he decided against it.

"Do you think I could be a permanent fixture on Onyx Abyss Alpha?" Scarlex asked as she opened the poetry book she carried everywhere with her.

"It's possible. It may take time though. What are you reading?" Balzar asked her, trying to read the title of the book.

"This? Oh, I found it in Mum's room. It's got some really good words in it, have a look," she replied sliding the book to him.

He opened the front page and was surprised;

'Aquilia,

I hope this book brings you some comfort when I'm not around. I know it helped me a huge amount when you went away.

Love you always.

Mum x'

He wished his parents had left him little mementos like this for when he grew up, but they didn't have the chance. He flicked through a few pages, not really paying much attention to the words before sliding it back to her. "You best not lose that," he smiled.

"Why?" She asked looking confused.

"Well, your mother might miss it if you do," Balzar replied. He turned to the first page and showed her the message inside.

"I didn't see that. Did you know my grandparents?" She asked.

"Not as well as some but I knew enough about them," he told her.

"I don't talk to them much. Mum says they are too busy all of the time," Scarlex hung her head.

"I'm sure they will make some time for you soon. I have to head off and check up on Mitzi. You keep reading," he told her. "Talk soon."

He walked away, leaving Scarlex to her book. He needed to talk to Aquilia about her, but it could wait. He needed to check on Mitzi and Zeke.

"Are you comfortable?" Zeke asked flattening the blanket down.

"I'm fine," Mitzi laughed. "Stop fussing."

Zeke smiled, "I'm just glad you're home safe."

"If it wasn't for all of you, I don't think I ever would have made it out of there, thank you," she said. "Can you hop up here with me? I feel a lot safer the closer you are."

Zeke jumped on the bed and Mitzi snuggled into his neck. "Thank you," she whispered.

"Any time," he told her. After seconds, she was sleeping, snoring softly.

There was a light rapping at the door and Balzar came in.

"Sorry, just wanted to check everything was OK," he whispered.

"She's sleeping now, but I'm worried about when we go back on patrol. Will she be OK?" Zeke whispered back.

"I'm sure she will be. We just have to be extra vigilant from now on," Balzar replied. "We gotta keep out eyes open wide."

"You got it," Zeke said.

Balzar smiled at him. "Get some rest Zeke. You deserve it too."

By the time he had finished his sentence, Zeke was asleep with Mitzi snuggled up into his neck. Balzar knew, right then and there, that Zeke had to stay aboard Onyx. Mitzi needed him to; she had a bond with him. One she hadn't had with anyone else. He slipped out of the door and closed it softly. Turning to walk away, he bumped into Benzyline.

"Sorry Ma'am," he said bowing his head.

"Stand up straight," Benzyline laughed. "How is she?"

"Sleeping. I worry about her a lot," Balzar replied.

"I can see how much. Your eyes tell a story," she smiled. "Zeke will be good for her."

"How can you be sure?" He asked. It wasn't that he didn't believe her; he just needed to be sure.

"Zeke is rare. A special type of being. One that comes once in every seven or so generations, the number deceives me most of the time, but he will not let her down. He would rather die than risk anything that would harm her," Benzyline replied. She began to wander off before he stopped her again.

"What do you mean by that?" Balzar asked.

"I mean exactly what I said. He would rather die than allow her to be harmed. Do you trust him?" She asked.

"Absolutely," he answered.

"Then never question an old woman," she laughed. This time she managed to wander far enough away that he couldn't stop her.

Balzar rested his back against the wall and breathed in deep. He wouldn't allow anything to happen to either Zeke or Mitzi.

"It seems the children are now part of the army Master," she hissed over the radio. "What's our plan?"

"Wait until they launch again, we will get them then. Queen Aquilia will have no choice but to bow to me," he replied.

"Yes Master. I will set up camp in the mountains. Somewhere I can see everything. I will report back at regular intervals," she said. Her amethyst purple eyes flashed orange for a brief second before returning to their original colour.

Closing the conversation off, she settled in a relatively leafy area of the mountains and watched the Palace's coming and goings. She sat for hours watching the occupants go about their business, unaware of the impending chaos that would soon endure.

Chapter Twenty-One - Saturn

Evadene and Janus watched on as The Wraith Doctors looked over Ammyn. They talked amongst themselves, in a language that neither of them understood.

After what felt like hours, one of the doctors turned to Evadene. She had a smile across her face and gestured for them both to join her. Eva and Janus, nervously, walked towards them. They could see Ammyn sitting up on the bed, smiling so broadly, something Eva had never seen before.

"Is there anything wrong with her?" Janus asked.

"It depends what you class as being wrong? Ammyn can, in a way, predict the future. What she sees in her dreams is a warning to everyone who is shown in them. You must listen if she tells you and warn others if she cannot tell them herself," the doctor told them.

"Predict the future? Is that even possible?" Eva asked.

"It's rare. There is only one other person we know of who can *see* the future," the doctor replied.

"Who is that?" Eva asked desperate to find out who else could share this with Ammyn.

"Unfortunately that is something we cannot disclose," they said. They smiled, bid their farewells and left.

"What do we do now?" Janus asked.

"I guess we go on as normal," Eva shrugged. She plucked Ammyn from the bed and placed her on the floor where she promptly ran off to join her sisters and brothers in the garden. Eva watched her go; it was as if nothing had happened. She watched as Ammyn laughed and rolled around with her siblings, it was as if the dream had never happened.

Enceladus

Balzar stopped his watch as he finished his fifth lap of the gardens. He felt as if someone were watching him. He looked around slowly. Something didn't sit right with him. He needed the help of Scarlex. Continuing on with his routine,

Balzar slowly made his way into the Palace in search of the young Princess.

"Excuse me Ma'am," Balzar stopped Halana in the corridor. "Have you seen Princess Scarlex?"

"Oh my so polite. You must be Balzar?" Halana asked.

"I am indeed. May I ask who you are?" He replied.

"Me? Oh, I'm Halana. Head dressmaker and closet nanny to the children," she laughed. "Princess Scarlex will be in the library. Mind how you go."

Balzar bowed his head and headed off on the direction of the library. He peered through the windows in the door and spotted Scarlex sitting in the corner, her head buried in a book. He made his way in quietly and approached her.

"Excuse me Princess. I don't know how to ask this but," he tried so hard to contain himself, he had never had to ask someone this question and it seemed such a strange thing to ask.

Scarlex looked at him with her head cocked to one side. "Spit it out," she laughed.

"I need your sight," he smiled.

"Finally, someone needs me for something," she exclaimed. She placed her bookmark inside the page and gently laid it on the table. "Let's go!"

Balzar led her towards a balcony on the far side of the Palace, one level up from where he had stood a little earlier. "There seems to be something or some being there. Can you see them?"

Scarlex looked. She narrowed her eyes and spotted the being hidden in the bushes. "Hmm, amethyst eyes. Dark, black, if not, purple hair. Yes, more dark purple. She isn't Enceladant. Looks more, Plydant. I could be wrong, but, and this is a big but, she could also be a shapeshifter."

Balzar's shoulders dropped. "We need to warn your mother."

"This way," Scarlex led him to Aquilia's office.

"Absolutely. I understand. We will sort this out once and for all. I'm sorry this has caused so much confusion Xink. Thank you for bringing it to my attention," Aquilia said. "I'll get onto it right away. Thank you." She ended the call just as Scarlex knocked on the door. "Come in."

"Good morning mother," Scarlex said. "Balzar has something he needs to tell you."

"Please come in and have a seat," Aquilia gestured.

Balzar sat at the seat across from her and thought hard about what he would say. He decided to just come out with it. "We have an intruder in the Kingdom."

"What do you mean?" Aquilia asked, instantly looking worried.

"There seems to be a being lurking in the mountains. Thankfully, using Scarlex's vision, we now have an accurate description," he replied.

"You know about her vision?" Aquilia asked.

"Yes Ma'am. She was the one who helped us locate Mitzi," Balzar replied.

"He was also the one who persuaded me to talk to you," Scarlex added.

"I see," she smiled. "I'm glad you gave us both a little nudge. Now, what does this being look like exactly?"

Balzar gestured for Scarlex to explain. "You saw more than I did!"

Scarlex laughed, "OK, she had really dark purple hair, and her eyes were the colour of amethysts. She doesn't look to be from here. Using the method that Eva taught me, I would guess she is from Plydar."

"You really did listen in Ancient History!" Aquilia said. "Let's get one of the artists to sketch up a picture and see if we have the right being." She sent for an artist who arrived within seconds.

As Scarlex described the being, the artist scribbled away. Aquilia joined Balzar at the window of her office. "What is it Balzar?"

"I'm worried Ma'am," he replied.

"About Mitzi?" She asked.

"I don't think she is here for Mitzi," he confided. "I believe she is here for you Your Highness."

Aquilia tried to stifle her gasp before it escaped her mouth but she was too late.

"What is it mother?" Scarlex rushed to her side.

"We need to get your mother into hiding. I believe the being is here for her," Balzar replied.

"How can you be sure?" Scarlex asked.

"He is right I'm afraid," the artist answered. "Judging by the picture, Princess Scarlex was correct in her assumption. This being is from Plydar. I can run background to check her identification."

"If you could, please, as fast as possible," Aquilia asked.

The artist bowed his head and left the room.

"We need to alert the others. Scarlex, please accompany your mother into her personal bunker until I give the all clear," Balzar ordered.

Scarlex nodded once and led Aquilia to the bunker. "I'll stay with you Mum."

Aquilia was too shocked to argue. She followed her daughter and allowed her to close and lock the bunker doors. Balzar then set about rounding up the troops and explaining the situation. He hoped Mitzi and Zeke would be recharged enough to help out.

"I think I have been spotted Master," she hissed into her radio.

"Then you have two choices. Either break cover and go for it, or return home and try again at a later date," he replied.

"I may have to go for it, it could be the only time we have to do this," she told him. "I may be silent for a while."

"Indeed. Contact when it is done," he ended the transmission.

She knew this was going to be a hard mission, but this was the only way to get back on the good side of Fresion. He was a formidable master but one who negotiated well. She had one chance to prove her worth, and this was it. She crept down the mountains, ducking for cover at every opportunity. She couldn't risk being taken out by anyone, luckily for her, she had excellent vision. Spotting a patrol officer up ahead, she diverted around the back. She had scoped out the Palace overnight and seen nothing on that side. She slithered around the side of the Palace, stopping when she spotted one of the Queens children. A boy. With a mass of scarlet hair. She pondered if kidnapping a Prince would put her in Fresion's good books. She would come back for him if she couldn't access the Queen. Just as she rounded the last corner, she spotted the Queen being led by a girl with electric blue hair, speckled with silver streaks. 'This must be the Princess,' she thought. 'I wonder where they are heading off to in a hurry." Unable to make her feet move as fast as her mind, she had just finished thinking as a door slammed shut just ahead of her and she heard a sliding bolt followed by a deadbolt. 'Too late,' she thought. 'It's going to have to be the Prince after all.'

Double backing on herself, she crept slowly towards the red haired boy; she cleared her throat before speaking.

"Your mother has told me to get you inside. There has been a breach within the Kingdom," she said.

"Oh Miss Halana, I didn't see you there. I'll just gather up my things and..."

Before he could finish his sentence, she had him bound, gagged and asleep. Gathering him up, she snuck into the undergrowth and back towards her own ship. Silently she lifted off and back towards Plydar.

"There seems to be an intruder in our Kingdom," Balzar commanded everyone's attention. "We are led to believe they are from the planet Plydar."

"Do we have any other information?" Celest asked from the front row.

Balzar had ordered all military personnel to convene in the hanger which housed Onyx Abyss Alpha. Mitzi and Zeke had been the first to arrive.

"We are currently waiting on additional information. The Queen and Princess Scarlex are currently safe and secure in the Queen's personal bunker.

"Are they here for me?" Mitzi squeaked. She began to panic that she was putting everyone at risk just being here.

"No. I don't believe they are. I believe they have a vendetta against the Queen, which why I ordered her to take cover," Balzar replied.

Just as he finished his sentence, one of the doors at the rear of the hanger opened.

"I'm very sorry to interrupt Mr Balzar sir. I was just wondering if Young Prince Eliontara was in attendance." Halana asked from the doorway.

Balzar's eyes swept the masses. "I don't see him Ma'am," he replied. This worried him because Eliontara was now part of their military. He pointed out to soldiers and ordered them to sweep the grounds in search of the Prince. They were not to return until he had been found.

"We will find him Ma'am," Balzar told her. "I suggest you take cover too. Being such a close ally to her Majesty, I wouldn't want you to come to any harm. Inform only who you think would be at risk and get them to safety."

Halana nodded once and turned to leave. As she spotted Zeke she smiled. He knew she would get his parents to safety too. As Halana left the room, the sketch artist arrived with more information on the being in the bushes. Balzar read everything before announcing to the troops who they were dealing with.

"Her name is Symese. She is from Plydar as we first thought, but according to her record, she can also shift, so I suggest extreme caution, she could shift into anyone," Balzar updated them. "She is currently on bad terms with Fresion so I would hazard a guess at her attempting to make peace with him."

Balzar's radio crackled to life. He didn't like what he was hearing through his earpiece. "Repeat."

"Prince Eliontara is not on the premises. Repeat, NOT on site. Wait! There's a note," the solider repeated.

"Bring it," Balzar ordered.

The soldiers arrived back at the hanger in mere seconds, one handing the note to Balzar.

'I have the boy.

Bring me the Queen and I'll let him go free.

Now, I don't expect a whole army to bring her, just the one ship will do, in fact, she could just bring herself. I shall leave the choice to you. Please don't make me choose for you. He's a sweet boy, but he's not what I want. Do you value him enough to trade?

You have less than twelve hours.

Sym'

Chapter Twenty – Two – Plydar

"This isn't Queen Aquilia!" Fresion boomed.

"Well, this is the closest I could get. By the time I had accessed the Palace, she was being whisked away by a girl with bright blue hair," Symese replied.

"Blue hair? Who has blue hair?" Fresion asked.

"I don't know sir," she replied. "I thought on my feet and grabbed the next best thing."

"You disobeyed me. I *ordered* you to being me Queen Aquilia and you bring me this," he shouted, pointing at a curled up Eliontara. "Who is he?"

"I believe he is a Prince sir," Symese said.

"So the child of Aquilia. Maybe we can make this work, but, if it doesn't your punishment stands. How long do we have?" Fresion asked.

"I gave them twelve hours," she replied. "I'll lock the Prince up in the holding cells."

Fresion watched her walk away, he shook his head and she went. Something, which should have been a simple kidnapping for Symese, she had done it many times before. His favourite had been the King of Voldum. It had taken her mere seconds to have him bound, gagged and hold up on her ship, and she couldn't even get a simple woman. He wondered how she had been spotted. Enceladant people weren't known for their vision. Only those from Alphir had the best vision. He would question Symese later. He didn't want anything to go wrong with this mission.

"How do we go about this?" Zeke asked Balzar.

The troops still stood to attention, awaiting further orders.

"I...erm...I don't know," Balzar admitted.

"Can I help?" Nymeria asked softly. "I don't want to stand on anyone's toes here but I know a few Plydants. I may be able to find out something."

"Really? How fast can you get a response?" Balzar asked.

"Normally within a few minutes. They owe me a few favours. Let me see what I can do," Nymeria smiled. "Don't panic. We will find him."

Balzar took a deep breath in. He hoped Nymeria was right. He didn't know how he would break the news to Queen Aquilia that her son had been kidnapped and may never make it home.

"Don't think like that," Mitzi whispered. "We will find him. Just like you all found me."

"It was simple to find you. We had Zeke and you had a phone. I don't believe the Prince has one of those that we can trace," Balzar smiled at her. "But thank you for trying to cheer me up."

Mitzi shrugged her tiny shoulders. "A Squink can try, right?"

"They certainly can," Balzar replied. He walked away from her and Zeke and sat a table alone. 'How am I supposed to lead an army when I'm blind myself," he thought out loud.

"You're only blind to the things in front of you," came a voice from beside him.

"Who?" He asked.

"Benzyline," she replied, holding out her hand.

"You shouldn't be here. This is for military personnel only," he told her.

"I come and go. Nothing is ever revealed. Just remember. The answers are not always right in front of you," she winked.

He looked away and then turned back to ask a question, but she was gone.

"Did anyone see that woman?" He asked.

"Benzyline?" Zeke replied. "She comes and goes. Don't be too scared of her. She is actually wiser than you would think. She's a little bit mysterious, for want of a better word, but she's great."

"Who is she?" Balzar asked.

Zeke sat next to him. "You met Lyra on Saturn right?"

Balzar nodded.

"Well, Benzyline is Lyra's mum. It doesn't explain much, but it explains the mysterious part," Zeke laughed. "Believe me; I was very cautious of her to begin with. Then she helped my mum with her inner Alphir magic. She's been great. Now, well, she just seems to appear and then, go!"

Balzar stared at him with his eyes wide open. "Where does she go?"

"No-one knows. Maybe back to Saturn, maybe she hangs around here," Zeke shrugged.

Balzar was confused. He had only seen this woman once before today and that was at an outhouse in the Palace gardens. "Zeke, the outhouse, what is that for?"

"My mother. She practices her magic there. She is Alphir and Benzyline helps her. Why do you ask?" Zeke said.

"I have only seen that woman once before today. Are you sure she is who you think she is?" He asked.

"I'm absolutely sure. In fact I can prove it," Zeke replied. He called Eva.

"Hey Zeke! What's up?" Eva answered after just two rings.

"Is Benzyline back on Saturn?" Zeke asked.

"She hasn't been back in over two months Zeke, why? Is everything OK?" Eva said.

"Everything is fine. Balzar was worried that's all," Zeke smiled.

"Has she been sneaking around again? I keep warning her not to annoy the military! I'm so sorry Balzar," Eva apologised.

"It's OK honestly. It just had me worried how she just appears and then is gone again," Balzar laughed. "Sometimes I wish I had that ability."

Eva smiled. "Benzyline is harmless. Well, depending who you ask. She would never put anyone there in harm's way."

"Thanks Eva," Balzar replied.

"I'll call you later Eva," Zeke said as he closed off the call.

Balzar went back to his own thoughts. How was he going to rescue Eliontara without giving up the Queen? He thought back to what Benzyline had said.

'The answers are not always right in front of you,'

What could she have meant? He decided to take a walk around the grounds. Maybe something would come to him.

<u>Saturn</u>

Eva stared out of the window and up at Enceladus in the sky.

"What's eating you?" Janus asked softly.

"Something doesn't seem right. Zeke is hiding something from me, I can tell," Eva replied.

"Why would he hide something, from you of all people?" Janus asked. He sat next to Eva on the window seat and gently held her hand, brushing the hair away from her eyes with the other. "Sweetheart, if something is bothering you, why don't you just ask him?"

Eva bit her lip. "I don't want him to think I'm being nosey. Maybe I should call Aquilia; she will know what's happening."

Eva dialled Aquilia and waited for her call to be answered. The waiting grinded on Eva so much. She hung up and tried again. "Why isn't she answering?"

"Try your mother," Janus said.

Eva dialled Halana and waited again. "This isn't normal," Eva began to panic. "I'm going to call Zeke back."

"Be gentle honey," Janus warned. He knew how fast her temper could fly.

Eva rolled her eyes at him. She dialled Zeke and waited.

"Eva? What's wrong?" Zeke said as he answered.

"You're asking me? What aren't you tell me and why can't I get hold of the Queen or my mother?" Eva hissed.

"Oh boy," Zeke whispered.

"Oh boy what?" Eva raised her voice.

"Calm down and I'll tell you. Let me get somewhere a little quieter," Zeke told her. He covered the mouthpiece and told Mitzi he would be back shortly. She nodded to him and bounced off to find Balzar. "You still there?"

"Obviously!" Eva replied.

"OK, promise not to freak out OK?" Zeke asked.

"I can't promise that Zeke," Eva told him honestly.

"OK," he began.

"Mum, are you OK?" Scarlex asked Aquilia.

"I'll be fine honey. It's just a shock that someone would come after me. I'm trying to think of anyone I could have offended," she replied.

Scarlex looked at her mother. For the first time in what felt like forever, she finally saw something different about her. She saw how scared she was. How worried she was that something she could have done could bring harm to the Kingdom.

"It will be OK Mum. I promise," Scarlex told her softly.

"Oh sweetheart, don't make promises you can't keep," Aquilia smiled. "I know you mean well, and I appreciate it, I really do, but until we know exactly what these beings want, we will have to make do with *hoping* things will be OK."

Scarlex gave her mother a strained smile. She didn't want to *hope,* she wanted to *know.* She wanted to *fix* everything. Wanted to *make* it all OK. She sat down on the far side of the bunker and pulled out her poetry book. The one her grandmother had left for her mother. Opening the book to page twenty-eight; she read quietly;

In times of battle,

Hear me cry.

A shout, a whoop, or a call.

But never fear,

For I cannot die.

Only cowards can fall.

Scarlex looked at her mother again. She had settled into her own chair and looked to be deep in her own thoughts. Scarlex never believed she would be the one to be protecting her mother. Yet here she was. Her only contact with anyone outside this room was the radio link. She lifted it to her mouth and said;

"Is there anyone there?"

"Scarlex? What is it? Are you OK?"

It was Halana. Scarlex breathed a sigh of relief.

"Yes, we are. Do you know what is happening?" She asked.

"I haven't heard anything yet. I am with Bella and Layson," Halana replied. "How is your mother?"

"I'm here Halana. I'm OK. I wish I knew who I had offended. I can't even think straight," Aquilia cried.

"Come now Your Highness. I'm sure it is a misunderstanding," Bella's voice floated through the speaker. "It will be fine. Within a few hours, we will all be back to our normal duties and this will all be forgotten about."

"I wish I could believe you Bella," Aquilia replied.

"Scarlex, I want you and your mother to get some sleep. I will call if I hear anything else," Halana ordered.

"Yes Ma'am," Scarlex agreed. She placed the radio onto the table next to her book, grabbed a blanket from the shelf and placed it over her mother as Aquilia laid down on the makeshift bed.

"Where will you lay?" Aquilia asked.

"I will curl up on the chair, don't worry," she smiled.

"No, you lay here with me. There is room for two," Aquilia smiled. She moved the blanket to allow Scarlex to join her. She pulled her daughter close and allowed sleep to claim her.

It felt like only a few minutes when they heard Chylla's voice through the radio.

"Your Highness, we have an emergency. You may exit the bunker, please make your way to the hanger."

Chapter Twenty – Three – Saturn

Eva placed the phone back on the table in a daze. She couldn't believe what Zeke had just told her. Janus noticed how she held on to every piece of furniture as she walked, as if she would fall down if she removed her hand. He gently took her hands and guided her to the nearby chair.

"What is it?" He asked.

"I don't think you would believe me if I told you. Can you get my book? The one my father left for me," she asked him.

He nodded and ran to their personal quarters and returned carrying the book. Eva quickly turned the pages, stopping on one which showed various versions of Plydant.

"This. This 'being' has been scoping out the Palace on Enceladus. Zeke believes they were there for The Queen, but they have kidnapped Eliontara in hope of Aquilia giving herself up or her people doing it for her," Eva told him.

Janus stood with his mouth open. "How did they get close to the Palace with so many guards?"

"Aquilia scaled back the protection after months of peacefulness. She didn't feel the need to protect the Palace as much. Obviously, the Kingdom has it protection," Eva explained.

"What's all the commotion?" Lyra asked as she walked in holding Avalynn.

Eva looked at Janus who nodded.

"Eliontara has been kidnapped by Plydants. They wanted Aquilia but her protectors, or namely Balzar, had worked out there was an intruder and sent Aquilia and Scarlex into their bunker," Eva told her.

"Oh no. No, no, not again," Lyra cried. "Janus, put Avalynn back in the playroom. Eva, come with me."

Eva and Janus exchanged glances, both looking worried. Janus took Avalynn from his mother and tickled her legs, she squealed with joy, her eyes flashing orange and green.

"Lyra, what do you mean by not again?" Eva asked as Janus walked away.

"There was a time, not long before I met Altair, that Plydants walked Saturn. They had their own part of the planet. Altair knew a few of them. Dodgy deals and such. When I met him and took an interest, he kept some of the deals quiet, some I overheard. I didn't question what he did, it was his business. When I fell pregnant with Janus, the deals became almost silent. I didn't hear a peep of Plydant. It seemed awfully convenient but I never spoke out of turn. Obviously you know what happened after that, but I don't believe Plydant ever fully left Saturn. There was one Plydant in particular, Fresion, if my memory serves me well, and it hasn't failed me yet. He and Altair had a particularly lucrative thing going. After Altair's untimely death," Lyra smiled, "I believe Fresion was captured for fraud."

"What does that have to do with Aquilia?" Eva asked just as Janus walked back in.

"What did I miss?" He asked.

Lyra quickly filled him in, a look of shock flowing over his face.

"Back to your question my dear. Aquilia killed Altair, so in theory, she was the one to end everything for him," Lyra explained.

Eva thought for a second. "So you mean this could be him? Could he have sent someone to do this?"

Lyra nodded. "You must tell her, but be wary. Someone may still be listening."

Eva was stunned. For something that happened a while ago, Fresion certainly dwelled on things. She had to inform Aquilia, but she had to do it in person.

"I will go there," Eva said.

"I'll come with you. Mother would you mind..." Janus began to ask.

Lyra waved her hands around and told them to go. "I've got the kiddies."

"Don't give them too much ice cream please," Eva begged.

"I can't promise!" Lyra laughed.

Eva and Janus made their way to their own secluded landing pad and prepared to take off. Eva worried about how Aquilia was taking the news.

<u>Enceladus</u>

 "What? Am I hearing you right?" Scarlex screamed "And no one helped him?"

"OK sweetheart, calm down," Aquilia grabbed her by the shoulders. "We know that your brother can look after himself."

"Calm down? Mum, Eliontara has been kidnapped and you're just sitting there!" Scarlex cried. Tears streaked her face.

Aquilia hadn't known what to say when Chylla had informed her. She had stared into emptiness. It had been Scarlex's shouting that had brought her back to reality. Aquilia sat at a nearby table and held her head in her hands.

"Your Majesty," Balzar held the note out to her. "This is what was left behind."

Aquilia took the note and stared at it. She didn't really take in the words. She held on so tight that the paper it was written on began to crumple and her tears began to fall. Her hands shook with grief and anger. She stood so quickly that the chair flew onto its back. Her eyes flashed red, "if there is some so called higher power, then I wish to it that it protects whoever *dared* lay a hand on my child!"

Everyone stood in stunned silence as Eva made her way to Aquilia's side. She gently laid her hand on her shoulder and guided her away from all the prying eyes.

"We need to find him Balzar," Scarlex said. "Before she does." She looked back at her mother as the door to her personal office closed behind Evadene.

"You're right. Let's get off the ground and search for him. Zeke, you good to join?" Balzar asked.

"Like you even need to ask," Zeke replied, pulling his rucksack over his shoulder.

"I'm good to go," Mitzi squeaked. It was clear she had been crying.

"You sure Mitzi?" Balzar asked.

"One hundred percent, I'm rested and recharged," she replied.

Balzar nodded. "Right, listen up. We take directions from Nymeria. We run everything through her."

"I'm coming too and there's nothing you can do to stop me," Scarlex told him.

"I wouldn't dream of it, climb aboard." Balzar told her.

As the troops began to board their ships, the atmosphere around the Palace had become thick and heavy. With one of their own taken, no one knew what to say or even what to do.

"Why are you here Eva?" Aquilia asked. She had become close friends with Eva ever since Halana had taken the job at the Palace well over twenty years ago.

"I spoke with Zeke. He told me what's happened," Eva said softly. "I then spoke with Lyra."

Aquilia turned so fast she made herself dizzy. "You spoke to Lyra! Why?"

"Sit down. Look, Lyra believes that this Plydant may have something to do with Altair," Eva explained.

"Why?" Aquilia asked again.

Eva took a deep breath before beginning her explanation. "You don't remember much about life on Saturn do you?"

Aquilia shook her head. "All my life's memories are here. It's like I never lived there."

"Lyra explained a few things to me. From before you were born and when she was just flirty with Altair. Plydants lived on Saturn for a while. According to Lyra, Altair was a little too friendly with a certain one, Fresion. She told me they had some pretty lucrative stuff going on, and when Altair died, Fresion took things a little too personally," Eva explained.

"You mean when I killed him?" Aquilia asked.

"I was trying to be gentle," Eva rolled her eyes.

"Why? That's what happened. I pulled his head off, there wasn't anything gentle about it," Aquilia shrugged.

Eva smiled and shook her head, "you never were one for subtlety were you?"

Aquilia shrugged her shoulders and looked out of the window. "Where are they off to?" She asked.

Eva joined her, watching the ships take off into the air. "I would hazard a guess and try to save Eliontara?"

Aquilia spun around to face her. "How did you know about that?"

'*Uh oh,*' Eva thought. "Zeke told me."

Aquilia stared at her friend. She was surprised that Zeke would tell Eva before he told her. Eliontara wasn't Eva's child. He was *hers*.

"Chylla, come here," Aquilia called over her radio.

"Yes Ma'am," she replied.

Eva worried she had said the wrong thing but she had always promised to be honest with Aquilia and she would stick by that promise. "I promised to never lie to you."

"I know, and I'm glad you told me. I'm just angry that I wasn't told sooner," Aquilia replied softly.

Chylla entered the room and bowed before Aquilia. "You called Ma'am?"

"Why wasn't I told sooner about Eliontara?" Aquilia asked.

"We didn't want to worry you Your Majesty," Chylla whispered.

"Worry me? He's my SON!" Aquilia shouted. "You had no right to keep it from me! Where are all the ships going?"

"I believe they are heading to Plydar Your Highness," Chylla replied.

"Bring Halana to me please," Aquilia dismissed her.

"You can't stay angry at them for long," Eva stated.

"I can try," she replied looking back out of the window as the last of the ships left the atmosphere.

Chapter Twenty – Four

"Where to now Nymeria?" Balzar asked as they rounded Quixon.

"We're still a way off. We need to head past Plystar then up towards Blystup," she replied.

Balzar nodded and stepped away from the visualizer.

"Still a while to go I take it?" Mitzi asked. She was sat at the front of the ship watching the passing galaxies. "I can't imagine what Queen Aquilia is going through right now."

Zeke sat quietly at the monitors, watching for any threats. He didn't feel comfortable getting involved in the conversation. He had felt some animosity when he and his mother had first arrived on Enceladus. She had his father holed up in some kind of prison, granted she said it was for protection. But how was he to know she was telling the truth. He had grown to trust her, it had taken a while but he would now fight to the death for the Kingdom. He may not have before, but after spending some time with Queen Aquilia, he truly believed she had the Kingdom's best interests at heart. Both Kingdoms.

"Zeke? You OK?" Balzar asked taking the seat beside him. "I noticed you didn't join in our conversation."

"I prefer not to talk of others personal lives without their prior consent," Zeke replied. "I was brought up to respect others privacy unless it was an emergency or their life were in danger."

"I'm sorry Zeke. I didn't think. I like the Queen. I really do, I was just saying I wouldn't know what to do with myself if I were in her shoes," Mitzi whispered.

"Oh Mitz," Zeke smiled. "I didn't mean you had to stop. I'm just not the type. That's all."

Mitzi jumped down from the chair and scurried towards him. She jumped up on his lap and looked him in the eyes. "I can see why she trusts you. I think we all do."

"Thanks Mitzi. I was a little lost when I first arrived on Enceladus, but after a while, I found my feet and well, the rest is history," he shrugged.

"Well, I think Mitzi is right. You're a good lad Zeke. Don't let anyone tell you otherwise," Balzar said. He stood and took his place at the front of the ship. Mitzi nuzzled Zeke's neck and joined Balzar.

Zeke watched her bound away. He wished he could take away the pain she felt. Maybe one day he could but for now, he had to concentrate on rescuing Eliontara.

"Zeke, are you there?" Nymeria called over the radio.

"Yeah, always. What's up?" He replied.

"I got a message back from the Plydants, you remember I said I knew some," she said.

"Yeah, what did they say?" Zeke asked.

"Well, it seems one of them has now be placed in charge of prisoners on the planet. She said a red haired boy had been placed under her care. She has been told that he can request anything except communication with the outside," she told him. "I asked her to send me a picture. This is what was sent."

Zeke stared at the image of Eliontara inside of a, relatively clean, holding cell. He had an amount of food with him but he had touched none of it. He looked physically unharmed but no one knew how he would be feeling emotionally or mentally. He was curled up in the corner, staring at nothingness.

"We have to get to him and quickly," Zeke said. "How far are we away?"

"We still have a bit to go, unless we Hyper Jump, it could take us another few hours," she replied.

"Then we have to do it," Zeke said.

"We need confirmation from Chylla," Nymeria told him.

"We don't have time. If we don't go now, I don't even want to think of having that conversation with Queen Aquilia," Zeke told her.

Plydar

"So, talk me through it again Symese," Fresion said. "I can't quite get my brain around what happened."

Symese sighed inwardly; she had gone through this more than three times already. She turned to him and placed her hands on her hips. "I couldn't *get* to Queen *Aquilia,* because she had been swept away by a girl with *blue* hair. How many more times do I have to explain?"

"Enough times that I *might* begin to believe you. Now, who is this boy again?" Fresion asked.

"The boy is Aquilia's *son!* The PRINCE!" She replied, throwing her arms up into the air. "I have gone over this so many times, why couldn't you just have believed me to begin with," she said through gritted teeth.

"What reason would I have to believe you without question? You have done over so many before. I am giving you a chance to redeem yourself," Fresion told her.

"I know that and I appreciate it. So why would I even *attempt* to go back on my word?" Symese asked. "You have no faith in my word?"

"Your word means nothing as you well know!" He fired back at her.

She turned from him and strode away. She couldn't believe that he would question her, after she had practically given her life to serve him. She made her way down to the holding cell, throwing open the door and pulling Eliontara to his feet.

"You are going to explain to Fresion exactly who you are, and don't try any crazy stuff, OK?" She demanded.

"Who is Fresion?" Eliontara asked.

"That doesn't matter right now, but he doesn't believe what I tell him so you can do the explaining for me," she said.

Eliontara nodded and followed her. His guard snapped a picture as he went. This confused him but then she smiled. He took this as a sign she would help him if he needed it. Dragging him into the large hall at the centre of Fresion's Palace, Symese presented him to Fresion.

"Now you can ask him," Symese said as she threw him on the floor.

"You don't treat him like a Prince," Fresion said as he looked down at her.

"He's no Prince here," she replied.

"Stand up," Fresion commanded.

Eliontara stood where he was. He kept his eyes down. He didn't seem to want to anger this person.

"Who are you?" Fresion asked softly.

"My name is Eliontara sir," he replied.

"And your family?" Fresion questioned.

"My mother is Queen Aquilia of Saturn and Enceladus," Eliontara replied as he looked into Fresion's eyes.

"Hmm," Fresion sighed. "Take him back."

"Come on, back to the holding cell," Symese said as she pulled on his arm.

"Why am I here?" Eliontara asked.

"Don't ask questions," she told him. She pulled him back to the cell and pushed him back inside, closing the door behind him.

Eliontara curled himself back into the corner of the cell and wished he was back home.

"Hey," his guard whispered. "Come here."

Eliontara made his way to the door, "who are you?" He asked.

"I'm Marixah. I'm going to try and help you. Nymeria and her crew are on their way," she whispered, "but you have to do exactly as I say when I say it, OK?"

Eliontara thought for a second. Could he really trust this being? He nodded all the same. He knew he had the ability to hold his own if it came to it.

"Now, quickly, back to the corner, she's coming back," Marixah smiled.

He made his way back to the corner and positioned himself exactly how he had been before. Symese looked at him and grinned. It scared him. She had the sharpest teeth he'd seen and it terrified him.

"Make sure he doesn't try anything. He is very important to Fresion's plan," Symese told Marixah.

She nodded in agreement and turned her back to Eliontara. He watched as Symese walked away and listened as a door slammed in the distance. He crawled towards the door.

"Marixah, how do you know Nymeria is on her way?" He whispered.

She didn't turn towards him. She kept her back straight. "I owed her a favour, she's calling it in. What makes you so special anyway?" She replied.

"I'm a Prince," he said sadly. "I'm Eliontara. My mother is Aquilia."

Marixah nearly dropped her guard. "What?" She hissed. "No wonder Nymeria had been insistent on photos."

"What happens now?" He asked her.

"I don't know yet. As soon as I hear anything I will tell you," she replied. "Now, go back before Symese returns."

Eliontara did as she said. He closed his eyes and drifted off to sleep.

<u>Enceladus</u>

"You sent for me Your Highness?" Halana asked as she entered the room.

"Did you know?" Aquilia asked.

"Know what Your Majesty?" Halana questioned. She looked at Evadene with a worried look.

"About Eliontara?" Aquilia replied.

"I'm sorry; you have completely lost me dear. Where is the young Prince? I've searched the Palace from top to bottom," Halana said.

Aquilia looked at Eva and then back at Halana. "You didn't tell her?"

"I didn't tell anyone else, other than Lyra and Janus but that's a given because we live together," Eva replied.

"Could one of you let me know what is going on?" Halana said, throwing her hands up in the air.

"Eliontara was kidnapped," Aquilia stated. "The note said we have twelve hours to make a trade. Myself for him."

Halana dropped to the floor with Eva and Aquilia rushing to her side.

"Mum, are you OK?" Eva cried.

"I'll be fine dear. I swore I would not allow something like this to happen whilst I was around. I have failed," Halana responded.

"Halana, you have not failed in the slightest. I don't think anyone has. I have taken out my anger on those closest to me and I was wrong. Now, I have to work out what to do," Aquilia told her.

Eva and The Queen helped Halana to a chair and sat her down. Aquilia walked to the window and looked out over the Kingdom of Enceladus. She promised never to bring war to this Kingdom or any other within her realm ever again, and she intended to keep that promise. She pulled a secondary radio from the desk drawer and placed it to her lips.

"Balzar, do you copy?" She asked.

"Balzar here Your Highness. How can we assist?" He replied.

"Is Zeke available? I need to speak with him," she asked.

"I'll pass you over now," he said.

"I'm going to get him back. One way or another," she told the two women in the room.

Chapter Twenty – Five

"What's the plan?" Balzar asked after Zeke had finished his conversation with Aquilia.

"You won't like it," Zeke told him. "None of us will."

"Is she taking his place?" Mitzi asked, her voice barely a whisper.

"No," Zeke replied. "It won't be as simple as that. She has given us permission to rescue him at any cost. Meaning we can go in all guns blazing."

"We have never worked like that," Balzar told him. "We have always tried to do things peacefully. It was the only way to make sure there were no repercussions on Enceladus. I don't know why she would say that."

"I think I know why." Nymeria said from the video link.

Everyone turned to face the camera. Nymeria closed her eyes and then opened them, focusing on Celest. She didn't dare look at the others.

"When Aquilia took over, she vowed to never bring war to our shores. Hence why she took the battle to Altair. This is the only way she can guarantee that Enceladus will be safe," Nymeria explained.

"But I don't get it. If we go in and start war, won't the Plydants just bring the war to Enceladus when we leave?" Mitzi asked.

"That is a fair point Ny. We can't risk leading them back there," Celest agreed.

"We don't. Our instructions are to decimate the planet and all who live there, as soon as we rescue Eliontara," Zeke replied. "That's why I said you all wouldn't like what she had said."

"But that's someone's home Zeke," Mitzi whispered.

It hurt him to see her upset. He scooped her up and placed her on his shoulder. "That's why I think we could come up with something a little more different. Do you think we could?" He asked everyone.

There were murmurs among those on the video link. A lot of discussions between different groups about ways they could go about it without blowing up a planet and killing its inhabitants.

"I may have something," Celest announced. "I don't know how well it will go, but it's a start."

"OK, shoot," Zeke smiled. He could feel Mitzi nuzzling at his neck. He knew she was scared and worried about what they would have to face when they arrived at Plydar. He would keep her safe, even if his life depended on it.

"So, we know that Nymeria has someone on the inside. We have to match the shift changes and rescue Eliontara when there aren't any guards," Celest began.

"But there is always a guard babe. Marixah informed me she has been placed on solitary duty to guard him," Nymeria told her. "She is our only hope of getting him out without a major struggle."

“Do you think we can pull it off?” Balzar asked.

“I don’t doubt it, but we will have to be very careful. I know Plydants have expert hearing,” Nymeria replied. “Hang on, I’m getting an update.”

Nymeria walked away from the camera to check out the message she had just received. Zeke tried to gauge her reaction but she was too smart for that. She turned her back on them but Zeke could see her shoulders rise and fall. This wasn’t normally good news.

“What’s happening?” Mitzi whispered to Zeke.

“I’m not sure yet Mitz. Nymeria has an update on Eliontara, we’re just waiting for her to relay what has been said,” Zeke replied. “You OK?”

“I’m a little scared, but you knew that, right?” She replied.

“Yeah, I knew. That’s why you’re sitting there and not up front on your own,” he smiled.

“You’re the best Zeke,” she smiled back.

Balzar watched the exchange between them. He was happy she had finally trusted someone enough to be able to take some comfort from them.

“OK, heads up. Marixah has told me that Fresion isn’t entirely sold on who Eliontara is. Symese was supposed to kidnap Queen Aquilia is retaliation for her killing Altair,” Nymeria told them.

"And she knows this how?" Balzar questioned. He was curious how she would know all this and not be in cahoots with Symese.

"When Symese took Eliontara up to Fresion, Marixah eavesdropped on the conversation. Look, I know you don't want to believe that she will help, obviously because she is Plydant, but she has her reasons," she replied.

"What would they be, exactly?" Balzar asked.

Nymeria took a deep breath, she didn't normally tell other's personal histories, but she guessed she didn't have a choice in this one. These were her crew. Beings she trusted with her life. "Her father was one of those killed in the battle between Aquilia and Altair."

"Wouldn't she attack Aquilia though?" Zeke asked.

Nymeria shook her head. "No. Misik was killed by Altair. Although he was fighting on Altair's side, it seemed Misik wasn't a good enough fighter for Altair and he decapitated him in one flick of his claws."

There was a collective gasp.

"So, yeah, she isn't exactly loyal to Fresion at the moment because he refused to believe it was Altair who murdered her father. She even had proof," Nymeria told him.

"OK. So we go with what Marixah is informing us. How do we manage to get to him though? I'm sure Plydants don't sleep that much," Zeke stated.

"They don't normally, but, there is another Plydant who is willing to help. She works in the kitchens. She has said she will mix up a concoction which will knock them out for a while, we do have one issue," Nymeria told them all.

"And that is?" Balzar asked.

"They want to come back with us," Nymeria said quickly.

Balzar was quiet, as was Zeke, Celest and Mitzi. It was Shlysta who spoke first.

"I don't think it would be a bad idea, especially as they would be helping us rescue Eliontara," he said.

"I see your point kid, but we have to think of the safety of the Kingdom before anything," Balzar explained.

"But these beings are placing their own lives on the line to save someone they don't even know, isn't in common courtesy to extend a kind hand and help them in their own situation?" Shlysta asked.

Balzar was stumped. This kid was wise beyond his years and it would take him far. He reminded Balzar of a young Matro. Full of knowledge, sense and compassion.

"We can think about it," Balzar replied. "I don't promise anything but to think."

"That's all we can ask for, for now," Nymeria replied.

They continued on their journey, skirting the various planets that stood in their way. All the while, planning their next move to rescue Eliontara and whisk him home.

<u>Enceladus</u>

"Your Highness! You can't do that!" Halana exclaimed.

"I can and I will if it protects my people. If Nymeria and her crew rescue him and bring him home, it will only lead to them following and causing war here, on Saturn or both. I can't risk that," Aquilia replied.

Halana had no words. For once she was speechless. She turned away from Aquilia and went back to her workshop. *'What has she become?'* Halana thought to herself. Eva watched her mother walk away. She had never heard Aquilia talk of decimating another planet.

"Why?" Eva asked.

"Why what?" Aquilia spat.

"Why would you command to decimate a planet you know nothing about?" Eva asked.

"I don't need to know anything about it. They kidnapped Eliontara, did you forget that?" She replied.

"No, no one's forgotten that," Eva said rolling her eyes. "But have you even thought about how Eliontara would feel when he found out?"

Aquilia sat at her desk and shuffled some of the folders around. Anything to keep her hands busy. "It wouldn't matter what he thought," she said quietly. "All that would matter is that he would be home. Back where he belongs," her voice broke on the last syllable.

Eva pulled her friend into her arms and allowed her the time to cry. "It will be OK. You know your army will find him and bring him home, but to wipe out a civilization, it's too much."

"How am I supposed to keep them safe?" Aquilia asked.

"As a parent, it's hard, but we can't protect them all the time. Aquilia, look what happened with you? Your mother sent you away and the trouble still found you," Eva reminded her.

Aquilia looked defeated. "I can't do it, can I?"

Eva shook her head. "It's not right, and you know it."

Aquilia tried to radio through to Zeke but there was no answer. She looked at Eva for help. "I'll get Janus to keep trying, but you need to go and see Mum."

Aquilia nodded and quickly ran off in search for Halana. She knew she had a lot of making up to do.

As Aquilia walked away, Eva worried that the stress placed on her shoulders was becoming too much for her to handle alone. She left Aquilia's office in search of Janus and Chylla. She ran almost head into the latter as she rounded the corner towards the Higher Elders' meeting room.

"Chylla, you need to contact Zeke and the others. Tell them the plan has changed, that they shouldn't act on Queen Aquilia's words," Eva told her.

"What plans were they exactly?" Chylla asked.

"Nothing to worry about now, but they will understand what you mean. Thank you," Eva smiled.

Chylla nodded once and ran off to the Comms Room. Eva carried on in her original direction and burst through the doors of the meeting room. Much to her surprise, the Higher Elders were already waiting for her.

"Come on in Evadene," Zyra said.

Eva closed the door behind her and took her seat at the table. "How did you know I was coming?" She asked.

"It's our job to know when you are making a visit. Now, what has summoned you Enceladus?" Zyra asked.

"I guess you know about Eliontara?" Eva asked.

A look was shared between all the Higher Elders and the look told Eva they hadn't a clue what was happening outside these four walls.

"What has happened?" Quintara asked.

"He's been kidnapped and taken to Plydar. Symese has him, along with Fresion," Eva stated. She watched for their reaction but found none. Not one flinched at the news of a child being taken from their home. "You don't even care, do you?"

"It's not a case of caring Evadene. Aquilia bring these things upon herself and hopes that we will dig her out of a hole, which we cannot do," Quintara replied.

"She doesn't even know I'm telling you!" Eva cried. "How can you not care? Eliontara is your GRANDSON!"

"Technically speaking, he isn't," Quintara whispered.

"Wow! Just. Wow." Eva stated. She then got up from her seat and left the room.

Eva couldn't believe what was just said. She needed to find Janus and fast.

<u>Chapter Twenty – Six</u>

<u>Plydar</u>

"Marixah, how long before Nymeria arrives? I wanna go home," Eliontara whispered.

"I know you do. I'm waiting for an update now. They shouldn't be too far away. I know they used their Hyper Jump

Technology to get here faster. Just sit tight, yeah?" She smiled.

He nodded and closed his eyes again. He couldn't tell if it was day or night. He just sat in the corner of the holding cell, waiting for news. Symese had given him some food a little earlier, which he had cautiously eaten.

"I wouldn't poison you," she had laughed. "What good would you be to me then?"

He drank the liquid offered to him and remembered his manners. Symese may have kidnapped him, but he was taught to say thank you. Symese thought it funny that he was being polite.

"Anyone else would have spat it in my face," she had said.

"Maybe those people should learn some respect and manners. I was taught to respect my elders," he had replied.

She had merely stared at him, took his tray and scarpered off towards the main part of the building. He didn't even know if he was in a castle, palace or just some empty old building. In fact, he had no idea what planet he was on, let alone how he got there.

"Psst, come here," Marixah called.

Eliontara crawled over to her. "What is it?" He asked.

"Nymeria and her crew are only a few minutes out. I have to nip away for a second. Don't make any fuss, otherwise the plan will go wrong, you hear me?" Marixah said.

He nodded his response and hurried back to his corner and laid down on the straw left for him, closing his eyes, he evened his breathing to act as if he were asleep.

Marixah smiled, then she radioed through to Symese, "I need the loo, can I just leave for a minute? He's fast asleep, he shouldn't be any trouble."

"You have precisely one minute. Move!" Symese snapped.

Marixah ran from the cell and into the nearby toilets, there she sent Nymeria the all clear and run the taps on the sink, singing at the top of her lungs.

"OK, it's time," Nymeria told them.

"You ready Mitz?" Zeke asked.

Mitzi was suited up and ready to go. She had her instructions. She nodded once and climbed into the blast shaft. This would send her through the bars on the holding cell wall; they just hoped that Scarlex had pinpointed the correct wall.

Zeke stood by the blast shaft, checking and rechecking Mitzi's restraints.

"I'm fine. Stop fussing," she smiled at him.

"Come back," he told her.

"I will," she replied.

Within a few seconds, Mitzi had been shot towards the gap in the bars and landed effortlessly next to a Prince.

"Hi there!" She called.

Eliontara opened his eyes and smiled. "You came!"

"Shhh! You'll get us both caught!" Mitzi laughed.

"Ahh it's too late for that!" Symese screeched from the shadows. "You didn't really think I would let you be left alone did you Princey?"

Marixah could hear the commotion from the toilets, she peeked around the corner to see Symese attempting to bound the wrists of a tiny being, one she could just about make out with white hair. She quickly sent a message to Nymeria.

M – We have a problem.

N – What problem?

M – I think your crew got caught.

N – What!?

M – I went to the toilets, to give you all time to get him out, but it seems Symese wasn't going to leave him on his own. I'll try everything I can to get them both out. I owe you.

Nymeria held her head in her hands. "It's all gone wrong," she whispered, hoping no one but Celest would hear her but she was wrong.

"What's happened?" Zeke called.

"Symese didn't leave the holding cells. She's got Mitzi and Eliontara now," Celest told him.

Zeke tried to control his temper. He could feel the anger rising. He closed his eyes for five seconds and focused on his breathing but he just couldn't control it any longer. "You promised us he would be OK. You PROMISED me Mitzi would be *safe!*" He shouted.

"I didn't know that Symese would trick Marixah," Nymeria jumped up. "Marixah helped us by getting us in there."

"And now, they have Mitzi too! Do you even realise how dangerous that is for her?" Zeke cried. "It would take *one* call to The Wigfya and Fresion would have the biggest payday of his life!"

"So, you're saying Mitzi is more important that Eliontara?" Nymeria threw back at him.

"To me? Yes," Zeke replied. He wasn't ashamed to say that. He held his head high and prepared for the backlash but none came.

Balzar clapped him on the shoulder and guided him away from the camera. He sat Zeke at the table in the tiny kitchen area and looked into his eyes.

"Don't say it if you don't mean it," Balzar warned him. "She's been through too much."

Zeke watched him for a brief second, looked deep into his eyes. "I know. I've seen it."

Balzar narrowed his eyes at him. "How?"

"Can I show you?" Zeke asked, holding his hands out to Balzar.

Taking Zeke's open hands, Balzar nodded. Zeke clasped his hands around Balzar's and closed his eyes.

"Not long now, my love," Hula smiled.

"Are you sure?" Balzar asked.

"I'm certain. Within the hour, you will be a father," Hula whispered in his ear.

Balzar looked at the calendar on the wall. It showed a date in the next few weeks.

"Are we ready for this?" Balzar asked his wife.

"More than ready," Hula smiled.

Zeke let go of his hands and smiled. "You have some excellent news coming soon."

"What kind of news? Please tell me," Balzar begged.

Zeke thought hard before he answered. "Do you have a way on contacting Hula?"

"Yes, should I call her?" Balzar asked.

"I think it would be best coming from her and not me," Zeke replied. "I'll give you some privacy."

Balzar pulled his phone from his pocket and called Hula.

"Balzar honey, is everything OK?" She asked after just one ring.

"Everything is going as well as it could be. How are you? I miss you," Balzar replied.

"Well, I do have something I needed to tell you about. I wanted to wait until you returned but since you have called," she began.

"What is it?" He asked.

"We are having a baby," Hula replied.

Balzar could hear the smile spread across her face.

"A baby?" He whispered. He looked over at Zeke who smiled to him.

"Yes. You are going to be a father Balzar," Hula replied.

Balzar continued his conversation with his wife for a while longer. Whilst everyone else tried to figure a way to rescue Eliontara and Mitzi, Scarlex tapped Zeke on the shoulder.

"What happened in there?" She asked, nodding towards the kitchen.

"I'm not sure how to explain it. Maybe one day when this is over, I will try," Zeke replied.

Scarlex tried to smile but it didn't reach her blue eyes. "I'm scared Zeke."

"I know. We will get them back, don't worry," he replied. He turned back to look out of the ships main window. He wished he knew of a way to get to them.

Enceladus

"Halana, are you here?" Aquilia called as she walked into Halana's workshop.

No reply came from within.

"Halana, please, I know I was wrong. I'm trying to fix it now, but fixing things with you is important to me," Aquilia said.

Halana rustled past all the vibrant fabrics that swung from rails built into the walls. "You knew it was a bad idea from the start! You just wanted to throw your weight around," she said.

Aquilia could see the tear stains that were left on her cheeks. She cursed herself for making Halana cry. She had been there for her through everything with Aquilia as she grew up. She had held her when she cried for her mother, was there to catch her when she found out her mother had passed, and she was there to aid her recovery after her epic battle with her uncle.

"You're right. I just want him home. I would do anything to just bring him home," Aquilia cried. She sunk to the floor as her tears fell.

"Oh child, you have been through the most testing of times and yet here you are, shining through the other side. They will bring Elion back, they have never failed before. For once, let someone else be the saviour," Halana whispered as she rocked Aquilia. "You will still shine out the other side."

As Aquilia calmed, her radio sprang to life.

"Your Highness, you are needed urgently," Chylla's voice echoed through the room.

Aquilia looked at Halana who had a solemn look on her face.

"Let's go," Halana instructed.

Chapter Twenty – Seven

Enceladus

"What do you mean?" Aquilia asked. She couldn't believe what she was hearing.

"Mitzi and Eliontara are now being held hostage Your Highness," Chylla bowed her head. She had been dreading telling The Queen this new information.

"How?" Halana asked.

Chylla sat them both down and explained what happened. Janus looked on from a distance and worked out that something must be wrong. The Stealth Raiders and Onyx Abyss Alpha had never failed in their missions.

"What's wrong?" Eva whispered, sliding her hand into his.

"Something is off about this," he replied. "The crew have never failed an extraction before.

"Do you think someone has gone rouge?" She asked, concern flooding her face.

"It's quite possible. Where is Layson?" Janus asked.

"I would guess he is in his office," Eva replied. "Why?"

Janus kissed her on the head and rushed off. She stared after him, unsure of what he was about to do.

"So they weren't going to carry out my instructions anyway?" Aquilia asked.

"It doesn't look that way Your Majesty," Chylla replied. "I didn't think they would if I'm honest."

Aquilia hung her head. "I know I was wrong to request that of them. I'm glad they didn't do it. What is our next move?"

Chylla shook her head, "I'm not sure Your Highness. Zeke has requested radio silence. I can't get through at all."

Eva sat next to her friend, the concern still etched on her face.

"What is it Eva?" Halana asked. She knew the look well.

"It's just something Janus said, that's all," Eva replied.

"What is it?" Aquilia asked.

"He thinks someone in the crew has gone rogue, giving information over to Symese and Fresion," she told them. "He is going to see Layson, probably to ask to see the crew list."

Aquilia sank back in her chair. She couldn't think of anyone who would go against her. She had a good relationship with all her military members; they were handpicked for their loyalty.

"Try not to think too much of it. He could be wrong," Eva offered.

Aquilia shook her head. "No, Janus has always had a good gut instinct. I need to talk to him."

With those last words, Aquilia ventured towards Layson's office. She needed to hear for herself what her cousin thought.

<u>Plydar</u>

"So, it seems I was followed back here. How fast does the military work in your world?" Symese grinned.

"We didn't follow you," Mitzi spat. "If we did, you wouldn't have made it back here."

"It squeaks!" Symese laughed.

Mitzi narrowed her eyes at Symese. She thought of all the nasty things she could do to this being and it somehow calmed her mind.

Symese paced back and forth for what felt like forever before she finally stopped and stood in front of them. She looked at Mitzi and cocked her head to one side. "Where are they then?"

"Where are who?" Mitzi asked.

"Well, the rest of your little crew members of course. There's no way you came all this way alone," Symese grinned.

"Why would you say that?" Mitzi questioned her.

"You're not exactly *built* for single combat, are you?" Symese laughed. "I could probably squash you with my shoe!"

"Ha, I'd love to see you try, in fact, I would *pay* to see you try," Mitzi smiled, she could feel the sharpness of her teeth with her tongue.

"You'd be no match for me. I've been a sorceress longer than you've been alive. Nothing and no one has *ever* outsmarted me," Symese said. "Eradicating you would be a vacation in my eyes."

"Vacation this you miserable witch!" Zeke cried as he crashed through the wall.

"Where, how?" Mitzi stumbled on her words.

"Ask no questions, get no answers. Now move," Marixah cried as she ushered Mitzi and Eliontara out of the cell.

"Take them to the ship, quickly," Zeke told her.

"I'm not going without you," Mitzi replied.

Zeke rolled his eyes. He should have known she would have refused to leave. "Fine, just don't die. I need you to survive, OK?"

Mitzi nodded quickly, placing herself by his side. The height difference making Marixah giggle a little. She quickly dragged Eliontara towards the exit before Symese could pick herself up from the floor, but as she rounded the corner, an angry looking Fresion made his presence known.

"Where are you going with the prisoner?" He demanded.

Marixah had to think on her toes. "Somewhere away from the commotion going on in there," she pointed back towards the holding cell where dust still lingered in the air. "I won't let him out of my sight sir."

Fresion looked at her ready to second guess her but quickly decided she could be more loyal than Symese, how wrong he was.

"Fine, there are four more holding cells on the west side of the Palace. Hold him there and I will be along as soon as I have cleared up in here," he told her.

She nodded once and headed off in the direction he had pointed. She looked back to see him heading into the holding cells and quickly diverted towards the open doors. She picked up the Prince and flew to the ship, placing him down at the foot of the steps.

"Quick, get him inside before Fresion comes," she told Balzar.

He grabbed the Prince and pulled him to safety, then returned for her, holding his hand out. "Are you coming aboard?"

Marixah stared for a second before grabbing his hand and climbing onto the ship.

"OK, Nymeria, we have Marixah but Zeke and Mitzi are still inside, what do we do?" Balzar radioed.

"I don't know whether to take them back or wait for Zeke to finish whatever it is he decided to do. Did you know he was going to go in there?" Nymeria asked.

"I didn't have a clue. I was talking to Hula, and she told me we are having a baby, and when I turned back to him, he was gone," Balzar explained.

"He's so sneak...What! You and Hula? Parents? Oh Balzar! That's fantastic news!" Nymeria cut her prior sentence short when she realised what he had said.

"You heard me right. I just have to make sure I get Zeke home before I can take off and see Hula," Balzar replied.

"We'll get him back, don't worry," Celest told him.

Saturn

Lyra paced the room gently bouncing Codex in her arms. She hoped that everything was OK up there as she stopped to look up into the sky. She hadn't heard from Eva or Janus since they had left for Enceladus. She sighed inwardly placed Codex back on the floor, luckily he had stopped crying and just wanted to run, which was caused his outburst in the first place, that and a mislaid ball. She watched him launch himself on top on his brothers, falling all over the garden in fits of laughter. She smiled, shook her head, picked up her phone and called her mother.

"Hello darling, what's wrong?" Benzyline asked as she answered within the first two rings.

"What makes you think something is wrong?" Lyra asked.

"Hmm, I can sense it. You don't have that same hike in your voice as you normally do," her mother replied.

Lyra looked down at the floor. "Where are you?" She asked.

"I'm up on Enceladus sweetheart. Why?" Benzyline said.

"Have you seen Eva and Janus? I haven't heard from them since they arrived there and I'm getting worried," Lyra told her.

"Well, there's no need to worry. Janus is with Layson and it looks like The Queen and Eva have just joined him. I wonder what that could be about." Benzyline informed Lyra. "If I hear any more, I will let you know."

"Thanks Mum. Will you come see us soon?" Lyra asked.

"Sooner than you would like," Benzyline smiled. She hung up on her daughter and crept up to Layson's office door. She placed her ear to the door and listened.

<u>Enceladus</u>

"So, you think someone up there," Layson pointed towards the sky. "Is giving Symese information?"

"It's a possibility," Janus replied. "I know it doesn't sound good but how else does it explain what's happened?"

Layson say back in his chair and placed his hand under his chin. He knew it made sense but he didn't want to think of someone up there putting his son in danger, let alone the Prince.

"All we need to see is the list of crewmates who travelled with the ships," Aquilia asked. "I think I can probably guess which one it could be."

Layson let out a sigh and handed her the list. "I don't like the idea of everyone being in danger up there, especially if this being could jeopardize everything."

"We know Layson and we appreciate it. This is the only logical explanation," Eva said gently touching his arm. "You won't get into trouble."

"It would be worth getting in trouble for. Has anyone heard from Zeke yet?" He asked.

Aquilia shook her head, "apparently he asked for radio silence."

Layson turned in his chair and looked up towards the sky, "come back to us kid."

Aquilia turned away from the others to swipe at a tear that had begun to slide down her cheek but Eva caught her. "It's OK to cry," she said.

"As a Queen I shouldn't be showing my emotions," Aquilia replied.

"I think, as a Queen, you should be able to do as you darn well please!" Eva smiled.

Layson and Janus laughed in unison. "She has a point," Layson said. "You are entitled to have some emotion about anything. Who told you otherwise?"

"No one really. I guess I watched my mother hide her emotion all the time and figured that's what a Queen should do," Aquilia replied.

"Nonsense! Why hide what every other being shows naturally," Janus said, pulling her into an embrace. "Always be you, that's the Queen they expect to see."

"You could be right," Aquilia smiled. "Let's get looking at this list then."

They all checked through the list each picking names that didn't seem to fit, but Aquilia honed in on one name in particular.

Alestra.

Chapter Twenty – Eight

Plydar

Symese dragged herself back to her feet, dusted off her jacket and turned towards Zeke and Mitzi. She had a grin across her face; it was the stuff of nightmares. Her huge fangs hung down and her tongue whipped in and out of her mouth.

"Do you really think that between the two of you, you can defeat me?" She hissed.

"That's the plan," Mitzi replied.

Symese laughed, it seemed to come from the pit of her stomach. "I've taken on bigger beings than you will ever take on. You're no match for me!"

Mitzi rolled her eyes, "so you've already said!"

Symese bared her teeth and pounced towards Zeke. He rolled to the left and she just missed his shoulder. With the opportunity open, Mitzi sank her own teeth into Symese's arm. Symese yelled in pain. She looked over at Mitzi who had quickly backed away.

"You're Slizard!" Symese hissed, her forked tongue flickered in and out of her mouth.

"First prize to *Slymese* here," Mitzi goaded. She backed herself into the corner and watched for her next opportunity to strike.

"Maybe I should just capture you and bargain you off to the highest bidder!" Symese shouted. She then leapt from her feet and landed mere inches from Mitzi. "I could get a fair price for you and I wouldn't even have to share it," she whispered.

"Do your worst witch!" Mitzi hissed, her full Slizard form coming to fruition.

Zeke was amazed by how big she became. Her tail whipped out from behind her, knocking Symese to the floor. He jumped out of the way as Mitzi pounced after her, swatting her across the room to the furthest wall.

"What is going on in here?" Fresion asked as he entered the holding cells. He stopped in his tracks as he took in the sight of Mitzi and Symese grappling all over the room. He aimed his next question at Zeke. "Who are you?"

Zeke wasn't prepared to face questions. He froze on the spot, looking awkwardly at Fresion.

"I asked a question boy, and from where I come from, we are normally obliged to answer!" He boomed.

Zeke blinked so many times he began to go dizzy. He then found his voice, "hopefully someone who isn't sticking around."

"You broke through *my* walls, attacked *my* guard and you expect me to just let you walk away?" Fresion asked, his eyes flicking back towards Mitzi and Symese. "What is that?" he pointed.

"Not my place to say, although, I'd say it's winning," Zeke joked.

Fresion grabbed Zeke by the throat and lifted him off the ground. Zeke's eyes rolled back into his head as the vision came flooding through;

The whole kingdom is on fire. The walls of the Palace are crumbling.

"What do we do?" Fresion screamed.

"That is your problem, not mine," came the reply from an unknown source.

"What did Symese lead here?" Fresion asked.

A shadowy figure emerged from the smoke, "seems your trusted advisor lead an elite force of destruction your way. How are you going to handle this one?"

Fresion crouched down with his hands over his ears, blocking out the screams and cries of his people slowly burning to death.

Zeke opened his eyes and looked Fresion deep in the eyes. "Your Kingdom will burn," he gasped.

Fresion stared at him. "Is that what you are going to do?" He asked.

Zeke tried to shake his head. "It will happen, but we won't be here."

"Then how do you know?" Fresion questioned him.

Zeke began to lose consciousness; he could just make out Mitzi and Symese trading whips and claws. Just as he blacked out, he worked out that Symese, too, was Slizard, she had begun her transformation just as Zeke closed his eyes for the last time.

<u>Enceladus</u>

"Are you sure?" Eva asked. "I thought she excelled through her training?"

"She did," Aquilia replied. "A little too well if I remember correctly."

"Do you think it could be her?" Janus asked.

As soon as Aquilia had said the name, Layson had begun his search on the being in question, bringing up all her back history, family and educational training.

"It seems we may have a slight problem," he said.

Everyone in the room looked at him.

"What problem?" Aquilia asked. She walked behind his desk and looked at the screen. All the information on Alestra had gone. Every last detail about her life, scrubbed from existence. "Do you think you can do something with this? Maybe do a deep search or something?"

"I can try. It may take me a little while though," Layson admitted.

"See how much you can dig up in thirty minutes," Aquilia told him. "We will be back then."

As the door swung open Benzyline almost fell on top of Aquilia.

"How long have you been there?" Aquilia demanded.

"Long enough Your Highness. I think I may be of some assistance," she smiled. "The girl you're searching up, I have much data on her family."

"Where is this data exactly?" Evadene asked.

"Right up here," Benzyline replied, tapping the side of her head.

"Let's go to my office," Aquilia led the way.

As Layson searched through the deepest depths of the Enceladant servers, it seemed every inch of data about Alestra had been wiped. The list of her family had disappeared, her education, even the list of her training had mysteriously disappeared. He decided he would have to hack into the system and see who had removed it. Only limited people had access to the servers, he knew he would be able to find out quickly, but he would have to cover his own tracks so that the same person didn't track him, providing that person hadn't covered their own tracks. As he typed in the commands to load up his cloaking software, his door opened slightly.

"Who's there?" He called.

"Just me," Chylla replied. "Have you seen Queen Aquilia?"

"I believe she went to her office," Layson replied. He quickly opened a different program before Chylla cold make her way around his desk.

"Still working on the numbers for the new telescope I see," she smiled. "Sinclair would have been so happy to work with you."

"He was a great man. A lot of what I have learnt, I picked up reading his work. He really did love his work," Layson smiled back. "If you don't mind, I need to get back to this."

"Of course. Sorry, I didn't mean to disrupt you. I'll go and find The Queen," Chylla waved as she closed the door.

Layson instantly became suspicious of Chylla. She had never entered his office unannounced before and she had always knocked first. He was glad he had changed programs before she could look at the screen. Layson quickly called ahead to Aquilia and informed her of Chylla's visit.

"Thank you Layson. I'll watch out for her," Aquilia replied. She replaced the phone into her pocket and gestured for everyone to take a seat.

Just as they sat down, there was a knock at the door.

"Come in," Aquilia requested.

Chylla opened the door and entered the room, quickly bowing her head. "Your Highness, we have word from The Stealth Raiders."

"Well, go on," Aquilia demanded.

"Eliontara is safe aboard Onyx Abyss Alpha," Chylla told them.

Aquilia let out a sigh of relief before collapsing into her chair. "That's fantastic news. When are they due to arrive?"

Chylla bit on her bottom lip.

"What is it Chylla?" Eva asked.

"Mitzi went in to save him and she got caught," Chylla began. "But then Zeke went in after her and they're both still there."

"Well, get them out!" Aquilia cried. "Zeke isn't trained in battle!" She began to panic. She had no idea how well or badly Symese could fight but she couldn't risk Zeke's life.

"They can't," Benzyline replied.

Everyone turned to look at her.

"Why?" Janus asked.

Benzyline sighed inwardly. "Symese is Slizard. Just like Mitzi. Slizard's don't mix well with other Slizard. It's a fight to the death kind of thing."

"So we just have to what, wait?" Eva asked.

Benzyline nodded. "I'm afraid so. If they are to battle, then that is the only way it will end."

"And Zeke?" Janus asked.

"Zeke will hold his own. He has a deeper talent than any of you know," Benzyline told them. She then fell quiet.

Chylla blinked twice and said "I will inform you of any changes."

Aquilia nodded at her. Chylla turned and left the room. Aquilia looked at Benzyline, sat forward in her chair and said, "tell me everything about Alestra. Then you can explain Zeke."

Everyone else sat around the table and waited for her to speak.

<u>Plydar</u>

Fresion dropped Zeke to the floor where he stayed. He didn't even flinch when his body hit the ground. Fresion looked down at him and nudged him with his foot.

"Get up!" Fresion demanded, but walked away when Zeke made no attempt to move.

Zeke didn't move. He laid there willing himself to breathe. In his head, he saw Mitzi, slain on the floor with Symese standing over her. He forced himself to gulp down multiple lungfuls of air. His eyes fluttered open in search of Mitzi. He looked left and right before finally spotting her pinning a flailing Symese to the floor. The only way he could determine the difference between the two creatures was Mitzi's hair. He tried his hardest to smile, but it hurt his head. He dragged himself into a seated position and, using the wall for support, dragged himself to his feet. As he took more and more deep breaths, his vision became clearer. So clear in fact, he could make out Fresion looking out over the Kingdom from the furthest window. Zeke tried not to draw attention to himself. He slowly made his way towards where Symese and Mitzi were fighting, drawing on the energy from Mitzi to build up his strength.

"Not so fast!" Fresion cried as he grabbed Zeke's arm. "Where do you think you're going?"

Zeke stopped in his tracks and looked back at Fresion with a new found hatred in his eyes. "Let me go!" He said through gritted teeth.

"You know too much!" Fresion whispered. "What are you?"

"I'm nothing. I'm just a technician," Zeke replied.

"Clearly you aren't a warrior," Fresion laughed. "There's nothing to you."

Zeke snatched his arm away from Fresion's bony fingers. He glanced over at Mitzi and Symese, now whipping tails and snapping teeth at each other.

"They will be at it for a while," Fresion grinned. "You may as well pull up a chair unless you're willing to jump in there with her."

Zeke had begun to despise this being. He turned and walked towards Mitzi and Symese. His first instinct was to grab Symese and throw her across the room but the closer he got to the two fighting beings, the bigger they became. He hadn't realised how big Mitzi could grow as a Slizard. When he had seen her before, back on Enceladus, she hadn't been this big. He watched as they tussled back and forth until Mitzi caught Symese's tail in her mouth and threw her through the outer wall and down on the courtyard below.

"Mitzi, wait," Zeke called.

Mitzi looked round at him. Gone were her blue eyes and gentle face, replaced by small orange beady eyes and a scaly skin, complete with a black, whipping forked tongue. "I have to go. Slizards fight to the death," she hissed at him. She then jumped through the hole made by Symese and down onto the ground.

He rushed to the gaping hole and looked down. He saw Mitzi prowling around a broken Symese lying on the ground, her tongue whipping in and out every other second. He looked away just as Symese attempted to stand up, but he saw enough to know that Mitzi had already pounced on her.

Chapter Twenty – Nine

Enceladus

"Your Highness, we have a video link coming through," Chylla called over the radio.

"Patch it through to my Heads Up," Aquilia replied. She opened it up and waited for the video to begin.

"Mum? It's me. I'm safe, thanks to Mitzi and Marixah. Mum, Zeke and Mitzi are still there. Mum?" Eliontara's face came over the screen. "How do I know if she can hear me?"

"I'm here Elion, I'm here," Aquilia replied. "What happened?"

"I wasn't hurt. Marixah helped Nymeria find me and tried to hep Mitzi rescue me, but that weird woman wouldn't let me stay in the cell alone, so she hid in the shadows," he began to explain. "But Mum, Mitzi and Zeke!"

"I know sweetheart. We are trying to think of a way to get them out," Aquilia replied.

Benzyline scoffed. "That's a joke."

Eva stared at her and put her finger to her lips.

"What? No one has even thought of how to rescue them," Benzyline whispered.

"We know, but we need to listen to Eliontara and see if there are any clues on how to get to them," Janus explained.

Benzyline shrugged her shoulders and shuffled towards the window. "They could just tranquilize Symese and then they could escape."

"Wouldn't work Mrs Benzyline Ma'am. Fresion, he's like some sort of King, he saw Marixah leading me off somewhere. He told her to take me to the other holding cells but she brought me here, to Balzar," Eliontara told them.

"Fresion?" Benzyline asked. "What is he doing on Plydar?"

"Is that a bad thing?" Aquilia asked.

"Absolutely. Fresion is Enceladant. He should be here. Enceladant people are only allowed to make home on another planet with written permission from the reigning monarch. That would be you my dear," Benzyline explained. "I shall return. I need to work this out."

"But Lyra said Fresion was Plydant?" Eva whispered.

"What was that dear?" Benzyline asked.

"Lyra, she said Fresion was Plydant. He and Altair had some dodgy deals going on," Eva explained.

"Ahh, she may well be confused. In fact, I'm sure of it, give me some time and I will prove it," Benzyline smiled, and with that, Benzyline shuffled down the corridor and out of sight. No one knew if she stayed on Enceladus or travelled back to Saturn.

"OK sweetie, where is your sister?" Aquilia said.

"Right here Ma'am," Scarlex answered. "Do you require my assistance?"

"Yes, I need you to see if you can work the computers on board, you know, the one Zeke would normally work at," Aquilia told her.

"I can't work that. Eliontara can," she replied.

"Oh? I didn't know he had tech knowledge?" Aquilia replied. "Fair enough. Tell him to load up the SincTelescope and aim it at where Zeke and Mitzi are being held, then he is to press the yellow button which will beam it down to me too," Aquilia explained.

"Got it Mum!" Eliontara called from the background. He jumped into Zeke's chair and searched for the SincTelescope and loaded it up. He took the controls and turned the scope towards the Palace. "Are you seeing it Mum?"

Aquilia gasped when she saw Mitzi fighting with Symese. "Oh my gosh," she whispered.

Eva and Janus looked over her shoulder just as Symese launched Mitzi into the wall. Mitzi fell to the floor, blood trickling from her nostrils. To their surprise, Zeke slid into view.

"What is he doing?" Janus asked.

"I don't know. He seems to be reaching out to Symese," Eva replied.

"I know what he is doing," Aquilia said. "I hope he knows how dangerous it could be."

Both Eva and Janus refused to ask what she meant.

<u>Saturn</u>

"Mum, you're back," Lyra exclaimed.

"I'm not here long darling. Now, where is that book I always had, you know the one," Benzyline asked as she bustled around the Palace.

"I know the one. I put it away after you left it out on the table. Codex couldn't sleep for nearly three days after reading what Trylox do with their dead!" Lyra cried. She walked over to the highest cupboard and pulled out the book. "Here." She passed it to her mother who grinned from ear to ear.

"Now my dear, a little lesson to learn. Never assume anyone that someone is a particular species unless you are completely certain. Now, let me show you." Benzyline opened the book to the Plydant page and showed her daughter the types of Plydant listed. "You see how none of them look anything like Fresion?"

Lyra looked over her mother's shoulder. "I see, but what has that got to do with me?"

"Well, young Eva said you mentioned that Fresion was Plydant?" Benzyline asked.

"That's what Altair told me," Lyra replied.

"Indeed. Nothing that man said was ever true. No, Fresion was, in fact, Enceladant. He was given permission from Quintara's parents to live on Saturn," Benzyline explained. "He and his family, along with a select few, were given a piece of Astrodia to settle in. They settled well but Altair saw a deal to be made and that's where they met. I believe Fresion may have slightly bent the truth about where he was from. I'm sure, if Altair knew he was Enceladant, he wouldn't have been so welcoming."

Lyra nodded. "I get it now. I'm sorry Mum. I just thought that...Don't worry. Thank you for explaining it to me."

"You only need to ask dear. Now, who did you say was threatening young Mitzi?" Benzyline asked.

Lyra sighed. "Shima. She told Mitzi that they didn't want the likes of Squink around there. It rattled her a little. Is she OK?"

"Of that last bit I am unsure, are you up to date on the situation up there," Benzyline said, pointing upwards.

"Not as up to date as I wanted to be. Tell me," Lyra said as she sat at the kitchen table. She looked out over the Palace gardens as all the children played happily. All except Xandr. He seemed to be looking up towards the emptiness of space.

"Is he OK Lyra?" Benzyline asked.

"I don't know. He seems to be fine at times, and then he just blanks out and stares upwards," Lyra replied. "It's only been happening since Mitzi and Balzar stayed, when Mitzi was first kidnapped."

Benzyline sighed. "Does he know we got Mitzi back?"

"I don't know if anyone told him. I don't want to overstep Eva and Janus, but I wonder if I told him, would it stop him looking skywards?" Lyra said.

"Why don't you give it a try?" Her mother said, gently pushing her in Xandr's direction.

Lyra walked over to the boy, wringing her hands together as she went. "Xandr honey."

The boy looked around at her with the biggest smile ever, "yes nana?"

"What's got your attention sweetie?" Lyra asked, settling herself on the grass next to him.

"I'm just seeing if Mitzi is coming back. She's been gone for a long time. What did the red-skinned man want with her? Is he her daddy?" Xandr asked.

"No sweetie, but Mitzi came back. She went back to Enceladus. Didn't we tell you?" Lyra replied.

"No. I'm glad she is back. Can we watch some stars?" He asked.

Lyra laughed and scooped him up in her arms. "Of course we can. Let's go."

She took him up to the highest part of the Palace and lined up the telescope. Xandr bounced up and down on the chair waiting his turn to see the stars. Lyra placed the eyepiece over his eye and he gasped in amazement at the star in front of him.

"This is a new set?" He asked.

"Absolutely! I show you a new set every time. Before long you will have seen the entire galaxy. We will have to ask

Layson to develop a new telescope for your birthday," Lyra replied.

Over the next hour and a half, Xandr continued to watch the stars. He asked questions about space and asked when he would be able to travel like the Space crews. Lyra hoped he would grow out of wanting to become part of the military.

<u>Plydar</u>

"What are you doing you crazy fool?" Symese cried as Zeke reached out to touch her back. She flicked her tail, just missing him by an inch.

Zeke narrowed his eyes and placed his hand on her scaly back. His eyes then rolled back as he viewed what would happen;

'"It's not supposed to be like this," Symese called.

"What is it supposed to be like? Enlighten me," Aquilia asked, pacing in front of Symese.

"You were supposed to trade with your son. Fresion should be killing you with his bare hands!" Symese grinned.

"I guess the plan didn't work," Aquilia smiled. "Now I get to kill you."

Zeke opened his eyes just as Mitzi regained her balance. She wiped the blood from her nose and launched herself at Symese.

"You did that on purpose," Symese screamed as she fell to the floor.

"Mitzi wait. We have to take her back with us. Tie her legs up tail up," Zeke called to her.

"And where do you think you will be taking her?" Fresion asked form the window he still stood at.

"Back to Enceladus. She will pay for her crimes there," Zeke said with his head held high.

"And what if I refuse to let you?" He said, turning to face Zeke.

Zeke contemplated his answer carefully. He wasn't trained to fight, but he knew how to defend himself. He knew he wouldn't be able to take on Fresion alone.

"Then we will force you," Balzar replied from behind him. "And you will end up coming with us and we will try you for similar crimes."

Fresion considered his next move, narrowing his eyes at Balzar who stood over two feet taller than him and Zeke. He finally waved his hand in dismissal. "Take her. She is no use to me, but tell Queen Aquilia that I will receive payback for what she did."

Balzar shook his head, threw a squirming Symese over his shoulder and stalked away. "Tell her yourself," he threw back.

Mitzi scrambled over to Zeke. "Are you OK?" She asked.

"I should be asking you that?" He replied with a smile. "This new look," he gestured to her Slizard form. "It's kinda growing on me," he laughed.

She slapped his shoulder and morphed back into her Squink form.

"But I like this one better," he whispered as she clung to his neck.

As they walked back to the waiting ships, she smiled. Happy to be back where she belonged.

Chapter Thirty

Enceladus

"What just happened?" Janus asked.

"It's not something I can tell. It is something that Zeke would have to explain when he is ready to," Aquilia replied. "Now, we must get things ready for when they return. Mitzi will need time to recharge." She called Halana over the radio and requested that the guest room be set up for Mitzi's return.

Eva wondered why Aquilia was so calm about everything that had happened on the screen. She didn't seem worried about anything that they had seen. She pulled Aquilia aside. "Did he see something?"

Aquilia looked at her, shocked. "What do you know?"

"I don't *know* anything but you didn't seem fazed when he touched Symese and closed his eyes, plus you mentioned that what he was doing would be dangerous," Eva whispered.

"I can't say anything. I promised him. If and when he wants to tell anyone, he will," Aquilia said before turning and walking out of the office.

Eva could tell she was hiding something from her, but she decided not to pursue it yet.

Janus walked alongside Aquilia as she strode through the corridors of the Palace. "What was that about?"

"What was what about Janus?" Aquilia sighed.

"You and Eva whispering in the corner. What aren't you telling us?" He asked grabbing her arm.

"It's more what I *can't* tell you. It's not my place," she replied shaking him loose from her arm. "I don't find it polite to interrogate me either." She turned away from him and walked towards the landing site. The ships would no doubt be Hyper Jumping back any minute.

"The guest room is ready Your Highness," Halana told her. She had managed to catch up with Aquilia at the landing site. "Are young Zeke and Mitzi OK?"

"They will be Halana. Mitzi will need to rest and recharge. Zeke will need to be debriefed and get lots of rest," Aquilia replied.

"Young Zeke is a strong soul," Halana whispered. "He takes on so much at once."

Aquilia turned to look at her, "I know he shared it with you," she said.

"Who shared what dear?" Halana replied.

"Zeke. I know he showed you his gift. He has shown me too. I didn't want to know what happened. I want it to be a surprise," Aquilia replied. "You knew I was going to be a mother before even *I* did."

"I didn't know for sure that it was you. In the snippet shown to me, there was someone with long red hair, much like yours, but I didn't see the face," Halana replied. "He told me I would have forever to enjoy you, Eva and the children."

Aquilia squeezed Halana's arm. "We aren't going anywhere." She looked back out at space, spotting the ships as they emerged from their Hyper Jump. "Here they come."

Onyx Abyss Alpha made its way through Enceladus' atmosphere, followed closely by The Stealth Raiders. Their descent from the skies above gripped the Kingdom. Touching down carefully, the ships shut their engines off and opened their doors. Halana was the first to Onyx Abyss Alpha, pulling Zeke and Mitzi into a huge embrace.

"Come, I have the guest room set up for you," she told them, pulling them towards the Palace.

Zeke looked over at Aquilia who just nodded her head. He then allowed Halana to guide the way.

"We have a guest," Balzar announced as he hauled Symese off the ship. "Which cell?"

"Let's see, we don't want her too comfortable, but we don't want to come across as mean, so...seven?" Aquilia grinned.

Balzar knew that cell seven was halfway between luxury and bottomless pit. He nodded his head and carried Symese to cell seven. He had just walked into the holding area when Nymeria and Celest disembarked their ship along with their crew and one added person.

"Who might this be?" Aquilia asked.

Marixah bowed in front of Aquilia. "My name is Marixah Your Highness."

"Should I know who you are?" Aquilia replied.

"Marixah helped us locate and rescue Eliontara, she was my inside source," Nymeria explained.

"And she is here because?" Aquilia asked.

"I didn't think she would be safe if we left her behind. No doubt Fresion would have killed her," Nymeria said. "I couldn't let that happen to her after she helped us."

Aquilia looked at Marixah, then back at Nymeria. "She is your responsibility."

"Yes Your Majesty," Nymeria bowed her head.

"Mum!" Eliontara bounded out of the ship and barrelled straight for her. "I missed you."

"And I you. I must say, you were very brave up there, taking over the tech side of things with ease," Aquilia smiled. She looked over his shoulder as Scarlex climbed down from Onyx Abyss Alpha. She looked every bit the Queen she would, one day, become. Her blue hair whipped around her face as she surveyed her surroundings. "Scarlex, come."

Scarlex looked towards her mother and made her way over to her. "Yes Mother?"

"I'm proud of you both. You have both shown how well you can handle any situation thrown at you and that you can both do it calmly. I may have some positions coming up for you both," Aquilia told them. "But first, we must debrief. My office in thrity."

"Yes Ma'am," they said in unison.

Aquilia walked away towards the holding area in search of Balzar. She found him just as she entered the building. He looked weary and worn out.

"You need some time away?" Aquilia asked.

"I may do soon. Hula is having a baby," Balzar replied.

"Well that's amazing news! Congratulations. I'll send a hamper to her immediately. How long do you need Balzar?" Aquilia exclaimed.

"I don't know for sure. I need to go and see the doctors with her and go from there, but if you need me here, then I can work out something," Balzar replied. He hadn't known how to ask for some time off. He'd never done it before.

"Let me know as soon as you find out. I may have someone who can stand in for you whilst you are on leave," Aquilia smiled. "Now, debrief in thirty."

"Yes Ma'am," he bowed and left the area.

Aquilia slowly walked past the cells before she reached cell seven. She looked in at a curled up Symese. Her green tinted hair coiling around her.

"Get up!" Aquilia screeched.

Symese almost jumped into the air. She got to her feet and turned to face Aquilia.

"Why?" Aquilia asked.

One simple question that could amount to a multitude of answers, but Symese offered none. She stared back at Aquilia, almost daring her to make another move.

Aquilia laughed. "You're pathetic. What did you think you would achieve? Kidnap me and all your wrongs would be forgiven? You realise that Fresion doesn't work that way? You will, forever, be in debt to him."

"He was going to make me his right-hand woman. I would have done everything for him," Symese sneered. "You would never understand. No-one will ever be loyal to you, Alphir!"

Aquilia didn't even flinch. "Do you know how many times someone has said that to me and yet, here I am, still Queen of both Saturn and Enceladus. The people aren't worried where I am from. They worry about how I will protect them. Especially from Plydant like you."

Aquilia then turned and left Symese alone in the dark. She made her way to her office and sat herself in her chair. She could feel the Phoenix battling to emerge but she kept it down with some silent persuasion.

"Are you OK?" Zeke asked Mitzi as he placed her on the bed.

"I think I'm good, maybe my ego is a little battered but I'll survive, you?" Mitzi replied.

"I'll survive. I'm not really a fighter. I watched Scarlex and Eliontara train, maybe picked up a few moves, but most of it is just instinct," he replied.

Mitzi snuggled up to his side and drifted off to sleep. His phone buzzed in his pocket. Pulling it out he noticed it was from Aquilia.

A – Don't worry about debrief. I'll bring you both up to speed later. Get some rest Zeke. You did good.

He quickly typed a reply.

Z – I'll be in the office in two hours. I'll just have a little sleep and settle Mitzi.

He then put his phone away and drifted into a fitful sleep.

"We can't hold them off, there's too many of them," Aquilia cried.

"I can only do so much Your Highness," Chylla replied.

"We have to try something else, this isn't working," Aquilia said. "Where is backup?"

"Backup is an hour out. I don't think we will make it through," Chylla replied. "You may have to unleash her."

"I can't. If I do, she'll destroy everything," Aquilia replied.

"There's no choice Your Majesty," Chylla cried.

"Zeke, wake up," Mitzi cried. "Zeke!"

Zeke's eyes flew open, his breathing coming in rapid succession.

"Zeke, what happened?" Aquilia asked as she gently touched his shoulder.

"There was destruction everywhere," Zeke whispered.

"Here?" Aquilia asked.

Zeke shook his head. "Saturn." He replied. "There was an army. I don't know who sent them." He stopped. Then he looked at Mitzi. "Fresion. He's going to send his army to finish the job that Symese couldn't. Your Highness we have to get Saturn into lockdown immediately."

"Zeke, we can't do that, and if Fresion is after me, why wasn't the attack here?" Aquilia asked.

"I don't know. I don't know how near or far in the future it will be, but we have to be careful with your every move," he told her.

"It was just a dream Zeke. I don't think anyone would threaten the people of Saturn," Aquilia finally dismissed the idea.

"I still think you should be careful," Zeke told her.

"Nonsense. Now, I've questioned Symese but she is refusing to speak. Mitzi, if you're up to it, I need your help," Aquilia replied.

"I think I can do it. It might be harder with Symese though, she is Slizard too. The same tactics might not work," Mitzi informed her.

"I'll do it. Symese has taken too much of Mitzi's energy as it is," Zeke offered.

"Do you think you can?" Aquilia asked. "It's a big thing to interrogate someone."

"I won't know until I try," Zeke replied. "Lead the way."

Mitzi and Zeke followed Aquilia through the Palace, across the landing pads and into the holding area. She walked to cell seven and stopped.

"Symese, get up," Aquilia demanded. "You have a visitor."

Symese looked up from her resting place, first eyeing Mitzi as she rested on Zeke's shoulder. "Oh, do I get another shot?" She grinned.

"No. You get me," Zeke said. "Aquilia take Mitzi back to rest some more, please."

"Zeke, I can stay," Mitzi defended.

"No, I'd rather you go and rest. Who knows when we will be needed again," Zeke told her.

She nodded slowly and jumped onto Aquilia's shoulder. "You don't mind do you Your Highness? The walk is awfully long on small legs."

Aquilia laughed. "Of course not. Let's go. Zeke, call me when you're done."

He nodded at her and waited for her to leave before turning his attention to Symese. "So, you won't answer Aquilia's questions? Why?"

"I don't need to justify myself to you," Symese snapped. "You're nothing more than my next meal."

"You couldn't digest me if you tried," Zeke grinned. He had her attention now.

"What makes you say that?" Symese asked. "There are only a few beings that we Slizards can't digest. Skylarks, Bycalf and Dark Wolf."

Zeke remained calm. He had done tests on himself a few years before to see if he too carried the Dark Wolf gene, and it flowed through his veins faster than a Hyper Jump.

"You can't be any of those. You don't look the type," Symese said. She slinked closer to the door.

"There's a look? I didn't know. Do all form have a certain look when they aren't morphed?" Zeke asked, he slid down the wall opposite her cell door, he didn't want to risk being too close in case she tried anything.

Symese looked at him through narrow eyes. "What are you?"
She hissed.

Zeke looked back at her, his brown eyes flashing green, then
orange and back to brown. "If I told you, well, a lot would be
at stake wouldn't it?"

"Dark Wolf," Symese whispered. "How?"

Zeke jumped to his feet, "it's simple really. Basic genetics."

"But the Dark Wolf has been extinct for centuries," she
replied.

"Hmm, I don't think so. It's only been laying dormant," Zeke
shrugged. "Now, back to my original question, why won't
you answer Aquilia's questions?"

"She asked me about Fresion's plans for her; I told her I
didn't know what he had planned. She then asked why he was
so interested in her, I refused to answer. I thought she would
have already known that answer," Symese shrugged. "She
killed Altair. Fresion had some really good deals going on
with him, which brought in a lot of money. After the big
battle and Altair's subsequent demise, Fresion's income dried
up. He blames her and he will exact his revenge."

"And you thought she would already know all this?" He
laughed. "Fresion clearly blind-sided you. Aquilia has lived
here on Enceladus since she was five. She didn't really *know*
her uncle. In fact, let me get her to explain."

Zeke radioed for Aquilia to attend the holding area.

"I'm on my way," came her reply.

"Does she know?" Symese asked.

"Does who know?" Zeke questioned her.

"The Queen, does she know what you are?" She grinned.

"Not yet, but she will soon," he replied.

They waited for Aquilia to arrive, neither making any move to speak to the other.

"So, where are we with this?" Aquilia asked as she walked into the corridor.

"I think you should explain the whole situation with Altair to our guest here. She has some, shall we say, views?" Zeke replied. He gestured to the floor next to him, where Aquilia gladly sat. "So, Symese here was under the impression, according to Fresion, that you killed Altair and that stopped all of his money."

Aquilia looked over at Symese, who, in turn, shrugged. "It's what he said. He told me that he and Altair had a pretty good deal going on and that it brought lots of money in. He said once Altair had been killed, the money stopped, you are to blame and he wanted you captured so he could kill you."

"I knew nothing of my uncles deals. I came here at the age of five, two years after my father died. We heard, from a source who will remain anonymous, that Altair was out to kill my mother and I. Being Queen of Enceladus already, my mother sent me here for my protection, little did she know that he would make numerous attempts on my life here too," Aquilia explained.

Symese looked at her inquisitively. "I am confused."

"What part are you confused at?" Aquilia asked. "It seems pretty clear to me. I grew up here, not on Saturn. I had relatively little to no contact with my uncle and didn't know any of his deals or partnerships."

"Fresion said you knew everything. Altair told him you did," Symese replied. "Are you insinuating that Fresion was lying?"

"I can almost guarantee it," Zeke added.

"So, where do you stand now?" Aquilia asked as she brushed a stray hand behind her ear.

"I must think. I need some time," Symese replied.

"We'll be back in an hour. I think that's plenty of time," Zeke said. He then took hold of Aquilia's hand and helped her to her feet. "Your Highness, if you have a few moments, may I speak to you in private?"

"Certainly Zeke. Come to my office, we can talk there," Aquilia replied, she looked worried. Zeke followed her towards her office, practising, is his head how he would start the conversation. She opened the door and gestured to the sofa overlooking the Kingdom.

As Zeke settled himself into the seat, he took a deep breath and looked her in the eyes."There is something I need you to know. I haven't told my parents yet but I think you should be the first to know."

"Zeke, you're worrying me. What is it?" Aquilia replied.

"I ran a blood test on myself. I needed to know if what I felt was natural or an infection. I got the results back a little over a week ago. I have Dark Wolf genes," Zeke told her.

Aquilia was shocked. She didn't have any words. She stared at him for what felt like hours before she spoke, "how will you tell your father?"

"That's why I needed to talk to you first. Will you be there with me, when I tell them?" Zeke asked.

Aquilia nodded. "Of course I will, but, I think we need some advice from Benzyline first. She has a deeper understanding of this than I do."

Zeke nodded briefly once and left the room, heading back to Mitzi. He needed to tell her before someone else did.

Chapter Thirty – One

Saturn

"Are you quite pleased with yourself Shima?" Benzyline called from the edge of the village boundary.

"In what way?" Shima asked.

"Well," Benzyline continued, inching closer. "I heard from a little star that you were quite nasty to a certain Squink."

We don't need the likes of that around these parts," Shima defended. "We have to protect our young."

"Oh Shima. Shima, Shima, Shima, you know, as well as I do, that Squink don't hunt the young," Benzyline grinned. "It's the elderly that they like. She would have been more interested in you or I."

Shima looked shocked. "That's not what I heard."

"What you hear and what you know, are two very separate things my dear. Now, you remember what it was like to be an outcast?" She asked.

Shima nodded.

"Good. Don't make me do it again. I could make quite the fuss about it this time," Benzyline warned her. "Mitzi is off limits to you and your little remarks, do you understand?"

Shima nodded and ran back into her house. Within a few seconds, Shima's husband, Fruga, had emerged.

"We don't take kindly to threats," he said before he looked up from the floor to face Benzyline. "I didn't...Shima didn't say it was you. What has she been up to this time?"

"Just threatening a Squink friend of the Royal Family's. I just wanted her to be aware that her actions will come with consequences if she continues," Benzyline replied. "You have a great day now Fruga."

He nodded towards her and made his way back into his house.

Benzyline shook her head and made her way back to the Palace.

"I'll get her to call as soon as she gets back. I don't even know where she went. Is everything OK?" Lyra asked.

"Everything is fine Lyra, try not to panic. Eva and Janus will be returning soon and I'll be down to visit too," Aquilia assured her.

"Wait, I think she has just come in the door. Mum is that you?" Lyra called out.

"Yes dear. What is it?" Benzyline replied.

"Aquilia is on the phone. She needs to speak with you," Lyra said.

Benzyline quickly placed her bags on the floor and shuffled towards the kitchen.

"Hello Your Highness. I was about to contact you regarding Fresion," Benzyline said.

"He is on hold at the moment. For now, we have something a little more pressing to deal with. How quickly can you get back here?" Aquilia asked.

"Within the hour Your Majesty. I shall leave at once," Benzyline replied. She placed the phone on the countertop and made her way to the landing pad at the top of the Palace. "I'll send Eva and Janus back to you; you look like you could do with a rest." She told Lyra.

"Thanks Mum," Lyra smiled. "Have a safe trip."

Lyra waved as her mother shoot of back to Enceladus, leaving her alone, once more, with her grandchildren. She returned to the gardens of the Palace and watched the children playing happily together; Codex pushing Ammyn on the swing; Xandr digging in the sand pit, Kodyn rode around on a tricycle and the others were climbing the climbing frame. Lyra couldn't be happier. She had finally been given a chance to be a mother and a grandmother to eleven beautiful grandchildren, all with their own personalities. She smiled as Zeryn waved to her from the top of the frame. She couldn't imagine herself being anywhere else.

Lyra looked up to see the remaining trail of her mother's departing ship; she wished she could have gone too but the children needed her. Eva and Janus would return soon.

As Benzyline looked down from her ship to Astrodia, she wished Lyra could join her. It had been so long since she had been able to travel. She settled back for the journey and looked through the book she had taken with her. It listed the different types of being throughout the galaxies and what things others should look out for when coming up against them. Unlike Eva's book, about Ancient Saturnese history, Benzyline's warned which creatures to avoid.

She finally arrived less than an hour later; landing gently at the private landing pad Aquilia had set up in the grounds of the Palace. Climbing down from the pod, Benzyline made her way to Aquilia's office on the second floor of the Palace. She knocked twice before being requested to enter. To her surprise, Zeke sat with Aquilia, a look of confusion and misunderstanding across his face.

"Oh young Zeke! It's good to see you. What's wrong?" She asked as she made her way towards him.

"This is what we needed to talk to you about," Aquilia began.

"I'm part Dark Wolf," Zeke finished before Aquilia had a chance.

Benzyline didn't look in the slightest bit surprised. She looked at them both and said "of course you are, Layson is Dark Wolf so why wouldn't it pass down to you. Did you think it would just stop?"

Zeke's mouth fell open. "I just thought that, with Dad's being dormant for so long, the genes may not have passed to me."

"My dear, genes can remain dormant for a very long time but still be passed down. Just ask our Queen here," Benzyline gestured. "The Phoenix gene jumped generations in her family, yet she has it."

"Does that mean Scarlex will have it too?" Zeke asked.

"That one is slightly more complicated. Now, about Fresion," Benzyline steered the conversation away from the subject of Aquilia and her hidden genes.

"We're holding Symese," Aquilia told her.

"What? She's here?" Benzyline looked surprised. "Mitzi?"

"She's asleep in the guest room," Zeke replied.

"And they both survived? What happened?" Benzyline asked. She placed herself next to Zeke and waited to be informed.

Fresion paced the Palace's Grand Ballroom. He couldn't believe how easily they had infiltrated his Palace. He had sent his own security out to re-evaluate the walls of the Palace. They had found some weakness among the walls closest to the holding areas. He had then instructed new walls be built immediately.

After watching the workers for a while, he remembered that he still had Prince Eliontara in his other holding cell area. He grinned to himself and started in the direction of the holding area.

"Well young Prince. It seems your friends seemed to have forgotten about you," he said as he swung his trailing purple cloak behind him.

He stood staring, wide eyed and open mouthed, at the empty cells.

"That conniving little wench!" He cried through gritted teeth. "I'll find you, you deceitful thing."

He stormed back towards his own personal quarters and slammed the door in anger. He loaded his computer up and pulled up his tracking software, typing in Marixah's codes, he found her to be on Enceladus. He summoned his army to prepare the ships. He would go to Enceladus and bring her back for punishment. He would not let her get away with blindsiding him.

"The ships are ready sir," his Captain said, saluting at the door.

"Then we travel at once. How long before we reach?" Fresion asked.

"It could take days or even weeks sir. Our navigations have never taken us far from Plydar," he replied.

"Then let's get a move on," Fresion commanded.

He led his Captain to the launch pads and commanded everyone to set their compass to Enceladus. They were ordered to attack if confronted but not on sight. His fleet of twelve ships launched in unison and they began their tedious journey towards The Milky Way.

<u>Enceladus</u>

"And that's about the jist of it," Zeke finished.

He had told Benzyline the whole story of Marixah helping them save Eliontara, to Mitzi being imprisoned, to how they both managed to bring Symese to Enceladus. She had almost hung off his every word.

"Wow. So this Marixah, what is she?" Benzyline asked.

"I believe she is Plydant, but I didn't ask," Zeke replied. "I think Nymeria would probably know."

"Well, I must go in search of her. Be aware though Your Majesty. I believe Fresion would not let Marixah go unpunished if she has betrayed him," Benzyline warned. "I would be prepared."

As Benzyline went in search of Nymeria and Marixah, Aquilia thought about what she had said. "Do you think there is any truth in it?" She asked.

"Fresion did say you would receive payback for what you did. I didn't take any of it seriously, but if what Benzyline said is true, then maybe we should prepare the city," Zeke replied.

Aquilia nodded once and got to her feet, radioing her army at the same time. "All meet in the barracks, I repeat, all meet in the barracks. You have three minutes!" She turned to Zeke, "get Eva and Janus home to their children. I can't risk anything happening to them whilst they are here."

Zeke nodded and ran off in search of them, bumping into Chylla as he rounded the first corner. "Have you seen Evadene?"

"They just left to head back, I was about to inform The Queen," she replied.

"Great, that makes things a little easier. How are your fighting skills?" Zeke asked.

"I can still throw you around young man," she smiled, but it faded fast. "Why do you ask?"

"Meet in the barracks and Aquilia will update you all," Zeke told her as he ran off again. He headed toward the guest room and found Mitzi just waking up. "We're needed in the barracks. How are your energy levels?"

"More or less back to normal. You don't happen to have any berries on you, do you?" She asked, her blue eyes shining in the light.

Zeke smiled and pulled out some of her favourite Elderberries from him pocket. "I saved them for you."

"Thank you," she smiled as she took them from his outstretched hand and slowly chewed on them. When she had finished, she scrambled up onto Zeke's shoulder. "Let's go."

Zeke laughed and jogged off to the barracks, joining up with a whole host of soldiers.

"Is it bad?" Mitzi whispered. "I feel like it's going to be bad."

"I only know so much, but I think Queen Aquilia is preparing for an invasion. Try not to panic. I'm here, and I won't let anyone hurt you," he said, gently nudging her nose with his.

"Thanks Zeke," she whispered.

They entered the barracks and waited for Aquilia to begin her speech. All eyes were on the front of the room.

Aquilia took a deep breath and looked around the room. She was amazed by how many soldiers attended after her call. She stood straight and tried to look into any many eyes as she could as she spoke.

"Thank you all for coming. I know a lot of you are on your family leave and I appreciate you cutting it short to be here. As I am sure most of you know, I sent The Stealth Raider and Onyx Abyss Alpha to rescue my son and they succeeded," she began.

The room erupted into applause for the mission completion.

Aquilia held her hands above her head, "but there seems to be some repercussions up ahead. We had some help with the rescue, a being by the name of Marixah. A confidential but reliable source has warned of a possible invasion by Fresion and his army. I called you all here to ask that you be on standby. The trip from Plydar could take weeks but we must prepare and be ready. The city will go into lockdown in just over a week. Please ensure your family is advised and ready when the order is given."

"Yes Ma'am," came a united call.

"Dismissed," Aquilia shouted.

Within seconds, the army of soldiers began marching towards the exit and back to their families to share the news and get them ready for the impending lockdown.

"You Highness, should we send word to Astrodia?" Chylla asked.

Aquilia hesitated. She hoped Fresion wouldn't invade Astrodia considering what he wanted was here, but she nodded. "Yes. Warn Eva and Janus and get them to prepare for any immediate lockdown of Astrodia. I trust they will do the correct thing."

"Yes Your Highness," Chylla replied running off to send the message to Astrodia.

"Your Majesty," Nymeria bowed in front of Aquilia. "What do we do about Marixah?"

Aquilia sighed. "Nymeria, you decided to bring her here and Fresion may well decide she has committed treason and he may well hunt her down. If she is an asset to us, then we must find a way to protect her, but that falls solely on you and Celest."

"Yes Ma'am. If we had any knowledge of Fresion hunting Marixah, we would have taken her somewhere else, but right now, we don't have the time to arrange that," Nymeria told her. "I will make sure she remains hidden."

Aquilia nodded. "See that you do."

Nymeria bowed and headed back in the direction she came. Aquilia shook her head and sat herself on the steps to the podium at which she had just spoken.

"Why do I do it?" She asked.

Neither Zeke nor Mitzi made any move to answer her.

"I've been here since I was five and in that time there has never been a full scale invasion. Other than The Neptunites hunting for The Phoenix, Enceladus has remained off everybody's radar. Symese comes here almost five years later and now Fresion wants to start an all out war because of one being that helped us rescue my son? It seems a little off, don't you think?" She asked.

"What are you thinking Your Majesty?" Mitzi asked.

"I don't know, but it seems this Marixah is more than just a watch guard," Aquilia replied.

Chapter Thirty – Two

Saturn

"Are you sure?" Eva asked.

"The Queen wouldn't have issued the instruction is she hadn't been sure," Chylla told her.

"What gave her the idea that Fresion would launch an attack?" Janus asked.

"Of that I am unsure. You would probably have to ask her yourself," Chylla replied. "Just be ready for further instructions."

"Of course," Janus replied. He closed the connection and sat at the table rest his chin on his hands. "Something seems really odd about this."

"What do you mean?" Lyra asked. "Do you think Aquilia is keeping something back?"

"In a way yes, normally she would have had Chylla explain the whole situation, but I don't fully understand why we would be on the verge of a complete lockdown if it is only a hunch," he replied.

"I'll call her personally, maybe she'll tell me," Eva smiled. "I'll be back in shortly." She took her call in the gardens looking over the Kingdom.

"Aquilia, what aren't you telling us? There's more to this than you are telling us and we need to know. Call me back." Eva left the message and returned to the kitchen to find it empty. That's when she heard the raised voices.

"Why would she tell her that?" Janus cried.

"I don't know. You know what she is like. The words are out of her mouth before she thinks," Lyra replied.

"You definitely think it was her?" Janus asked.

"I would put my life on it," Lyra replied.

"It was Benzyline, wasn't it?" Eva asked, bursting into the kitchen. "Were you even going to tell me?" She asked Janus.

"Yes I was, but I needed to be sure first," Janus told her. He reached out for her hand but she snatched it away.

"If I hadn't overheard you, neither of you would have told me," she said through gritted teeth. She turned and left the kitchen, leaving them both staring after her.

"We should have waited until she had finished her call," Janus said. "It's going to take time for her to forgive me for this."

"She will come round. You'll see," Lyra told him. "She's hurting now but in the end she will understand."

"I hope so Mum. I really do," Janus replied as he continued to stay in the direction Eva had just ran.

"I can't believe they were going to hide it from me," Eva cursed to herself. "It's as if he doesn't trust me!"

She threw herself into her finger knitting to calm her anger down. She had never been so angry with him. He had always told her everything. She knitted with so much force her fingers began to cramp up and she dropped a number of stitches. She threw the yarn across the room and broke down in tears.

"Why Mama cry?" Ammyn asked from the doorway.

Eva jumped not knowing someone was standing there. "Mama is just a little upset and tired, that's all sweetheart. How are you?"

"Not good Mama. I don't feel good," Ammyn replied.

"What's wrong honey?" Eva asked, getting up from her chair and kneeling next to Ammyn.

"Something feels strange in my tummy Mama. Like something is trying to get out," she replied.

Eva pulled Ammyn top up a little and nearly jumped back as she saw something moving just under the skin. It moved in circles. Going around and around. It didn't make any moves to break through, just circled. "OK sweetie, we're going to have to get the doctors again, is that OK?"

Ammyn nodded and hugged her mother hard, "I'm not scared Mama. It just feels strange."

"I know sweetheart and that's because you are strong and brave," Eva told her, tears pricking at her eyes. She scooped Ammyn into her arms and ran back to the kitchen. "We need to get the Wraith Doctors, quickly."

"What is it?" Lyra asked. "Is Ammyn OK?"

Eva lifted Ammyn's top slightly to show the same thing as before, whatever was under her skin just circled and circled.

"Oh dear. Oh no, no, no," Lyra whispered.

"Lyra, what is it?" Eva demanded.

"Oh, I'm afraid to say without confirmation," Lyra replied.

"Tell me," Eva demanded again, this time more forcefully.

Lyra closed her eyes for a second and said, "She has the Serpent curse."

Eva's mouth dropped open but no words emerged.

"I'll get the Wraith Doctors, they can confirm or deny it," Janus said.

And with that he ran out of the room. Eva sat holding Ammyn close to her, slowly stroking her long emerald hair. "It will be OK baby. I promise," she whispered.

<u>Enceladus</u>

Zeke and Mitzi were sat in the library when Aquilia found them. They were deep in conversation and she debated disturbing them with this news, but she felt they needed to know.

"Zeke, Mitzi, could I have a word?" Aquilia asked.

They sat back in their chairs and waited for her to sit with them.

"We have had some new information sent over to us from Grazille Swirl," she began. "It seems that there is an army of around twelve ships heading this way. They believe Fresion is at the helm."

Zeke let his head drop back. "Why? Why does he insist on revenge? Altair was a bad person, he deserved what he got!"

"I understand Zeke, believe me I do, but I think we need to be realistic here. He isn't here for anyone but me," Aquilia told him. "Maybe I should face him alone."

"Excuse me Your Majesty but don't you think that is rather silly?" Mitzi asked.

Aquilia looked at her with a sharp turn of her head. "Absolutely! But, as Queen, and as the real target of this attack, I must do what I can to protect the Kingdom."

"Then I will stand by your side," Zeke said defiantly.

"WE. WE will stand by your side," Mitzi corrected him. "No matter what, we will be by your side."

"As will I Your Highness," Chylla added from the doorway. "You are requested in the barracks."

!I appreciate your sentiments. All of you," Aquilia said and she rose from her seat. "Join me?"

Zeke and Mitzi nodded and followed her to the barracks where the whole military was waiting, headed up by Nymeria and Celest.

"Your Highness, we heard that Fresion has just passed Grazille Swirl. We are ready on your orders," Nymeria announced. "Where is Balzar?"

"Balzar is having some well needed time off. Hula is having a baby and Balzar is needed there," Aquilia told her.

"Who will head up Onyx Abyss Alpha?" Nymeria asked.

Aquilia turned to the blue haired girl in the front row. "Scarlex, come here please."

Scarlex nodded once and joined her mother at the front. "Yes Your Highness?"

"I want you to head up Onyx Abyss Alpha. Do you think you can?" Aquilia asked. She clearly thought Scarlex had leadership qualities.

Scarlex thought for a second. She looked around at the room full of soldiers, all hanging on to hear her answer. She nodded quickly. "Yes. I think I can."

"That's settled then. Anything that needs signing off or confirmation goes through Scarlex. I do not expect you to treat her any differently than you would Balzar. When she is aboard Onyx Abyss Alpha, she is the captain, not a Princess," Aquilia told everyone.

"Yes Ma'am," they said in unison.

"Now where is that son of mine, I have a job for him. Zeke, accompany me? Bring Mitzi too," Aquilia said. She walked from the barracks in search of Eliontara.

As she rounded a corner, she almost knocked Halana over.

"Oh my, I'm dreadfully sorry Your Majesty. I should hold my head up when I walk," Halana apologised.

"It was my fault Halana. Have you seen Eliontara?" Aquilia replied.

"I haven't actually, but I have an idea of where he might be," she replied. "Please follow me."

Aquilia followed along with Zeke and Mitzi as Halana led the way towards the Comms room.

"He spends a lot of time in here. I found him a few weeks back, watching the screen much like you used to when you first arrived Zeke," Halana smiled. "He looks up to you."

Zeke smiled back and slowly opened the door. "Hey Elion," he whispered so as not to startle him. "What'cha watching?"

"Oh hi Zeke! I'm just watching this pod of ships just to the east of Mars. I think they came from Earth, see their trail?" Eliontara replied.

"I see, did you track it?" Zeke asked.

"No. I can do that?" He asked.

"Of course. Sinclair taught me how, let me show you," Zeke told him. He used a series of codes and brought up a different camera angle which showed the trajectory of all ships nearby. "You have to keep it a secret though." He said, placing his finger over his lips.

Eliontara smiled at him. "It's our secret."

"What's a secret?" Aquilia smiled as she came into the room.

"Zeke showed me how to track ships!" Eliontara blurted out and then quickly covered him mouth. He looked at Zeke who raised his eyebrows in shock. "Sorry," he whispered.

Zeke laughed so hard he almost fell off the chair. "It's OK Eliontara. Your mother knows how to track them too!"

"But you said it was a secret!" Eliontara cried.

"I know. I'm sorry. I couldn't resist, you were so excited to learn something new," Zeke tried to contain his laughter which was futile as it burst through multiple times.

Aquilia looked at him and shook her head all the while a massive grin crossed her face. "Eliontara, I have something to ask you. You can say no, if you feel it isn't for you, but how would you feel about becoming my technician?"

Eliontara looked stunned. He exchanged looks with Zeke and Halana before turning back to his mother, his eyes wide with shock. "Really? Me? Do you think I can?"

"I have no doubt you can. Zeke can train you for a while," Aquilia replied, looking at Zeke for confirmation.

"Absolutely. We can start right away," Zeke confirmed. "You just say the word."

Eliontara stood and walked over to where Zeebrakaan's picture hung. "I'll do it for you sir," he saluted to the picture then turned to his mother. "I accept your offer Your Highness."

"I'm glad. I will leave you in the capable hands of Zeke. You know where to find me should you need anything," Aquilia stood and left the room, leaving Zeke to pass on his knowledge to Eliontara.

A scream from the workshop caught Aquilia attention. She spun around and began running towards the workshop.

"Halana? Halana what is it?" Aquilia cried out. She ran round three corners and down two corridors before bursting through the door of the workshop.

Halana sat on the floor, tears streaming down her face and her phone lay on the floor beside her. Aquilia quickly ran over and dropped to her side.

"Halana, what's happened?" Aquilia asked, gently taking Halana's face in her hands.

Halana pointed to her phone, but her words refused to come out. Aquilia picked up the phone and almost dropped it after reading the message from Eva.

E – Mum, we've just found out something about Ammyn.

H – What is it sweetheart?

E – I feel sick just thinking about this Mum.

H – What is it Evadene – Dionne?

E – She has the Serpent Curse. The Wraith Doctors confirmed it.

Halana hadn't replied after the last message from Eva.

"I don't understand. How would Ammyn have got the Serpent Curse?" Aquilia thought out loud.

"Ohhh that will be Lyra's side. Her great-great grandmother was Serpent Eagle," Benzyline answered Aquilia's thoughts.

"Excuse you?" Aquilia asked her.

"Serpent Eagle. It's part Serpent, part..." Benzyline began.

"I know what it is!" Aquilia shouted. "Why didn't anyone warn Eva and Janus that it could have been passed on?"

"Well, because we believed it extinct!" Benzyline shrugged.

"Clearly it isn't!" Aquilia hissed. "Halana, do you want to travel to Saturn?"

Halana couldn't speak but she nodded hard.

"I will travel with you. We leave in a few minutes," Aquilia told her. She stood, turned towards the door and left to inform Zeke and Eliontara that they would be leaving imminently.

"Are you sure about this Your Highness?" Zeke asked. "It could be dangerous."

"We will be fine Zeke. You are took look after the Kingdom whilst I am away. The relevant people know who to find if something requires attention. We will be gone a couple of days at least. I am trusting you," Aquilia told him.

He nodded and showed Eliontara how to ready the launch system. Aquilia made her way back to Halana, who was ready to go but her hands were shaking. She hated flying.

"I'll be with you every step of the way," Aquilia told her, holding her hands to calm them down.

And with that they walked to Aquilia's ship, settled in and closed the hatch. Aquilia passed Halana a tablet.

"Just in case it gets too much, take this. It will make you sleep for the journey," she explained.

Halana nodded and Aquilia gave Zeke and Eliontara the all clear sign.

"And launching in 5, 4, 3, 2, and 1," Eliontara announced before pressing the launch button. "Stay safe Mum."

Chapter Thirty – Three

Saturn

"And that's definite?" Eva asked the doctors.

They nodded.

Lyra sat in the corner of the room, he head in her hands. Eva walked to her and looked down at her.

"You knew this could happen, didn't you?" She asked.

Lyra shook her head. "We thought it was extinct."

"Clearly it isn't. Mum what if I've got it," Janus whispered.

Lyra looked at him and shook her head again. "It only runs through the female bloodline."

"So you have it?" Janus asked.

"I have the Eagle part," Lyra confirmed.

"And Benzyline?" Eva asked.

"She has the Serpent part," Lyra answered.

As Eva walked to the window, she looked back at her phone, worried that her mother hadn't replied to her last message.

"Are you OK?" Janus asked, placing his hands gently on her shoulders.

"I wish mum would reply," Eva whispered. "I've not heard from her since I told her."

"I'm sure she is just busy or trying to process it all," Janus replied.

"I hope you're right," Eva said, she turned into his arms and took the embrace he offered.

"What's that?" He asked, looking out of the window. "Are we expecting anyone?"

"Not that I know of," Eva replied, turning to look out of the window.

The landing craft made its way towards the far side of the Palace. Eva took off towards the landing pad in search of answers, but as she arrived she was greeted by Halana and Aquilia.

"I had to bring her, she just wasn't saying anything. I think she needed to be here," Aquilia explained to a confused looking Evadene.

"Mum?" Eva whispered. She could see her mother was still a little shaken, she just couldn't tell if it was from the flight or the news. "Shall we go inside?"

Halana nodded and took hold of Eva's outstretched hand as Janus stepped around them and kissed Aquilia's cheek.

"Thank you for bringing her. Eva has been going out of her mind," Janus told her as they watched Eva and her mother walk into the Palace.

"What prompted you to call the doctors? Aquilia asked as they followed along behind.

"Ammyn was complaining that her tummy felt funny, like something was in there. Eva took a quick look and saw something circling just under the skin. The Wraith Doctors have said that it doesn't look like it will attempt to break free anytime soon but we have to keep a close eye on her," Janus explained. "Then Mum mentioned that it was supposed to be extinct, or so they thought. Benzyline has the Serpent side, Mum has the Eagle side."

Aquilia shook her head, "I can't believe they didn't even mention it, whether it is extinct or not, there is always the risk."

"I know. Eva has already gone into a rage with Lyra," Janus told her.

"It seems we think alike. I flew into one with Benzyline," Aquilia confessed.

Janus laughed. "Like two jewels in a crown you two!"

Aquilia and Janus continued to walk into the Palace when a wave of children came running from all rooms of the house.

"Nana! Auntie Quilia!" Came the shouts.

"Whoa! Hey you lot!" Aquilia laughed. "Why don't we head outside and give Mummy and Nana some time? Last one out is a human!"

The children ran from the Palace and out into the gardens before Aquilia could start. She looked at Janus and shrugged, "I guess I'm the human!"

He laughed at her and ran off in front of her, almost tripping over Xandr in the process.

"Are you OK Xandr?" Aquilia asked as she bent down to his level.

He shrugged his shoulders. "Is Mitzi home?"

"Yes she is, why do you ask?" Aquilia said as she sat on the floor.

"Nana Lyra said she was but I wasn't sure," Xandr replied.

"Would you like to speak with her?" Aquilia asked.

Xandr nodded so hard Aquilia worried his head might roll off.

"OK, let's give Mitzi a bell," Aquilia smiled.

Xandr climbed up onto her lap, eager to see Mitzi on the screen. The phone rang for a few seconds before Mitzi answered her white hair and blue eyes filling the screen.

"Your Majesty. Is there something I can help you with?" Mitzi asked.

"Xandr here just wanted to check that you were definitely home," Aquilia told her. "He wants to speak with you."

"Hi Mitzi! Are you OK?" Xandr asked.

"Hey, I'm good. How are you?" She replied.

"I'm better now. I was worried and I'm sorry," Xandr said, hanging his head down.

"Now what do you have to be sorry for?" Mitzi asked.

"Well I saw the man who took you and I didn't do anything. I should have screamed or something, I'm so sorry," Xandr said, tears rolling down his face.

"Xandr, look at me," Mitzi said.

Xandr looked up at the screen to see Mitzi with a wide smile.

"I don't blame you. I don't think I would have been able to scream either if I saw what you did," Mitzi told him. "So there is nothing to be sorry for."

"Thank you. Will you come and visit us soon?" He asked.

"I will," Mitzi replied.

Xandr waved and ran into the garden with his father and siblings.

"Your Highness, is Xandr going to be OK?" Mitzi asked.

"He will be now. Thank you Mitzi," Aquilia replied. "I will be in contact soon."

Mitzi nodded and the connection clicked off. Aquilia got up from the floor and went off to find everyone in the garden. The children were climbing all over Janus while he just lay on the floor laughing so much he couldn't even get up. Aquilia was reminded of the times she would play with Plexys and Paxy on the same floor when she was a child. It seemed so long ago now.

"Hey," Eva said as she nudged her in the side. "What's going on up there?" pointing to Aquilia's head.

"Just memories of a time long ago," Aquilia laughed.

"Hmm, memories of being a child?" Eva asked.

"Yeah. I guess my childhood wasn't as amazing as I would have thought," Aquilia replied. "So, how are you?"

"Honestly, I don't know. Ammyn hasn't let it change how she is, why should I let it change me?" Eva asked.

Aquilia looked at how Ammyn played with her siblings and how, whatever harboured beneath her exterior, didn't allow her to stop being a child. "Maybe, in time, she will learn to control it. Like I do with The Phoenix."

"Well, we all know you can't always control that," Eva smiled. "But, you try."

"I do control it!" Aquilia grinned.

Eva nodded and laughed whilst they walked towards where Halana sat at the garden table. She watched her grandchildren with the deepest love any Grandmother could have, as they climbed and swung, slid and rolled over. Tears escaped her eyes as she smiled.

"Mum, are you OK?" Eva asked, gently touching her shoulder.

"Hmm? Oh yes dear. I just love to watch them play. I wish I could clear some time to stay a while. Just to be near them," Halana replied.

"Time off can be arranged. How are you on the dresses for the upcoming banquet?" Aquilia asked.

"Oh they were finished last week. A few alterations hat would take me no more than a few hours, and they would be complete," Halana replied.

"And the children's schooling?" Aquilia said.

"They are done for the year. Nothing more for another three months," Halana answered.

"Then it's settled. Halana, you will stay with Eva, Janus and the children here on Saturn, at least for the next two months. Lyra will come back to Enceladus with me whilst you all enjoy your time together," Aquilia stated.

Halana didn't have the words to express her gratitude; she simply let the tears fall from her eyes. Aquilia smiled at her and went off to find Lyra.

<u>Somewhere Just Outside Of The Milky Way</u>

Fresion looked out towards The Milky Way as it came into view. "Ah, a place I never thought I would see again."

"Sir?" His captain questioned.

"I used to live. Not so long ago but it feels like millennia since I was here last," Fresion replied.

As the army neared the outskirts of Pluto, a vast icy blast of air made its way through the vent of his ship, cooling the air temperature rapidly.

"Quick, fire up the heaters! We don't want the electronics to freeze. Pluto air is easier in sub temperatures, you wouldn't want to be caught out there," Fresion called out to his ship hands.

Every member of his crew dashed around turning heaters up and placing ice blockers around the windows. Fresion continued to look out over the Galaxy as they neared Neptune and skimmed past its hidden rings. The blue planet looked amazing from above, but Fresion knew exactly what that planet harboured. The Neptunites were not the types of beings you made dodgy deals with. They were tough and menacing.

As they travelled towards Uranus, Fresion allowed himself to admire its stillness. The Uranese beings were quiet in their ways. Hardly ever heard from, or seen, unless something major happened in the Galaxy. Its rings made of the finest space dust, polar circled the planet. Fresion had always been amazed by its difference.

"Let's slow the boosters a little. We're not in a rush," he told his crew.

They shut the boosters down to minimum and admired the Galaxy before them.

Saturn

Lyra and Aquilia settled themselves in for the flight back to Enceladus. It hadn't taken much persuasion for Lyra to come with her. They bid goodbye to Eva, Janus, the children, and Halana and closed the hatch. Within seconds the pod had risen to a reasonable height.

"Everything always looks so different from up here," Lyra said as she looked out of the windows.

"It never seems any different to me," Aquilia replied. "Maybe I should travel more."

Lyra nodded and laughed. "Maybe. You do spend too much time on Enceladus. There are so many places you could visit. Is there anywhere you wish you could go?"

Aquilia thought for a second, "Earth? Bella and Layson visited once and she brought these seeds back with her. Lavender I think. They smelt amazing."

"You should go. Take the children. I'm sure they would love to be able to travel too," Lyra told her.

"I wish that could happen, but, unfortunately, it will be a while before that trip gets off the ground," Aquilia told her. "Eliontara is now my head ground technician and, whilst Balzar is on paternal leave, Scarlex is in charge of Onyx Abyss Alpha."

Lyra looked surprised. "Do you think she is capable?"

"Oh I have no doubt she is. If there was any doubt whatsoever, I wouldn't have asked her," Aquilia said. She turned to look towards Enceladus just as a radio message came in.

"Your Highness, Fresion has arrived in The Milky Way. Be safe travelling back," Eliontara called.

"We are on final approach now," Aquilia replied.

Just as she had finished her transmission, the pod rocked with a force unknown to her before.

"Zeke, what was that?" Aquilia called.

"Checking now Your Majesty," Zeke replied.

"You don't think.." Before Lyra could finish her sentence, another jolt rocked the pod, this time sending it into a spinning frenzy.

"Zeke, I need answers. We're spinning out of control," Aquilia radioed.

"Your Highness. It seems Fresion has found you; I will try to take control of your pod from here and bring you in for a safe landing. Our soldiers are gearing up as we speak," Zeke replied.

"Then get with them, I need you on that ship with Scarlex. Eliontara can guide us in," Aquilia ordered.

"Yes Ma'am," Zeke responded.

"How is this going to work?" Lyra asked.

"Sinclair devised a system that can control spacecraft from Enceladus. He has all the ships in our fleet connected to it. Eliontara should be able to control us from there and guide us down safely," Aquilia explained.

Lyra strapped herself in and prepared for any further hits from Fresion's army.

Enceladus

"Eliontara, you need to utilise the system I showed you earlier. Connect to your Mother's ship and guide it into the far landing pads. I have to go, but I trust you," Zeke told him.

Eliontara nodded fiercely and pulled up the guidance system, connected to Aquilia's ship and took control. By the time he turned to confirm with Zeke, he had gone and Onyx Abyss Alpha was taking off towards the sky. He centred himself and began guiding the ship in slowly. Above him, he could hear explosions and fast moving ships whizzing past. He closed his eyes and focused on his task. Little by little he managed to guide the ship to its landing spot.

Aquilia and Lyra emerged from the pod unharmed and rushed towards the Palace. Aquilia made her way to the Comms Room while Lyra found Chylla asking what she could do to help.

"Elion, you did so well, now I need you to focus on what's happening out there and keep everyone informed of Fresion's army's movements," Aquilia told him.

"You got it," Eliontara replied, placing an ear bud in his ear and testing the frequency. Once everyone had confirmed they could hear him, his real job began; keeping everyone up there safe.

Lyra had joined the ground troops in fending off the approaching army. She had learnt to fight with a staff and was happily swinging it high above her head, slowly picking off soldiers, one by one with Chylla showing her acrobatic skills with her red-feathered spear.

"Nymeria, six o'clock," Eliontara shouted over the radio. "Onyx, twelve o'clock."

"Got it," they both shouted.

Eliontara watched as the swooped and swerved their way out of danger, dodging lasers and flames along the way.

"Mathias, behind you," Eliontara called. He watched as Mathias's ship ducked and dived away from the chasing ship. Swaying left and right to dodge its penetrating lasers.

With so much going on in front of him, he didn't notice that his mother had left the room. He continued to shout advance warnings to anyone he saw in danger.

Aquilia watched from the sidelines as her army battled an angry Fresion. Of what he was angry about, she was unsure, but she knew he wouldn't stop until he had his revenge. She contemplated bringing The Phoenix into play, but feared it would do more harm than good. She allowed her army to pick off as many as it could before she decided for certain.

"There's too many of them Zeke," Scarlex called form the controls of the ship.

"We can do it, don't worry," Mitzi told her. She had regained her full energy balance and was ready for war. She grabbed the weapons system and switched them to defence mode. This allowed her to move freely between each attack weapon without worrying about being shot at.

Onyx Abyss Alpha had been fitted with the highest defence mechanism Sinclair could create. Along with added technology from Layson, it was almost indestructible. Mitzi had worked the weapons systems since the day she arrived on board; she had never missed a target.

"Zeke, I need info," she called.

"Seven o'clock, slightly off to the left," he shouted. "Ready, FIRE!"

Mitzi fired off a shot that knocked the chasing ship off course be nearly half a mile.

"BULLSEYE!" Mitzi shouted.

"Twelve o'clock," Zeke called out.

"Got it," Mitzi replied. She fired off two shots which both hit their intended targets, one after the other, sending both ships falling from the sky in balls of flames, landing far away from the Kingdom.

"Zeke!" Scarlex called from the front of the ship, "where did they all come from?"

Zeke looked towards the front of the ship to see around twenty or more smaller ships all aiming their lasers towards

Onyx Abyss Alpha. "They are a lot smaller, so they should be easier to take out. Mitzi, straight ahead."

Mitzi turned her turrets towards the front of the ship and change the weapon to a flamethrower. She fired and swayed the turret from left to right, taking each ship down as she went.

"I hate to be the bearer of bad news but..." Scarlex pointed towards the side of the ship.

"Oh shooting laser, where are they all coming from?" Mitzi gasped.

"It seems that with each ship you destroy, the mother ship releases smaller ones," Eliontara said over the radio.

"Thanks Elion," Zeke replied. "OK, we need to take out the mother ship. It's the only way we can avoid having more of the smaller pests getting in the way."

"How are we going to do that?" Scarlex asked. "The ship is running low on power as it is."

"Then we need to source some power from somewhere," Zeke said. He looked around at what he could easily switch off to harvest power but everything they had powered up was needed. "This is going to be harder than I thought."

"I've got an idea," Mitzi said as she scrambled up Zeke's leg. "Mathias, are you there?"

"Right here Mitz, what's up?" Mathias replied.

"We need power. You still carry that harvester?" She asked.

'Harvester?' Zeke thought.

"Like I would go anywhere without it. What do you need?" Mathias laughed.

"Steal as much power from the enemy ships as you can, then we'll hook you up and take what we need," Mitzi replied.

"You go it," Mathias replied. "See you in a while!"

"Hey Mathias," Mitzi shouted. "Don't be too long!"

Mathias could only laugh as he flew his ship in the centre of the battle, dodging falling ships as he went.

"You think he can do it?" Scarlex asked.

"I know he can, we just have to be patient," Mitzi replied.

"Nymeria, give us some cover. Power is low, we're waiting for backup," Zeke called.

"I'm off to your left. Where are you going to get power from? You have to land and recharge," Nymeria replied.

"Mitzi had an idea and I'm rolling with it," he shrugged.

"OK, well, if it works, do you think we could get some too?" Celest asked.

"Sure things gals," Mathias replied. "Ante up Mitzi!"

Mitzi ran to the controls and opened the rear hatch, she scurried towards the waiting sensors and turned then towards the rear. Mathias lined up and beamed the power through to them. Scarlex watched as the bars filled rapidly to max power.

"Thanks Mathias," Scarlex called out.

As Mitzi closed the rear hatch, Mathias made his way to The Stealth Raiders ship and did the same with them.

"Now go easy with it. Don't drink it all at once, it'll go to your head," Mathias laughed as he flew back into battle.

"Let's get back into it," Zeke commanded.

"OK, we need to work out how we are going to take the big ship out," Scarlex said.

"We could use the cloaking technology to sneak up on it," Mitzi suggested.

"I don't know if it will work," Zeke confessed. "The cloaking technology is good, but it will drain the power rapidly and I don't think Mathias can do another power up."

"This isn't helping. These ships are spawning from nowhere. How many more can that ship send out?" Scarlex asked.

They looked out of the windows surrounding the ship; there were more than a hundred now.

"This is going to be difficult," Zeke whispered. "We need something or someone to help."

The crowd of ships surrounded them. All weapons aimed at Onyx Abyss Alpha.

Chapter Thirty – Four

Saturn

"I feel bad sending Lyra back with Aquilia," Halana said as she sat at the kitchen table with Xandr and Codex.

"I'm sure she will be grateful for the break," Eva laughed, "and it's good to have you to ourselves for a while."

Halana smiled. She loved being around her grandchildren. Helping them find their feet and their skill sets. Ammyn was quite the artist with some chalk.

"It will be nice to cook for someone different too," Janus called from the stove. "So what will it be Madam?"

Halana laughed, "oh Janus, you know I would be happy with anything plated up by you."

"I know, but I just wanted to make you something special, you know, you're first night staying over for a while. What do you say kids, what can we cook Nana that she will love?"

"Squish burgers with flat bread with a side of crisp salad from the garden!" Codex announced.

"Well, squish burgers it is!" Halana laughed.

She watched as the other children played in the gardens, running left and right, throwing balls and dancing around, but something caught her eye. Something high above seemed to explode, sending a beam of orange and black back into her eyes.

"Janus, Janus, what's that?" Halana asked. She pointed up towards the sky.

"Eva, get the kids in the safe room and send out the alert. Get the Kingdom into lockdown now," Janus ordered.

Eva rounded up the children and ushered them into their safe room. "Now, you remember what Mummy and Daddy told you?"

"Don't move until you give the all clear," they all replied.

"That's right. Now, you have the radio. I will stay in contact," Eva told them as she closed and locked the door behind her. She leant against the door for a few seconds more before running to alert the Kingdom of a total lockdown.

"Please make your way quickly and safely to the bunkers provided. This is precautionary at the moment until we have further information. Quickly and safely to the bunkers, thank you," she called out over the speaker system.

The people of Astrodia calmly made their way to the nearest bunkers, filing in until each was filled and the Kingdom was empty.

"Everyone is in lockdown. Do we know what is happening yet?" She asked as she returned to the gardens.

"I can't contact anyone there. I'll try Aquilia again," Janus said as he walked away.

"I hope it isn't too serious," Halana said as she bit on her nails. "I couldn't bear it."

Eva grabbed her mother and held her tight. "It'll be OK Mum. You'll see."

"I can't get her, either she doesn't have her phone or..." Janus trailed off.

"Don't say it. She's not," Eva said her face straight and serious. "She wouldn't put herself in harm's way. She has the children to think of."

"You're right. Of course you're right. What was I thinking? She's probably down in the bunker waiting it all out, just like she would have told everyone up there," Janus smiled. Inside he had other thoughts.

"Wait!"Eva cried. "Sinclair made Xandr a telescope. Maybe we can see what's going on through it." She ran off to grab it and brought it back to the gardens.

Janus set the telescope up on one of the garden tables and pointed it into the direction of the latest fireball they had seen.

"It doesn't look good," he said as he pulled away from the eyepiece.

Eva looked through and instantly recognised Onyx Abyss Alpha. "Oh no. Zeke!" She whispered.

"What about Zeke?" Halana asked.

"Onyx Abyss Alpha is there. This isn't something small Janus, we need to get in contact with them," Eva said.

"Who is in the Comms Room?" Janus asked.

"Eliontara," Halana replied. "Zeke has just finished teaching him all about it."

"Then I'll try the old radio, see if it still works," he said. He ran off towards the main living room and into the cupboard when he always put the old things. He found the radio and powered it up, hoping that it would still go through.

"Hello?" He called. "Is there anyone there?"

<u>Enceladus</u>

"They are off to your left Celest, be careful," Eliontara called out."

"I got it," Celest replied. She spun The Stealth Raiders ship around and fired straight into the main window of the attacking ship, rendering it useless.

Eliontara watched the whole thing unfold in front of him on the mass amount of screens. He worried about his sister as she guided Onyx Abyss Alpha through the skies above Enceladus.

"Hello? Is there anyone there?"

Eliontara could hear the voice, but had no idea where it was coming from. He searched around the small space, finally laying his hands on what looked like a really old piece of space junk. He almost dropped it when a voice boomed through it again.

"Eliontara? Are you there?"

Elion held down the button on the side before replying; "Yes."

"Elion, its Janus! What is going on up there? I've been trying to reach you mother," Janus asked.

"Well, where do I start?" Eliontara asked.

"Start at the beginning," Janus replied. "And make it quick. Halana is getting agitated."

"Are you not in the bunkers?" Eliontara asked frantically. "Nymeria, five o'clock."

"No, the people of Astrodia are and so are the children, but Eva, Halana and myself are watching everything from down here," Janus explained.

"I will have to be quick. I'm everyone eyes here. Fresion attacked Mum's ship before she had a chance to land. I had to guide her and Lyra down. Zeke has gone up with Onyx Abyss Alpha and Scarlex is in charge," Eliontara rambled. "I'm scared Janus. I can't get hold of Mum."

"OK Eliontara, you are doing so well. Keep everyone informed of everything. I'll stay on this line and keep you company," Janus tried to comfort him. "Try calling your Mum again."

"OK," Eliontara went quite whilst he tried to call Aquilia. Again there was no answer. "Nothing. I don't know where she is."

"Try not to panic. Could she have gone into the bunkers?" Janus asked.

"I doubt it. Lyra is out there fighting," Eliontara told him.

"My mother is fighting?" Janus asked almost dumbstruck.

"I'm afraid so. She's pretty good with a staff!" Eliontara told him.

"Who would have thought?" Janus laughed. "OK, Elion, I'm going to go back out to the gardens and look through the telescope again. I'll be quiet for a while."

"You got it. I need to check on our troops," Elion replied.

Eliontara looked back over the screens to see where everyone was. He noted the Nymeria and Celest were out of harm's way for now, but Onyx Abyss Alpha was heading straight for the main ship.

"Scarlex, what are you doing?" Eliontara called.

"We have to take it out," she replied. "Every time we take out one of the bigger ships, this one spawns smaller ones. There's too many."

"You can't! It will be catastrophic," Eliontara told her.

"I know, but we have to. I've tried calling Mother but she isn't answering. Where is she?" Scarlex asked.

"I don't know. I've tried her and so had Janus. She isn't answering anyone," Eliontara told her.

"Look, unless you can think of another way to do this, then we have to get on to it," Scarlex said. "I will stay in contact as long as I can."

"Scar..." Eliontara began, but before he could finish what he was saying, the main ship seemed to spawn some sort of long robotic arms from its underbelly, grabbing hold of Onyx Abyss Alpha.

Aquilia looked up when she heard a rapid amount of lasers going off. She could see that Onyx in the hands of something robotic.

"No," she whispered. Seeing her daughter in the hands of Fresion made her mind up for her. She ran, full speed towards the end of the landing pad, launching herself into the unknown, transforming herself in The Phoenix.

She swooped and dived, dodging lasers and flames as she went, directing herself towards the main ship of the Fresion's fleet. She stretched her talons wide, grabbing the ship in one foot and flying high above Enceladus. She lifted the ship until she was within eye level with the main window.

"Drop them immediately," she commanded.

"Under who's orders?" Fresion asked.

"By order of Queen Aquilia," she replied, allowing her eyes to flash from their ruby red colour back to their original electric blue.

"Well, isn't this a turn around?" Fresion grinned, a sly grin that reminded her of Altair.

"Let. Them. Go," she said again, this time allowing her eyes to show their flame form.

"As you wish," Fresion laughed, signalling to his crew members to let the ship go.

The robotic arms dropped Onyx Abyss Alpha into a freefall.

"I guess it's you against me?" Fresion laughed. He took over the controls of the robotic arms and grabbed The Phoenix by the neck.

Eliontara watched from the Comms Room, unable to do anything for his mother. "Janus, Janus!" He called.

"I'm here. What is it?" Janus answered.

"It's Mum. She's transformed. Look," Eliontara told him.

Janus ran to the telescope, looking up just in time to see Fresion's ship throw Aquilia across the sky.

"Get everyone back to safety Eliontara, get them out of there!" Janus told him.

Eliontara did as he was told and made sure every ship landed safely and that everyone made it to the bunkers for safety. He then went back to his seat and hoped his mother would fight back with everything she had.

Scarlex tried her hardest to restart the engines but nothing would work. She frantically pressed a combination of buttons, hoping something would trigger the starter.

"I can't start it," she cried. "We're going to crash. I'll have to glide it away from the city."

"Oh I wish I'd watched Balzar more," Mitzi said, holding her head in her hands.

Zeke searched up the manual via the onboard systems, scouring the pages until he found the failsafe.

"Look, all we need to do is, press this," he said as he pressed a yellow button, "turn this three times," he said turning a sliver dial, "and then press this," he finished, pressing the ignition. Onyx Abyss Alpha sprung to life.

"Thanks Zeke," Scarlex smiled. "I guess I'd be stuck without you."

"Or dead. We'd probably be dead," Mitzi shrugged.

Zeke smiled. "It was just patience. Now, we need to help The Queen.

"No, you need to land and get into the bunkers," Eliontara's voice came over the radio.

"Not going to happen bro. We need to help Mum," Scarlex replied. "I'll see you soon." And with that she switched all contact with the outside off.

"Scarlex...Scarlex please don't," Eliontara called, but it was no use. He took his headset off and sunk into his seat. It was only when the Comms door opened he realised that Scarlex really meant business.

"She switched it all off," Chylla told him.

"I know. She said she is going to help Mum. I can't lose them both," Eliontara allowed one solitary tear to fall from his eye.

"You won't lose any of them. Your Mother is one of the greatest warriors to ever grace the land of Enceladus, I should know, I know the assassin who trained her. Scarlex won't be alone in anything she does. Zeke won't let her put herself in danger. Let's just see how things go," Chylla told him.

Eliontara turned back towards the screens and watched with hope that his family would be OK.

Chapter Thirty – Five

Saturn

"I can't sit here and watch this, I have to get back. The children will be going out of their minds," Halana said as she began bustling around trying to find a way to get back to Enceladus.

"Mum you can't go back there. All travel is suspended until they give the all clear. I'd feel better if I knew you were safe here," Eva said, hugging her Mum tight. "I know you care about them a lot."

"Oh Eva, what if something happens to them?" Halana cried.

"Then we will deal with it then. Until such time, let's just stay positive," Eva said.

They sat in the gardens for a while watching the drama unfold above them, each taking it in turns to use the telescope to get a better view. A sudden explosion from above shocked them all. The fireball so big, it rivalled the shine from the sun.

"That didn't look good," Eva whispered to Janus.

"I'll see what I can find out," he replied, grabbing the old radio and heading inside.

"Elion, what was that?" he called.

"It was one of the other ships in Fresion's fleet. It collided with one of our obsolete satellites," Eliontara replied. "I don't know how much more of this I can watch."

"Are you alone?" Janus asked.

"No. Chylla is here too," he replied.

"Put her on," Janus told him.

Chylla came on the radio within seconds. "I don't know much more than Eliontara. We were fighting with the ground troops when Aquilia transformed."

“How is my Mother?” Janus asked.

“A bit bruised but she is alive. She is getting checked over by the medics, she isn’t severely injured, like I said, just bruises,” Chylla replied.

“I’m worried about Eliontara. He feels helpless in this battle,” Janus told her.

“He is in a depressed state. I am trying to bring his hopes up, but he doesn’t seem to share my enthusiasm of his Mother’s strength,” Chylla told him. “This worries me a lot.”

Janus thought for a moment. Eliontara had always been very sensitive when it came to his Mother and sister. “He is growing into a protective man. Who are we to stop that?”

“You could be right. We will stay in contact. Please stay safe,” Chylla signed off.

Janus headed back to Eva and Halana and informed them of the extra news. He refrained from mentioning how Eliontara was. For now.

Enceladus

“So what’s our plan?” Mitzi asked as she sat on Zeke’s shoulder.

"I don't know yet," Scarlex replied. She had placed the ship far enough away that Fresion couldn't spot them, but close enough to see what was happening.

"I think we should just wait it out a little. I know Queen Aquilia can fight. I've seen it," Zeke told them both. "Right now, we would probably do more harm than good."

Scarlex hung her head. She knew she had to help but she didn't know how. Everyone had told her about how well she defended herself against Altair.

"Do you think she will be OK?" Mitzi whispered.

"She has to be. She's the captain," Zeke replied.

"You didn't think it would be as easy as killing Altair, did you?" Fresion laughed. "Altair was weak."

"Weak? How does *this* make *you* any better? Coming to another's world and wrecking havoc upon it inhabitants," Aquilia roared.

"I only sought out you. The fact your army interfered, well, that's a *you* problem," Fresion grinned. "Now, shall we do this the hard way or the easy way?"

"The easy way being that you take your fleet and leave unharmed?" Aquilia asked.

"Oh no my dear. The easy way being that you give up and accompany me back to Plydar and be punished was causing me to lose so much, well deserved, money," Fresion screamed. "Before you took out Altair all those years ago, I was lined up for a very comfortable windfall."

"Well, I was unaware." Aquilia replied. "I'm not sure if you know, but I grew up on Enceladus. I knew nothing about my Uncle's tactics."

Fresion shook his head. "I don't think you are being completely honest now, are you?"

"Fresion, we aren't all as gullible as you. My Uncle had an army out for mine and my Mother's blood. Do you really think I would even *care* what my Uncle got up to?" Aquilia asked. "At that young age, I just wanted him to leave my Mother alone."

Her words hit harder than she thought they would as Fresion swung one of the huge robotic arms and backhanded her across the sky. She used her left wing to ease the pain in her neck.

"If you think that you can use all the emotions to make me feel sorry for you, then you are sorely mistaken. Altair told me that you are an exact replica of your Mother. Vindictive and cunning. Quintara used her charm to win over Elio and claim the throne as her own, and she did exactly that when Elio died. She had no right to take over the throne," Fresion said. "Altair should have been next in line."

Aquilia rolled her red eyes, allowing a little of the flames to escape, "Did Altair tell you that?"

"Absolutely," Fresion replied.

"And you believe him?" Aquilia asked.

"I had no reason not to. He was the second son. The throne was supposed to be his," Fresion explained. "As a Queen, I would have thought you would know the line of succession by now."

"He really duped you, didn't he? Altair was removed from the line of succession for marrying a commoner," Aquilia laughed. "And to think, you believed every single word that came out of his mouth. Maybe it was for the greater good that I killed him."

Fresion's skin changed from green to violet the angrier he got. He took controls of the robotic arms and plucked Aquilia's phoenix form from the sky. He held her with one hand as he slowly plucked a few of her golden feathers from her wings. "You won't need these where you're going."

Aquilia writhed in pain, but Fresion found this amusing. He plucked another and then another, laughing whilst she screamed. Something within her stirred, an anger building up inside. She closed her eyes and let the feeling take over her body. Her eyes turned black and her feathers became engulfed in flames causing Fresion to let go of her.

"What is this?" He asked, a look of fright covering his face.

Aquilia couldn't answer him. She didn't know herself. She flapped her wings and glided back away from the reach of the robotic arms. She raised her head and looked down on him.

"What's happening?" Eliontara asked Chylla. He had turned his head from the screens when Fresion had begun to pluck his Mother's feathers from her wings.

"I really don't know how to explain it," Chylla replied. "Your Mother's form has changed again."

"What?" He asked, spinning in his chair and staring at the screen. His eyes were wide as he stared at the new form glowing in the sky.

"What has he done to her?" Eliontara screamed. "He's pulled at her feathers!"

"Your Mother can regenerate her feathers, but I won't lie and say it didn't hurt her," Chylla told him.

"Zeke, what are you lot doing?" Eliontara called over the radio, completely forgetting that he had switched off all contact. Eliontara held his head in his hands and sobbed. "He's going to kill her!"

"I don't think anyone could kill your Mother, believe me, plenty have tried," Chylla said she she rested her hand gently on his shoulder. "We have to believe that she will OK."

"I don't know if I can," he whispered. He looked back at the screen just in time to see Fresion reach back out to Aquilia but she had backed too far away from him.

Fresion grabbed at her, narrowly missing her flapping wings. "Stupid bird," he seethed. He moved the controls of his ship forward just enough to be able to grab her again. "The change in form may have startled me a little, but I will finish what I came here to do."

Aquilia flapped her wings faster, trying her hardest to free herself from his grip but it was no use, the harder she flapped, the tighter he gripped.

"It's no use; you might as well give up. No one is going to rescue you. Your entire fleet has retreated back to their hidey holes. You're all alone," he laughed.

Aquilia looked around nervously, realizing he was right. Everyone had left her. She was alone. She looked back at him and tried to arch her neck towards the arms that held her tight, but she couldn't reach, they were just out of reach.

"Poor Queen Aquilia," he spat. "You don't deserve that title."

As he finished his sentence he her her up and brought one of the arms crashing down onto her head, shocking her into paralysis. Her eyes rolled back into her head and her breathing became laboured. She struggled to open her eyes, focusing hard on the window of Fresion's ship. She summoned an unknown power from somewhere deep within her and snapped at the robotic arm as it came crashing down once more, just missing the main electrical wires which controlled it. She snapped again and again, each time taking a little more out of it.

Fresion screamed and used the controls to grab her with both arms. He held her up in front of the main window of the ship and stared at her. "You give me no choice. I wanted to torture you and laugh at your pain, but now, now it's just taking too much time!" He aimed his laser at her, pulled back the power controls and watched at the meter powered up. He smiled as it finally made it to eighty percent, grinning as it hit one hundred. He double checked that the aim was correct and fired.

Just as the laser erupted from the gun, Onyx Abyss Alpha flew up in between the laser and Aquilia, causing it to miss its intended target.

"Did we do it?" Mitzi asked, her head buried in Zeke's shoulder.

"I don't know. We have to fly back around and check," Scarlex replied. She guided the ship into a dive and aimed back towards Fresion's ship. "Oh no, he didn't let go."

"We try again," Zeke called out. He watched his screens for any attacks from Fresion's fleet. Finding nothing, he told Scarlex to go for it.

She powered up the ship and aimed the nose directly for the side of the ship, making contact just as Fresion shot off another laser beam at Aquilia. His ship rocked from side to side but he still held onto Aquilia.

"What is going on?" Fresion called out to his crew. "I thought that fleet went into hiding?"

"It seems this one didn't Sir," his captain replied.

"Then get rid of it!" Fresion shouted.

"We can't Sir. Our entire additional fleet has been wiped out. It's just us Sir," he replied.

Fresion shook his head. He looked back towards Aquilia, noticing how he had managed to hit the side of her head. He grinned as feathers floated to the ground and Aquilia's head lay lopsided and unmoving. From deep within, he could feel laughter building up. It made its way to his mouth and he laughed like he had never laughed before. Using the controls, he dropped Aquilia's phoenix form from the sky and watched as it fell to Enceladus landing with a bone shattering crunch.

"Mum," Scarlex screamed. She jumped from her seat, leaving Onyx Abyss Alpha without a controller, and ran to the back window, watching as her Mother fell to the ground. She slumped to the floor of the ship, sobbing and punching the floor.

Zeke climbed into the front seat of the ship and guided it away from Fresion whilst he worked out what to do next.

Mitzi looked between them both and decided to go and check on Scarlex. Zeke looked out towards Fresion. He knew he had to do something to avenge his Queen. After everything she had given him these past few years, he couldn't let her death be in vain. He looked back at Scarlex who was still sobbing and made his decision. He turned the ship away from Fresion and headed back to the Palace.

"Why have we come back here?" Mitzi asked.

"Scarlex needs her brother. Take her to him please," Zeke told her.

"But Zeke..." Mitzi began.

"Please Mitzi. I'll wait here," Zeke replied.

Mitzi scurried towards him and nuzzled his nose with hers. "Wait for me," she whispered.

Zeke nodded and she ran off, gently pushing Scarlex's legs to usher her off the ship.

As the back of the ship opened up, Mitzi continued to coax Scarlex off the ship and into the Palace to find Eliontara. As she entered the main doors from the landing pad, she heard the engines roar to life and just as she turned, Zeke took off into the sky.

"ZEKE!" Mitzi cried. "ZEKE WAIT!"

"What? Where is he going?" Chylla called from behind her, she had her hands wrapped around Scarlex's shoulders.

"I don't know. He said he would wait for me," Mitzi said with tears in her eyes.

"Come. Let's see if he switches his comms back on," Chylla smiled. "Come one."

Mitzi, reluctantly, followed her back into the Palace and on to the Comms Room. She looked at the array of screens in front of her, amazed by how much they could really see in here.

"Eliontara, I think you should go with your sister. Go and find Layson and Bella and meet me in the main meeting room in an hour," Chylla told him.

He nodded and took Scarlex away from the room and off to find the others. She was still sobbing.

"He killed her Elion. I won't let him get away with it," she said.

"I know sis. We'll get him. Both of us," Elion promised her.

They searched for Layson, finding him with Bella in the outhouse.

"Chylla said to meet her in the meeting room in an hour," Elion told them with tears in his eyes.

"What's happened?" Bella said, instantly bringing them both in close.

"He killed Mother," Scarlex cried out. "Fresion killed our Mother!"

"What?" Layson asked.

"Mother is dead. Fresion shot her with a laser and then dropped her from the sky like she meant nothing," Eliontara explained.

Bella looked at Scarlex. She could see something deep inside her that she hadn't noticed before. "Why don't we take a walk Scar? Leave the boys to talk?"

Scarlex allowed herself to be guided away by Bella. She had stopped sobbing, replacing it with hate and anger.

Chapter Thirty – Six

Saturn

Janus continued to look through the telescope, but everything seemed to have gone quiet. There were no more fireballs, no more explosions. Just silence. He could see that some ships lingered and that some had gone from sight. Fresion's ship remained. He called up to Chylla.

"Janus, I can't speak right now," Chylla cut him short.

"I need to know what's happening. Halana is having squids here," he said.

"We have to check on everything before we give any information. I will let you know as soon as I know what's happened," Chylla told him. She wasn't polite with her words.

Janus turned back to Evadene with a blank expression. "I don't know what's happening and Chylla won't tell me."

"She's hiding something. Chylla is never that short with anyone," Halana whispered. "You don't think...Aquilia?"

"I told you not to think like that Mum. You know Aquilia wouldn't put herself in danger like that," Eva said. "We have to find a way to communicate with someone else up there."

"Layson!" Janus cried out. "I have a direct line to him."

He walked away from his wife and mother-in-law and made the call. It rang almost seven times before Layson answered.

"Hello?" Layson said.

"Layson, it's Janus. What is going on up there? Chylla won't tell me anything and Halana is going out of her mind," Janus explained.

"I think Eliontara should explain everything. Is Halana with you?" Layson asked.

"I can go to her. Just give me a second," Janus replied.

"Are you sure about this Eliontara? We haven't even had confirmation," Janus could hear Layson asking.

Eliontara must have nodded because Layson replied with, "I'll be just outside."

Janus put the call on speakerphone and allowed Halana to speak.

"Elion, what's happened?" Halana whispered.

"He killed Mother," Eliontara told them. "We watched on the screens. He shot her in the head and dropped her from the sky. Scar was right in front of him."

Halana fell to the floor. Huge sobs rising from her chest.

"Elion, are you sure?" Eva asked.

"There hasn't been a confirmed body yet, but I'm guessing it will only be a matter of time," Eliontara replied. "Scarlex is with Miss Bella."

"Wait, Scarlex is there?" Eva asked.

"Yes. Zeke brought her back," Eliontara replied.

"Where is Zeke now?" Eva asked as she looked through the telescope still sitting on the garden table.

"I would guess he would be with Mitzi and Chylla," Eliontara replied. "Why?"

"No reason. I will be there as soon as the all clear is given to travel. I love you," Eva said.

"Love you too Auntie Eva," Eliontara replied as he cut the connection.

"Eva, what's up?" Janus asked tentatively. He always knew when she wasn't telling the full truth.

"Zeke's gone back up there," she replied, gesturing to the telescope. "See for yourself."

Janus looked through the eyepiece just in time to see the trails from Onyx Abyss Alpha as it travelled from Enceladus into the skies above. He watched as the ship circled the remaining pod of Fresion's fleet more than five times before coming to a stop in front of the largest of the ships. Even from his viewpoint on Saturn, Janus could see that Fresion's ship outsized Onyx Abyss Alpha by more than three times.

"What is he doing?" Janus whispered. He turned to find that Eva had taken her mother inside to lie down. He looked back through the scope, settling himself on the one of the nearby benches. "Come on Zeke. Don't do anything stupid."

<u>Enceladus</u>

"I thought you went back to safety?" Fresion laughed. "Your ship is *nothing* compared to my fleet. You are alone."

"I don't need any help with what I'm going to do. You killed our Queen. We will take revenge," Zeke told him.

"I don't think you understand what you're up against," Fresion said. "Show yourself."

Onyx Abyss Alpha had been fitted with a two way window. As Zeke set the window to 'clear', Fresion grinned from ear to ear.

"So I'm up against a boy. A mere child thinks he has what it takes to seek revenge for Queen who couldn't even kill me herself," he laughed.

Zeke narrowed his eyes at him, a flicker of flames at the centre caught Fresion off guard. He changed the glass of the window so Fresion couldn't see in, but Zeke could see out.

"Bring all we have to the front. Cover me so I can leave," Fresion ordered his fleet.

Ships of all sizes began moving from their holding places in an attempt to distract Zeke from his own vendetta against Fresion. He watched as each took up a different position, putting distance between him and Fresion. He noted all the positions and entered all into the missile control panel. Each of the twelve missiles onboard could be programmed individually. He sprang from one control panel to the other, selecting different sequences and re-routing controls to the main control yoke. Doing this enabled him to be front and centre and not have to worry about missing the big finale.

One of Fresion's fleet made a move to Zeke's left, but made no attempt to attack. Zeke flicked multiple switches and, accidentally, switched his comms back on.

"Zeke. Can you hear me?" Janus's voice came over the radio.

He tried to ignore it but Janus was persistent in his calls.

"Yes, I can hear you," Zeke finally caved and replied.

"What's your plan?" He asked.

"I...I don't know. He killed Aquilia. By oath I have to seek revenge for our Queen's murder," Zeke rambled on. "The oath was to protect the Kingdom should anything happen to the Queen and that's what I'm doing."

"Alone?" Janus asked.

"Yes," Zeke squeaked.

"Why not with your crew?" Janus said.

"I...I can't let them get hurt," Zeke replied.

"But, didn't they take that same oath? Don't they get to choose their own destiny?" Janus said.

Zeke stared at Fresion's ship. He hadn't thought this through but he knew he had to do something.

"Zeke?" Mitzi's voice broke through his thoughts. *"I'm not on comms so don't speak, just listen. I know why you went back, I understand, but why didn't you wait for me?"*

"I can't let you get hurt. You are too special," he thought.

"But I want to help. I can heal," Mitzi said. *"I should be there with you."*

"I don't want you to be here. I need you to stay safe," he thought.

"What if I don't want to be safe? What if I want to be with you on that ship, fighting against the being that killed our Queen?" Mitzi asked.

"I don't want you to die Mitzi," he thought. *"I love you."*

Mitzi opened her eyes. Tears had begun to fall.

"What is it Mitzi?" Chylla asked.

"I need to get up there," Mitzi replied. "How can I get there?"

Chylla had to think fast. How to get Mitzi to Zeke without the risk of her being shot down by Fresion's fleet. "Give me a few minutes."

Chylla ran, as fast as she could to Layson's office. Throwing the door open as she entered, she struggled to catch her breath. "We need the cloaking technology to cover Aquilia's pod."

"Why?" Layson asked.

"Mitzi needs it," Chylla replied. "She needs to get to Zeke."

"ZEKE!" Layson cried out, spinning in his chair and looking out towards the sky. "What is he doing?"

"That's what we are trying to determine. Mitzi has telepathic capabilities, she spoke with him. He says he is standing by the oath he took to seek revenge on his Queen's murder," Chylla told him.

"But Chylla...never mind...I'll set up the tech straight away. Have Mitzi ready in less than two minutes," Layson told her. He left the room and headed down to the launch pads. Opening the hatch to Aquilia's personal pod, he entered the codes for the cloaking tech and readied the pod for launch.

As Mitzi approached, Layson took her in his arms and whispered something in her ear. Her eyes widened with shock. "Are you sure?"

Layson nodded, helped her climb into the pod, "bring him home Mitzi," he said as he closed and locked the pod door.

Mitzi nodded from inside, still in shock about what she had been told.

Giving the all clear, Mitzi was launched to the co-ordinates of Onyx Abyss Alpha. Everyone watched from the Comms Room as she ascended towards Zeke undetected by Fresion. She entered through the under hatch, with the pod returning back to the launch pads.

"Zeke," she whispered. "You can't do this."

"Somebody has to avenge her. Everyone else went into hiding without a second thought," he replied. His eyes focused on Fresion's larger ship.

From his viewpoint, Zeke could see Fresion barking orders and pointing off into various directions whilst his crew ran about aimlessly. He sat at the main controls, arguing with himself over what to do next. He launched one of the missiles, striking the first ship in his way. Within seconds the ship had begun to swarm around Fresion's ship, attempting to protect it against any attacks.

"Zeke! You're putting us in danger!" Mitzi cried. She hurriedly sat the seat next to him, realising, too late, that her seat restraints were on the seat to the other side of him.

"To kill him, I have to pick off these, one by one," he explained.

"But Zeke, even if you kill him, what will that achieve?" Mitzi asked. She tried to pry his attention away from Fresion but he wouldn't look at her.

"If I can take out those two," he said, pointing at the two on either side of Fresion's ship, "I have a better chance of taking Fresion out."

Mitzi looked towards the unsuspecting ships, hovering just in front of Fresion's main window. "Zeke, I need you to listen to me."

He ignored her. Inputting the co-ordinates of the two ships in question, he fired the missiles into them, causing the rest of the fleet to break for cover. Fresion was defenceless. Zeke powered up Onyx to full power and pushed the yoke forward. The ship propelled forward, building speed as it went. Mitzi looked through the front window, her blue eyes widened at the speed they were approaching Fresion's ship.

"Zeke you have to stop. Please," Mitzi pleaded with him.

"FOR QUEEN AQUILIAAAA! I WILL HAVE VENGENCE!" Zeke screamed.

As they sped towards Fresion's ship, Mitzi jumped from her seat into Zeke's lap and pulled the yoke as hard as she could possibly muster to the left.

"She isn't dead Zeke!" She cried out.

<u>Chapter Thirty – Seven</u>

<u>Enceladus</u>

"How long will she be like this?" Scarlex asked The Wraith Doctors.

"It is unclear at this moment. It could be days, weeks, or even months," they replied in hushed tones. "We will have to monitor her closely. Something like this could also cause the Phoenix to try and gain more control over her than she has over it."

Eliontara raised his head from his hands. "You mean the Phoenix could break out while she's...unconscious?"

The smallest of The Wraith Doctors sat next to him. "If it does try, we can medicate it back into sleep mode, but because we don't really know how powerful she is, it could overpower us and break free."

Scarlex closed her eyes, a solitary tear falling from her right eye. "You have to wake up Mum. We can't keep her hidden forever."

Eliontara stood and placed his arm around his sister. "We will do everything we can."

They stood together for a while, begging their mother to wake up. Chylla stood watch at the door, under strict guidance from The Wraith Doctors that only necessary visitors should be granted entry.

Layson continued to watch the screens of the Comms Room when Chylla was called away to guard Aquilia's room. He hadn't a clue what was going on up there but he watched as Onyx Abyss Alpha sped towards Fresion. He hoped and begged to a higher being, that Mitzi had told him the news and that they were just speeding up for a smoother landing, but then the explosion lit up the screens and the skies above Enceladus.

"No," Layson whispered. "Please no."

He used the program he and Sinclair had built and magnified the images by nearly one hundred times. The tail end of Onyx Abyss Alpha had shattered the main window on Fresion's ship and ripped a gaping hole in the side. The smoke and flames made it difficult to see anything else.

Layson ran from the room, heading down to the launch pads, hoping to find out what had happened. Upon seeing Nymeria and Celest, Layson ran to their side.

"What did you see?" He asked.

"Nothing. We just came out here a few seconds before you. Did you capture it in the Comms Room?" Celest asked.

Layson nodded, "but I haven't watched it back."

"OK, let's go and take a look," Nymeria smiled. It was a forced smile, a way to attempt to make Layson feel a little more at ease. It seemed to work for a second or two.

They returned to the Comms Room and loaded up the video footage of Onyx and Fresion, rewinding it to a few seconds before Onyx sped up. They watched as Onyx Abyss Alpha powered up and began to move.

"Wait! Go back about half a second," Nymeria said.

"Did you see it too?" Celest asked.

Nymeria nodded.

"I didn't see anything," Layson said rewinding just slightly.

"There," Celest pointed. "It turned just slightly left before hitting the other ship."

"Is it possible that it could be...?" Layson didn't want to jinx anything.

"I don't know. It all depends on how close in proximity Onyx was to Fresion and at what angle to the left they turned. We won't know for sure until the dust settles," Nymeria said softly.

"How long?" Layson whispered.

"I wouldn't want to guess. It was a big explosion," Celest added. "Why don't you find Bella and go to see Aquilia?"

Layson nodded, holding back as many of his tears as he could. "Should I...explain to Bella? Prepare her?"

"As best you can Layson." Nymeria told him, gently laying a hand on his shoulder.

<u>Saturn</u>

"What was that?" Eva cried as she ran from the kitchen to the garden.

Janus moved away from the eyepiece and sat on the bench facing the Palace. He couldn't look at the aftermath of the explosion he had just witnessed, knowing that Zeke was a part of it.

"Was that?" Eva's words caught in her throat.

Janus nodded.

"Zeke," she whispered. "Oh Zeke."

Janus held Eva tight as she sobbed tears of orange and red. She slipped to the floor with Janus's arms still wrapped around her.

Janus looked skywards, willing the cloud of dust to dissipate, but it lingered. He could see the fire burning aboard Fresion's ship and he secretly hoped that Fresion had been burnt alive, but he had a deeper feeling that Fresion would have likely found another route off of his ship.

Halana stood in the doorway to the gardens looking up towards the sky. She closed her eyes, crossed her heart and held both hands up to the sky. "Fly high young Zeke. You made an old woman very happy." She swiped at a tear which had escaped her eye and walked over to where her daughter sobbed and crouched down and taking her from Janus's arms. "Contact Enceladus and find out what's happening." She told him.

Janus nodded and walked back inside the Palace. He wiped a few tears from his eyes and called ahead to Chylla.

"Chylla, is there any news?" He asked.

"I should probably put Scarlex or Eliontara on to fill you in," she replied, handing the phone to the outstretched hand on Scarlex.

"Uncle Janus?" She asked.

"It's me. Are there any updates? Has your Mother been found?" He asked.

"Mother is unconscious. She isn't dead. Fresion's laser pierced her skull and just grazed her brain. The Wraith Doctors say she could be down for a while. I'm scared Uncle Janus," Scarlex admitted. "When can you all come?"

"As soon as someone gives the all clear. The explosion still hasn't settled so I'm going to guess that it won't be anytime soon," Janus told her.

"What explosion? Chylla, find out," Scarlex barked.

"It seems Zeke may have taken matters into his own hands and attempted to bring Fresion down himself," Janus explained. "Wait! Does he know about Queen Aquilia?" He heard some muffled talking in the background. "What's happening Scar?"

"Layson says...Mitzi went up to bring him home. Janus...please tell me they aren't..." Scarlex couldn't bring herself to finish the sentence.

"Let's try not to think that way just yet. We have to be positive," Janus told her. "Have Chylla keep an eye from there and I will watch from here. Stay positive Scar."

"I'll try Uncle Janus," she replied before she cut off the call.

Janus turned back to the two women on the floor of the garden. "Halana, please take Eva inside. Give her something to eat and settle yourselves in. This could take some time."

Halana nodded, gathered her daughter up and took her inside. She sat Eva at the kitchen table and went about making some food. "Janus, can we let the children out?"

He had almost forgotten about them in the bunker. "Yes, bring them out but make sure the stay in the Palace."

Halana and went to gather to children. Janus turned back towards the telescope and gathered himself before looking through. The flames seemed to be settling but the dust cloud was still lingering. There were no signs of any life coming from beyond. Janus moved the telescope in t he direction he thought Onyx Abyss Alpha would have flown, but again, he saw no sign of anything. He swung the scope back towards Fresion's ship, just in time to see a fleet of ships heading towards the outer reaches of Enceladus' atmosphere.

"I knew you'd slink away you spiteful thing," Janus whispered. "We'll find you one way or another."

"He fled," Chylla informed Scarlex. "Fresion jumped ship and fled with his fleet."

"Thank you Chylla. Can someone maybe track him in the Comms Room?" Scarlex asked.

"I can," Eliontara replied softly. "It will probably do me good to have a break for a while. You should too sis. Chylla will watch over Mum."

Scarlex turned to her brother and sighed. "I don't want to go and she wake up. I don't want her to think we ditched her."

"She won't. Deep inside she knows you are here," said The Wraith Doctor who had volunteered to take first watch over Aquilia whilst the others went back to work.

"Come on sis. Get some rest, even if it's just for a few hours. You need it," Elion encouraged her.

Scarlex finally gave in and followed her brother towards the main Palace, taking one last look back at her mother as she lay on the table surrounding by a protective field.

"Come quick Your Highness'!" Celest called.

Scarlex and Eliontara exchanged glances and followed her towards the launch pads. As the exited the building, Nymeria pointed towards the sky.

"What are we looking at Nymeria?" Scarlex asked, searching the skies for something significant.

Nymeria handed her a set of binoculars and pointed in the direction of a trail of smoke. Scarlex was confused so she passed the binoculars to Eliontara in the hope that he could spot what Nymeria was pointing out.

"I see it! Oh my word I see it!" He exclaimed.

"Where?" Scarlex cried. She searched the skies until she finally spotted them.

Onyx Abyss Alpha was practically falling from the air.

"They're going too fast. How quickly can we get up there Celest?" Nymeria asked.

"Not fast enough to slow them down," Celest replied, but as she finished her sentence, a ship flew past her and up into the air.

Mythias had boosted his ship past the point it could realistically go at and aimed his grapple to what remained of the back of Onyx and pulled hard to slow it down. The grapple struggled to start with but then with a little bit more power, he managed to bring the ship under control and bring it safely down to the landing pads.

Scarlex, Chylla and Eliontara held their breath as Mythias pulled open the door to Onyx Abyss Alpha and peered inside.

"We need the medics and fast," he shouted.

Chapter Thirty - Eight

Enceladus

"Zeke?" Mitzi whispered. "Zeke are you OK?"

"M y head hurts. Are *you* OK?" He replied, his leg stuck on the leg braces of the captain's seat.

"I think my arm is stuck under your neck," she said, trying not to move too much. She looked at Zeke's head from where she lay and could see a gash across his left eye, running down towards the top of his cheek bone.

"Did you mean what you said?" He asked. He winced at the shooting pain down his right side.

"About what?" Mitzi asked.

"That's enough chit chat you two. We're going to get you out, but you need to bear with us. It's a little...er...banged up in here," Mythias told them. He stepped over what remained of the technical console, over the trashed crew beds and bent down to where Mitzi and Zeke lay. "You first Mitz."

He and Celest carefully lifted some of the debris from Mitzi's small body, allowing enough room for Nymeria to pluck her from the wreckage and carry her off to medical. Mythias didn't want to look but could see that her left leg was in a bad way.

"You're up next big boy!" Mythias said. He reached around the chair and carefully unhooked Zeke's legs from the braces. "Easy now. I won't lie to you man. You're legs aren't in the best of ways. What were you thinking?"

"Vengeance?" Zeke replied, gritting his teeth together as Celest tied his legs to a stiff back board. "I had to get vengeance. For Queen Aquilia."

"OK buster, time for you to get to medical too," Nymeria called out. "Maybe they can check for a brain while they're at it!"

"Please, don't make me laugh. It hurts too much," Zeke tried to smile.

"Well," Nymeria spun around to the sound of Bella screaming Zeke's name. "Don't say I didn't warn you of this but..."

Bella barged past Celest and Nymeria and stood with her hands on her hips looking down at Zeke. "What were you trying to achieve exactly?"

"Mum, I'm sorry. I...I needed to avenge Queen Aquilia's death," Zeke replied, a few tears escaping his eyes, stinging the open wounds.

"You...You're just too loyal!" She cried.

"We'll look after him Ma'am," Mythias smiled as he carried Zeke away.

Bella watched as Mythias carried her son away. She pleaded with every higher power she could think of that he and Mitzi survived.

"We have another issue," Chylla reported to Scarlex.

"Is it something The Stealth Raiders can deal with? Onyx will be out of action for a while whilst we make repairs," Scarlex asked.

"I'm unsure. It seems Xeno hasn't given up on his hunt for Mitzi," Chylla informed her.

Scarlex spun around to face her. Braids of blue hair tangling themselves around her waist. "Xeno?"

"You don't know who he is, do you?" Chylla asked.

Scarlex shook her head. "Should we be worried?"

Chylla led her away from other prying ears. This wasn't something she wanted everyone to hear. "Xeno is Zeke's grandfather."

Scarlex raised her eyebrows. She had never even heard Zeke speak of his grandfather. "Why is he hunting Mitzi?"

"I think we should gather Layson and Bella and talk in your Mother's office," Chylla said. "He is probably one of the only other people who can explain."

Scarlex nodded. She hunted for Eliontara and briefly explained what was happening. He decided to join them. He needed to be aware of what could possibly happen, just in case they needed to move Aquilia to somewhere safer.

Scarlex closed the door to the office as soon as Layson, Bella and Chylla had arrived. She couldn't bear to sit in her Mum's seat so she sat at the window seat overlooking the wreckage of Onyx Abyss Alpha.

"Who is this Xeno?" Eliontara asked.

Layson sighed. "He is my Father. I was told he had died when I was only a young child, probably not much older than Zeke is now. It seems he didn't actually die. He went off to join The Wigfya."

"Which is?" Scarlex asked.

"A community of beings who hunt Squink. They capture, torture and extract their DNA to breed clones. They will use those clones to carry out their evil deeds, thus passing the blame to the Squink community," Bella explained. "We learnt a little about them back in Alphir."

"So Mitzi is Squink?" Eliontara asked.

"Yes. There aren't many of her kind left, but Mitzi is different. I know I shouldn't normally give away this information but this is an emergency. Mitzi is part Squink, part Slizard. She is rare, this is why Xeno wants her so bad," Layson replied hanging his head in his hands. Zeke will hit the atmosphere if he finds out Xeno is coming for Mitzi."

"We have to provide a defence barrier between her and him. Elion, find Nymeria and Celest and explain everything, be sure to be out of ear shot of Mitzi and Zeke and anyone who doesn't need to know," Chylla told him.

"I'll sort the radars out, I have been working on a code that enhances their vision by at least eight times," Layson said. "I made need a hand though Bella, if you're not busy that is."

"I can help. I think. Yes I can. Let's go," Bella replied.

Layson walked with Bella to his office, grabbed his paperwork and headed back towards the Comms Room. "We have to code it from here. Can you read the first two lines of code for me?"

"Err...sure. A8T572F86. D5P274G7K." Bella read out. "What do they mean?"

"They don't really *mean* anything as such. They don't stand for anything, it's just the right combination of numbers and letter to enhance the vision. See?" He said, offering for her to look at how much further they could see.

"Oh wow! Layson, what's that?" Bella asked, gesturing for him to look.

"Oh no! Xeno has arrived sooner than we thought." Layson pulled his radio from his pocket, calling to Chylla to ready the ship. "Xeno is about fifteen minutes out."

"On it," Chylla replied. "Scarlex, how are you feeling about going back up?"

"I'm ready. Just keep an eye on Mum for me?" She replied.

Chylla nodded and Scarlex ran towards the launch pads.

"OK everyone. This is a defence tactic only! Only fire when fired upon. Hopefully we can re-route this threat before it becomes anything more," Scarlex said as she boarded the ship.

Nymeria and Celest nodded their agreement and begun to power up the ship. Scarlex sat with them, watching as the launch pads slipped away beneath them.

"So no, firing?" Celest smiled.

"Not yet. Chylla doesn't want us to bring around a panic, but, I don't think he will leave without some sort of fight. Elion, did you explain?" Scarlex said.

"Yes. They know as much as we do," he replied. "We have to get rid of him. We can't let him find Mitzi."

"We won't. It will be hard not being able to fire though. It seems to be the only way that beings listen these days," Nymeria laughed.

"Let's see how things go. We can decide later. And if Chylla asks, I'll take the blame," Scarlex shrugged.

"Sorry to interrupt," Marixah whispered. "What can I do to help?"

Celest looked back at her. Her hair was a golden blonde/brown mix and her eyes were as green as emeralds. She stood a few feet back from the front of the ship.

"I'm unsure how you help for now, but what skills do you have?" Scarlex asked.

"I'm trained in aikido. I can jump almost triple my own height, I've worked with swords," Marixah explained. "I have a few others that I'm not ready to mention just yet."

"Those will work just fine. If I need you, I'll call you up," Scarlex smiled at her.

Marixah nodded and sat back in her seat. She looked out of the window, out towards the vast reaches of space. Her sight settled on something moving rapidly towards them. She stood and walked towards the front of the ship. "I think we have company."

Nymeria ran to the window. "We have to do something. Man the weapons systems!" She shouted.

"We can't fire yet! We're too close to Enceladus. If we open fire, debris will rain down and Chylla will lose her temper!" Scarlex warned them. "Wait until we have, at least, tried to talk them into leaving."

"I don't think that is even going to be an option at this point," Nymeria called out.

Scarlex looked towards the the speeding ship, its laser guns pointed straight at them. "They're not going to make this easy are they?"

"It doesn't look that way," Marixah whispered. She closed her eyes, took three deep breaths and disappeared.

"What...Where did she go?" Eliontara asked, scanning the remaining faces in front of him.

"Maybe that is one of her other hidden talents!" Celest laughed.

Scarlex didn't know whether that would be a good thing or a bad one. "Keep an eye on them. If you smell so much as battery acid, you fling up the shields. We can't fire until we are higher up."

"Yes Ma'am," the crew said in unison.

All eyes were on the ship ahead of them. No one dared to move an inch.

<u>Saturn</u>

"Any news?" Eva asked as she sat next to Janus on the garden bench.

"They made it back, battered and bruised but they are home," Janus smiled at her.

"What happening up there now?" Eva asked as she looked through the telescope again.

"There shouldn't be anything happening up there. Why?" Janus asked.

"There's some sort of ship. Big thing. I'll just see if I can see the tail code," Eva replied. "X3W185."

Janus opened an app Layson had stored on his phone. It was a way for him to check codes of ships passing Saturn. "It comes up as being registered to a being called Xeno."

"Why are you talking about Xeno?" Halana asked as she stepped into the garden.

"You know him?" Eva asked.

"Of course I do darling. He was your grandfather," Halana replied.

"What? But you told me he died a really long time ago," Eva said.

"He did dear," Halana said, sitting down next to her.

"Then why is he ship, up there?" Eva pointed up.

"Maybe there is a different Xeno?" Halana shrugged. "I mean, we haven't seen this Xeno."

"This doesn't feel right." Janus said as he walked back inside the Palace. He couldn't think why but something just didn't sit right. After Fresion had slinked away and Onyx Abyss Alpha had almost crashed landed, *who else could be making there was to Enceladus?* He thought.

Chapter Thirty – Nine

Enceladus

"Layson, Janus is on the screen. Hi Janus!" Bella informed him.

"Ow!" Layson hit his head on the underside of the desk as he tried to climb out from underneath. "Janus! What a surprise! How are things?"

"Hi Bella. Layson, what's happening?" Janus asked.

"I'm just re-coding the scopes," Layson replied.

"I mean up there," Janus replied.

"Oh up there...I think The Stealth Raiders are doing a training..." Layson looked at Janus. He didn't believe a word he was saying. "You used the app, didn't you?"

Janus nodded. "Ship is registered to Xeno. Layson, what's going on?"

Layson hung his head. "We can't say at the moment. Chylla has sworn us to secrecy."

"Really? When Saturn could be at risk from falling debris too?" Janus cried. "When will she understand that what happens up there has repercussions for us down here too? Everyone is still in their bunkers so I guess they are safe for now."

"I'm sorry Janus. I wish I could tell you," Layson began to explain, but Janus cut off the connections. "He's angry and I don't blame him. Why we have to keep this a secret I'll never know, he knows all about Mitzi."

"I'll talk to Chylla, maybe she will allow us to explain to Janus and Eva about things," Bella said. "I'll be back soon."

Bella practised things to say to Chylla in her head whilst she went in search of her, but each time she thought she had the perfect line, it then didn't seem to be right. Bella was set on changing Chylla's mind. She felt Janus should know, as Duke of Astrodia, he should know everything that could affect the Kingdom below them. She rounded the corner to Aquilia's office and heard a voice. A voice she recognised.

"Yes I know what you said to do, but I cannot control her," Chylla said.

"It is your duty and the only remaining Elder to make sure she doesn't bring trouble to this Kingdom and she has done exactly that," Quintara exploded.

"She's your daughter," Chylla threw back.

"But that's just it isn't it? She's not my daughter! She is Alphir! Nothing to do with Enceladus or Saturn in the slightest. Sent from another planet to take over," Quintara shouted. "You make sure you do as I have instructed."

"Yes Ma'am," Chylla whispered.

"Repeat you instructions," Quintara demanded.

"Lure The Wraith Doctors from Aquilia's room and switch off her life support, unplug from the mains and claim a malfunction, by the time anyone arrives, she should be dead," Chylla replied.

"Let's see if you can get this right," Quintara said.

Bella almost screamed. She turned around and ran back to the Comms Room. She had to inform Layson, Janus and Eva before it was too late.

"He won't tell me anything. Says Chylla won't allow it. I know he is keeping something from me," Janus said as he paced the kitchen.

"Maybe you should just sit down for a bit. You'll wear out the tiles if you carry on," Halana smiled. "Try not to worry yourself too much. It could be something and nothing."

"It's more likely something rather than nothing. I could tell by the way he was talking that he knew more," Janus replied. He looked out into the garden and watched Eva as she continued to look through the telescope. He wished he could give them both some answers as to who this ship belonged to.

Eva twisted the viewing scope from left to right, trying to get a better look at the ship above but it was no use. No matter what she did, nothing made the ship any clearer. She sat back on the bench feeling defeated. She looked back towards the Palace and sighed. She hoped that this was a different Xeno and not Halana's father. After seeing her face when she said he had died, she could see how much he meant to her.

She chanced a glance back towards the skies over Enceladus in time to see The Stealth Raiders ship circle the other ship. She peered through the telescope again, blinked three times and looked back again. Had she really seen what she thought she had? A flicker of light jumped from one ship to the other.

"Everything OK dear?" Halana whispered as she edged closer to Eva.

"I don't know Mum. I don't, or more can't, comprehend what I just saw," Eva replied.

"Explain it to me darling," Halana said as she gently lay her hand across her daughters.

Eva looked at their joint hands, realising how long they had been apart. "There was a flicker of light. It jumped from The Stealth ship to the other ship, but I can't be sure if I actually saw what I thought I saw."

Halana thought for a second. She only knew of one being who could do those sorts of things. "Eva, you remember the book that your father gave you? Where is it?"

"It's on the bookcase. Next to the one he gave me on Saturnese art, why?" she replied.

"I need you to go get it. I need to check something before I tell you this," Halana told her.

Eva rose from the bench and ran inside to find the book. As she watched her daughter go, Halana stole a look through the telescope and up into the sky above where The Stealth gently glided. She twisted a few of the reels and looked closer at the ship Stealth surrounded. She focused on the tail fin. It's blue and red swirls triggering a memory from deep inside. She remembered looking at the paint with her father, pointing out the range of different shades of red, green and blue. He settled on a sapphire blue and a garnet red, saying they matched Halana's tints in her hair.

"Got it Mum," Eva's voice broke through her thoughts.

"Ahh," Halana smiled. She turned the book towards her and searched the index, turning to the page she needed with ease. "Whatever and whoever that was, they are called Dharzoids."

"I've never heard of them. What traits do they have?" Eva asked, clearly eager to learn more about them.

"They are the only species that we know of that can teleport from one place to the other. Only short distances mind you, but they do it with stealth and silence," Halana told her.

"I don't know anyone on Enceladus who can do that, at least, no one who's told me they can," Eva replied.

"It looks like we will have to wait until someone informs us who this being is and where they came from," Halana smiled. They both settled back on the garden bench and took turns looking through the telescope.

Janus watched them from the window of Xandr and Codex's room, the two boys setting their beds up for the night. He was glad Halana had stayed. Eva had missed having her around. Just as he was about to turn away, a bright light caught his eye. He ran to the window and shouted for the two women to take cover.

❑　❑　❑

<u>The Skies Above Enceladus</u>

"What was that?" Scarlex screamed as she covered her eyes from the light.

"I have no idea but it came from that ship!" Nymeria replied. With Nymeria's exceptional eyesight, she could bare the blinding light and continued to search for the reason behind it whilst everyone else shielded their eyes or ducked for cover. As she looked through the light, she spotted Xeno taking cover under the control panel of his ship whilst Marixah stood in the centre, glowing the brightest white she had ever seen. "It's Marixah!"

"What is she doing?" Scarlex asked. She slowly tried to see through the light.

"I'm not sure. She is just standing there. Xeno is hiding under the control panel but she hasn't moved from that spot. Now is our time to fire!" Nymeria replied.

"We're still too close to Enceladus. If Chylla..." Scarlex began.

"To Dionne with Chylla! If we don't knock him out of the sky now, he will be able to attack us first," Nymeria shouted.

Scarlex was taken aback by Nymeria's outburst. She looked between Nymeria and Celest, getting confirmation from Celest that Nymeria was right. "How do we do it? We can't risk any debris falling down to Enceladus."

"We have to use the HollowLaser. It's the only one that creates a vacuum to eliminate debris at the same time as eliminating the enemy," Celest offered up. "We haven't used it before, but we have been assured it works exactly as it should." She added quickly when seeing the look on Scarlex's face.

"If we do this, we have to protect Marixah too. We can't risk losing her!" Scarlex said. "She has risked her life to help us. Make it worth it!"

Nymeria and Celest both nodded and went about setting up the HollowLaser. Scarlex looked around her remaining crew and took a deep breath in. This would be the first time she would be ordering them to do things and she didn't want them to get hurt. She began giving out orders, telling some to spot from the windows; they needed to make sure that they didn't hit any other passing ships and another team to ready up so that they could rescue Marixah at the same time. Each team prepared themselves for their assigned tasks, each helping the other out with their protective gear. Once the teams were assembled, Celest and Nymeria aimed the HollowLaser towards Xeno's ship, and together they pulled the trigger. Within seconds Xeno's ship had a big chunk missing from the port side. Just as the spotter team turned to inform Scarlex of the damage done, Marixah appeared in front of them.

"We were just about to send a rescue team. You have a lot of explaining to do when we get back. Join the spotter team and, please, don't disappear on us again," Scarlex smiled.

Marixah nodded and took her place next to the rear window. She looked out just as Celest aimed the laser at the front of Xeno's ship. She pulled the trigger sending a beam of light towards the ship, pulling the remnants of his ship into a hidden holding tank.

"What happens now?" Scarlex asked Nymeria.

"We take it back and filter the contents. Xeno will be there and we question him," Nymeria smiled. "It was a good call Scar. You should be proud of yourself."

The ship erupted into applause for her and her face blushed a shade of purple. She felt like she belonged here.

"Let's head home now Celest. We have to find out what this Xeno wanted," Scarlex told her.

"Yes Ma'am," Celest smiled. She turned the ship and headed back towards the Palace.

Scarlex sat with Marixah on the return trip. "So what are you exactly?" She asked.

"I'm Dharzoid. From the planet Dharmak. Fresion made a stop there over three decades ago and enslaved my parents whilst my mother was carrying me. I was born on Plydar," Marixah explained.

"What happened to them?" Scarlex asked.

"It's been a while but they both died not long after I was born. Fresion took control of my life and I was employed as a guard. Fresion would tell people I was his daughter but really I think he was waiting for me to die so he could harvest my power just like he did my parents. There are so many things that he did wrong, but I couldn't speak out," Marixah replied, a single tear slid down her cheek.

"We will work things out for you. Maybe you could stay with us on Enceladus?" Scarlex replied with a smile.

"I'd love that," she whispered.

They settled back for the remainder of the trip. They didn't expect what they found when they arrived.

Chapter Thirty – Nine

Saturn

"What was that?" Eva asked as she and Halana finally made their way back into the house.

"I don't know but are you both OK?" Janus asked.

"I think so, but that was so bright," Halana replied. "Where are the children?"

"Most of them are in bed. Ammyn is having trouble getting comfortable; maybe her Nana can help her settle?" Janus smiled.

"I'll go and check on her. She is probably a little out of sorts with everything that has happened recently," Halana said. She grabbed a warm cup from the stove and headed up to Ammyn's room.

"Is she really struggling to settle or did you want her out of the room?" Eva asked.

"No, Ammyn really is struggling to settle. Anything I do for her doesn't help in the slightest," Janus said, his face showing clear signs of distress.

"I'm sure things will settle once the medication she has been taking starts to settle into her system," Eva smiled. "Do you think we will ever find out what's happening up there? I know Mum is really worried about Zeke and Aquilia."

"We will go up there as soon as we get the all clear," Janus reassured her. He pulled her into his arms and held her close, stroking her green hair slowly. "I promise we will find out soon."

"Now now my little Ammyn, why won't you settle for Daddy huh?" Halana asked as she sat gently on the edge of Ammyn's bed.

"I want to sleep Nana. I'm so tired, but this thing," she replied, pointing to her tummy, "won't stop wriggling!"

"Have you tried taking your medicine?" Halana asked.

Ammyn began to nod but then shook her head. "It tastes like mud," she grimaced.

"Sometimes, the best medicine tastes the worst because it's doing its job," Halana smiled.

"But it's gross. It looks like mashed up grass and Xandr said it's probably doesn't work," Ammyn told her.

"Oh Xandr," Halana shook her head. "He wouldn't understand. Now, I'll get it, and when you take it, I will read you a story."

"Will you create one Nana?" Ammyn smiled.

"Only if you take your medicine," Halana countered.

Ammyn nodded her head viciously. Halana rose to collect the medicine from the bathroom cabinet and perched herself back on the edge of Ammyn's bed. She held out the spoon and waited for Ammyn to take the liquid down. Ammyn closed her eyes tight, took a deep breath and swallowed the medicine down without any hesitation. A disgusted look crossed her face but she had finally taken her medicine.

"And how was that?" Halana asked.

"Disgusting to begin with, but, thinking about it now, there's a hint of apple blossom there! I love apple blossom!" Ammyn smiled. "Thank you Nana. Can you make a story now?"

"Settle down under the covers, and prepare your imagination," Halana smiled as she snuggled down next to her granddaughter.

Enceladus

Nymeria and Celest landed The Stealth ship with ease, positioning it so the collection tank could be filtered and emptied.

"Place the prisoners in the holding cells, and leave a gap between each one," Celest called out.

The guards behind her dragged each soldier and Xeno into the cells, slamming the doors and locking them.

"So, anyone want to volunteer to question him?" Celest asked.

"I could, but I don't trust myself not to rip his throat out, maybe you should do it," Nymeria replied.

"I guess I don't have a choice in this do I?" Celest replied. She looked towards of Scarlex. "Wanna sit in?"

Scarlex looked surprised. "Can I?"

"Of course! Come on. Let's set up the interview room," Celest replied.

Scarlex smiled at her and turned to Nymeria, "could you check on my Mum?"

"Sure. I'll let you know if there have been any changes," Nymeria replied.

"Thank you," Scarlex smiled. She then followed Celest towards the interview rooms.

"So," Celest said. "Have you ever been in here before?"

"No. Mum told me it wasn't really the nicest place, but it looks pretty decent," Scarlex replied.

"Believe me, they aren't all like this. I chose this one particularly because it has the shackles on the floor under the table," Celest pointed out. "We don't normally use them, but I have a feeling we might need them for Xeno."

"I think this will be fun!" Scarlex said. "Has my Mum done this before?"

"Oh yeah, with Layson!" Celest replied.

"Layson?" Scarlex questioned.

"How much do you know about Layson?" Celest asked.

Scarlex thought back to what her Mother had told her about discussing others' forms without prior permission.

"It's OK. I know about him myself. I was here when he first came to attack your Mother," Celest said, sensing the hesitation in Scarlex's silence.

"I know he has the Dark Wolf deep down inside and that it is controlled by monthly injections, but..." Scarlex stopped.

"But what? What are you thinking inside that head of yours?" Celest asked.

"Has anyone checked to see if Zeke has the gene?" Scarlex whispered.

"Without anything happening for them to check, no one would know," Celest replied. "Something would need to happen for anyone to even consider testing him for it."

Just as the words had left her mouth there was a gut wrenching roar followed by a loud crash and screams.

Celest grabbed Scarlex's hand and led her to the closet window, pushing Scarlex to the floor below her. She peeked around the window frame, looking for the source of the sounds but found nothing. Just as she pulled Scarlex to her feet, Eliontara crashed through the door.

"Something bad has happened. We need to get into the bunker," he said, pulling his sister behind him. "They will need you in there, Celest. Nymeria can't hold him off by herself."

"Who?" Scarlex asked.

"I'll tell you in the bunker," he replied, grabbing her hands and dragging her behind him.

"Wait!" She shouted. "Celest, do you think you will need help?"

Celest thought before she answered. She looked over Scarlex's shoulder at Eliontara who looked genuinely frightened.

"I'm sure it's nothing. I'll come for you before I bring Xeno in and we can question him together," Celest smiled.

"You know I will help. You just need to call for me," Scarlex told her.

Celest nodded once and ran off in the direction of all the commotion. Scarlex watched her run, then turned to her brother and said, "You have a lot to explain." Before turning and heading towards the bunker.

Eliontara rolled his eyes behind her back and followed her. He wondered how he would explain this to her and which words he should choose to explain it.

Celest made her way through the destruction, noticing how close she was to the medical wing. She looked around to find Nymeria, spotting her on the far side of the debris, Celest clambered over to her.

"What happened?" She called out.

"You wouldn't believe me even if I told you!" Nymeria replied, pulling her wife in an embrace.

"Seriously, what happened?" Celest asked again.

"Well, how about you take a look inside the medical wing and tell me who is missing?" Nymeria pointed to the door.

Steeling her spine, Celest made her way towards the door; she pushed it open and surveyed the destruction around her. It looked as if a huge monster had ripped open the side of the medical wing. There were claw marks along the walls and huge footprints in the dust leading away from the building. Celest couldn't fathom what could have made these tracks until something clicked in her memory.

"Has anyone checked if Zeke has the gene?"

'What if Scarlex is right?' She thought to herself, but then quickly pushed the thought aside. There was no way Zeke would destroy the medical wing. 'But what if he isn't thinking straight?' She thought again. Celest shook her head clear and focused on the debris in front of her. She walked towards where the tracks ended and held her breath before she slowly peeked around the side of warehouse. Her eyes swept left and right, landing on nothing but dust. The tracks had completely vanished. She walked slowly around the side of the warehouse, sticking close to the walls, her eyes darting in every direction. They landed on nothing until she reached the far side of the warehouse. Creeping slowly, one step at a time, she rounded the last corner and stopped. Something was sobbing in the corner, something with short brown hair, naked and clearly afraid.

Taking a deep breath, she slowly made her way towards the hunkered down being. Stretching her hands out, palms facing out to show she wasn't a threat.

"Hey. Hey are you OK? You really shouldn't be out here alone. Maybe I can help?" She said softly.

The being stopped sobbing with a gasp. Slowly turning to face her. Cheeks streaked with tears.

"Celest?"

Celest gasped and threw her arms around the being.

"Zeke!" She whispered.

Chapter Forty

Saturn

"And that's clear?" Janus asked.

"Fully," Chylla replied. "When will you leave Saturn?"

"As soon as we can find someone to watch over the children, unless we bring them with us," Janus replied.

"Bring them! Maybe they can sit with Aquilia whilst we rectify everything out here," Chylla said.

"OK. I'll send for the pods to be readied, and we will leave as soon as possible," Janus told her. "We will see you soon."

Janus placed the phone back into its cradle and turned to face Eva and Halana.

"Chylla wants us to travel to Enceladus. She would like us to bring the children and to leave as soon as possible," he told them.

"Bring the children? With everything that is going on up there?" Halana cried. "What is she thinking?"

"I'm sure everything with be fine. Chylla wouldn't recommend us bring the children if she didn't think it would be safe for them," Eva said. "Plus, Scarlex and Eliontara will be there."

"Oh them poor children. If Chylla says it's safe then maybe it is. I guess we will have to go and find out," Halana shrugged.

Janus hugged them both then hurried off to round up the children.

"Are you sure you're ready to go back Mum?" Eva asked.

"Oh darling. Enceladus is my home, as much as I love being here with you all, I'm needed back there," Halana smiled. "it will be an honour to be there with the children on their first visit to Enceladus."

Eva smiled. She had never seen her mother as home sick as she was right now. She knew her mother's heart belonged to Enceladus, she just wished she would visit more often and stay with them longer. She gathered her mother into an embrace and then went off to pack the children's things, unsure how long they would be staying for. She knew there were supplies on Enceladus for her children, so she decided not to pack too much.

Halana watched as her daughter pack things for each child in a military style, making sure each little rucksack was packed with each child's favourite toy and book. She admired how she had passed down her love of reading to her children. Remembering how Eva could never sit still unless she had a book in her hand. The memories of a time before now came flooding back to her. Watching her daughter be the only child to be overexcited at the opening of the library, being the first one through the door to search for books and being the only person left to still use it long after technology evolved beyond anything anyone could have ever imagined. She was proud of her daughter for keeping her traditions alive and she hoped those traditions would travel from generation to generation.

<u>Enceladus</u>

"It's OK Zeke," Celest said as she held him close. "How long have you known?"

"For a while, I wanted to see if I could control it, you know, like Queen Aquilia does with The Phoenix. I guess I can't," he said as he hung his head low, fresh tears appearing in his eyes.

"Who else knows?" Celest asked.

"Aquilia, Benzyline, and Symese guessed," he replied. "I'm so sorry I didn't trust you or Nymeria with this information. I don't even know how to handle it myself."

Celest looked at him. He looked barely a child having to deal with the weight of the world on his shoulders. "You haven't told your father?"

Zeke shook his head. "Not yet. I was hoping to before all this happened and I had asked Queen Aquilia to be with me when I did, but I guess we didn't have the time."

Celest shrugged off her jacket and hung it around his shoulders. "I know it's not quite your style but it will do while we get you back inside. I'll take you the back way, that way you get to keep some of your dignity."

Zeke smiled at her. "Thank you."

Celest helped him to his feet and helped him back to his quarters through the rear of the Palace. There he pulled on a pair of jeans and a sweatshirt. She averted her eyes whilst he dressed, unsure why as she had seen everything out near the warehouse, but she assumed he wasn't aware of it, so he would allow him some privacy.

"So do you think we should tell you father?" Celest called out as she looked over the pictures he had hanging on the walls. She picked up a piece of paper that had been left on the kitchen table and turned it over. On the other side was a sketch of Mitzi.

"Erm, I guess I don't have much choice now, do I?" He replied, walking through into the kitchen. He saw the paper she was looking at and froze. He knew he had sketched a picture of Mitzi on it.

Celest replaced the paper and turned to face him. "She got you bad huh?"

"Is it that obvious?" He blushed.

"There is no shame Zeke! We don't choose who we fall in love with. I had never thought of being with another of the same gender until I met Nymeria and after that, well, she was all I could think about," Celest explained. "Just because she is a different species, it shouldn't hold you back."

Zeke couldn't find the words to reply. He knew Celest was right, she normally was, but it still worried him. How would everyone else take the news? How does Mitzi feel?

"I have to see Mitzi," he said. "I have to find out if she is OK. I have to tell her."

"OK, hold your space dust. We will get to her, but first, you need to speak to your parents and the Wraith Doctors," Celest told him. "No exceptions!"

He hadn't even begun to protest, but he had thought about it. "Do you know where they are?" He asked.

"I would hazard a guess at your father's office. I'll just let Nymeria know what's happening," Celest said as she began to walk away.

"Please, don't tell her about me. Not yet," Zeke pleaded.

"I won't say anything until you are ready. I'll say I found you near the warehouse and that you must have been sleep walking," Celest smiled. "You can trust me Zeke."

Zeke had always had trouble trusting others. Even when he was at school, he had trouble believing that the teachers were there to help him.

"Nym, you there?" Celest said into her handset.

"Hey, yeah. You find anything?" She replied.

"Nah, I looked all over. If I'm honest the only thing I found was Zeke huddled by the warehouse. I think I startled him though, he was sound asleep," Celest told her.

"Oh wow, to sleep through that noise is astonishing. He must have had some strong painkillers!" Nymeria laughed.

"Probably, hey, do you know if Layson and Bella are in Layson's office?" Celest asked.

"i believe they are. Why?" Came the reply.

"Zeke wants to go up and see them, and I said I'd go up with him, that's OK right?" Celest asked.

"Hey why are you asking me?" Nymeria laughed. "If we need you here, then I'll call. Tell him Mitzi is doing OK."

Celest smiled. "I will do."

Celest placed the handset back into her pocket and turned to Zeke. "Mitzi is doing OK. Let's go and see your parents."

Zeke took a deep breath in and steeled his spine. He knew he would have to tell his parents sooner or later but he was dreading it. Every step he took towards his father's office felt like he had the weight of the universe hanging from his feet.

"It'll be OK Zeke. I'll be right here with you," Celest assured.

As Zeke neared his father's office, the lump in his throat became bigger and bigger. He knocked on the door and waited for an answer.

As Enceladus came into view, each child became more and more excited to visit this new place.

"Calm down children. There will be plenty of time to explore when we have settled in," Halana explained.

The closer they got to the landing pads; more and more of the destruction could be seen.

"Oh my, what happened?" Halana exclaimed.

"I don't know. Chylla mentioned something about the medical wing, but she didn't mention anything to this magnitude," Janus replied. He looked out of the window, surprised by how much debris lay around below. "When we land, Halana, please take the children off to the far side of the Palace."

"Absolutely," Halana replied.

They landed softly and Halana swiftly took the children off to the far side. Eva looked around the destruction. Tears formed in her eyes. This had been the place she had built up a bond with Aquilia. She had become a sister to her and a very close confident. Eva ran off to seek out Chylla. She needed to see Aquilia for herself.

"I'll find some of the others whilst you find Chylla," Janus shouted after her.

Eva waved her hand but continued running. She had to find out where Aquilia was. Janus began walking around. He moved rocks out of the way and picked up multiple different pieces of furniture. What he had once remembered at the medical wing was now just rubble and debris. He finally noticed Nymeria in the corner of the medical suite. Waving at her, he picked his way through the debris, making his way towards her.

"What happened?" He asked as he finally made it to her.

"Something ripped the side of the wing open like it was a packet of snacks! Luckily everyone is safe, but it seems Zeke managed to escape. Celest found him on the far side of the warehouse, sound asleep," Nymeria told him.

Janus was surprised, "how could he have slept through all this?"

"I don't know. Celest says he was asleep when she found him and that she startled him when she found him," Nymeria told him. "She has taken him to see his parents."

"How is Mitzi doing?" Janus asked. He looked around the room to see her sitting up on the bed. She looked well.

"She's doing OK. Worried about Zeke though, personally I think there is something going on between them," Nymeria said.

Janus instantly remembered what Mitzi had told him when she visited, but that wasn't his story to tell.

"Hey, I kinda lost you for a second there, you OK?" Nymeria said and she grabbed his shoulder.

"Oh, yeah, sorry, I just thought of something. Layson still in the same office?" Janus asked.

"Yeah, hasn't moved and still has the picture of Sinclair on the wall," she replied. "I guess he feels at home there."

"Thanks Nym. I'll catch up with you soon," he said as he jogged away.

Janus made his way towards the office, along the white marble walled corridor and across the landing which separated the two wings of the Palace. He turned right at the next corner and stopped just outside Layson's door when he heard voices from within.

"Are you sure?" Layson asked.

"Positive Dad. I had the tests run a while ago. I thought I would be able to control it, like Queen Aquilia does with The Phoenix, but I don't think I can," Zeke confessed.

Layson turned to Celest and said "how long have you known?"

"Not long, I only found out about five minutes before we arrived here," Celest replied.

"I wish you had come to us sooner darling," Bella whispered. "We will have to get you seen to and see what The Wraith Doctors say."

Janus opened the door slowly and walked in. "Were you planning on telling everyone?"

Chapter Forty – One

Eva looked down at Aquilia as she lay peacefully under the shield. "Hey you. You better not sleep too long; I've brought the brood to see their Auntie Quilia!" She let the tears fall from her eyes.

She couldn't believe that her best friend now lay, unconscious and protected because of a grudge. She hung her head down and let her pain flow through her.

"Hello?"

Eva jumped up, her head spinning left and right but finding nobody there.

"Hello?"

"Who's there?" Eva shouted.

"Eva?"

"Yes, who's that?" Eva replied.

"It's me, Aquilia. I need you to do something for me," she said, her voice sounding distant.

"Like what? Do you want the children? I can get them," Eva almost stumbled over her voice. She looked down at Aquilia, who still remained in a peaceful trance.

"No, please, leave them where they are. I need you to look out for them. I don't know how long I have left. I don't know how long I can hold on for. The pain is unbearable and I don't think I can repair myself," Aquilia told her.

"You will not go anywhere until you have told those kids you love them!" Eva cried. She sent one of the Wraith Doctors to find Scarlex and Eliontara.

"I don't know how long Eva," Aquilia whispered.

"You will not leave here until you have said goodbye properly," Eva cried. Her tears fell like meteors to the floor. "Don't give up yet," she whispered. Pulling her phone from her pocket, she sent her mother a message asking her to leave the children and come quickly.

Within minutes, Scarlex, Eliontara and Halana had arrived, closely followed by Janus, Layson, Bella and Zeke. Each had messaged someone else, until the room had barely enough space to breath.

"We're all here," Eva whispered.

The room grew dark. A collective gasp rose from the gathered crowd. From where Aquilia lay, a bright light emitted, rising high above the room. Everyone looked up to the sight of The Phoenix.

"You must not be sad my precious ones," she said to Scarlex and Eliontara as she settled beside them. "Eva and the others will be here every step of the way, just as they were with me."

"But Mama, you can't go. There's so much more we need to do," Scarlex cried. Huge red tears escaped her eyes.

Aquilia reached out her hand and held Scarlex's face gently. "And you will do so many more things. I have every faith that you will become a magnificent Queen."

Eliontara hugged his mother hard. "I don't want you to go," he cried.

Aquilia embraced her son and kissed his head. "Elion, you were named after the greatest person I ever knew, my Father, and I know you will be every bit the King he was. You have both made me the proudest, richest and most loved Mother of all time, and for that I am grateful."

Scarlex held her brother tight as Aquilia made her way towards Halana who bowed instantly.

"Oh Halana. You have been and still are, the greatest Mother to Eva, and the most wonderful mother figure for me whilst I was growing up, I cannot thank you enough for everything you have done for me and my family. I hope you will continue to do the same for my children," Aquilia whispered.

"Oh you," she said, swiping at a tear, "you kept me on my toes, but you, well; you are a pleasure to have known all these years. To watch you grow from a mere child to a mother and a Queen, it had my heart bursting with so much pride." She allowed the remaining tears to fall with grace.

"Eva, my one true friend and someone I class as my sister. I am entrusting you to keep my babies safe. I wouldn't trust them with just anyone. You made growing up without my parents bearable and fun, but you also helped me find the right path and stick to it. I love you, so, so much," Aquilia said as she held Eva close.

"You don't have to go. You could fight. We know how strong you are. We...we don't want you to go. We need you here," Eva cried.

"I won't be far away. I'll always be in your heart and in your soul," Aquilia smiled. "Look after her Janus."

Janus couldn't speak. He let his tears fall as he held his wife close and she snuggled her face into his neck.

Aquilia rose again to the ceiling, followed by another glow of light.

"Are you ready Your Highness?" Marixah asked.

Aquilia nodded. "Yes, I think I am."

"Then take my hand," Marixah said as she held out her hand. "From where I will take you, you will be able to watch over everyone."

Aquilia took her hand and the bright light grew to an immense size, before slowly fading out replaced with the sparkles of glitter as it fell over the shield which shrouded Aquilia's body. The room fell silent. No one dared to utter a word. For everyone who had watched Aquilia grow from a five year old child into a formidable Queen, this was a moment they never dreamt of living through.

Scarlex stepped towards Halana and leant her head on her shoulder. "What happens now Miss Halana?" She whispered.

Halana took a deep breath. "Now we must visit the Higher Elders and seek their guidance. I'm surprised no one has appeared as of yet."

Halana stood, took Eva by the hand and led her and Chylla to the meeting room. Scarlex stayed with the others, holding her brother tight.

"Mama, I'm not sure I can do this. The way Quintara and Elio have been towards Aquilia is despicable," Eva explained as they walked the marble halls.

"I know darling, but we must inform them," Halana explained. It still deeply concerned her that none of the

Higher Elders had made themselves known during Aquilia's ascent.

As they stood before the large door, Halana input a code on the keypad and waited for an answer. She kept her head low in respect for their recently departed Queen. With Chylla to her right and Eva to her left, Halana waited for a reply to her call.

"Why have you come?" Zyra asked through the intercom. "We have no meeting planned."

"We have news to convey," Halana replied.

"Enter, but please be brief," Zyra allowed them to enter the room.

Chylla followed Halana and Eva into the room, closing the door behind her. Within seconds of sitting down, all the Higher Elders had converged across the walls.

"What news do you have? And where is Queen Aquilia?" Zyra asked.

Eva stood to answer but knowing she was still angry, Halana gently told her to sit down.

"Queen Aquilia was involved in a battle with Fresion. She has been unconscious for a number of days," Halana began. "She sadly departed us not more than twenty minutes ago."

The room fell silent but for the loud thudding of Eva's heart.

"I feel you have something more to add young Eva," Zyra said as she looked down upon her.

Eva's breathing became rapid. She rose to her feet and placed her hands on the table in front of her. "Where were you all? Were you even watching what happened? Why weren't you there when she left us? WHY DIDN'T YOU CARE?"

"Eva, calm yourself down," Halana told her.

"Let her speak Halana. She is angry and she has every right to be," Quintara said.

"I do have every right to be. As soon as you found out she was Alphir, you wanted no part of her life, NO PART! You never ask about Scarlex, who, by the way, commanded Onyx Abyss Alpha in the fight against Xeno, or Eliontara who now runs comms. When have you EVER attempted to make time for them?" Eva shouted. "NEVER, that's when!" She slumped down in her seat and sobbed into her arms.

"You don't understand how it affected us Eva," Elio tried to explain. "When we found out she wasn't truly ours, things changed. We felt less of a connection to Aquilia."

"Less of a connection? LESS OF A CONNECTION? Why would you say such a thing? Regardless of whether a child is your own bloodline or not, but..." Eva stopped.

"Eva, what is it?" Chylla asked.

"But she must be your bloodline Quintara, otherwise, how would she have the Phoenix gene?" Eva asked. "Unless there is something we don't know about you?"

"Well, my dear, there isn't anything I have been hiding, if that is what you are implying," Quintara said.

"What will happen now?" Chylla asked.

"As they are twins, Scarlex and Eliontara must rule together unless one decides they wish the other to rule alone," Zyra replied. "Halana, you are tasked with delivering the news."

Halana bowed her head once and when she looked up, they were gone. As they left the room, Celest was waiting outside.

"Is everything OK?" Eva asked.

"Yes. The Wraith Doctors have prepared Aquilia's body, with the help of Scarlex and Eliontara. You should see her. She is a picture of peace and power," Celest replied, a solitary tear falling from her eye.

Eva linked her arms with Celest and they walked towards the embalming room. Here Aquilia's body would be committed to rest for all eternity.

"Are you alright?" Mitzi asked as she nudged Zeke's nose.

Zeke didn't trust his voice. He shook his head too hard that it made him dizzy.

"I'm so sorry Zeke. I know she was very special to you," Mitzi whispered. She snuggled into his neck and he gently laid his head on her.

"She trusted me in Zee's room. Trusted me to look after the comings and goings of all the ships. I just can't believe I couldn't save her. I should have been able to save her. I saw it all happen, up here," he said, tapping the side of his head.

"This isn't on you Zeke. Don't ever believe that. Aquilia was a strong willed being. Someone I looked up to. I didn't know her as well as you did, but when I saw her, I wanted to be like her," Mitzi replied. "You can't blame yourself."

Zeke held Mitzi in his hand and held her up to his face. "You are every piece as strong as Aquilia was, and you are every piece a Queen like she was." He nudged her nose with his and looked deep into her eyes. He could see himself and could see how much he loved this being.

Mitzi blushed, her pale face showing a slight tinge of red. She snuggled herself back into his neck and there she remained. "It will be OK Zeke. I won't leave you. Ever."

Zeke smiled, he always smiled around Mitzi. He looked out over the masses who had filed in to pay their respects to their fallen Queen. Nodding his greetings to those who passed by. He watched as his mother and father bowed their heads to Aquilia, a single tear falling from his mothers' eye. He wanted to reach out to her but he knew his father would be her rock.

"It's OK to cry young Zeke," Halana whispered into his ear.

"I saw this happening. She touched my hand a few weeks back and I saw it all. I tried to stop it. I didn't want it to come true," he cried. "Why couldn't I stop it?"

"It wasn't for you to decide," came a voice from beside him.

He turned to see Marixah standing just off to his left.

"What do you mean?" Scarlex asked.

Marixah turned to face her. "There would always be a time when your mother's time would come. I was sent to guide her to the other side."

"Is that why you saved me from Fresion?" Eliontara asked.

Marixah nodded. "I was recruited by Atona Goddess of Bravery, to bring Aquilia to her. It was her time to go, but I needed to get you back to safety before recovering Aquilia."

"You will take care of her. Won't you?" Scarlex whispered.

Marixah bent slightly and looked Scarlex in the eyes. "Your Mother will be held in the highest regard. She will be cared for, and loved by many, and she will be able to visit. You may not see her when it happens, but she will be there."

"Thank you," they both replied.

Marixah smiled, gently touched each of their faces and floated up towards the sky before fading into nothing.

Scarlex buried her face into Halana's shoulder and sobbed. Huge, heavy sobs.

Eliontara sat beside Zeke. "I really shouldn't cry, but I feel like a part of me is missing."

Zeke turned to him, tears streaming from his eyes. "You shouldn't hide your emotions Elion. It's OK for us to cry too."

"In fact, it's advised!" Mitzi squeaked from Zeke's shoulder. She smiled at them both. "You shouldn't bottle up your emotions. It can have disastrous effects on those closest to you."

"Thanks Mitzi, I'll definitely remember that one," Eliontara smiled. He rose from his seated position, walked towards Halana and Scarlex and opened his arms wide, embracing them both and letting his tears run free.

"You're quite the being aren't you?" Zeke whispered to Mitzi.

"I like to think so, yeah," she replied, cocking her head to one side.

"Promise you'll stay?" He asked.

"Always," she replied.

Chapter Forty – Two

Lyra watched from the sidelines as numerous people paid their respects to Aquilia, their fallen Queen. She had chosen to stand away from the crowd and allow everyone their own time. She would pay her own respects when everyone had left.

"Mum," Janus said as he slowly walked up behind her.

She turned to face him, smiling and swiping at her tears as she did.

"There's no need to hide how you feel Mum. We all completely understand," Janus smiled back at her.

"Oh Janus. She was so kind to me. Welcoming me back and allowing my people to rejoin Astrodia. I never thought I would belong to a community again," Lyra replied. "It's so hard to see someone who has worked so hard to build something up, just be knocked down."

Janus pulled his mother into an embrace, kissing her on the head as he did. "We will get through this Mum. You, me, Eva, and the children. We have a huge family. Everyone up here is family too; don't be afraid to lean on them once in a while." He let her go and went off to find Eva. He knew she was angry and why she was, but he needed to check she was OK. Aquilia had been more of a sister than a Queen to her.

Sitting by the crystal fountain, Eva trailed her fingers in the clear water below, letting the cold liquid flow over her fingers. Her tears flowed like the river on Dionne.

She looked up towards the sky, "why did you have to leave us? The children were looking forward to getting to know their Auntie Quilia. I needed you to stay. We all needed you to stay."

Janus walked up behind her slowly and gently placed his hand on her shoulder. As soon as he did, her tears came again, harder than before.

"I know you're angry baby. I understand why, but even though Aquilia has gone, she will always be a part of our lives. No matter what we do in life," Janus told her.

"We have to tell Scarlex and Eliontara that they must rule together unless one allows the other to take full charge. How can we put this on them?" She asked him.

"In a less torturous way than Aquilia had it thrust upon her? We will always be here for them, exactly like you were for Aquilia," Janus told her.

"I know. I just feel so bad. It's like history repeating itself all over again," Eva cried. "They shouldn't have to do this."

Janus pulled her into his arms and held her whilst she cried. He understood her pain, he was close to Aquilia when she was a youngster and hated everything his father had done to her, but she had flourished into a grand young woman and a Queen who held the attention of everyone in everything she did. "I'll be with you every step of the way," he whispered.

Eva nodded and took a deep breath in, "let's go and find Mum and deliver the news to Elion and Scar. It's going to be hard, but we have to do this."

Janus led her by the hand and they went off in search of Halana. They had to let the children know sooner rather than later, and let them decide, together, what they would do. Memories danced around in Eva's head. The time she first met Aquilia; when she offered her home to Halana and herself with the joint aspect of head dressmaker. Allowing them to keep their family as a gift, to walking the markets with her just before her sixteenth birthday; so much had happened between them, she vowed to stay by Scarlex and Eliontara's side's, no matter what they chose to do with their new found power.

As Eva and Janus walked the corridors of the Palace, every little thing reminded them of their departed Queen; the colour on the walls, the paintings which hung on the walls and the smell of fresh jasmine that lingered in the air. Everything just screamed Aquilia. They found Halana standing under the portrait of Aquilia with Scarlex and Eliontara.

"Mum, we need to do it," Eva said, attempting to smile but it never reached her eyes.

"Do what?" Scarlex asked.

"Children, why don't you both sit down? Eva and I have something we need to discuss with you," Halana smiled.

They sat on the small bench under their mother's portrait, holding each other's hands. Not knowing where to start, Halana struggled with the words.

"We...Well...We have been told to tell you..." Halana struggled.

Eva placed her hand, gently, on her mother's shoulder and knelt down in front of the two children. "We want you both to know, that we are all here for you. We will be by your side no matter what paths you choose. The Higher Elders have stated that you are to both rule over Enceladus together, unless, you decide together that one rule alone. Now, don't decide straight away, go off together and talk about it. I know you will make a decision together as you work so well as a team."

Scarlex and Eliontara hugged Eva and Halana hard. "Where will we find you?"

"Anywhere and everywhere. I will not leave until you have made your choice," Eva told them.

"I will probably be with the children in the nursery area," Halana smiled.

Both children went off together, just as twins would do.

Zeke sat with Mitzi curled up on his shoulder. She had dropped back off to sleep a few minutes after the last person left the embalming room. As he stood, Mitzi stirred slightly. He slowed his pace to allow her to sleep. Walking towards Aquilia's peaceful looking body, tears began to escape his eyes. He placed his hand on the tomb that guarded her body.

"You ruled this world with so much kindness and care. Everyone looked up to you. I tried so hard to protect you. I tried to take him out before he did anything. I failed and I shouldn't be able to carry on. I beg of anything that is higher than anything to punish me with immediate effect," Zeke said.

"No-one will punish you Zeke."

Zeke spun around so fast, Mitzi almost flew from his shoulder, but he caught her just in time. He looked up to see Aquilia's spirit hovering just above him. She, angelically, sunk to his level and placed her hands on his shoulders.

"You defended me as best you could. It was pure luck on Fresion's part that he managed to get that fatal shot off. I need you to head up the team interviewing Xeno. I know who he is to you and I hope that will not dampen your views on his mission. Keep Mitzi away from him, we know that is part of why he is here," Aquilia told him. "I expect to see great work."

"I will try my best Your Highness," Zeke whispered.

"That's what I expect and I expect you to serve my children in exactly the same way you served me," Aquilia smiled. She rose, again, high in to air, and faded slowly.

"Who were you talking to?" Mitzi asked, mid yawn.

"Myself," Zeke smiled. He carried her off to the confines of the Palace in search of a bed for her to rest in. He walked the Palace corridors, examining the portraits and art as he went, finally arriving at a guest room, equipped with a fully made bed. He laid Mitzi on the pillow and draped a small blanket over her.

As Zeke left the room, he ran into one of the Palace guards.

"Keep guard of this room. No one is to enter," Zeke told him.

The guard nodded briskly and stood guard at the doorway.

Safe in the knowledge that Mitzi was protected, Zeke went in search of Celest. He needed to begin the interview with Xeno, whether he wanted to or not.

He wandered the Palace in search of Celest. He checked back in at the, now run down, medical wing. His heart hurt at how much destruction he had caused. He made a mental note to help with the rebuild as soon as this part was over. As Zeke re-entered the Palace from the far side of the landing pad, he bumped into Eva and Janus.

"Have you seen Celest?" He asked.

"The last time I saw her, she was heading towards the repair bunkers," Janus replied. "Is everything OK Zeke?"

Zeke looked down at the floor and then brought his eyes up to meet Janus's. "I have something dark inside of me, and I fear that what I am about to do, after I find Celest, will be terrible. Can you help me?" He whispered.

Janus glanced at Eva, who seemed to know exactly what to do. They each took hold of Zeke's arms and almost frogmarched him to the Wraith Doctors.

Slamming Zeke onto the table, it took almost ten beings to hold him down as they restrained him as best they could.

"You will probably need to fetch his father," the youngest doctor told Janus.

Janus headed off in search of Layson.

"What's wrong with him?" Eva asked quietly. "I've never seen him like this."

"This could be an infection of some sort, we need to run tests to be sure," another doctor replied.

Of all the years Eva had known these doctors she had never once thought to discover their names.

"It isn't an infection," Layson said as he stopped just inside the doorway. "Zeke has the genes of the Dark Wolf. Just like me."

The Wraith Doctors all rushed to their various stations, mixing chemicals together in various beakers and tubes. They moved in absolute silence, all seeming to know exactly which part they each played in this conveyor belt of chemistry. Their act lasted no more than half an hour and a dose was complete.

The eldest of the doctors hovered forward, he held in his hands, a syringe filled with a white liquid.

"He will need these monthly, just like you, to keep the Dark Wolf at bay," he told Layson. "Ensure she receives them."

Layson nodded and allowed the doctor to inject the liquid into Zeke's neck. As soon as the plunger was pressed, Zeke's flailing slowed, and his heart rate returned the normal. He panted heavily trying to catch his own breath. He looked around at those in the room, silently thanking Eva and Janus for getting him here in time.

"He will need a few hours rest," the youngest doctor smiled.

Everyone left the room except Layson. He sat with Zeke whilst he slept, ensuring the concoction worked. It wasn't until Layson awoke from a nap that he realised the horrible truth.

It hadn't.

<u>Chapter Forty – Three</u>

"Well, where is he?" Bella cried. "Surely he can't have gone far."

Layson had awoken to an empty bed where Zeke had been restrained. The restraints had been ripped from their tethering and discarded on the floor.

"I've sent out a discreet message to Nymeria and Celest, they have been searching for him for over an hour," Layson replied. "There has been no sign of him."

Bella paced the medical suite. She couldn't imagine where he could have gone. Onyx Abyss Alpha was still being repaired as were majority of the other ships. She thought of the outhouse where she had been practicing her magic, would he have gone there? She fled from the room and began heading for the outhouse. Weaving her way across the gardens, she pulled out the key and attempted to unlock the door. As she slowly opened it, a figure sat hunched over the table.

"Zeke?" She whispered. "Is that you?"

"No dear, it's just me. Is young Zeke lost?" Benzyline asked, turning on the table lamp.

"Oh Benzyline! Have you seen Zeke?" Bella asked, clearly frustrated.

"No dear. How is it you've come to lose him? Is he not with little Mitzi? Them two are almost joint at the hip recently,"

Benzyline said as she shuffled towards the bookcase and withdrew a large dusty book.

"I didn't think of that, but then again, I don't even know where she is," Bella wondered out loud.

"That's simple dear. Fourth bedroom along the white corridor, there's a guard on the door, won't let you in mind, but you may be able to wake Mitzi if you call out to her," Benzyline shrugged.

Bella rolled her eyes, chuckled to herself and made her way back to the Palace. Wandering the corridors, she listened out for any tiny noises, it helped having hearing better than anything in this universe. She picked up on shallow breathing coming from three doors down. Benzyline was right; there was a guard on the door. Zeke must have had a reason to have one placed there. She walked, cautiously, towards the door.

"I'm sorry, I'm under strict orders not to allow anyone to enter," the guard announced.

"Orders from whom?" Bella asked, looking in deep in the eyes.

"Zeke Ma'am. He told me that under no circumstances was anyone to enter this room," the guard replied.

"Very well, I will have to call her from here. Mitzi! Mitzi are you in there?" Bella called out.

"What's all the shouting?" Mitzi called out from beneath the guard.

"I'm sorry Miss. Did this lady wake you?" The guard asked her.

"No, this is Zeke's mother. You really ought to know that," Mitzi told him. "Bella, what is it?"

"Can we walk and talk?" Bella smiled.

"Sure, erm, would I be able to hitch a ride? Legs are a little small to keep up," Mitzi smiled coyly.

"Absolutely," Bella smiled as she bent down to allow Mitzi to climb up.

"So what's up?" Mitzi asked as she settled herself on Bella shoulder, gently wrapping Bella burnt orange hair around her shoulders, "Your hair is amazing!"

Bella laughed, "I wish it was! I wanted to ask you about Zeke. Have you seen him?"

"Not since he and I were in the embalming room together. I overheard him speaking with someone, it sounded like Queen Aquilia, but I cannot be sure," Mitzi replied.

"Can you remember what was said?" Bella asked as they passed the entrance to the sacred gardens on the far side of the Palace.

"Hmm, if my memory serves me, I remember a name," Mitzi closed her eyes as if reaching into the depths of her brain to recover the name she heard. "Xeno? I don't know if that name means anything to you."

Bella stopped. "Xeno? He's in the holding cells? I'm sure I overheard Celest invite Scarlex to the interview."

"That could be, but, I can't go near there," Mitzi began to shake. "He is Wigfya. He's here for me."

Bella turned her head slightly towards her. "You're Squink. Oh my. We must put you into hiding."

"I would be safe in a bunker, if there is one available?" Mitzi asked.

"Then we will find you one. Hold tight," Bella told her. As soon as the words left her mouth, Bella began running through the corridors in search of Halana and the others.

"Who's there?" Xeno called. "I know you're there."

Zeke stalked out of the shadows, his huge, seven foot frame, filling the space between the floor and ceiling, his amber eyes staring straight into Xeno's soul.

"You can't be," Xeno whispered. "You simply can't be."

"Recognise anything? Grandfather," Zeke snarled.

"But it no longer exists," Xeno said softly.

Zeke laughed; the sound resonating from the pit of his stomach. "Even you don't believe that!" He strode towards the cell which kept his grandfather separated from him and placed his paws around the bars. He leant back, bending the bars slightly but not too much.

Xeno backed away from the cell door. "W...what do you want?"

"Just a chat, seems we never really got the chance to meet considering you lied about dying," Zeke grinned.

"You're Layson's boy?" Xeno asked, daring to step closer.

Zeke let out a gut wrenching laugh. "You finally worked it out! Why did it take you so long?"

Xeno backed away from the cell door once again, this time cornering himself in the furthest corner from the door. He watched in horror as Zeke ripped the door from its frame and squeezed through what remained. As he stood in the centre of the room, his eyes focused one Xeno.

"You. You are NOT what Enceladants should be! You make us look bad! Why are you part of the Wigfya?" He shouted.

Xeno laughed. "Are you worried about that little *thing* that hangs around you? Once I have her, you won't have to worry about her anymore. She's no help to you or this world, you'll see. Life will be better without her."

Zeke's eyes flashed from amber to black and remained that way, baring his teeth and let out a deep growl. "You know *nothing* about her."

Xeno smiled a sly smile. "I see where you're going with this. She means something to you, doesn't she? She's important to you."

Zeke refused to allow him the pleasure of an answer. He continued to glare at him until he could no longer bare it. Zeke pounced from his standing place and pinned Xeno to the ground. "I should rip out your throat, and then send you on a one way trip to Gydex. They would love someone like you out there." He continued to show his sharp teeth, white foam dripping from the two sharp fangs at the front.

Xeno cowered under Zeke's large frame, his arms shielding his face. He curled himself in the smallest form he could, hoping Zeke would eventually back down.

"Zeke, come on son. Let's go," Layson said softly, touching Zeke's back gently.

Zeke spun around wildly almost knocking his father flying, his hind legs moving precariously closer to Xeno's torso.

"I can't let him take her Dad," Zeke told Layson. "He can't have her."

"We won't let him Zeke. Don't worry," Layson whispered, taking two steps towards him. "She's safe."

Zeke took one more step back, stepping straight onto Xeno's torso, a loud crack stunning both into a deafening silence. Zeke looked at his father. Layson looked down at the floor. A pool of green spilling from between Zeke's back paw.

"I...I didn't mean to Dad," Zeke said, looking at his father with tears in his eyes. "I'm sorry."

Layson took Zeke's hands in his own and looked his son in the eyes. "He was always dead to me. This, will make no difference at all. You need to realise how many beings you have probably just saved, not only Mitzi, but her entire species.'

"But there are others Dad. Others that will want to hunt Mitzi," Zeke said, clearly still worried for Mitzi's safety.

Layson laid his hand on Zeke's arm. "When news gets back to them on *how* Xeno died. I can guess that *no one* will even think of coming for her."

"Can you guarantee that Dad?" Zeke asked, his form slowly returning to normal.

Layson looked at a now broken Xeno, "I won't lie to you. I can't guarantee it, but I will bet my life that they won't venture here the whole time you walk this planet."

Zeke stood next to his father, back to his original form and asked, "Will they ever find a way to control this?"

"The Wraith Doctors never give up son. They will find a way. Until then, you will need to control it," Layson told him. "But don't worry, your mother and I will be by your side every step of the way."

Zeke hugged his father hard. He knew that his parents would never let him down. Layson allowed a single tear to escape his eye. His only child was now facing a truly ominous future. Zeke would need to learn how to control The Dark Wolf. Only he could do it. Zeke's inner form was more powerful than Layson's; it would take all of Zeke's strength to keep it at bay.

As they walked back towards the Palace, Bella appeared from the main doors, followed closely by Mitzi, Celest and Nymeria. Zeke wondered how to tell them but as his father placed his hand on his shoulder, he knew he had the closet bond with these people.

"I have something I need to say but I need everyone in attendance. Celest, can you gather those closest and meet me in the library?" Zeke asked.

"Sure thing kid," she smiled, turning and running off towards the Palace.

"Are you sure you want to do this son?" Layson asked.

"I need to Dad. I need to let people know what could happen," Zeke replied.

Layson nodded his head once. He understood what Zeke meant; he just worried about how people would react to it. He was happy that his son was so confident; it showed him that Zeke would be able to handle anything thrown at him.

Chapter Forty – Four

Zeke sat at the furthest table back from the door, watching as the selected beings filed in, sitting where they could find room or standing to the sides.

"I know you must all be wondering why I asked Celest to bring you here. This is not going to be an easy thing to hear and, believe me, it's not an easy thing to admit," Zeke began, "but there is something I need you all to know. I have the gene for The Dark Wolf."

The room was silent. Not one being spoke, let alone breathed.

"I saw it in you," a voice spoke from the back of the room.

Everyone turned to allow Scarlex to walk forward. She placed her hands over Zeke's and looked him in the eyes.

"The day we spoke together, on that very table," she said pointing to the table behind him. "I saw something in your eyes."

Zeke thought back to the day. He had hugged Scarlex and seen something himself. He remembered her saying something about Mitzi. Mitzi!

Hr turned to see Mitzi sitting on the table, her head hanging down. "Mitz?"

She looked up at him. Her eyes shining with tears. "How long have you known?" She whispered.

"For certain? About three months. I haven't shifted before. The medical wing was my first time. I was terrified," Zeke told her softly as he sat on the chair beside her.

"I could have been there for you. Just like you were for me," she said, blue tears falling from her eyes.

"Oh Mitzi. I couldn't let you see me like that. It's not a pretty sight," Zeke replied, fresh tears appearing in his eyes.

Mitzi climbed up onto his shoulder and pulled his face towards hers. "Nothing would stop me looking at you Zeke. Not a wolf, not an alien, not even a human," she told him, bumping his nose with hers. "I love you," she whispered in his ear.

Zeke smiled. He stood tall and proud and turned to face the gathered crowd. "Does anyone have any questions or comments?"

The crowd was silent. He looked across the face of every being gathered and saw no fear or judgement. He saw faces of trusting aides, and supportive friends.

"I think it's clear to say that nobody is, in the slightest, bothered," Nymeria laughed. "But, you do need to help us fix the medical wing. Wolfie!"

The crowd erupted with laughter and being slapped Zeke on the back whilst shaking his hand and congratulating him on being brave.

"That was a really brave thing to do Zeke," Elion told him.

"I guess I learnt to be brave from some other brave beings." he looked between Scarlex, Eliontara and Mitzi. "You have all taught me so much."

"We do have some news to announce also, if you could all just stay for a few more minutes," Eliontara asked. He took hold of his sister's hand and pulled her atop the nearest table.

"Together, we have decided who will rule over Saturn and Enceladus," he said, looking at Scarlex. She nodded to him, urging him to continue. "We have decided that Scarlex will be the overall ruler. I will be by her side at all times, but she has vowed to remain a fighter for this planet and Saturn."

"NONSENSE!" Zyra's voice boomed around the room. "As a Queen she will remain on Enceladus during battle and be confined to the bunker until it is safe."

Scarlex jumped from the table and made her way to the meeting room. She thumped on the door as hard and her dainty hands would allow. As the door slide open, she forced herself inside. She slammed her hands on the table and waited for someone to reply to her.

Zyra's face appeared first, followed by Quintara and Elio.

"What is it Scarlex?" Zyra asked.

"You don't get to tell *me* what I can and cannot do as Queen," she announced.

"Oh stars above she sounds just like her mother," Quintara exclaimed.

Scarlex spun her head towards her, the electric blue braid winding itself around her waist. "My legendary 'grandmother and grandfather,' both of whom have had little to no interest in mine or my brothers' lives. You didn't care when my mother was alive, you didn't ask about us or even worry when we were both in the skies above Saturn and Enceladus, trying to protect OUR MOTHER!" She shouted. "You, none of you, will dictate to me or my brother how this Kingdom will be governed."

"Young lady. We are the Higher Elders. We can dictate whatever we please. Now, you go back to that little meeting of yours and you inform them all the same," Zyra raised her voice.

"If memory serves me right Zyra, it is up to the reigning monarch as to whether we remain in our positions or not," Elio whispered.

Quintara and Zyra both glared at him. He shrugged his shoulders and faded from the wall.

"Is that true?" Scarlex asked.

"Within reason, yes," Zyra said sounding defeated.

"And the reasons being?" Scarlex asked, sitting in her mother's chair.

"The reigning monarch must prove that we are no longer fit for purpose," Zyra replied. "But we are still fit for purpose."

"Is that what you think?" Scarlex asked. "Where were you all, exactly, when my mother died? Why didn't you instigate the shield around the planets when there was word that Xeno was hunting Mitzi? Where have *any* of you been when we have needed you? Nowhere! That's where! You are no longer fit for purpose, and when I find out how to remove you from your positions, your help will no longer be required." She then stood and strode from the room.

"Do you think they made the right choice Mum?" Eva asked Halana.

"Only time will tell my dear. She will have an army of people behind her, she knows that," Halana replied with a smile. "Exactly like her mother had when she arrived here."

Eva watched Eliontara as he sat with Zeke and Mitzi. She admired how well he interacted with others considering how quiet he was when he was younger.

"MUMMY!"

Eva spun around, amazed by the smiles that greeted her. "Look at the state of you all!" She laughed.

Each child was covered from head to toe in paint and clay and feathers.

"I'm sorry Duchess. I tried to keep them away from the art supplies but, I just couldn't watch them all at once, even have twelve eyes didn't help," Duscha told her.

"Oh don't worry Duscha. It's great that they are exploring their artistic sides," Eva laughed.

Duscha didn't know whether Eva was serious or angry but really great at hiding it. She didn't want to risk smiling in case Eva snapped at her. She kept her head down.

"Duscha, it's OK, really. My children have a habit of exploring every single thing and I enjoy seeing what they have been up to in my absence," Eva said as she placed her hand on Duscha's shoulder. "Have you ever considered a job looking after little ones?"

"It was something I dreamed off as a young Spritelet," she replied.

"That's settled. You can come back to Saturn with us and pick up some experience. You will be paid well," Eva smiled.

Duscha stared, wide eyed, at Eva. "Really? I wouldn't want to put the Countess out of place," she began.

Eva laughed, "I think Lyra will be grateful for the help and the break. Speaking of the Countess, has anyone seen when she went?"

Duscha looked around the room, spotting Lyra heading off towards one of the far corridors of the Palace. "I believe she is heading towards the East Wing."

Eva turned and looked in the direction Duscha pointed. She was surprised to see Lyra hurrying out of the room and down the corridor; her head hung low and her hair flowing behind her. Eva jogged after her, gently calling her name as she went.

"Hey," Eva said as she managed to catch up with Lyra. "Where're you off to?"

"I...I just needed some space to process everything," Lyra replied, trying her hardest to avoid looking into Eva's green eyes.

"Lyra, you have every right to be upset about Aquilia's death too," Eva soothed.

"I know. I just don't feel like I should mourn over her in front of everyone considering my background," Lyra said softly.

Eva placed her hands either side of Lyra's face, and forced her to look at her. "Ignore what people say. Aquilia forgave you and allowed you and your people to reside back in Astrodia. She wouldn't have allowed that if she believed you were dangerous."

A single tear slid from Lyra's eye. She knew Eva was right. Aquilia had a deeper soul than anyone she had ever known. Lyra made a decision there and then that she and her people needed to do something to mark Aquilia's life on Saturn.

"When we return to Saturn, we will mark Aquilia's death with a celebration of her life. There will be music, colours and a mass of laughter," Lyra whispered. "I know she loved to laugh."

Eva smiled. "Duscha will be travelling back with us. She will tend to the children whilst you continue with your plans. She will be staying with us to fulfil her dreams. Is that OK with you?"

Lyra smiled. "I will be grateful for the help. Duscha is a lovely soul, someone who will put anyone before herself. Let me know when we are to leave." Lyra turned from Eva's hands and walked out towards the crystal fountain.

Eva sighed. She hoped Lyra would be OK. She had a lot of hidden feelings.

<u>Chapter Forty – Five</u>

<u>Saturn</u>

"So," Eva said as she spread her arms wide. "Here are your quarters. There are no limits as to where you can go. Our home is your home."

Duscha looked around the bright and airy room with is lilac voiles and its freshly made bed. "It...It's amazing. Thank you."

"Lyra normally has the children up, dressed and ready for their lessons by eight. As you have already seen, each child has their own way of getting ready," Eva laughed at Codex placed his shoes on his hands and tried walking on them.

"They each have their own personalities and that is a unique thing. I'm sure we will get into a routine," Duscha smiled. She bent down to Codex and held his legs up, enabling him to walk on his hands.

Eva smiled. She knew deep down she had done the right thing in bringing Duscha to Saturn. She looked out of the window that overlooked the courtyard, spotting Lyra walking with the Sun Healer Leader. Lyra seemed to be describing where she wanted something placed. Since returning from Enceladus, Lyra had busied herself with arranging a huge celebration for Aquilia. A way for the Kingdom of Astrodia to celebrate their Queen in all the ways they could possibly imagine. Lyra had arranged a parade, a book of memories and lots of other things that would involve the people of Astrodia.

Lyra had made it her sole responsibility to show her appreciation of Aquilia in any way she could.

Turning from the window, she gasped as Xandr slid along the floor on his bottom.

"Weeee!" He exclaimed as he slid passed her.

Eva giggled to herself. All her children had their own way of travelling as well as their own unique personalities. She walked back towards the kitchen and out into the gardens, joining Janus as he relaxed in the afternoon sun.

"It feels strange going back to normal after everything," she whispered as she laid her head on his shoulder.

"It does, but it's what Aquilia would have wanted," Janus smiled, kissing the top of her green hair. He looked back up towards the sky just as a trail of smoke shot across the sky.

Grabbing the nearest SkySearchers, he followed the trail back towards Enceladus and then back towards the ship, only to be greeted with the back end of Onyx Abyss Alpha. He shook his head and lowered himself back to his seated position.

"Onyx is back in the air. I wonder how Scarlex is getting on with Zeke and Mitzi." Janus whispered.

"I'm sure she is doing great. She had the most amazing teacher and Zeke respects her," Eva replied.

"Ready the VisionScope," Scarlex ordered.

"VisionScope ready and online," Zeke replied.

Scarlex stepped towards the eyepiece and looked through. Despite having telescopic vision of her own, she opted to use the tools to hand. She changed the magnification multiple times and moved the scope left to right on more than three occasions.

"What is it Ma'am?" Mitzi asked as she watched Scarlex work.

"I'm unsure. There seems to be an object about three light years to the west of us and approaching at a rate of nearly fifteen hundred miles an hour," Scarlex informed them. "We have to get word back to Elion."

"On it Ma'am," Zeke said as he turned back to face his monitors. He pulled up the newly installed video communication system and placed the call to Enceladus.

"Enceladus here, what's up Zeke?" Elion asked as he beamed from the screen.

"Trace an object three light years west of our current location, travelling pretty fast in our direction. Any information you can get would be great," Zeke relayed.

"Yes Sir. I'm on it as we speak," Elion replied.

Zeke watched as he typed various codes and commands into the system, many of which he knew himself, others had been recently coded in. His eyes wandered from screen to screen as various amounts of information loaded in front of him. Elion finally sat back in his chair, his eyes wide with shock.

"What is it Elion?" Zeke asked. "You look like you've read something surprising."

Elion swallowed audibly, "I have. According to the trajectory of your location and the incoming object, there is a possibility, a rather large possibility that you will collide if you continue at your current speed and heading."

Mitzi bounced over and landed on Zeke's shoulder, a place she had spent so much time over the past few months. "What do you mean?" She asked.

"I'll show you what I have in front of me," Elion said as he tapped multiple keys.

Within a few short seconds, Zeke's screen was displaying the tracking system Elion had used to trace the object. He followed the direction of the object and noticed how it would intercept their path within the next week.

"Where is its origin?" Scarlex asked.

"It seems to have originated from Earth, or in that vicinity," Elion replied. "Judging by bounce back signals, it is an empty vessel."

Scarlex returned to the VisionScope and peered through again, this time using her added vision to gather more intelligence. She noticed the absence of windows and the fact that the object looked as though a human would be compacted inside it.

"I don't see any signs of life from the object. There are no viewing points and the vessel looks too small to even be able to hold Mitzi comfortably enough," Scarlex told them.

"Is it really that small?" Mitzi asked.

"Believe me, you would feel cramped!" Scarlex smiled."Let's alter our course by half a mile, see if we can avoid contact. Elion, keep track please. You are my eyes."

"You got it!" Elion replied before closing off the link.

Zeke stood, stretched his back and his arms and walked around the ship. He looked back towards Enceladus, the events of the past few weeks slamming into him like poison darts. He had been slowly learning how to keep The Dark Wolf at bay, give or take a few times when his ugly head had reared, but luckily it was just his head and it was swiftly put back into its box.

"You OK?" Mitzi asked as she nuzzled into his neck.

"I am now," he smiled. "I'm glad you stayed."

"I promised didn't I?" She said as she jumped from his shoulder to the desk in front of him. "What's wrong Zeke?"

"I don't know. Something feels strange," he replied. "I knew things wouldn't be the same after Aquilia died, but I don't even think it is that. I can't seem to put my finger on it."

Mitzi's eyes glazed over as she watched him struggle with his feelings. She wished she could figure things out for him so that he would be feeling this way. She noticed how he would flex and unflex his hands when he couldn't find the right words to say and she wished her hands were big enough to cover his and help him. In some ways, she felt incomparable to the bigger beings around, but Zeke seemed to calm down more when she was around compared to anyone else. As he wandered the rear of the ship, Scarlex sat next to Mitzi.

"Is he still struggling?" Scarlex asked.

"MmmHmm. I don't want to sound like I'm talking behind his back, but I'm worried about him," Mitzi replied. "Since your mother passed, I feel that he hasn't been himself."

"Oh Mitzi. That isn't talking behind someone's back, you clearly care very deeply for Zeke," Scarlex said. "What is it that is worrying you about him?"

Mitzi thought for a second. There were so many things that she had noticed about him, she didn't know where to start. "I think the whole Dark Wolf thing is genuinely hard for him to control. I wish The Wraith Doctors could make this concoction quicker. I really feel that it will do him the world of good."

"I fear you may be right. Zeke is a strong part of this team, but I fear something will throw him off course. I'll get a message back to Enceladus for The Wraith Doctors to step up their research," Scarlex told her.

"Thank you. Could I do a little research myself?" Mitzi asked. "I have had an idea that I would like to check up on."

Scarlex gestured the computer in her private quarters. "Take all the time you need. Zeke and I will be able to navigate from here."

Mitzi scrambled towards the computer, closing the door quietly behind her. She clambered up onto the chair and began researching The Dark Wolf. She had the ability to access far darker websites than others. She trawled through page after page of information, storing it all in her head. She searched up on cures and preventions, finally landing on a page which caught her attention. She read each line as carefully as she could. Once, twice, almost three times. She couldn't believe what she was reading. Could it work? Would it work? She searched harder for any trials that had been completed, anything that would give her the results she so desperately wanted to read.

When the page finally materialized, she was amazed. It seemed what she had read had been correct! Now she just had to talk Zeke and The Wraith Doctors into trying it. That would be the hardest part.

Zeke emerged from the kitchen area, his hands stuffed with snacks which he then placed into the lower drawer of his desk.

"Planning on moving in?" Scarlex laughed as she watched him blush.

"It's just in case I get snowed down," Zeke said as he lowered his head. He had hoped no one would be around to see him stash the snacks away.

Scarlex smiled. "You don't have to explain yourself Zeke. The snacks are there to be eaten, even if you do stash most of them away in that drawer."

"What drawer?" Mitzi asked as she crept up on them both. "What'cha got stashed away?"

Zeke blushed even more. Not because he had been caught out stashing food, but because most of the food was for Mitzi. She climbed up onto the edge of the drawer and looked inside.

"Ohhh! Smarshies!! My favourite! Almond Halves and Batch Pieces! I didn't know you liked them too!" She exclaimed.

Scarlex looked at Zeke slyly. She had worked him out, but she wouldn't let on. For now.

"So did you find out much?" She asked Mitzi.

"I did, but I don't know how to approach the subject," Mitzi admitted.

"Approach what subject?" Zeke asked as he perched himself on the edge of his desk.

Mitzi looked at Scarlex who raised her eyebrow just slightly. "He would find out sooner rather than later, maybe best coming from you."

Mitzi stood up as tall as she little frame would allow. "I have been checking up on ways that could prevent The Dark Wolf. I know that you're going to tell me that The Wraith Doctors are doing all they can but I don't think they are."

"What makes you so sure?" Zeke asked calmly.

Mitzi was surprised he hadn't snapped at her. "Because they haven't found out what I have."

"And what would that be?" Zeke asked his eyes kind and gentle.

"Well..." Mitzi began.

Chapter Forty – Six

Enceladus

"It's out of the question. There is no way on this rock that I will put you through that!" Zeke told her. "I don't care how long I have to put up with this until The Wraith Doctors find something but there is no way I am putting you at risk just to *try* something out.”

“But Zeke, I don’t want you to worry anymore. I don’t want you to be afraid of going far away and not being able to control it. Even if we just try once. If it doesn’t work then I will forget the whole thing,” Mitzi begged. “Please Zeke. I need to be able to help, or at least feel like I am.”

“All I need is for you to be with me. Nothing more and nothing less. You alone can keep The Dark Wolf at bay,” Zeke told her.

“But I can’t Zeke. You and I both know that,” she replied. “Please, let me try.”

Zeke stopped walking and Mitzi almost walked into the back of his legs. He hung his head and shoulders low. “I can’t ask you to do this Mitzi. It’s too much to ask.”

“I bet your Mum would do it for your Dad if she could,” Mitzi whispered.

She looked down at the ground and allowed a few tears to escape at a level where they couldn’t be witnessed falling to the floor. She turned away from him and walked, quietly towards the library. She figured he would rather be alone for a while. She sat alone in the library, swinging her legs under the chair. She wanted to make Zeke see what a difference it would make to his life. She *needed* him to see the difference, but she knew it would take more than just her word alone.

Dropping to the floor, Mitzi went in search of the only people she knew that could help her persuade Zeke into trying this outrageous thing; Layson and Bella.

"So what are you thinking?" Celest asked Zeke after he had explained Mitzi's idea to her.

"I can't let her do that. What if it doesn't work? I would feel guilty for the rest of my days," Zeke explained.

"But, don't you think it should be up to her what she does? I mean, if she is willing," Nymeria shrugged. "I know I'd do anything to help Celest out if I could."

"I get why she wants to help. I really do, but I can't risk losing her. She means too much to me," Zeke replied as he hung his head low.

Celest stood, walked to where he was sitting and sat beside him. "Be honest with yourself here Zeke. Who are you more afraid of losing? Mitzi or The Dark Wolf? Have a think about it."

With those parting words, Nymeria and Celest left Zeke to ponder his own thoughts. He sat with his head in his hands, allowing his mind to wander. He hated having to make decisions which could ultimately hurt those he loved, but he knew Nymeria and Celest were right. They would do anything to help each other. It was part of their bond. He wanted that bond with Mitzi. He *needed* that bond with her. Every time he closed his eyes, her face would come into view. He knew what he had to do. Zeke climbed to his feet, made sure all the chairs were tucked in under the table and went in search of Mitzi.

As he made his way along the corridor, he came across Halana, peacefully sitting beneath the portrait of Aquilia and her children.

"Miss Halana?" Zeke said softly, not wanting to startle her.

"Oh young Zeke, come, sit with me. You seem troubled. What's wrong?" She said as she patted the seat beside her.

Zeke obliged in sitting with her, but was unsure how to begin the conversation about Mitzi. It had been so easy with Celest and Nymeria.

"Let me guess, seeing as though you can't seem to summon the words to speak. Mitzi?" Halana asked.

Zeke nodded. "I...She has offered me something and, oh, I was so angry when I told her no. She went off by herself and...I guess I feel so guilty, and after speaking with Celest and Nymeria, I know I was wrong to just say no without thinking it through first."

"Zeke, as we grow older, we make rash decisions, especially when it concerns someone we care very deeply about, and I can tell Mitzi means a lot to you. What is it that she is offering?"Halana asked.

Zeke thought hard before he answered. "She has done some research with regards to holding off The Dark Wolf. It seems that there is a way in which she can help, but I instantly refused. I don't want her to risk her getting hurt if it doesn't work."

"Don't you think that should be up to Mitzi to decide?" Halana asked.

"Maybe, but what if it doesn't work? I will always feel guilty for asking her," Zeke admitted.

"It will work," Benzyline said as she bustled by.

"What will?" Zeke called after her.

"Everything! Everything will work out in the end. Mark my words!" She called back.

Zeke shook his head and sat back down, "she is a strange one," he laughed.

"But she could be right. Why not give it a go?" Halana asked.

"Would you come with me? Please?" Zeke asked.

Halana stood, linked her arm with his and smiled. "Lead the way Zeke. Let's see what we can do."

They walked along the corridor, smiling to each being as they passed by. Unaware of how things would go, Zeke allowed his hoped to rise slightly. The closer they got to where Mitzi had left him not too long ago; they could hear the sound of voices, ones that he could pinpoint in the darkest of rooms.

"I really want to help him, but I don't think he will let me. I can understand why he won't but I really want to try," Mitzi was saying.

"Have you asked him why he won't let you?" Layson asked.

"He said he doesn't want to feel guilty if it doesn't work, but I won't let him feel guilty. It should be me that would feel guilty that I couldn't help, but I really want to try," Mitzi said.

"Zeke is a very independent young being. He likes to be able to work things out for himself. When we see him, we will have a chat and see how we can move on from this," Bella smiled. "You are thinking of doing a very kind thing Mitzi."

Mitzi smiled. She hoped Zeke would see that what she was trying to do was for his happiness as well as her own. She hoped that Bella and Layson could help Zeke see that. Mitzi had nothing to gain from this experiment, not personally anyway, but she would gain the chance to be able to travel with Zeke again without him having to worry about The Dark Wolf making an appearance.

"Thank you for listening to me. I...I guess I'll head back to Onyx and wait for our next mission," Mitzi said as she turned and headed out the door.

"She has a deep soul Layson," Bella whispered. "Deeper than any I have seen before."

"Her heart is in the right place, but it is a huge risk," Layson replied. "She is such a wonderful being, so caring and loyal."

Bella and Layson watched as Mitzi as she sauntered back towards the loading area, her white hair billowing in the sudden winds which had picked up. Layson looked up towards the sky. It had turned a scary shade of orange. He could see flashes within the clouds. Sprites of red and green jumping from cloud to cloud. He watched as the clouds swirled above, throwing raindrops down like knives towards the surface. The more he watched the faster things changed. He noticed how Mitzi had begun dodging the rain, cowering when one drop landed on her head and another on her shoulder. The rain fell harder and harder, forcing Mitzi to seek shelter under one of the taller flowers in the gardens. She huddled down to the ground, as low as she could just as a bright white light lit up the area. She flinched slightly, only to then be terrified of the low rumble that followed shortly behind.

Bella noticed how scared Mitzi looked, she opened the door to go and bring her back in, but as she did, another bolt of bright light appeared. Layson held Bella's arm.

"But Layson...I have to get her," Bella insisted.

"No darling. If you go out there, the sprites with catch you," Layson told her. He had seen this phenomenon before. The sprites hunted their victims but how much they stood out in the storm. They watched from the window as the flashes became more intense and the rumbles got louder.

"Mum, Dad, where's Mitzi?" Zeke shouted over a deep rumble that seemed to be coming from the depths of the planet.

Layson pointed towards the flower underneath which Mitzi still cowered.

"Why is she out there in this?" Zeke said as she ran to the window. "I have to bring her back."

"Son, believe me, if there was a way, I would bring her myself, but weather like this is not like playing Dodge The Drop," Layson warned him. "This is something that doesn't happen often but when it does, it makes up for times it has been away."

Zeke placed his hand against the window in the hope that just by him watching, she would be safe. He watched as she huddled under the flower, her eyes darting left and right as she calculated the falling raindrops. He placed his hand on the door handle and prepared to throw open the door.

Mitzi counted as the drops fell. One, two, three, four, and then a gap of five seconds. Another set of drops. One, two three, four, five, six. Another gap of six seconds this time. Back to the drops to the count of four and back to the five second gap. Mitzi waited for the same cycle to circle three times before placing her own fate in her hands and running for the door which Zeke held onto. She hunched down ready to sprint, arched her back and in the blink of an eye, sprinted towards the door. Zeke counted her steps and threw the door open when she was exactly two steps from the door. Mitzi stretched her hand out to Zeke, ready for him to pull her into the Palace, but just before their hands locked, a bright light lit up the sky and struck Mitzi at the top of her spine, the light blinded Bella and Layson temporarily.

Zeke stood motionless as Mitzi's limp body fell to the floor, her white hair now streaked with gold, and her eyes almost welded shut. He stared at her still body as the skies above Enceladus cleared to reveal the same azure blue they were accustomed to.

Chapter Forty – Seven

"Zeke?" Nymeria called for what felt like the thousandth time.

"Maybe we should just leave it for now babe," Celest said as she tried to guide her wife away.

"No! He has to hear this," Nymeria cried. She grabbed Zeke by his shoulder and spun him around. "Mitzi needs you to be strong. Get your head out of Jupiter's gases and get it back here where it belongs!"

"I can't do anything for her Ny! What can I do? The Wraith Doctors aren't even sure if she is going to make it and they have been working on her for what feels like days now. I just..." Zeke sighed. "I just want Mitzi back." Tears began streaming from his face.

Nymeria pulled him into an embrace. Never one to shy away from showing her maternal side, she held him whilst he cried, slowly soothing him into a gentle sob. "She's going to be OK. She's made of stronger stuff than we give her credit for."

A swishing sound caught Celest's attention and she turned to see two of The Wraith Doctors enter the room. She gently nudged Nymeria and Zeke and gestured their arrival.

"How is she?" Zeke asked, swiping at the tears that refused to stop flowing.

"We need you to come with us," the smaller doctor said. "It is important but you must come alone."

Zeke looked between Nymeria and Celest, begging one of them to come to his aid, but they both nodded in agreement with the Doctor. He turned from them both and followed the Doctors to an aqua coloured room at the end of the longest corridor he had ever seen.

He braced himself at the door before entering. Mentally preparing himself for what he would see. He looked up from the floor to see the remaining Wraith Doctors looking down at Mitzi as she lay on a white table. Her golden streaked hair spread around her head in a halo effect, her blue eyes staring straight up at the skylight above.

"Is she going to be OK?" He whispered.

"Zeke, please, join me here," the tallest Wraith Doctor said, gesturing the left side of him. "We need you for the final part of Mitzi's journey."

"Journey? To where?" Zeke asked as he slowly made his way to his appointed place.

"Back home of course," a small woman said from the right side of him. "You and Mitzi have a strong bond. To bring her back to this world, we need you here."

"Where is she now?" Zeke asked, taking the hand the smaller Wraith Doctor held out.

"In between worlds. She has no form of escape. To bring her back, it will take the love of another to drag her back. Are you ready?" The tallest Doctor asked.

Zeke nodded. He would do anything he could to bring her back.

"Try not to worry. Your power will not work on us. We have no future or past to show," the smaller Doctor smiled, noticing how nervous Zeke was as holding her hand.

He took a deep breath and closed his eyes. He could feel his hands begin to tingle, the sensation slowly making its way up his arms before settling in his chest. He slowed his breathing down and his vision adjusted to the bright light in front of him.

"Zeke? Is that you?"

"Mitzi? Where are you?" He called back.

"Follow the sound of my voice," she replied. "Don't think, just listen."

Zeke allowed his ears to guide him to the far side of a stark white room, where Mitzi sat on what looked like a throne. Her white hair still streaked with gold and her blue eyes sparkling in the light. Gone were her dark clothes and boots, replaced with a white jacket, white trousers and white platform boots. Her lips were painted with a light silver colour which highlighted her lips.

"You look different," he told her.

"I may have to stay this way," she said as she hung her head low. "They told me only love can send me back, but no one loves me enough to bring me back. I just wanted you to know, that if this is the end. You have to try the research."

Zeke gathered her up in his arms, nudged his nose against hers and looked her deep in the eyes. "No one could love you more than I do."

"But is it enough to send me home?" She asked looking hopeful.

"I guess we have to wait and see," Zeke replied, looking up towards the light above them. He held on to her tight as the light got brighter and brighter.

For what felt like hours the light shone brightly in his eyes, but he refused to let go of Mitzi. He could still feel her in his arms. The light gradually dimmed, revealing The Wraith Doctors still standing in their circle with him, still clutching hands, but as he looked down towards Mitzi, he found her smiling up at him with her blue eyes sparkling in the light.

The tallest doctor was the first to break contact. He reached down and checked Mitzi over, making sure she was breathing and that her heart was beating. Zeke watched on as each doctor made their checks nodding to each other in the process.

One of the doctors took Zeke aside and sat him down at one of the stations. "Mitzi mentioned something in her slumber that we took note of. Something to do with some research, do you know which research she was referring to?"

Zeke nodded. "Yes. She has been conducting her own research into preventing The Dark Wolf and it seems she found something that would require her bone marrow and some of her blood. I point blank refused because I didn't want to risk our bond or risk hurting her."

"Let me find the research she came across. I will cross reference everything and give you the best odds," the doctor smiled.

"OK. Thank you," Zeke replied, before heading back over to check on Mitzi. "How is she doing?"

"It seems the bond between you both pleased the other world enough to allow her to return. She may not be herself for a few more days but she is back," the tallest doctor told him.

Zeke reached for Mitzi who scrambled up to his shoulder, wrapping her arms around his neck. "I told you, didn't I?"

Mitzi didn't trust herself to reply, so she nodded into his neck.

"Let's get you into one of the guest rooms to rest. We are grounded for the next three weeks whilst everything on Onyx Abyss Alpha is upgraded. Dad is fixing a new radar system and upgrading all the software on the computers," Zeke told her. "It will give you ample time to rest and recharge."

Mitzi clung to his neck as he walked from the room and along the corridors. She barely made it halfway along the first corridor before she was snoring softly in his ear. Zeke smiled as he rounded the second corner, he couldn't believe how much he had missed the sound of her snoring. He found an empty room and placed her gently on the pillow, covering her with blanket. He would allow her to rest whilst he went to find something for her to eat.

"Do you think she will be OK?" Bella asked Layson.

"I hope so sweetheart. No one would be more devastated than Zeke if she didn't pull through," Layson replied. He plugged the power into the computer aboard Onyx Abyss Alpha and waited for the machine to boot up. He had made several upgrades and adjustments to the system in the time Mitzi had been down.

Bella began drumming her fingers on the workstation. She hated when she had something in her head but couldn't figure out how to act on it. She began pacing the ship, before finally slumping to the floor next to the chair Layson had perched himself on.

"What's wrong darling?" Layson asked. He had seen her rattled like this too many times to know something was wrong.

"I wish I could do more to help them. I don't know what though," Bella replied as she crossed her legs and closed her eyes.

Layson kept quiet. He knew she had placed herself into meditation. It was always best to leave her be whilst she became one with her thoughts. He watched as Bella's eyelids flickered in quick succession. He continued with his work, knowing that she would alert him to anything that showed itself to her after her meditation.

As Layson typed in the new codes to allow the radar system to scan the furthest reaches of the universe, he suddenly felt the air shift around him. Having it felt it many times before, he tried to continue his work, but something seemed off with the atmosphere. He looked back at where Bella sat, horrified when she wasn't there. He jumped from his seat and looked out of the door of the ship. She was nowhere in sight. Layson locked the ship door and went in search of her. He began to panic when she wasn't in her normal places. He searched the outhouse, the kitchen and the library. He asked a range of different people if they had seen her, only to be met with head shakes and apologies for having not seen her.

Layson searched the Palace from top to bottom. He searched every room and every cupboard. As he left his office to search the next room, he ran into Zeke.

"Hey Dad, what's the rush?" Zeke asked.

"Have you seen your mother?" Layson asked.

"Yes, she is sitting with Mitzi. Why what's wrong?" Zeke said, a look of concern crossing his face.

"I don't know son. All I know is the atmosphere shifted and your mother was gone. Where are they?" Layson asked.

"This way," Zeke said as he gestured to the far reaching corridor.

Layson took off at a sprint down the corridor, with Zeke close on his heels. As they ran, beings parted ways to allow them a clear path. Layson was first to arrive at Mitzi's room, scanning the area quickly and finding no sign of Bella.

Zeke approached the bed where, just a few moments before, he had laid Mitzi down, only to find the space empty.

"She's gone," he told his father.

"Gone? How long ago did you leave her?" Layson asked.

Zeke shook his head, "only a few moments before I ran into you. She can't have gone far surely?"

As the words left Zeke's lips, there was a crash outside in the courtyard. Rushing to the window, Zeke and Layson spotted Bella running across the open area, with Mitzi swinging from her hands. Zeke looked at his father, the anger bubbling deep within.

"I know what you're thinking son. We have to get there and fast," Layson said. He threw open the window and dived out, closely followed by Zeke.

They both took off at speed towards the outhouse, knowing exactly where Bella would take Mitzi. Running around the outside of the Palace, they made it to the outhouse before Bella arrived. They crouched down behind one of the lion statues that flanked the doorway and waited for her to arrive.

"Why are you taking me here?" Mitzi asked, the constant swinging making her head hurt and her stomach flip.

"You promised to help Zeke so that's what you will do," Bella replied, continuing at her fast pace towards the outhouse.

"Does Zeke know?" Mitzi asked, trying to turn herself around but failing.

"He will find out after we have done the procedure and put the prevention into a syringe and into him," Bella smiled. "You better hope it works," her eyes flashing with orange flames.

"What happened to you?" Mitzi asked, her voice becoming a whisper.

"Things. Just things. Now, let's get you in this house and work my magic," Bella laughed. She continued on her way, unaware that Layson and Zeke were waiting for her.

"Bella? Bella is that you?"

Bella stopped in her tracks, attempting to hide Mitzi behind her.

"Benzyline. What can I do for you?" Bella smiled.

Benzyline wandered towards Bella, shaking her head as she walked. "Now I know, you aren't hiding something from me, are you?"

"Why would I be hiding something from you?" Bella asked, slowly backing towards the outhouse.

"I can smell something. Something *sniff sniff* different," Benzyline said as she sniffed the air. "Smells like, Squink."

Bella spun on her heels and ran towards the door of the outhouse, only to be confronted by Layson and Zeke.

"Hand her over Mum," Zeke demanded, holding his hand out.

"No! She promised to help you and that is what she will do. You cannot promise something and not keep that promise," Bella replied, placing Mitzi behind her back once more.

"Honey, listen to me. Mitzi promised, but Zeke didn't agree. We can't force him to do something he isn't comfortable with, you know that," Layson smiled.

Bella shook her head. "No. I know, but if she can help him, why isn't he accepting that help?"

"It's because I don't want to Mum. If I have to live like this for the rest of my life then so be it, but I won't have anyone testing anything out on Mitzi," Zeke replied as his eyes flashed black. "Hand her over!"

Bella's hands and her head shook as she backed away from her husband and son. "No."

She turned to run back towards the Palace but Benzyline had remained firmly in her place. "Come now Bella. This isn't you."

"Maybe you don't know the real me Benzyline. Maybe, I'm more of a witch than you will ever be," Bella hissed.

"Now that would have to be proven," Benzyline narrowed her eyes.

Whilst Benzyline distracted Bella, Zeke crept up behind her and managed to slip Mitzi from her hands, it seemed that all the debate on her power had made her loosen her grip. He bundled her into his coat and slowly crept away.

"What's happened to your Mum Zeke?" Mitzi whispered. "She was saying some really strange things earlier."

"I don't know. All I know is that I need to get you away from here before she notices," Zeke replied, keeping his eyes on the entrance way.

Layson watched from the sidelines as Benzyline prepared to defend herself against Bella. He began to worry. He knew his wife wasn't as powerful as Benzyline and he worried that she would be hurt as a result of the impending attacks, what he was unsure about, was whether this was actually his wife.

Chapter Forty- Eight

"So what actually happened out there?" Scarlex asked as Zeke rushed Mitzi back to The Wraith Doctors.

"I don't know what's coming over my mother, but that, that *being* out there wasn't her," Zeke replied through gritted teeth. "If she has hurt Mitzi anymore than she already was, I swear I'll..."

Mitzi nudged his nose with hers. "You won't do anything because she didn't hurt me. The Doctors will prove it to you and you won't have to do anything."

Zeke sighed audibly. "I don't know what I would do without you."

Mitzi smiled before walking into the examination room.

Scarlex walked towards the only window in the corridor and looked out over the courtyard. She scanned the area for threats, knowing deep down there were none to find. Just before she looked away, something caught her eye. Something, or someone, with orange hair in the crystal fountain. She turned to Zeke only to find him pacing in front of the exam room door.

"Zeke, I need you to look at this," Scarlex said softly. "But don't panic."

Zeke stopped his pacing and carefully made his way to where she was standing. "What is it?"

Scarlex pointed at the fountain. "Can you see that?"

"See what?" Zeke asked, unsure what she was pointing at, other than the fountain.

Scarlex wondered how to make him see what she could see, but there was no way of doing it. "Your Mum has orange hair, right?"

"Yeah, why?" Zeke replied looking confused.

"Wait here. Don't go anywhere!" Scarlex told him. She turned away from him and ran off in the direction of the fountain. "Please don't be her, please don't be her," she whispered the whole way there.

Zeke continued his pacing, back and forth more than fifty times before The Wraith Doctors made an appearance from the examination room.

"She is absolutely fine. Try not to worry young Zeke," the tallest doctor smiled. "She has plenty of life left in her yet."

"Thank you doctor, thank you for everything," Zeke replied, shaking the doctors' hands.

"Got room for another?" Scarlex panted and she heaved Bella's dripping wet body through the doors.

"MUM!" Zeke cried out. He ran towards the door and swung his mother up into his arms.

"Through here please," The Wraith Doctor instructed.

Zeke carried his mother through to the exam room and placed her gently on the table. He turned to Scarlex, "find my Dad. He will be by the outhouse. Be careful, this means someone had cloned my Mum."

Scarlex nodded once and bolted from the room. Mitzi climbed up onto one of the workstations and kept her distance from the commotion that had begun in the centre of the room. She knew there was nothing she could do, but she felt a sense

of need from Zeke. He *needed* her there. She watched on as
The Wraith Doctors attached monitoring cables to Bella's
chest all the while Zeke paced and rubbed his hands together.
Mitzi didn't dare reach out for him; she knew he would refuse
to take his eyes off of his mother's body. He knew she was
there, and that is all she needed to do.

The closer Scarlex got to the outhouse, the louder the shouts
and screams became.

"I told you I was more powerful," Bella screamed.

"But you are yet to prove it," Benzyline replied, sending a
bolt of lightning towards her.

Bella dodged the bolt, sending it hurtling towards the door
behind where Layson had stood not more than five seconds
before. He watched as the bolt flew past his hiding spot
behind the statue.

He chanced a look around the statue's head, spotting Scarlex
as she ducked behind a nearby wall and began creeping
slowly towards him. She made her way around the back of
the outhouse and crouched beside him.

"Your Highness, you shouldn't be here," he exclaimed. "It
isn't safe," he said as another bolt whizzed past their heads.

"I can see that now!" Scarlex replied. "But I have a message from Zeke."

"Zeke? What's happened? Please tell me Mitzi is OK?" Layson spluttered.

"She is. It's Bella," Scarlex replied.

"But Bella is..." Layson looked towards the being in the midst of a power battle with Benzyline and then back at Scarlex. "You mean that isn't..."

Scarlex shook her head. "That," she pointed over to the two locked in battle, "is someone else."

They both looked across just as Benzyline summoned the strength to send of a fireball straight in the chest of the other being. Falling to the floor, the being screamed in pain as her disguise slowly faded away.

"Ahh, Symese. I wondered what happened to you. Tapping into others heads is NOT what we do here on Enceladus," Benzyline explained.

Layson and Scarlex emerged from their hiding place just in time to see Symese fade to dust and ash, a flurry of wind whisking it away.

"Take me to Bella," Layson told Scarlex.

"This way," she replied, gesturing to the doors on the far side of the courtyard.

Benzyline tagged along behind them, dragging her feet as she went. Scarlex chanced a look behind in time to see Benzyline collapse. She turned to help her but Benzyline waved her away.

"I shall be fine Your Highness, take Layson to his beloved. I will catch up soon," Benzyline told her. "Go."

Scarlex hated to leave her all alone, but she knew Benzyline wasn't a woman you argued with, so she reluctantly left her in the corridor, but mentally promised herself to return for her. Layson followed Scarlex along the corridor and into the exam room; there he saw how panicked Zeke was and how worried Mitzi looked.

"Layson. Welcome, please, take a seat," the smallest Wraith Doctor said, pointing to the chair placed at Bella's head. "I will need you assistance on the next part of the procedure."

Layson swallowed audibly. "Procedure?"

The Wraith Doctor looked at him. "How are you with blood?"

Layson dropped to the floor.

"Is he OK?"

"I'm sure he will be fine. Many beings have the same reaction to blood. It is very common."

Layson tried his hardest to open his eyes but the light hurt his head. He shielded his eyes from the bright light, before someone dimmed it down.

"Welcome back Layson. Did you enjoy your impromptu nap?"

Layson blinked his eyes as they adjusted to the darkness.

"I am so sorry. I don't know what happened," he explained.

"That is an easy explanation. You fainted."

"Bella? Is that you?" Layson whispered.

"I hope so. If it's not, then I want to know where I am and how they cloned you," she laughed.

Layson struggled to get to his feet, eager to reach his wife but clearly unstable on his feet.

"Go easy Dad. You hit your head pretty hard," Zeke smiled. He took hold of his father's arm and led him to Bella.

Layson pulled Bella into an embrace, looked down at her orange hair and noticed how some of it was not silver. "What happened?"

"An oversight of the procedure I'm afraid. Bella's blood reacts to her hair colour and causes streaks of silver to appear. It may never grow out," one of the female Wraith Doctors explained.

"So you will be Bella with orange and silver hair," Layson said, a tear streaking down his face.

"I will always be Bella, just with a new twist," she smiled.

"When can she be discharged?" Layson asked.

"Anytime she feels comfortable with, but she needs plenty of rest and relaxation," the tallest of the doctors explained. "Plenty of bed rest!"

Bella laughed, swung her legs over the edge of the bed and stood on her own two feet. "I think I'm ready to head home now. Thank you, for everything you have done for me. I am eternally grateful."

"As ever, it is what we are here for. Go safely everyone," The Wraith Doctors replied in unison.

Layson held his wife's hand as they left the exam room, followed by Mitzi and Zeke. It felt good to be together again. As they rounded the second corner, Benzyline sat on a bench with Scarlex by her side. Scarlex looked worried.

"Benzyline, what is it?" Bella asked, crouching down beside her.

"Oh Bella, it is so nice to see you," Benzyline coughed. "I fear the end is near."

"What do you mean?" Mitzi cried, jumping down from Zeke's shoulder and onto Benzyline's lap.

"Ahh Mitzi. You have a lot more left in you yet, and what you will discover will bring new meaning to life on Enceladus. You and Zeke will discover a whole new world out there somewhere, and you will make it your own," Benzyline smiled.

"But..." Mitzi began to speak before something crashed over her. She tried to jump from Benzyline's lap but she just fell. A shining light filled the corridor, blinding them all.

Mitzi felt strange. She looked at her hands and arms, noticing something very different.

"You, my child, are build for bigger things. Zeke and his Dark Wolf will be controlled, not by you, but by my gift to him. He will know about it when he needs to know. Until then, travel the universe, discover new worlds and enjoy his company," Benzyline whispered.

Mitzi didn't have any words to reply with, silver tears flowed from her eyes and onto the floor where they quickly dissolved. The light slowly faded along with Benzyline's body. Mitzi rose from the floor and stood behind Zeke. Finally at the same height as him, she tapped him on the shoulder. Zeke turned to her, his face a look of confusion.

"How?" He began to ask.

"Benzyline," Mitzi whispered.

Zeke turned back to where Scarlex now sat alone on the bench. "She was quite the being."

Mitzi nodded.

When the light had faded completely, looks of shock and sadness filled the room. Benzyline had been a sold part of all of their lives, coming and going, staying and leaving, for as long as any of them could remember.

"I should call Lyra," Scarlex said as she stood, dusted herself down and walked away.

Zeke held his hand out to Mitzi, "I'm prepared for what I will see."

Mitzi gripped his hands and closed her eyes.

"It's not working Zeke."

"It will, give it a chance."

"I have. I've given it too many chances."

"Then we will have to reboot and try again."

"If you say so. Rebooting now, Scanning surrounding area. Got them!"

"I told you it would work."

As the vision holder turned, two silver haired beings bounced into view.

"What have we told you two about bounding off into the wilderness."

Zeke released her hand and smiled at her. "Life will be great."

"Of course it will be. I mean, I'm here aren't I?" Mitzi laughed. She threw her arms around his neck and nudged his nose with hers. "Promise me we won't stop doing this?"

"Promise. It's our thing right?" Zeke whispered, as he kissed her for the first time.

Chapter Forty – Nine

Six Months Later.

"Be careful out there. I want you both back in one piece. Your mission lasts for three months and I want regular interactions," Scarlex told them.

Scarlex had arranged for Mitzi and Zeke to take Onyx Abyss Alpha off to Palioxis Hyperbius to test out the new radar and telescopic systems Layson had installed. She allowed them to go alone as part of a new trial she had begun. Most crews would travel in twos, with a maximum of four on board. She had commissioned Layson and a few of the beings he trusted to design and build a new fleet of ships capable to protecting the skies above Saturn and Enceladus whilst Onyx and The Stealth ship went off in search of new resources and allies.

"We get it. Constant contact and back in three months," Zeke replied. "Is there anything in particular we should be searching for?

"Life. Any beings who would be willing to become an ally to Enceladus in exchange for something reasonable," Scarlex replied. "Be careful who you make dealings with and do not, under any circumstances, allow yourself to be followed back here by anyone considered a threat."

"So this is solely on us?" Mitzi asked. "Is there a punishment if we fail?"

Scarlex laughed. "There is no such thing as failure, only discovery. Now go, before Bella brings more snacks."

Zeke laughed as he closed the door and fastened the locks in place. "You ready?"

"As I'll ever be," Mitzi replied.

Just as she settled herself next to Zeke at the controls, a video call came through on the HUD.

"Hey you two!" Balzar cried. "Woah, Mitz, what you been eating?"

Mitzi laughed. "How's Hula?"

"It's a girl! We have a bouncy, top of the range, girl!" Balzar exclaimed. "I'm sorry I wasn't there for you guys."

"It's fine Bal. Hula needed you. So, what's her name?" Mitzi asked.

"Aquinta," Balzar replied. "Hula wanted something to remember Queen Aquilia by and well, that's what she got!"

"That's a lovely name. Have you told Elion and Scarlex?" Zeke asked.

"That was my next call. You two stay safe out there OK. Call if you need anything and I'll be on the next ship up there," Balzar replied. "Love ya both! Bye!" Balzar signed off.

Mitzi looked at Zeke as he made the final pre-flight checks. She really felt like they could do anything together. She imagined their life on some distant planet, building their own Kingdom and having their own family. Being able to to live without fear and enjoy their lives.

"You ready?" Zeke asked.

"Huh? Oh yeah, let's hit the skies!" Mitzi laughed.

Zeke pulled back on the controls and the ship lifted into the air, steering it into position, he manoeuvred the ship from its holding pad and slowly rose into the sky. Mitzi looked ahead and held onto her vision of a hassle and stress free life as they powered, full throttle, into the sky. She closed her eyes and prepared herself for what lie ahead for them both.

"They are entering the far reaches of The Milky Way now. They will be out of radar reach in less than an hour," Elion told his sister.

"OK. Thank you. Keep me informed of anything that shows up, oh and Elion?" Scarlex asked.

"Hmm?" He replied, looking around from the screens.

"What I told you remains between us," she smiled, placing her finger to her lips.

"You got it sis," he said, throwing her a salute as he turned back to his monitors.

Scarlex walked away, safe in the knowledge that her brother wouldn't breathe a word to anyone until Zeke and Mitzi were ready. She walked towards her office, once her mother's, and sat behind the desk. She pulled a folder from the bottom drawer and began to work through the daily duties and tasks which needed to be addressed. After everything that had happened over the past year, Scarlex felt alone. She turned to the picture of her mother and smiled.

"I'm trying Mum, but I don't feel like I'm succeeding," she whispered as tears fell from her eyes and onto the desk below.

A cool breeze whipped at her hair. "There is no failure Scarlex, only discovery."

Scarlex let out a sob as the words rang in her ears. "I miss you Mum."

"I am always here. Just look for me, and there I will be," Aquilia's voice whispered.

Scarlex looked at the picture on the desk, smiling as her mother winked at her from the frame. She straightened herself up, flipped the folder shut and called Chylla to announce an annual holiday. No one would need to work and there would be a celebration in the town square due to begin at two p.m.

As she made her way to her own personal quarters, Elion called her over the radio so she diverted to The Comms Room.

"What is it?" She asked as she entered the room.

"Zeke and Mitzi. They have exited The Milky Way but are requesting a video conference with Layson and Bella, requesting us to be in attendance and also linking Eva and Janus in too?" Elion told her.

"I'll fetch Layson and Bella, you contact Eva and Janus. Reply to Zeke and ask them to call in ten minutes," Scarlex replied. She left the room in search of Layson and Bella.

Elion dialled Eva.

"Hey Elion, what's up?" Eva smiled.

"I have a request from Zeke and Mitzi for you both to join the video conference he and Mitzi would like to hold. I'm just waiting on Bella and Layson to arrive with Scar, is Janus there?" Elion explained.

"Right here Elion," he waved from behind Eva. "Just settling Codex and I'll be with you."

Scarlex knocked at Layson's office door before entering, finding them both sitting across from each other and looking at blueprints.

"Sorry to interrupt. Elion received a message from Zeke requesting a video conference with you both, plus Eva, Janus, myself and Elion," she explained.

"Let's go," Bella replied as she and Layson got to their feet.

They made their way back to The Comms Room and settled in to wait for the call. Exactly ten minutes later, Zeke called.

"Hey honey. What's up?" Bella asked.

"Hey Mum. Everyone. We wanted you all to hear this together," Zeke replied, panning the camera out more.

He stood next to Mitzi and placed his hand on her stomach.

"Mitzi and I are going to have a baby." He announced.

Bella almost screamed before Layson calmed her down.

"Oh honey. Why didn't you say something before you left?" Bella asked.

"I...well...we knew you wouldn't let us fly and we wanted to travel together first," Zeke replied.

"I'm happy for you son. Welcome to the family Mitzi."

Mitzi smiled. She finally felt like she had been accepted. She rubbed her growing stomach, happy to finally be normal.

"Oh Mitzi, look how you're glowing!" Eva exclaimed.

"It will be..." Lyra began from behind Janus.

"Shhhh!" Everyone shouted.

"We want it to be a surprise," Mitzi replied. "I have a lot to learn about my own species before this little one arrives. Eva, could you forward some reading material to me, preferably about pregnancies and birth?"

"I'm on it sweetie. Zeke! You take care of her," Eva warned with a smile. "I'm proud of you."

"We will all be here for you. All three of you," Scarlex told them. "Now, go and enjoy yourselves."

Elion ended the link with Onyx whilst the rest stayed connected.

"Oh my baby is going to be a Dad. That means...." Bella gasped. "I will be a Grandma!"

"And you will make a fabulous Grandma," Elion told her.

"Do you think that went well?" Mitzi asked as she settled herself back into her seat.

"It was a better reaction than I thought it would be. Let's see where this journey takes us. You, me and bump," he smiled. He pulled her close and kissed the top of her head before nudging her nose with his.

Setting their course to Palioxis Hyperbius, Zeke and Mitzi settled back and allowed the ship to guide them there. Mitzi rested her hand on her stomach with Zeke covering hers with his own, and there they sat whilst the travelled through far off galaxies in search of new life.

The End